President Darcy

A Modern Pride and Prejudice Variation

Victoria Kincaid

ISBN: 978-0-9975530-8-6

Chapter One

"It is a truth universally acknowledged that a single president in possession of an enormous civilian bureaucracy and a nuclear arsenal must be in want of a wife," Elizabeth Bennet said to her sister Jane with a grin.

"And why shouldn't he?" her mother asked with some aspersion. "He is handsome, rich, and powerful. Why shouldn't he want to get married?"

Why do people see presidents as almost super-human? Elizabeth wondered. "He's just another guy," she said. "Even if he's president, he puts his pants on one leg at a time."

"I'd like to watch him put on his pants," Kitty Bennet, the second youngest sister, uttered in a suggestive tone. Then she shivered as another gust of wind blasted over the family.

The youngest, Lydia, glanced sidelong at Kitty. "Or take them off!" They burst into wild giggles that attracted disdainful stares from others in the line. Truthfully, the Bennet family—with their expensive, but flashy finery—already contrasted with the men in bespoke suits and the women in furs.

Elizabeth, the second oldest sister, murmured ruefully to Jane, "Of course. If anyone would talk about undressing the president, it would be my sisters." Jane simply sighed; as the oldest, she probably had not expected much better.

The two parents and five daughters of the Bennet family were waiting in line to go through the security scanners at the entrance to the White House. Ever since invitations to the state dinner had arrived months ago, their mother had greeted even passing acquaintances with the news of the honor. Of course, Fanny Bennet hadn't anticipated an hour of standing under the towering White House portico waiting to be admitted— along with a hundred other "honored guests."

"How much longer will we be waiting?" Lydia whined as she shifted from one foot to the other in her too-tall heels and yanked at her too-tight, sparkly hot-pink sheath dress (with matching tiny hat). "I have to pee!"

Is it too late to pretend I don't know her? Elizabeth wondered.

Their mother ignored her. "Now you girls remember everything I told you about the president—everything he likes and doesn't like." She clasped her hands to her bosom while Elizabeth rolled her eyes at Jane.

Their father hunched over in his tuxedo jacket, trying to stay warm. "I don't see how he concerns our daughters."

"He's single!" Fanny Bennet's tone suggested that she expected her husband to find it obvious.

"I don't think the president wants to get married," Elizabeth said.

"He does," Fanny said with a superior nod. "He just may not know it yet."

Kitty's squeal drew looks from the surrounding partygoers. "OMG! I bet the last single president had a different woman in his bed every night."

Mary, the middle daughter, spoke up for the first time without raising her eyes from her iPad. "The last bachelor president was James Buchanan, who served from 1857 to 1861—right before the Civil War."

Of course, Mary would know, Elizabeth thought.

"So most of the other presidents were married fuddy-duddies. How boring," Lydia observed. "At least we get an interesting one."

"And a young one!" Kitty exclaimed. "Presidents are usually old and gray." At thirty-seven, William Darcy was the youngest man to ever become president, which made him an object of fascination to many single women.

Her mother adjusted some of the many ruffles on her bright green dress. "I don't see why President Darcy wouldn't be interested in one of you girls. You're all pretty enough." She shot a quick, dubious glance at Mary in her drab brown floor-length gown. "You two really should devote more time to finding Mr. Right." She eyed Jane and Elizabeth meaningfully. "Your eggs aren't getting any younger. Why, you're practically forty!"

Jane spoke through gritted teeth. "I'm thirty-one, Mom! Thirty-one! And Elizabeth is twenty-nine."

Fanny didn't so much as blink. "Women age more quickly than men, dear. It's like dog years."

There was a pause in the conversation as everyone digested that pearl of wisdom. The line inched forward. Elizabeth had been in a long-term relationship until nine months ago, but it wouldn't matter if she reminded her mother of that fact. Elizabeth tried a different approach. "President Darcy has a reputation for being aloof and snobbish. Probably not good boyfriend material."

"He might be a little…reserved, but that's because he's thinking deep thoughts about foreign policy and budgets and Easter egg rolls."

Fanny patted hair into place that was so heavily sprayed a tornado couldn't have dislodged it. "Besides, he's a billionaire. That excuses many eccentricities."

The line moved again. "At least Mom has her priorities in order," Elizabeth mumbled to Jane, who grimaced in agreement.

"And his life is so romantic!" Lydia sighed. "With his parents dying in the plane crash when he was still in college—and how he raised his sister."

"I'm can't imagine it felt very romantic to him," Elizabeth said.

"I'm f-freezing!" Kitty complained loudly. Despite being older than Lydia, who was still enjoying the drinking and sleeping around parts of college, she didn't seem much more mature.

"You should have worn your coat," said Jane, who had had the foresight to bring a faux fur-lined wrap.

"Lydia said it wasn't that cold for February," Kitty said peevishly. Which was true, Elizabeth reflected, but it was still damn cold for someone with bare shoulders. Elizabeth snuggled gratefully into her coat.

"I don't know how much longer I can stand here," Lydia whined. "My shoes are killing me."

They weren't even in the building, and already Elizabeth wanted to escape. She gazed longingly at the taxis zipping along 17th Street. *I could catch one now and avoid this whole fiasco.* Although her mother and sisters loved the fancy-dress occasions the family's recently acquired wealth entitled them to, such events often brought out their worst tendencies. Elizabeth had stopped attending any and all social events with her family as soon as she was old enough to put her foot down. After enduring weeks of pleading from Fanny, however, Elizabeth had agreed to the state dinner.

Sometimes Elizabeth imagined she'd been switched at birth. Everyone else seemed very happy to work in the family business, which made and sold high-end processed food. Even Lydia worked there on summer breaks. Kitty and Mary still lived at home as well. However, that was far more family togetherness than Elizabeth could stomach. She had obtained her own job and her own apartment—and was considered a bizarre aberration by everyone except Jane. They loved her, but did not begin to understand her. Elizabeth watched Kitty and Lydia tussle over a tube of lipstick. Sometimes the non-comprehension was mutual.

By now the Bennet family had arrived at the front of the line with its security gates and metal detectors. After clearing that hurdle, the family was ushered through a large set of double doors, opened ceremoniously by two uniformed doormen.

The entrance hall was designed to inspire awe with a marble checkerboard floor, a row of pillars along one wall, and an elaborate crystal chandelier. Uniformed staff relieved the Bennets of their coats and wraps. Elizabeth herded her younger sisters closer to the rest of the family. In a space this enormous it would be easy for seven people to get lost in the shuffle.

Kitty hugged herself. "I can't believe we're meeting the president!" Elizabeth said a quick prayer that Kitty wouldn't squeal when she met him, but she noted the exits just in case she needed to make a quick escape.

Mrs. Bennet bustled through the entrance hall. "Where is the president?" she demanded of one staff member. The young woman directed them into an enormous room with high ceilings and tall windows framed by golden draperies. Although there were plenty of people milling about, talking and eating hors d'oeuvres, the room was so huge that it dwarfed the occupants.

Mary nodded knowingly. "The East Room. This is usually where they put guests until dinner is ready."

Along with leaders from five African countries, the dinner honored some charities that worked in that region, including Oxfam, Doctors Without Borders, and the Red Cross. Around the room's perimeter, large screen televisions displayed rotating images of projects from the various organizations.

Elizabeth's heart swelled with pride as she caught a glimpse of the display for the Red Cross—her employer for the past five years. But tonight the organization was being represented by its higher-ranking employees; Elizabeth attended solely in her capacity as her parents' daughter. She knew nothing about which images had been chosen for the display and belatedly hoped the guests would not be treated to a larger-than-life picture of Elizabeth covered in mud and digging a latrine. Fanny Bennet would still be complaining about that on her deathbed.

Her mother bustled over with their place cards in hand. "We're at table eighteen," she announced, scanning the room. "What a pity it's not closer to the president's table—"

"John!" a voice boomed out.

They all turned to find Walter Lucas bearing down on them. Founder of the prestigious Lucas and Lucas public relations firm, Walter was John Bennet's oldest friend. Politically connected, he had been instrumental in involving Elizabeth's father in fundraising for President Darcy's campaign—and obtaining their invitations to the state dinner.

Walter pumped their father's hand and gave air kisses to all the women of the family. "The president isn't here yet. Of course, it's his prerogative to be late!" His hearty laugh could have made the windows vibrate. "But I can introduce you to a couple of other people…" Her parents followed Walter like ducklings after a mother duck, but Elizabeth shuffled over to the edge of the crowd. She didn't need to meet all the movers and shakers; in fact, she preferred to avoid them altogether.

After grabbing a few stuffed mushroom caps from a table of appetizers, Elizabeth scanned the room for her younger sisters; her mission for the night was to prevent them from humiliating the entire Bennet family. What was Lydia doing in that deserted corner at the far end of the room? Too far away to prevent it, Elizabeth watched helplessly as the youngest Bennet sister opened a door that had been designed to blend into the wall. Elizabeth felt sure this was a bad idea. Surely a door that was not supposed to be noticed should not be used by random dinner guests.

Suppressing a desperate urge to run, Elizabeth walked toward Lydia as swiftly as decorum allowed, praying her sister wouldn't be foolish enough to disappear through an unknown door. But Lydia was exactly that foolish. She had disappeared through the doorway by the time Elizabeth opened the door. The interior was dimly lit but revealed Lydia's retreating form. Sweat trickled between Elizabeth's shoulder blades and dampened her brow as she leaned in, calling to her sister. "Lydia! Lydia come back right now." If her sister heard, she gave no indication.

There was no choice; the only way to retrieve Lydia was to follow her. Elizabeth slipped through the opening and left the door slightly ajar behind her.

The hallway was long, narrow, and dim, clearly intended as a service corridor for the staff's use. Dust on the bare wood floors and a slight musty odor suggested that it wasn't used often. A few closed doors dotted the walls, but otherwise it was empty—except for Lydia's rapidly dwindling shape. Elizabeth raced to the end of the corridor, reaching Lydia right before she arrived at a T-intersection.

"What the hell are you doing?" she hissed, panting as she grabbed Lydia's arm.

Lydia smirked. "Well, you heard Mr. Lucas. If the president isn't there"—she pointed to the East Room—"maybe I can find him *alone*." Her voice dipped suggestively on the last word. "You can just scurry back to the party." Her hands made little shooing motions.

Lydia no doubt could have devised a more embarrassing ploy than to ambush President Darcy with her amorous attentions, but at the moment Elizabeth was hard-pressed to conceive of something more mortifying.

"If the Secret Service finds you back here, they could arrest you!" Elizabeth exclaimed.

Lydia waved this objection away. "I'll just explain I wanted a selfie. They'll understand."

Elizabeth was not so sanguine that the "selfie defense" was an all-purpose excuse, but she took a deep breath to calm the nerves that had her jumping out of her skin. Yelling at Lydia was always counterproductive. "This corridor probably only leads to the kitchen, you know," she said.

Lydia pouted. "You are such a Debbie Downer! God, Lizzy!" But then she smiled impishly. "You know what? It doesn't matter. I bet I can find the president once I'm in the kitchen."

Not if the workers in the kitchen called the Secret Service first. But Elizabeth didn't want to provoke a screaming match with Lydia; who knew what kind of scrutiny that would bring? There had to be a quicker way to entice her back to the East Room. "Did you know they have bacon-wrapped scallops?" Elizabeth asked.

Lydia's eyes lit up at the mention of her favorite appetizer. "Really?"

"Of course, they might be gone by the time you get back," Elizabeth sing-songed.

For a moment Lydia waffled, torn between two different impulses. "I'll see the president later," she muttered under her breath. Lydia did an about-face and rushed down the hallway toward the East Room. Elizabeth sagged against the wall, limp with relief at a disaster averted. After her pulse returned to normal, she followed Lydia at a more sedate pace, marveling at how fast her sister could move on those heels.

Lydia had just disappeared through the door and Elizabeth was about halfway down the corridor when voices rumbled from the other end. Deep, masculine voices. Secret Service? White House staff? Whoever it was, they would be unhappy to find Elizabeth in an unauthorized area.

There wasn't time to make it to the East Room. The only concealment options were behind the various closed doors along the corridor, although Elizabeth had no idea where they led. She yanked on one. It didn't budge. What if they were all locked? The voices grew louder. Damn it! Sweat trickled off Elizabeth's brow and into her eyes; she dashed it away impatiently with the back of her hand. The next door was also locked. Maybe she should just run for it.

However, the next door opened easily, revealing a closet full of mops, brooms, and buckets soaked in the stringent odor of cleaning supplies. What a mundane thing to find at the White House. Elizabeth hurriedly stepped inside, taking care not to knock over any of the brooms, and pulled the door closed behind her.

The interior was completely dark except for a golden strip of light under the door. Her ragged breaths were harsh in her ears no matter how she tried to quiet them. She hugged herself around her waist as if that could keep her still, but her hands trembled violently. Finally, holding her breath, Elizabeth strained her ears for any sign of discovery.

Firm footsteps echoed on the wooden floors—at least two sets. "We really shouldn't enter this way," said a male voice. "Everyone expects a grand—"

The second man's voice was deeper and tinged with irritation. "I'm late, Bing. I'd rather slip in unnoticed."

The shaking of Elizabeth's body intensified, and sweat trickled between her shoulder blades. One of the men was Charles Bingley, the president's chief of staff and widely considered the second most powerful man in the White House. Shit. Shit. Shit. He was the last person she wanted to find her in the presidential broom closet.

Bingley's tone was soothing. "You have a good reason for being late—"

One of the mops chose that moment to topple over with a thump. *I hope that was quieter outside the closet than inside.*

"What was that?" the second man asked. His voice was vaguely familiar.

Guess not.

"Something shifting in one of the closets," Bingley said, unconcerned.

"Kinski wouldn't want us to ignore it," the second man said with a rueful laugh. "You know 'constant vigilance is everyone's duty'?"

"Yeah, all right," Bingley said with a good-natured laugh. "We'll send a Secret Service agent back to investigate."

Yes, Elizabeth tried to convince the other man telepathically. *Listen to Bingley. Send someone back.*

"To investigate a closet?" the other man asked incredulously. "It'll only take a few seconds."

"You're not supposed to—"

Footsteps rapidly approached the closet. Elizabeth was no longer trembling; now she was frozen, rooted to the spot—and all her perspiration had turned icy. Even her teeth chattered. *What will they do to me? Please don't shoot me on sight. Please let me explain.*

The door opened, flooding the closet with light. Elizabeth blinked in the sudden brightness and then blinked again at the person before her. She'd been wrong, she realized. Bingley was not the last person she wanted to find her in the closet. He was standing in front of her.

She stared into the face of President William Darcy.

Chapter Two

President Darcy's head jerked back, and his mouth dropped open when he saw who was in his broom closet.

Television doesn't do him justice. In person, he was far more attractive. In person, he was breathtaking...with those gray-blue eyes and dark, almost black, hair falling in soft waves over his forehead. The lines of the tuxedo accentuated his broad shoulders and lean, muscular physique. The features of his face were classic and patrician, almost like a Roman statue come to life. But his lips were sensual, soft and full, contrasting with the clean, straight lines of the rest of his face. *I bet he's a good kisser with lips like those. And the intensity of those eyes...*

Which where glaring at her.

What am I thinking? I'm staring at the president. *And thinking lustful thoughts about* the president. Instead, she should be explaining. Talking her way out of the situation. At least making her mouth move. "Um...hi?" She gave him a little wave and what she hoped was her most nonthreatening smile.

"Who the hell are you?" he barked.

"Shit! There's someone in there?" Charles Bingley's blond head appeared over the president's shoulder. He was the same age as the other man, but his shaggy hair and relaxed surfer dude smile made him seem younger.

Elizabeth rattled out an explanation—before they shot her. "I'm Elizabeth B-Barnett...no...B-Bennet. I'm a g-guest at the party—you know...the state dinner thingy. And my sister ran off and I had to find her and then you were coming, and I knew I shouldn't be here...and so I hid," she finished lamely. Jeez, the explanation sounded ridiculous even to her ears.

President Darcy took a moment to stare at her like she should be under psychiatric care, which, to be fair, was a reasonable assumption under the circumstances. "Is your sister in there, too?" He peered into the closet's depths.

"No. She, um, went back to that really big room—" God, what was the name of it? She couldn't think coherently when the President of the United States was glowering at her. *Go figure.* "You know, with the tall drapes and stuff." *Good one, Elizabeth, that probably described every room in the White House.*

"The one with the state dinner thingy?" he asked with a raised eyebrow.

He's mocking me. Does that mean he believes me? A presidential assassin would probably be way smoother and less confused.

The president gave Bingley a sidelong glance. "Maybe we should call the Secret Service."

Elizabeth grabbed the doorframe. *Please, no.*

Bingley sighed. "She obviously isn't carrying a weapon, Darcy."

The president scrutinized Elizabeth from head to foot—his gaze lingering over every curve in her long black gown. It wasn't particularly revealing, but it was form-fitting enough that she couldn't have concealed anything bigger than a tube of lipstick.

He cleared his throat. "I suppose not."

What a monumental embarrassment to her family if she were arrested at the state dinner. "I'm so, so sorry! Please don't have me arrested or audited or drafted or anything!" she babbled. Elizabeth clapped her hand over her mouth before she said anything stupid. Stupider.

A corner of the president's mouth quirked upward. "Well, I promise not to have you audited or drafted."

"All the guests were vetted by the Secret Service, Darcy," Bingley pointed out. "Perhaps we can skip the arresting this time."

The president regarded her seriously for a moment. *He really did have the most amazing blue eyes, like a storm at sea. And...wow...was now an inappropriate time for that thought!*

"An arrest would not be an auspicious start to the state dinner," Bingley warned.

Elizabeth held her breath as he deliberated. Profiles of the president portrayed him as being very charismatic when he chose to be, but some people described him as aloof and cold. He must have chosen otherwise because the temperature of his glare was glacial—as if showing up in a White House broom closet were tantamount to murder. Elizabeth wanted—very badly—to forsake his presence immediately.

Finally, he threw his arms up in the air. "All right. But if we find you doing anything else...unexpected, I *will* have the Secret Service arrest you." With one arm across his chest, he pointed an accusing finger at Elizabeth.

She nodded eagerly. "That's great. Thanks. That makes sense. Yeah, the next time, go ahead and arrest me." His eyes narrowed. "Not that there's going to be a next time." She held up her hands. "Absolutely no next time."

He snorted in disbelief. *What a jerk!*

With a slight shake of his head, the president extended his hand to her. She stared at it. *Why...? Oh, he's offering to help me out of the closet.* Clearly, her brain had gone offline since entering the White House. Releasing the doorframe, she stretched out her trembling hand, which he engulfed in his warm, firm grip.

***

As the woman—Elizabeth Bennet— stepped out of the closet, brooms and mops went crashing to the floor. She flinched, and Darcy tightened his grip on her hand, drawing her closer to him as if the cleaning implements represented a serious threat to her safety. It was ridiculous and inappropriate, and Darcy had no idea why he did it.

The woman seemed to provoke unexpected reactions from him. How else could he explain his unwarrantedly casual reaction the potential danger she might represent?

As he double-checked to ensure she was unharmed, Darcy was struck by her eyes—a deep, mossy green he had never seen before on another human being. With such a uniform color...they really were quite fine. He couldn't look away. No, it would be more accurate to say he didn't *want* to look away.

She was about average height for a woman, which meant that she peered up at Darcy, who came in at around six feet. A sweet, heart-shaped face accentuated those marvelous eyes. Lustrous, wavy dark hair tumbled over her shoulders and down her back. And that dress—a floor-length black silk sheath that skimmed all her curves without revealing too much. In fact, it revealed just the right amount of her creamy skin...

Rather pointedly, she cast her eyes down at her hand. Which he was still holding. He noticed her fingers, delicate and tapered and so small, nestled in his grasp.

The touch of her hand was the single most wonderful sensation he had ever felt.

His fingers caressed her fingers.

Her hand trembled in his.

He had no desire to release her.

The rest of his body also responded to her proximity. Leaning toward her, he scented a vaguely floral fragrance...perfume or shampoo perhaps. He flushed with a warmth that had nothing to do with the temperature in the hallway, moisture collecting on his forehead and the back of his neck. His mouth was suddenly parched, and his tongue licked dry lips. Her eyes followed the movement. *She is staring at my mouth.*

If only I could touch more than her hand. Darcy's hand rose, needing to learn if her hair was as soft as it appeared. But then the (apparently very small) part of his brain that was still sane reminded him that the woman was a stranger, and he aborted the movement.

I should probably say something. His lips were parted, ready to speak, but all his thoughts appeared to have melted away at her touch.

Bing cleared his throat. "We should get to the dinner."

The words worked their way through Darcy's sluggish brain. He understood their import, but the thought of releasing Elizabeth Bennet's hand horrified him. He desperately needed to touch *more* of her, not less.

"Just a second, Bing," he snapped.

Elizabeth blinked, her eyelashes fluttering. *Is she as affected by the touch as I am?* "I-It's a pleasure to meet you, Mr. President," she said with a note of finality that suggested she preferred he return her hand. Damn. Could she guess he'd been thinking improper thoughts—when he knew literally nothing about her except her name? It seriously had been too long since he'd had a date.

Dropping her hand as if it had burned him, he stepped backward, putting more distance between them and trying to collect thoughts that seemed to have been scattered by a powerful wind.

Why was he reacting this way to this woman? She was pretty— well, more than pretty. Beautiful. And that dress displayed a body he would certainly describe as "hot." But he saw beautiful, well-dressed women every day.

And she'd been hiding in a closet, he reminded himself. It wasn't normal behavior. She also didn't appear capable of assembling coherent sentences. It truly was a shame she wasn't more …eloquent. Lack of intelligence was always a deal-breaker for Darcy.

Although it was probably a good thing. If she were smart, too, she'd be irresistible.

Bing cleared his throat loudly.

Finally, Darcy tore his eyes from her vivid, dark green ones, but he was still rubbed raw by her proximity. He didn't know why she affected him like this, but Darcy couldn't let her—or anyone else—notice the results.

Taking out his handkerchief, he blotted his brow and mopped the back of his neck before discreetly wiping his sweaty hands and returning the handkerchief to his pocket. Elizabeth stared, likely marveling at how profusely the President of the United States could sweat. Bing regarded Darcy warily; he knew how out-of-character this behavior was.

He had embarrassed himself sufficiently; remaining any longer would only produce more shame and more perspiration. It was past time to appear at the dinner and get away from the spacey woman with the lovely eyes.

Without another word, he turned on his heel and strode down the hallway. Behind him, he heard Bing ask, "Will you join us at the dinner, Ms. Bennet?"

Damn! I should have asked that. She had me too flustered.

"Um...sure," she said uncertainly.

No regrets, he told himself sternly. The woman couldn't string two sentences together. Her beauty was nothing but a momentary distraction.

Darcy tugged his cuffs into place and straightened his bow tie. Taking the service hallway was intended to help him make up time after his last meeting ran late, but the encounter with Ms. Bennet had further delayed his schedule. Time to focus on the dinner and his political priorities for the evening.

Although he was technically there just to make a speech and have a good time, a dinner was never just a dinner for a president. He hoped to buttonhole Senator Kirkpatrick about supporting his transportation plan. And a couple of CEOs wanted to complain about the Federal Election Commission. He wasn't planning to do anything about it, but they would be happy if he listened.

And then there was Congressman Ostrevsky on the Foreign Relations Committee and his crusade for humanitarian aid for African refugees. Encouraging the government's refugee efforts was one of the purposes for the dinner. *Keep your thoughts focused on that, Darcy.*

There was a strategy behind all of it. Darcy's predecessor in the Oval Office had left him with a lot of international relationships to repair. One of Darcy's top priorities was restoring the reputation of the United States abroad. He had just returned from a two-week tour of Europe and was gearing up for a trip to Asia in a few months. Their allies needed a lot of reassurances.

Darcy didn't have the luxury of time to be confused by a pretty woman. *Very well*, he resolved as he stepped into the hubbub of the East Room. *Time to get my head in the game.*

***

Elizabeth watched President Darcy's retreating back. On the bright side, he didn't seem inclined to have her arrested, but he had taken off like she had the plague. His contempt for her was so glaring that she practically needed sunglasses. What had she done to deserve that?

Besides venturing into a restricted area, hiding in his closet, and nearly giving him a heart attack. Oh, yeah. *Oops.*

What she wouldn't do for a time machine. Or failing that, a complete memory wipe of the past half hour. Since no amnesia was forthcoming, Elizabeth turned to face Mr. Bingley. No doubt her cheeks were bright red, and her hair was a dusty mess. Nevertheless, he gave her a reassuring smile. "Will you join us at the dinner, Ms. Bennet?" The chief of staff had a reputation for being far more affable than the president, and Elizabeth could see why.

"Um…sure…" It was as if she were caught in the White House version of good cop, bad cop.

He continued to smile pleasantly as he gestured for her to precede him down the hallway. As she hurried toward the East Room, Elizabeth wondered if anyone would see them emerge from the hidden door. Or would the president tell his friends about her mishap and laugh? She swallowed hard. What could she possibly say to her family?

Dad, I consider it an honor to be smirked at by the president. Most Americans couldn't claim that distinction. Mom, someday it will be an amusing anecdote to tell my children about the time the President of the United States thought I was an idiot.

That would not go over well.

I wasn't expecting to see the freaking President of the United States, so forgive me if I use words like "thingy" and can't remember the name of the East Room. That infuriatingly superior grin had grown wider with her every mistake and fumble. The bastard had enjoyed her consternation.

He had been chivalrous enough to help her exit the closet with some grace, but then he had wiped his hands clean of her germs. And what man under sixty carried a handkerchief in this day and age?

"Will the president report me?" she asked Bingley as they neared the East Room door. It would be a terrible blow to her family. And Elizabeth had worried that *Lydia* would embarrass them!

"No," Bingley said immediately. Then after a moment, he said, "I don't think so." *How reassuring.*

By the time Bingley and Elizabeth emerged through the concealed door, the president had disappeared into the crowd. *That's good. Maybe I can avoid him for the rest of the evening—and the rest of my life.*

However, Elizabeth's hopes were quickly dashed. The moment she became visible, her mother marched up to her, grabbing her by the wrist and dragging her away. "Where have you been?" she whispered harshly. "Walter is introducing us to the president!"

President Darcy's eyes, cool and assessing, perused her as she joined the semicircle of her family arrayed before him. Ugh. Elizabeth did not have any interest in another encounter with the man. *On the bright side, at least he's not out searching for the Secret Service to have me arrested.*

As Elizabeth and her mother slipped in next to John Bennet, everybody stared; Lydia smirked, no doubt pleased by her timely escape from the hallway. The president gave her father a superior smile. "Do you often misplace your daughter?"

As if she were a wallet or a puppy. *Could he be more condescending?*

Her mother curtsied—curtsied!—and said: "We're so sorry to keep you waiting, your highness." This was followed by a violent coughing fit from Bing and a disdainful look from President Darcy.

Walter hurried to make introductions—as if anything could cover up for that faux pas. "Mr. President, Mr. Bingley…" He gestured to the Bennets. "Please allow me to introduce John Bennet's wife Fanny, and his daughters: Jane Bennet, Elizabeth Bennet, Mary Bennet, Kitty Bennet, and Lydia Bennet." He chuckled a bit over Lydia's name as if to acknowledge that yes, there were a lot of Bennet sisters.

President Darcy's smile was tight and pained as if such introductions were a necessary duty, but the chief of staff gave the whole family a relaxed and easy grin. "What a lovely family!" Bingley exclaimed to Elizabeth's father. "You are a lucky man." His eyes lingered on Jane's face. Unsurprisingly, Jane blushed, which, naturally, made her even lovelier.

The president, on the other hand, surveyed her family and their bewildering array of colors and styles of dress with a slight curl in his lip. Elizabeth added "snob" to her list of nouns describing the man.

Bingley had already commenced shaking hands with the assembled Bennets. The president followed suit, plastering on a grin and slowly offering his hand to Elizabeth—the first in line. *What an "honor" to meet a man who grimaces at the thought of shaking my hand.* "Pleased to meet you, Ms. Bennet," the president said mechanically.

Their hands met, and as before, the touch triggered a strange reaction. Her entire body loosened, with knees so weak that they threatened to collapse. A lock of dark hair had fallen over his forehead, and her fingers tingled with the desire to touch it. His eyes darkened as he regarded her searchingly as if she represented some mystery to him. He was near enough that she caught a whiff of something spicy, perhaps an aftershave.

The president seemed to have an adverse effect on the speech centers of her brain. Her lips couldn't even manage to form words such as "pleased to meet you." But if she'd been capable of speech, she might have blurted out something about the color of his eyes. And that would have required her to flee the country in shame.

He was still squeezing her hand—it felt so right—but there was no actual handshaking. *I really should say something. And maybe smile. Or am I already smiling?*

His lips parted as if he needed to catch his breath. "Ms. Bennet—"

Chapter Three

Before he uttered another word, Elizabeth was pushed to the side as her father, tired of waiting, waved his hand in the president's face. "Mr. President? John Bennet."

President Darcy dropped Elizabeth's hand so he could take her father's. Freed from the power of his gaze, Elizabeth stumbled backward and a few feet away from the knot of people surrounding the president— which now included a couple Secret Service agents and Press Secretary Bob Hilliard.

Yet the rest of the world seemed to continue apace, unaware that a man had set her senses reeling. And not just any man—the president! Jane conversed animatedly with Mr. Bingley while Kitty and Lydia fidgeted impatiently as they waited to greet the president. Beside them, Fanny absently patted her shellacked hair, no doubt scanning the room for famous faces.

Hadn't they noticed the difference in Elizabeth? A simple touch of his hand had reordered her world. *Well, of course I had a powerful reaction to meeting him. He's the president. Duh. The leader of the free world and all that. Naturally, he's charismatic and holds people's attention. That's what politicians do.*

Still, Elizabeth had the niggling sensation that *he* had been the one to prolong the contact—that *he* had been unwilling to release *her* hand. No. That was absurd. A trick of her imagination. In fact, he was probably desperately wishing for some hand sanitizer right now.

Her father's voice—always the loudest in any room— intruded on Elizabeth's thoughts. "I'm the founder and owner of On-a-Stick, Inc.," he said proudly.

President Darcy didn't seem like the kind of person who had eaten anything off a stick in his entire life. "On-a-Stick?" the president repeated blankly.

Elizabeth winced. There was no stopping her father now.

"Surely you know about Meatballs On-a-Stick?" her father said eagerly.

The president managed a polite smile. "Your company makes those?"

"That was our first product," Mr. Bennet explained. Elizabeth could have recited his next words along with him. "We now sell 106 separate On-a-Stick products." The president nodded, but his eyes scanned the room as if hoping for a rescuer. "We have Ravioli On-a-Stick, Cookies On-a-Stick, Granola Bars On-a-Stick, Eggs On-a-Stick — the eggs are hard boiled, of course." Her father paused for the same little chuckle he always gave at this point in his spiel.

"Of course," the president responded dryly. Maybe politicians took classes in how to feign interest in boring topics.

"You have a younger sister, don't you?" her father persisted. "We could send her a case of Doughnuts On-a-Stick that she could share with her little friends."

President Darcy gazed down at John Bennet. "Georgiana is a sophomore at Harvard and rows crew. She has to watch her carbs."

Elizabeth's father continued, undaunted. There was something almost impressive about his ability to remain oblivious to scorn. "Soup On-a-Stick!" he announced. The president's eyebrows shot up. "We put it in a little cup and put the cup on a stick. It's frozen until you're ready to eat it."

"I see..." the president said slowly. "Does this enhance the soup-eating experience?"

His tone was so dry that her father missed the hint of disdain, but Elizabeth was offended on his behalf.

Mr. Bennet continued, "Lasagna On-a-Stick was a real misstep; I don't mind admitting that to you..."

Did he plan to describe the marketability of each of the 106 items? Elizabeth's stomach twisted, and her cheeks burned. Why did he have to do that *here*? She hardly needed additional reasons for embarrassment.

The monologue continued: "Cheese On-a-Stick makes a great appetizer. You should consider serving it here at the White House. We have cheddar, American, mozzarella, and brie..."

President Darcy's lips curved into a cold imitation of a smile. Elizabeth noticed his gold cufflinks and Patek Philippe watch; his tuxedo was bespoke and must have cost thousands. As a child, he had probably eaten his lollipops with a knife and fork.

Her father was in full-on marketing mode now. "Sticks are a big improvement over toothpicks when serving cheese...More sanitary and..."

If Elizabeth had to endure one more minute of this humiliation, she might scream. She sidled up to her father and tried to catch his eye.

"I'm sure *children* enjoy your products," the president murmured. It was not a compliment. *Oh no. Now he's done it.*

"Not just children," her father corrected sternly. "Our research shows that 65 percent of our products are consumed by adults—"

"Indeed?"

"Yes, and—"

That diatribe could go on for five minutes, and President Darcy's eyes already had a glazed and distant look. Elizabeth grabbed her father's elbow. "Dad, we should let the president greet other guests."

Her father eyed the rest of his family awaiting their turns. "Oh. Yes. We can continue this conversation later," he reassured the president.

The other man's lips twitched. "Of course." Elizabeth had barely drawn her father away before President Darcy reached for Jane's hand with a rather fixed smile on his face.

At least Jane could be relied on to be gracious and appropriate. However, Lydia was now talking to Bingley, making grand, sweeping gestures that suggested raucous storytelling. *I don't want to know.*

Her father wandered off in search of food. After a brief conversation with the president, Jane stepped away and joined Elizabeth as she observed the Bennet family from a safe distance.

Jane clutched Elizabeth's arm in horror. "Lizzy, look!" Lydia drew a selfie stick from her purse and proceeded to buddy up next to President Darcy. His smile could best be described as zombie-like. Elizabeth groaned. By the end of the evening, the president would be commissioning a Bennet family dart board for the Oval Office. *Ten points for Lydia, fifteen for Mr. Bennet, and 200 for Elizabeth right in the bullseye.* Of course, why should he be any different from anyone else who had met the Bennets?

Elizabeth covered her eyes with her hand. "At least we won't be compelled to attend another of these events."

"At least not during *this* administration," Jane agreed with a sigh.

Awed by the president, Kitty navigated her introduction rather sedately. Hallelujah. However, as their mother prattled to President Darcy, she pointed to her various daughters in different parts of the room.

"Do you think she's explaining how our eggs are getting old?" Jane asked in a low, horrified voice.

"It's like we're prime breeding stock she wants to sell," Elizabeth moaned.

Jane snorted. "I don't think he's in the market."

Indeed, the president's face had gone quite still, and he responded to their mother with fewer and fewer words. He said something to her, abruptly turned in the opposite direction, and hurried toward the dining room, Secret Service agents trailing in his wake. Their mother watched him leave with a bemused expression.

Glancing up from her conversation with Bingley, Mary appeared crestfallen that she had missed her opportunity to meet the president.

"Okay, I do support his policies," Elizabeth growled. "But the man is slime."

"Maybe it was an emergency," Jane said faintly.

"Right," Elizabeth scoffed. She turned her back on the scene. "I'm not sure how much longer I can stand this."

Jane's eyes widened. "We haven't even had dinner yet." She motioned toward the spectacle of Lydia taking a selfie with an unamused Secret Service agent. "And don't you think we need to provide adult supervision?"

Elizabeth allowed her shoulders to sag. "We're fooling ourselves if we think we're having an effect," she said tonelessly. "It's probably better if we don't know what's happening." She stared at the fiasco with Lydia for a moment. "Let's go."

Jane bit her lip. "Maybe in a little while? Bing was going to tell me about the administration's plans to combat child hunger." As the director of On-a-Stick's marketing, Jane was always reaching out to children's charities, and she served on the board for the D.C. chapter of Help Our Children Eat.

So he was "Bing" to her already? Interesting. "The president's chief of staff wants to chat you up?"

"You know that's an issue I care about." Jane had a sudden, intense interest in her shoes.

"Charles Bingley seems nice, but he's from an old-money family just like President Darcy." The Bennets had found that old-money families tended to form a united front against the "upstart" newly wealthy like themselves. With a bad track record when it came to dating, Jane could be so easily hurt.

"I'm just talking to him about childhood hunger. Not hopping into bed with him." Jane's voice was sharp.

Elizabeth held up her hands. "Of course."

In the next instant, Jane's face lit up with a soft smile; Bing approached with an iPad at the ready. His hand landed on Jane's elbow as he aimed a blinding smile in her direction. The man wasn't quite as handsome as the president, but his blond surfer look was quite attractive.

Jane glanced sidelong at Elizabeth. "Go ahead. I need to visit the restroom anyway," Elizabeth whispered in her sister's ear.

After giving Jane a little push in Bing's direction, Elizabeth wended her way slowly through the crowd, wishing she knew more people at the event. Although the success of her family's company had catapulted the Bennets into the upper echelons, the old-money families often snubbed them, and Elizabeth usually preferred the company of people like her coworkers. Unfortunately that often left her isolated at events like this.

Perhaps I should just be thankful I'm not hiding in the broom closet or on the receiving end of the president's glare.

At least she could escape to the restroom. Getting to the "ladies' lounge" required crossing to the opposite side of the entrance hall and traversing a short hallway. Decorated in shades of peach and cream, the room boasted frilly curtains, little baskets of toiletries on the sink, and cloth towels. This early in the event it was blissfully deserted, allowing Elizabeth to sink gratefully onto a small padded bench near the door. Taking deep breaths, she tried to relax muscles that were tied into one big knot after two encounters with the president.

Alas, the quiet was short-lived. As Elizabeth washed her hands, Lydia entered, accompanied by her "bestie" Maria Lucas, Walter's daughter. The minute Lydia glimpsed Elizabeth, her voice dissolved into high-pitched squeals. "Ohmygod, Lizzy. Did you come to the ladies' room *alone?*" She shuffled a little closer and sniffed. "Why do you smell like cleaning supplies? You are so *weird.*"

Elizabeth gritted her teeth, reminding herself that she loved Lydia and did not want to drop her sister's phone in the toilet.

Lydia had already moved on to a new topic. "Did you see me with the president? I took a selfie with him!" She waved her phone in Elizabeth's face. "Although I didn't get the best angle. I think it makes my nose look big. Don't you think it makes my nose look big? And my dress really is a brighter shade than it looks in the picture. But still…it's the president!"

Her voice was so shrill that Elizabeth winced. "I posted it on Twitter and Instagram. It's been retweeted 243 times already!" She tossed her head. "No one at school can top that!"

During this monologue, Elizabeth dutifully viewed all the pictures she had witnessed being taken only five minutes ago. When Lydia started hyperventilating from lack of oxygen, Maria had a brief opportunity to speak. "You are soooo lucky!" she enthused to Lydia. "I haven't even met President Darcy yet, and he and my dad are, like, best buds. It's so unfair!"

"You know what's unfair?" Lydia cried, regarding herself in the mirror. "Have you seen my hair?" She alternately fluffed and scrunched a curl on the side of her face. "I'm like, hello? I'm meeting the president and everything—and *now* I have to have a bad hair day?"

"That sucks!" Maria chimed in.

Lydia adjusted the hot pink monstrosity on her head. "And after everything I spent on this hat! People won't even see it." Elizabeth thought that would be an improvement. "All they'll notice is disaster hair!" Maria knew her lines in this play and rushed to reassure Lydia that her hair was the best in the whole ballroom. After what seemed like an eternity of watching Lydia preen in the mirror, they were finally ready to leave.

The bathroom door had just closed behind them when Elizabeth threw out her arm to stop the other women—as if they were heading into heavy traffic. She pointed emphatically down the hall. President Darcy, his back to them, was consulting with Bob Hilliard. They were surrounded by a small knot of Secret Service agents. Nobody had noticed the three women yet, so Elizabeth crowded them back into the alcove created for the restroom door where they wouldn't be visible.

They couldn't go anywhere without pushing past the president and his agents. Awkward, to say the least, and Elizabeth had no desire to remind President Darcy of her existence. If only they could return to the restroom! But the men in the hallway—who obviously believed they were alone—might hear the door open. They were trapped.

From her hiding place, Elizabeth could glimpse only a slice of the president's back, but his words were quite clear. "No, I won't!" he said to Hilliard.

"Okay, then someone else." The press secretary's tone was half pleading and half I'm-trying-to-be-reasonable. "This is the perfect opportunity."

She would have paid good money to be anywhere else. How had she managed to eavesdrop on the president twice in one evening?

"Damn it!" President Darcy shifted from one leg to the other and then back as if preparing to sprint out of the hallway. "Bob, I have important things to do. The transportation plan—"

"Your public image is important long-term," Hilliard said in a low, soothing tone. "The presidency is a marathon, not a sprint—"

"Yes, I know," the president interrupted. "But how will any of your ideas advance my agenda—?"

Lydia and Maria stifled giggles behind their hands, amused to be eavesdropping on the president. *I should feel guiltier about it than I do*, Elizabeth thought. But his arrogance hadn't made her charitably inclined toward him. Hopefully he wouldn't reveal any classified information. Elizabeth wasn't at all confident she could prevent Lydia from tweeting it.

Lips pressed tightly together, Hilliard consulted his iPad. "Mr. President, you saw your latest poll results. People see you as unapproachable and proud." Elizabeth smothered a snort; that was putting it mildly. Hilliard continued, "We discussed finding opportunities to soften your image. Dancing with a woman at an event like this will show you can loosen up and have fun. If the press picks up on it, the optics are good. Particularly if she appears to be an ordinary American."

Lydia listened with her hand over her mouth as though she might burst with excitement at any moment. This certainly was more interesting than hearing about the transportation bill.

The president's hand rubbed the back of his neck. "Bob…"

"Just a dance or two. Nothing more."

"No."

"The rumors are getting bad again," Hilliard said in a warning tone.

The president exhaled forcefully. "Who did you have in mind?"

Hilliard scanned his iPad. "How about one of the Bennet girls you just met? Elizabeth Bennet? Her father donated to your campaign. She's pretty, and you seemed taken with her when you shook her hand."

Elizabeth froze in horror while Lydia and Maria shot her amazed looks. Would he tell Hilliard about the broom closet?

President Darcy snorted. "Ha! I don't think so. You didn't have to speak with her. I don't think there's anything going on upstairs." He tapped the side of his head. "Intellectual lightweight. And she's not *that* pretty."

Elizabeth stumbled further into the alcove until she couldn't see the men anymore. Lydia convulsed in silent laughter, her hand stuffed in her mouth to muffle the sounds, while Maria gaped at Elizabeth, wide-eyed. Elizabeth reviewed the words in her head, but they remained the same. Yes, the president—the *president!*—thought she was ugly and stupid and had voiced the sentiment out loud.

She heard President Darcy blow out an exasperated breath. "Bob, I know you have my best interests at heart, but would a few dances with some wallflower from a nouveau riche family make much of a difference to your average voter?"

Elizabeth peeked around the corner again in time to see Hilliard sigh and tuck the iPad under his arm. "Will you at least dance with *someone*? Pretend you're having a good time for a few minutes?"

"Fine," the other man muttered. "I'll dance with Caroline again, okay?"

"Caroline is not an ordinary Amer—"

"Enough, Bob." The president's voice brooked no disagreement. The conversation was over. He straightened his jacket. "Now, if you'll excuse me, I have some governing to do." As the president started to walk, the whole group of men moved en masse down the hallway. Soon they were gone.

Elizabeth remained frozen in the alcove, plastered against the wall. She probably should have bolted for the exit, but her muscles felt loose and unattached as though she might fall to pieces if she tried to move.

Finally, Lydia grabbed her arm, pulled her through the ladies' room door, and pushed her up toward the sinks. "OMG! You just got *dissed* by the president!" she laughed.

Maria viewed Elizabeth with a kind of awe. "Presidential dissing. Executive dissing. Wow."

Elizabeth fell onto the padded bench and drew her knees up to her chest despite the tightness of her dress. "Can't we just forget it—?"

Eyes glued to her smartphone screen, Lydia interrupted. "Nah. It's too good. I already texted Amy about this. She'll scream."

"Please don't!" Elizabeth pleaded.

Lydia regarded her sardonically. "Yeah, uh, that's not going to happen."

Shit.

"She's not *that* pretty." Maria imitated the president's precise tones perfectly.

Lydia giggled. "I've got to send it to Jordan, too!"

Maria nodded vigorously. "Ooh, ooh! And Olga! It'll crack her up."

First the closet, now her father, and then this… Was it possible to induce a heart attack through accumulated mortification? Her chest ached, and she couldn't catch her breath. "What did I do to deserve that?" she wondered aloud.

Frantically texting away, Lydia snorted. "Some people get presidential pardons. You get presidential shade." Her phone buzzed. "Ryan thinks you should get a picture with him. Then we could add speech bubbles and…"

Great. The group of people in the know included Ryan, whoever he was. "Maybe we should go back to the East Room. Dinner will be ready soon," Elizabeth said.

Perhaps she should slip discreetly out the back door, but that seemed cowardly like she was allowing his rudeness to chase her away. *Instead, I should stay and show the president I'm not vapid and unattractive. Even if he doesn't know I overheard him.* As revenges went, it was rather feeble, but it was all she had.

"Ooh! I wonder who I'm sitting with!" Maria exclaimed in a too-loud voice. "I bet they'll think it's hilarious."

"By all means, tell everyone you can find," Elizabeth remarked dryly.

Lydia gave her an ironic salute. "I'll do my best."

As they opened the bathroom door, Elizabeth scanned the corridor, but it was empty. "You don't really mind if we tell everyone, do you?" Lydia asked breathlessly as they hurried toward the East Room.

Elizabeth's feelings were moot at this point, so she bit back an angry retort. Being a good sport would give her family less fodder for future teasing. "Nah. It's kind of funny," Elizabeth said through gritted teeth. "It's not like he knows me."

"Yeah," Maria agreed absently as she thumbed another message into her phone. "I mean, you're not as pretty as I am, but you wouldn't make someone lose their lunch or anything."

"I feel better already," Elizabeth mumbled.

"I'm glad you're being so mature about this," Lydia said in all seriousness as they reached the entrance to the East Room. "'Cause I already posted it on Twitter, and it's been retweeted 168 times already."

"Twitter—!" Elizabeth sputtered. But Lydia and Maria had already disappeared into the crowd, no doubt in search of a greater audience for the tale of Elizabeth's humiliation.

Elizabeth ambled around the edges of the room, avoiding eye contact and seeking a dark corner. *It's not like I ever thought of myself as a great beauty, so that part shouldn't rankle. He doesn't know the first thing about my intelligence or conversational abilities. He's just making assumptions. Most people would get tongue-tied when caught in a White House broom closet. Arrogant jerk.*

Of course, most people wouldn't get caught in a White House broom closet. Maybe that did say something about her....

No. It would be stupid to get upset.

Just stupid.

Chapter Four

Darcy hurried back toward the East Room, refusing to slow his stride for Hilliard's shorter legs. It was petty, but Darcy didn't care. So what if polls found him aloof? The way to fix that was creating policies and drafting legislation that helped the American people—not dancing. The press secretary's prodding had pushed Darcy to say something indiscreet and, worse—something he didn't mean. As someone who prided himself on his honesty—a quality the voters also appreciated—he was annoyed at Hilliard and even more angry with himself.

If Hilliard had just shut up about the dancing! That Bennet woman was a hot button for some reason. The memory of luscious dark hair and moss-green eyes caused his breathing to grow ragged. *I wonder where she is? I could find her and invite her to sit at my table…*

Perhaps this was the result of reading too many briefing books in too short a time: you began to hallucinate an instant connection with a stranger. Maybe he and Elizabeth enjoyed some…chemistry, but it was nothing more and would be easily dismissed.

She hadn't managed to say anything intelligent to him, not even "nice to meet you." Dancing with her would require him to attempt conversation. It would also foster rumors. Having his name associated with an inarticulate, pampered nouveau-riche princess whose father hawked excessively processed foodstuffs? No, thank you. Not the family background he sought in a romantic partner.

Of course, he wasn't seeking a romantic partner. The presidency occupied all his time and energy. Damn Hilliard for observing his reaction to Elizabeth! Hopefully everyone else remained oblivious.

Although who wouldn't have noticed her in that dress? Understated and elegant—so flattering to her slim figure. Completely unlike the gowns worn by her mother and sisters. Despite her superior taste in dresses, she was probably one of those empty-headed daughters of wealth who lived in tasteless McMansions until they met the right rich guy to father their precious babies. Shallow, uninformed, and self-centered.

Darcy could practically write the script for what women like that would say to him. She would flatter him excessively while discreetly touting her own virtues and accomplishments. He shuddered, recalling the woman at a recent reception who couldn't stop bragging about which sorority she had pledged.

Certainly, he'd dodged a bullet with Elizabeth Bennet.

Darcy braced himself for the onslaught of noise as he crossed the threshold into the East Room. It was a magnificent room, beautifully decorated to convey a sense of history and tradition, but after more than a year in office, Darcy still felt like a visitor—as he did in most of the White House. Technically it was his home, but many parts were used for ceremonial or official functions and didn't feel like "home" at all. Even the Residence was more like a well-decorated hotel than his actual domicile.

The mingled sounds of approximately 120 voices blasted him. The band at the other end of the room couldn't compete with the hubbub. One hundred and twenty voices, and every single one of them wanted to talk to Darcy. Each one thought they knew him. Each one had some idea or grievance they wanted to share. If he contemplated it too long, the sheer scale would overwhelm him.

His eyes were caught by an image on the large-screen television opposite the entrance. Elizabeth Bennet stared down at him. The picture appeared to show a refugee encampment, probably in Africa. Elizabeth's thick dark hair was tied up in a ponytail, but loose strands fell around her face and stuck to her cheeks with sweat. She sat on the ground feeding a small girl about two or three years old from a bowl in her lap.

Darcy allowed himself a second to admire the trim physique displayed by her cargo shorts and Red Cross t-shirt. Then he contemplated the revelation that she was a Red Cross staff member. The dirt smudged on her face…the sweat…the rip on her shorts. This was someone who worked hard in difficult circumstances. And looked hot doing it.

Maybe she wasn't as much of a spoiled princess as he had assumed. The Red Cross only hired the best. She had to be pretty damn good, particularly to be working for them at her age—which looked to be her late twenties. She was seemingly smart and compassionate as well as beautiful. And he had massively misjudged her.

He tried to ignore the tightening in his chest. It didn't matter; she would never know what he had said about her. Still, he couldn't help staring at the image until it faded from the screen and was replaced by one of a middle-aged man carrying a box of supplies. Only then did he notice many pairs of curious eyes watching him. Thirteen months into his first term and he still wasn't used to the scrutiny.

I need to stop this. I'm busy leading the free world. I don't have time to worry over maligning a woman who doesn't even know about it.

Pivoting, he strode toward the head table. Two Secret Service agents in front of him cleared a path—one perk of the office. Darcy considered his political priorities. So far he hadn't managed to buttonhole anyone he needed to talk with. That was unacceptable. His administration had accomplished a lot in his first year, but he needed to keep pressing forward. So much more needed to be done.

As he walked, Darcy's eyes skimmed over the dance floor where Jane Bennet was partnered by Bing, doing his usual goofy flirty thing. She was smiling and eating it up. Bing always knew the right thing to say to a woman. He even managed to remain friends with all his exes.

That kind of charm was missing from Darcy's DNA. He could cajole governors into supporting his environmental initiatives and persuade independent voters to cast ballots for him, but he evidently didn't have the temperament for flirtation—or the qualities necessary for a successful relationship. He'd only had a few serious girlfriends, and one had been all too happy to bad-mouth him to the press during the election.

He'd resigned himself to singlehood while in the White House. Dating in office could lead to all kinds of rumors and conflicts of interest. Plus, he simply didn't have time to meet eligible young women. Darcy grimaced. It hardly mattered if he'd misjudged Elizabeth Bennet; she could never have been more than a spin around the dance floor anyway.

The self-enforced celibacy had led to rumors he was gay. Hilliard was concerned the rumors were gaining more traction and that they would hurt his favorability ratings among Republican voters, who, sick of his predecessor's failures, had supported him in big numbers. Hilliard wanted to showcase Darcy's heterosexuality whenever possible—another reason to be seen with female dance partners. Darcy personally didn't care what people believed about his sex life, but it was galling when stupid rumors interfered with the good work of his presidency.

On the other hand, dancing with a single woman could provoke crazy rumors; he had danced with a single congresswoman at a Christmas party, and within hours the Internet buzzed with stories about a secret engagement. Darcy sensed the beginnings of a headache. There was only one woman he'd known long enough that their association wouldn't raise eyebrows.

But the prospect was not enticing.

"Will!" a female voice trilled from behind him. Perfect timing. Darcy managed not to wince. Most of his staff called him Mr. President in public, but Caroline Bingley insisted on using his first name to demonstrate how closely their families were connected.

Darcy slowed but didn't turn, allowing Bing's sister to reach him. She teetered in her high heels, always seemingly on the verge of wiping out completely. "Hello, Caroline," he said with something resembling a smile. Uninvited, she tucked her arm into his and pressed herself against his side. He could feel his muscles tense. Caroline had set her sights on becoming first lady, and her persistence had become an irritant.

Over the years, he had dropped many subtle and unsubtle hints that he viewed her solely as a friend, but she clung to the delusion that he might change his mind. Unfortunately, as a member of the White House communications staff, she was involved in Darcy's life on a daily basis. She was damn good at her job and extremely loyal, but that didn't compensate for the ground-down teeth and elevated blood pressure he experienced in her presence.

However, at that moment Darcy didn't see any of the legislators he needed to speak with, so he might as well get one unpleasant chore out of the way. Tall and fashionably skinny—with her brother's blonde good looks—Caroline was attractive enough. But her dress (no doubt from the latest Milan designer) was boldly colored and sequined, far too ostentatious for Darcy's taste.

He rewarded her expectant look with what he knew she wanted. "You look exquisite."

"Thank you," she purred.

"Would you dance with me?" Darcy asked, trying not to sound like he was requesting surgery without anesthesia.

The big smile on Caroline's face attested to his success. "I would love to, darling!"

She slid a perfectly manicured hand into his, obviously expecting him to escort her to the dance floor at that exact moment. Very well.

Just as they stepped onto the dance floor, the band struck up a slow song. Pressing his lips together, Darcy resisted the urge to curse. He had anticipated keeping her at arm's length, but now he would need to perform what his friends in high school laughingly called "the bear hug," holding her close while rotating in minute circles.

She smiled like a wolf that had just caught its prey, wrapping her arms around his neck and pulling him so close that he was forced to put his hands on her waist. Yeesh, there was nothing to it; she was so skinny. Hopefully Caroline would one day find a man who appreciated that build.

Darcy much preferred a woman with some curves, fine green eyes, and a headful of dark, lustrous hair…

He dragged his attention back to Caroline with an effort of will. She likely expected some conversation. Darcy cleared his throat. "The band is quite good." There. Inane, but sufficient.

Fortunately, Caroline was quite eager to bear the burden of future conversation. "Oh yes! You should have heard the band at my mother's birthday party. Was it her fiftieth or fifty-fifth? Well, we had them set up in a tent in the backyard…"

Why did slow songs always last approximately five times longer than fast ones?

When a new song began, Darcy mumbled something to Caroline about needing to find Bing. She was prepared with a request that he fetch her a beverage, one of her favorite ploys to prolong their time together. But Darcy's patience was exhausted. Peering over her shoulder, he announced, "There's Senator Ostrevsky! Bing and I need to talk to him." Without awaiting a response, Darcy hurried away in search of Bing.

Fortunately, Bing was nearby. Unfortunately, he was chatting with both Jane and Elizabeth Bennet. Darcy's words to Hilliard echoed mockingly in his head. They were even less true now. Learning about her Red Cross job had rendered her much more intriguing.

Aware of Caroline's eyes on him, Darcy sidled up to Bing as though he had Important Presidential Matters to discuss. Naturally, the moment he appeared, all conversation ceased—one distinct disadvantage of his office.

The moment all eyes turned to him, Darcy recalled how horrific his small-talk skills were. Elizabeth's frank gaze particularly weighed on him, seemingly demanding that he be witty and charming, but Darcy's communication skills were more along the lines of wonky and policy-driven. He wondered if he could wow her with a sharp analysis of the economic implications of historical ethnic divisions in the Balkans.

"Are you ladies enjoying the evening?" He managed not to cringe (outwardly at least) over asking the world's most inane question.

Jane raised her voice to be heard over the music. "Oh yes, it's lovely. So many interesting people, and the food is delightful!"

In the following pause, Darcy thought Elizabeth might chime in, but she regarded him with an indecipherable expression. This did nothing to lessen her attractiveness; instead he was intrigued by the alteration in her behavior.

Finally, Bing cleared his throat. "The prosciutto melon balls are great."

"I haven't had any yet," Darcy said. If only he had a drink to serve as the focus of his attention. Elizabeth's silence was disconcerting. The flustered, chatty girl was gone, and in her place stood a woman with a cool, detached gaze, which contrasted sharply with her sister's polite I'm-trying-to-please-the-president smile.

"Ms. Bennet," Darcy addressed Elizabeth. "I saw an image of you on the Red Cross screen. I didn't realize you work for them."

"Yes," she said, holding herself very still and taking deep, even breaths.

After a few moments, everyone realized that Elizabeth had no intention of elaborating.

"Elizabeth has been all over the world with the Red Cross. She's part of their refugee crisis team," Jane volunteered. Elizabeth didn't even nod in agreement with her sister's observation. It was an odd change in behavior for the previously uncontrollable babbler. Was she embarrassed about her previous behavior? Or about her family's? God knows, Darcy would be mortified by such relations.

He still found himself desiring her good opinion. "I'm sure that's a very rewarding career," he said, holding her gaze.

Her lips pressed tightly together, but a muscle twitched in her jaw. "Yes."

When it became clear that Elizabeth would say no more, her sister gave a nervous little laugh.

Darcy was once again that ninth-grade boy who had been ridiculed by Catherine Hopkins. Of course, he had made a strategic error by asking her to homecoming in front of all her friends—and he had mispronounced it so it sounded like comb-humming. Still, he would like to believe he had acquired more communication skills since then, but it was quite possible he hadn't. He *had* expected that becoming president would come with some privileges, like pleasant conversations with intriguing women.

But he hadn't gotten elected president by giving up easily. *Let's try a different approach.* "The White House is considering a new refugee initiative. What do you think is the area of greatest need?" Darcy smiled pleasantly at Elizabeth.

Her eyes were cold and flinty as she stared back. "I doubt you could benefit from my opinion. I'm a bit of an intellectual lightweight, as you know."

Jane's eyes widened in shock. Bing started coughing. Before anyone spoke, Elizabeth held up her phone. "Sorry, urgent call. Please excuse me." She turned away from them and was immediately swallowed up by the crowd.

Jane's eyes were focused on her wine glass. "Elizabeth, um, wasn't feeling well today."

"That's too bad," Bing said sincerely, careful not to look in Darcy's direction.

Darcy did not respond. "Intellectual lightweight." The phrase niggled at his memory. Where had he heard it recently?

Not that it mattered anyway. He'd probably imagined any connection between them—wishful thinking brought on by too many lonely nights in the Residence. Firs, she babbled, and then she acted like he'd killed her cat. Perhaps she was just a strange person.

Then he recalled he had used the phrase in describing Elizabeth to Hilliard. And somehow, she had heard him.

Shit.

Double shit.

No wonder she had been icy and distant. Darcy was lucky she hadn't flung a drink in his face. His cheeks heated and his chest tightened as he imagined her overhearing his uncensored remarks. Now that he knew she wasn't a pampered rich girl, his comments were even more egregious. He grappled with an intense desire to leave the room—or hide behind one of the eight-foot-high floral arrangements.

The proper course would be to follow Elizabeth Bennet and apologize. But he certainly couldn't chase after her, Secret Service agents in tow, begging for a moment of her time to explain—what, exactly? He couldn't claim he hadn't meant the words; there was no denying he had said them. She probably wouldn't even listen to a convoluted explanation about his annoyance with Hilliard, let alone believe it.

However, it was equally unimaginable *not* to apologize. Darcy started after her, but a hand on his elbow pulled him back. Bob Hilliard yet again. One glimpse of the man's white-lipped frown and tense shoulders prevented Darcy from voicing his complaints.

Without a word, Hilliard pulled Darcy to an unoccupied table, where they were immediately joined by Caroline. Hilliard handed Darcy a scotch on the rocks—a bad sign. Hilliard spoke in a low tone. "Sir, we have a potential situation on Twitter."

Darcy frowned at Caroline, who handled social media. His predecessor in the office had been a disaster on Twitter, but most of Darcy's tweets—posted by his social media staff—were about his policy positions.

"Not *your* Twitter account," Caroline clarified. "There's a guest here tonight by the name of Lydia Bennet." Darcy couldn't recall which sister she was. "She has a picture of herself with you." Darcy shrugged; people posted pictures with him all the time.

"She also complains that you 'threw shade'"—Bob used air quotes—"at her sister Elizabeth. Supposedly you said 'she is stupid and not pretty enough to dance with.' It's been retweeted 800,000 times." He checked his iPad. "Wait a minute...800,015."

Darcy was suddenly nauseated. Not only had Elizabeth overheard, but her sister had tweeted it? "That's what I said when—" Hilliard nodded knowingly. Darcy gratefully gulped scotch before scowling at Hilliard. "That area should have been cleared before we talked."

Hilliard grimaced. "The Secret Service should have cleared it, but apparently they didn't check the ladies' room."

Darcy tossed back some more scotch. "Elizabeth Bennet heard me insult her in person?" Hilliard nodded, and Darcy stifled a groan. He had harbored a small hope that she had heard it from a third party. *I'm lucky I got off with a cold shoulder instead of a slap to the face.*

"*The Washington Post* wants to know if we have a comment," Caroline said.

How soon was too soon to leave his own state dinner? This had been a series of fiascos. "They want us to respond to a tweet from a high school student?"

Caroline consulted her phone. "Her profile says she's at GW University. *The Post* wants to know if you actually said her sister was 'ugly and stupid' and if you said it to her face."

"No!" Darcy practically yelled. "I would never—" Several heads pivoted in their direction; Darcy lowered his voice. "Obviously I didn't know she was there."

Caroline frowned. "Her father is a big donor. Can we issue a denial?"

Darcy's predecessor had been notorious for his falsehoods, and Darcy had been scrupulous at avoiding any appearance of being less than truthful. It was one of the ways he had gained the public's trust and restored faith in the presidency. "No," he said wearily. "I did say it. I haven't lied to the press before. I'm not starting now."

Caroline took notes with brisk efficiency. "We can say 'no comment,' but perhaps we should get someone working on damage control." She shot a quizzical look at Hilliard, who nodded.

Darcy rubbed the back of his neck where the headache had now taken hold. He couldn't help imagining Elizabeth's reaction when he had uttered those words. How had her face looked? What had she thought? Had he made her cry? God damn it! Darcy scrubbed his face with his hands. "Can I issue an apology?"

"What?" Hilliard's voice squeaked, and Caroline barked a laugh.

"I was irritated at you." He waved at Hilliard. "And it was an insensitive thing to say. I didn't even mean it." Darcy's breathing constricted just thinking that she might believe those ill-considered words. They were beneath him and beneath the office of the president.

"No, you can't *apologize!*" Hilliard hissed. "An apology would only confirm that you said it. That would be the surest way to transform this into a media circus. It would be breaking news on the cable stations. Rule number one of the presidency: don't admit mistakes."

"Stupid rule." Darcy hated to maintain a façade of infallibility. Presidents were human and made mistakes. Pretending otherwise was idiotic and counterproductive, but admitting to errors gave your enemies too much ammunition. He gripped the scotch glass so tightly that his fingers turned white.

"If we don't say anything, it will likely die down," Hilliard said.

Darcy stretched his neck, willing the muscles to loosen. Hilliard was right, but still. "Can I at least apologize to Elizabeth Bennet?"

"Why bother?" Caroline asked sharply.

He drained the last of the scotch and slammed the glass down on the table. "Because it was rude and inaccurate. She's neither stupid nor ugly," he growled at Caroline, not even caring when she drew back slightly.

Hilliard shook his head sadly. "No. You can't apologize to her. It would be the first thing she'd mention if the media contacts her. It would be best if you didn't have any conversations with her at all."

Darcy thumped the glass on the table, startling Caroline. "Great. Just great," he muttered to himself.

Elizabeth would continue to believe that he thought she was unattractive and dumb, and the whole world would think he'd insulted a woman he barely knew. And he'd been barred from speaking with the most intriguing woman he'd met in years.

Sometimes being president sucked.

Chapter Five

Elizabeth's mother sounded frantic on the phone. "It's a disaster! We'll soon be begging in the streets! Starving in the hedgerows!" Elizabeth didn't even know what hedgerows were, let alone why they would cause starvation. Every question she asked was drowned out by wailing and dire predictions until her mother claimed that a racing pulse and faint feelings would keep her from speaking. Mr. Bennet came on the line and begged Elizabeth's presence at home, hanging up before she could ask for an explanation.

As Elizabeth navigated her Prius across Roosevelt Bridge and into the Virginia suburbs, she tried calling Kitty and Mary—the two sisters who still lived at home—but neither answered her phone.

Her biggest concern was that it had something to do with that stupid incident at the White House three weeks ago. Was it possible that the event was somehow having repercussions now? Lydia's tweet had been retweeted more than 1.5 million times, and Elizabeth worried that her name would be forever linked with the president's. Her days were haunted with visions of *People* magazine covers showing her and the president side by side in little rectangles and cable news shows with psychological experts diagnosing her state of mind at the time of the insult.

And if the media ever learned about the closet incident…? Elizabeth winced whenever the thought crossed her mind.

Fortunately for Elizabeth, the day after the state dinner, a senator had been arrested with a prostitute and North Korea had nearly hit an American ship with a missile. So Lydia's tweet and Elizabeth's identity were relegated to late-night comedy show punchlines, and even that quickly withered away when no more information was added to the story.

However, Elizabeth had not escaped unscathed. On social media she was known as "POTUSdissgirl," and her coworkers teased her about it unmercifully. She always laughed along as though she never tired of the reminder that the leader of the free world thought she was stupid and ugly.

The disastrous evening had produced one good result, though. Jane had been on four dates with Bing, and their relationship was flourishing. Jane hadn't been lucky in love, and Elizabeth rejoiced to see her sister so optimistic.

After twenty minutes of speculating about the nature of her mother's disaster, Elizabeth's neck and shoulders were stiff with tension by her arrival at her parents' house. She navigated her car between the large faux gold-leaf lion statues guarding the end of the driveway, marveling once again how she could have been raised by two people who thought they were an essential part of a "dream house."

Another unfortunate design choice was echoing the lions' gold leaf on the roofs of the rhomboid "turrets" at the front of the house. The shiny gold turrets, not to mention the gilt dolphins by the front door, were a rather jarring contrast to the house's otherwise staid suburban colonial architecture with its slate gray shingles.

Elizabeth had been only thirteen when her parents designed and built the house, but when she thought of "home" she still pictured the modest split-level they had occupied in her early childhood. That house had been small for a family of seven, and the zip code wasn't close to being fashionable, but Elizabeth still missed it.

Elizabeth was barely through the front door when she encountered Jane juggling a tea cup, an aromatherapy candle, and a hot water bottle. Yup, her mother was having another one of her "episodes."

Jane's shoulders sagged when she spotted Elizabeth. "Oh, thank God you're here! Please tell Mom it isn't as bad as it seems." That always seemed to be Elizabeth's role in such crises. For various reasons, the other sisters weren't very effective during Fanny's fits of anxiety; only Elizabeth ever managed to calm their mother through a combination of cajoling and tough love.

"No problem," Elizabeth retorted. "As soon as I find out what 'it' is." Jane nodded sympathetically but rushed up the wide marble stairs before she could answer any questions.

Elizabeth shrugged out of her coat and hung it in the front closet before following Jane upstairs and down the plushly carpeted hallway to the master bedroom. The bedroom could serve as a parking garage for at least two cars; its grand scale was matched by the adjoining master bathroom, which could have held fifteen people comfortably—although Elizabeth had no idea what good that was.

The bed was faux French Provincial with an enormous white wood canopy that was accented with gilt furbelows. In her pink bathrobe with the fake fur hood around her face, Elizabeth's mother was dwarfed by the enormous bed, surrounded as she was by dozens of pillows and blankets. "Lizzy! Thank God you have come! Nobody understands how I have suffered. I have a nervous condition, you know."

Elizabeth nodded solemnly. "I know."

"Here, Mom." Jane handed her the tea cup. "It's chamomile. And I brought your lavender candle and your hot water bottle."

Mrs. Bennet patted her daughter's hand. "You are very good to me, but I doubt it will be of much use. My nerves are completely shot."

"Have you taken your Xanax?" Elizabeth asked.

"Of course!" Fanny lifted her head indignantly. "I remember what Dr. Burgeron said. I had one right away."

"Just one?" Elizabeth asked.

Mrs. Bennet fluttered her hands. "I didn't want to sleep until you arrived. It's important that you understand how we're all ruined!"

Such words should have struck terror in Elizabeth's heart, but her mother was prone to doomsday pronouncements, and Elizabeth had developed something of an immunity so was only mildly worried. "Mom, you can tell me later. You should rest."

"No! No! I can't rest until you understand."

Jane shrugged helplessly at Elizabeth. With a sigh, Elizabeth sat on the edge of the bed. "So what's the problem?"

"Do you remember Stanley Yerger?" her mother asked in a quavering voice.

"The accountant?" He did the finances for On-a-Stick, Inc.

"He isn't an accountant!" her mother shrieked, wiping her eyes with a tissue. "He is a devil sent to torment us."

Huh. Elizabeth remembered him as short and plump with saggy jowls. "What did he do?"

"He took the money! He took *all* the money!" Mrs. Bennet blew her nose noisily into a tissue.

This response was just vague enough to produce maximum anxiety while providing minimum information. Elizabeth took a deep breath. "What money?"

"All of it!" Her mother waved impatiently. "It's gone!"

"He drained the reserves," said Mary from behind Elizabeth.

Elizabeth turned as her sister joined her at their mother's bedside. She was again wearing all brown, but today her blouse and pants were uncharacteristically rumpled.

"The reserves?" Elizabeth asked.

"On-a-Stick was setting aside money for new factory equipment. Stan skipped town with it."

Elizabeth's stomach lurched. Stan Yerger was a friend of John Bennet's from college, and his firm had done the books for On-a-Stick, Inc. since its founding.

Mary's lips were set in a thin, white line. "We found out yesterday. Charlotte Lucas came over."

Elizabeth suddenly remembered that Stan also did the books for Lucas and Lucas. Her hand flew to her mouth. "Oh no!"

"Yeah. Walter found some accounting 'irregularities.' When Walter went to Stan's office for a meeting, he was gone." Mary grimaced. "He cleaned out Lucas and Lucas, too, and then took off for parts unknown. The police have a warrant out for him, but if he's smart, he went to a country that doesn't have an extradition treaty with the U.S."

"We're ruined!" her mother howled. "We'll be homeless! We'll be living in the poorhouse!"

Mary put her hands on her hips. "Get real, Mom. They don't have poorhouses anymore."

Their mother wailed even louder.

"Just a thought, Mary, but don't take up counseling," Elizabeth said.

Mary shrugged.

"It's not that bad, Mom." Elizabeth raised her voice to be heard over her mother's cries. "I'm sure it's not that bad." She glared meaningfully at Mary.

"Oh! No, it's not that bad," Mary assured her hastily. "We'll be able to weather this without halting construction on the fourth factory or laying off workers or selling the house. I'm almost sure. Mostly sure."

Their mother continued to bawl. Elizabeth was beginning to remember why calming Fanny wasn't Mary's job.

"Mom," Elizabeth used her most soothing voice, "why don't you take another Xanax and try to sleep?" She gave another pill to her mother with a glass of water from the bedside table. "We'll talk about it when you wake up." From long experience, Elizabeth knew her mother would be more willing to listen to reason and less frantic after she rested.

Her mother nodded and swallowed the pill. The daughters waited at Fanny's bedside until she fell asleep and then quietly filed out. In the kitchen, Jane put on the tea kettle.

"How bad is it really?" Elizabeth asked Mary.

Mary pressed her lips together. "It's bad. Dad's been using the cash reserves to capitalize the launch of Spaghetti On-a-Stick…and…well…we've been having development problems with it."

"Whose idea was Spaghetti On-a-Stick anyway?" Elizabeth asked. Surely there were hundreds of foods that were better candidates for being put on a stick.

"Dad's," Mary replied. "He's very enthusiastic. He had this idea for wrapping the noodles around the stick that was very innovative—something nobody has ever done in the industry." Elizabeth exchanged a glance with Jane and knew they were thinking the same thing: maybe there was a reason nobody had tried it. "But it turns out that spaghetti is kind of slippery, so R&D has been having trouble getting it to stick to the stick. And with building that new factory out in Duluth…We're out on a limb financially."

"Shit," Elizabeth said, feeling suddenly unmoored. She was the only Bennet who didn't depend on the food company for a livelihood; if the business cratered, the whole family would be in straitened circumstances.

"Without new products to market, sales have been lagging. And we lost the City of Chicago contract to On-a-Rod, Inc. I don't know what we'll do if sales don't pick up. Dad doesn't want to sell to one of those big conglomerates, but—"

"He can't sell the company!" Jane cried. "It's all he ever dreamed about. And now it's finally a success!"

Mary shrugged. "I don't know how we're going to survive. We only have about a couple months' of business expenses in the bank, and nobody will give Dad another loan." She slouched into her chair. "What we really need is a steady customer to provide a stable stream of income."

"Weren't you going to apply for the USDA contract?" Elizabeth asked. The application for the U.S. Department of Agriculture's school lunch program had been the sole topic of conversation within the family for at least a month. She smiled her thanks at Jane as her sister handed her a cup of tea.

Mary brightened a little. "Yeah, that's a huge contract. It could save us, but we won't even know whether we won it for at least a month."

"All right," Elizabeth said. "I'll try to dwell on the positive when I talk to Mom."

Jane patted her hand. "Thank you for coming. Sometimes you're the only one she'll listen to."

"Better you than me." Mary rolled her eyes. "And you probably know this, but Dad wants to keep it quiet, so you can't say anything to Lydia—that would be like taking out an ad in *The New York Times*."

"What's going on at Lucas and Lucas?" Elizabeth asked. The PR firm was the pride and joy of her friend Charlotte's life.

Mary shook her head sadly. "Charlotte seemed upset on the phone. I guess business has been slow since her dad has been doing so much volunteering for the Democratic National Committee."

Elizabeth sipped her tea. "I wish there was something I could do. She's kick ass at PR."

"You know anyone who needs a PR guru?" Mary asked.

Elizabeth gnawed on a fingernail while she considered, but Jane spoke first. "Maybe Bing does! Politicians always need good PR or know someone who does."

"That's a great idea," Elizabeth said. "I'm sure Charlotte would appreciate being recommended."

Mary nodded slowly. "Now, if only we knew someone who can get spaghetti to stick to a stick…"

***

The phone rang. And rang again. Elizabeth rolled over and groped for it on her bedside table. "Hello?"

"Lizzy?"

The strained quality of Jane's voice put Elizabeth on instant alert. "Jane? What's wrong?" Her first thought was another financial emergency like the one a week ago.

"I…um…hurt my back again."

"Oh no!" Elizabeth bolted upright in bed. The last time Jane injured her back it had turned out to be a herniated disc which had prevented her from walking for almost three weeks. "How bad is it?"

Jane gave a humorless laugh. "Pretty bad." If Jane admitted to being in pain it must be excruciating. Elizabeth's mouth was suddenly quite dry.

"Are you lying down? Do you want me to come over? I could bring my heating pad. Is your prescription up to date?"

Jane chuckled without mirth. "Yeah, my prescription is up to date. Unfortunately, it's at home."

"And you're not?" Where could Jane be at—Elizabeth squinted at her clock—1:36 a.m. on a Saturday night? Well, technically it was Sunday Monday. Had she gone to Bing's place?

"I was hoping you could go to my apartment, pick up the medicine, and bring it here." Elizabeth could tell Jane was trying to keep the pain out of her voice. Each word was carefully enunciated.

"Of course. Where are you?" Elizabeth stood, pulling off her pajama bottoms and struggling into her jeans.

"Um, that's the thing. I'm at the White House."

Elizabeth dropped the phone. And hastily picked it up. "The White House? Why are you at the White House?" She froze with her jeans halfway up her legs.

"Bing invited me to a dinner at the Residence. Just the president and a couple of his friends and their wives. Then I fell and hurt my back. I thought it would be okay, but then…it wasn't." The slight slurring of Jane's words told Elizabeth how much pain her sister was experiencing.

Elizabeth took a deep, centering breath. "Tell me where the prescription is, and I'll be there as soon as I can."

"Hold on." There was a pause and some muffled voices.

Despite Jane's relationship with Bing, Elizabeth never expected to have an occasion to return to the White House. And she'd been content with that thought. In fact, she had planned to avoid President Darcy for the rest of her life. The last man in the world Elizabeth wanted to see, and Jane was stuck at his house. But it was Jane. And Elizabeth would do anything for her sister.

Then Jane was back. "You'll also have to give Bing your Social Security number. The Secret Service needs to do a quick background check even though you were at the White House before."

Bing makes Jane happy. This is worth the trouble. "No problem." She kept her voice as positive as possible.

"I'm sorry," Jane said somberly. "Maybe Bing could go to my apartment instead—"

"No, that would take a lot longer," Elizabeth said. She would not leave her sister in pain and vulnerable in a strange place. "I'm coming. Just tell me where the medicine is, and then I'll talk to Bing."

***

An hour later Elizabeth was riding in an elevator with a Secret Service agent whose expressions ranged from blank to grim. Jane had assured Elizabeth that she could simply drop off the medicine, but Elizabeth needed to see Jane herself. Bing was a nice guy, but Elizabeth knew nothing about his nursing skills.

The elevator doors slid open, revealing a small vestibule and front door that might lead to an ordinary apartment in a rather old-fashioned building. The agent knocked, and the door was quickly opened by Bing. He usually was immaculately dressed and collected, but his wrinkled shirtsleeves and disheveled hair suggested that he'd been caring for Jane.

His smile for Elizabeth came and went in a flash. "Thank goodness you're here!" As he opened the door wider for Elizabeth, the agent returned to the elevator. Bing closed the door behind them with a decisive click.

They were in the entrance hall of what Elizabeth assumed was the Residence, the part of the White House where the president actually lived. The hall was decorated with gray tile flooring and dark wood paneling. The ornately carved furniture dripped historical authenticity, but it was all on a residential scale—not the grand scale of the White House's public rooms. While this room was still formal, it was far more intimate and livable.

She had no problem envisioning President Darcy in this room. She bet he could give detailed information about the provenance and time period of each piece of furniture. What she couldn't imagine was someone running around the Residence barefoot in ratty sweatpants or cut-off shorts, but the president probably wouldn't do that anywhere.

Bing gestured down the hall. "Jane is resting in one of the spare bedrooms."

"What happened?" Elizabeth asked as they walked.

"Just a freak accident," Bing said. "One of her high heels caught on a bit of broken tile in the kitchen. She went down like a sack of potatoes." He shuddered at the memory. "I knew she was in trouble when she didn't stand up again right away." He squeezed his eyes shut and massaged his forehead with one hand. "She was wincing at the pain and trying not to cry; it was awful. I wanted to send for the White House doctor, but she swore all she needed was her medicine."

"She doesn't like having a fuss made over her," Elizabeth said. "The medicine makes her sleepy, and she shouldn't try to walk until she's rested her back, at least for the night."

"That's what I thought, too. Jane said otherwise."

"She's trying not to be a burden," Elizabeth observed.

They stopped outside a closed door. "To hell with that!" Bing said in a low voice. "She can stay all night if she needs to. Nobody else needs the room, and I don't want her to make it worse."

Elizabeth heartily approved. Bing had his priorities in place.

When Bing swung open the door, they entered a dimly lit bedroom straight from the colonial era. The dark wooden bed had a white lace canopy and blue covers in a floral pattern. Jane was lying flat on her back in the middle, her face pale and drawn. She turned her head as Elizabeth approached the bed and attempted a smile. But the lines around her eyes suggested the effort it cost her. Just like the last time. Elizabeth was not pleased with the similarities.

"Lizzy," Jane moaned. "Thank you for coming."

"Of course." Elizabeth took her sister's hand and squeezed it gently. Bing brought in a glass of water from the adjoining bathroom and left the two sisters alone.

Helping Jane into a sitting position provoked gasps of pain, but it allowed her to take the pill. "Thank you, Lizzy," Jane said after swallowing. "I'm sure I'll start feeling better soon, and then I can leave. You might need to drive me—"

Elizabeth scowled. "You are in no shape to leave tonight. You can't walk, and I doubt you can sit in a wheelchair. I'm not even confident you can leave in the morning."

Jane shook her head emphatically. "I can't stay here! It's the *White House*. Bing doesn't even live here."

Bing slipped into the room during this declaration and was at Jane's side in an instant. Tenderly, he brushed hairs from Jane's forehead. "Don't worry about any of that. It's not a problem to stay with you overnight, my dear. I've stayed over plenty of times when Darcy and I had a late night working on a project." He glanced at Elizabeth. "Can you help her settle down while I use the bathroom?"

Jane was silent until the bathroom door closed but then said, "No, I can't possibly stay." She tried to swing her legs to the edge of the bed but gasped in pain.

"You can't possibly go." Elizabeth put her hand on Jane's shoulder. "Remember how walking made it worse the last time?"

Jane nodded, biting her lip. Tears glistened in her eyes as she fell back against the pillows. Naturally, Jane was anxious at the prospect of being alone and vulnerable in a strange place. Her relationship with Bing was still fairly new, and Jane hated to impose. But Elizabeth had done this before. "Would you like me to stay?" she asked softly.

Hope shone on Jane's face for a moment, but then she averted her eyes. "I can't ask that of you."

"You're not asking. I'm offering," Elizabeth said firmly. "And *I* would feel better if I could stay. Just in case you need me."

Jane allowed her head to flop back onto the pillow. "It *would* be nice to have someone help me get into the bathroom and change clothes. Bing and I aren't quite at that stage yet."

Elizabeth patted Jane's hand. "No problem. You should sleep if you can. I won't go far."

Jane nodded wearily before her eyes fluttered closed. Bing emerged from the bathroom, and he and Elizabeth padded out of the room and closed the door softly behind them. Forehead creased with worry, Bing turned to Elizabeth. "What do you think?"

"Well, it's not exactly the same as when she herniated her disc, but she needs to be careful. She should sleep now. The medicine usually tires her out. I told Jane I would stay the night since I've been through this before. And I can help her leave in the morning."

"Thank you," Bing said earnestly, anxious eyes fixed on the door. "Maybe I'll go in and sit with her." He gestured down the hall. "The living room and kitchen are down there. You can help yourself to some coffee or food. Whatever you want."

He was turning her loose in the Residence with only those instructions? Elizabeth hesitated. "Is the president—?"

"Oh, he's working on a refugee issue in the Treaty Room." Bing pointed to a door. "It serves as his study. The man never sleeps. He won't emerge for a couple of hours—and then he'll head for bed."

"I don't want to be in the way," Elizabeth said, although that was not at all her real objection.

Bing waved his hand airily. "Darcy likely is oblivious to everything except foreign policy." With that reassurance, Bing disappeared into Jane's room and left Elizabeth in the surreal position of being alone in the White House Residence at three in the morning.

She wandered down the hallway until she came to an open door and peered in, finding an oval room. The White House architect sure liked his oval rooms. This one wasn't an office, though. It was set up like a formal living room with pale green sofas and chairs upholstered in gold and cream arranged around a fireplace. At the far end of the room were three floor-to-ceiling windows hung with gold drapes. Like everything else in the building, the room radiated history and formality—not a place to kick back to watch a football game. In fact, there was no television.

After turning on a lamp, Elizabeth tiptoed into the yellow room, feeling like an intruder but unable to resist a once-in-a-lifetime opportunity to explore. It was more interesting than the broom closet and less likely to get her arrested.

Venturing further into the room, she soaked in every detail. It looked a little familiar; perhaps she'd seen photos of presidents hanging out here. Peering out the window, she didn't see much except the railing for a balcony—underwhelming until she recognized it as the Truman Balcony.

This is actually happening, she reminded herself. *I'm not dreaming it or imagining it or watching it in a movie.* But it was still hard to believe.

A muffled thump from the hallway caused Elizabeth to freeze. *Please, please, don't let the president come in here*, she prayed silently. After discovering her in his broom closet, what would he think if he found her in the Residence? At the very least she would cement her reputation as a stalker.

Even if he accepted her presence here, she would still be exposed to his razor-sharp tongue. Exhausted and worried about her sister, Elizabeth had no desire to fend off a torrent of disdain at three a.m.

Continued silence from the hallway helped slow Elizabeth's heartbeat, but the scare had quenched her desire to explore. Avoiding the president was her highest priority. Her eyes searched the dimly lit Oval Room, finding a high-backed sofa in the rear, facing the windows. If she stretched out there, Elizabeth would be practically invisible from the hallway but still close enough to Jane's room.

The Victorian-style sofa had a curved back and striped silk fabric. Sturdily constructed, the piece was probably a reproduction rather than an antique. Still, sitting on it seemed presumptuous without written permission from George Washington. She snickered at her own hesitation and very deliberately flopped onto the cushions.

Despite its formal appearance, the sofa was quite comfortable, enveloping her in softness. Although she had no intention of sleeping, she positioned a cushion behind her back and another behind her head and commenced reading the news on her phone. However, the sofa was cozy and the hour was late, and soon Elizabeth was asleep.

Chapter Six

Darcy stood up at his desk and ran his fingers through his hair. 4:12 a.m. Well, he'd certainly had later nights. He'd made progress on a number of fronts, although he was still stymied by the problems in Zavene. His staff didn't seem to include anyone who truly understood the country's convoluted tribal structure and how that affected its politics.

Plodding to the door, his body protesting like a far older man, Darcy again swore he would curtail the late nights. But there was always so much to *do*. Walking into the hallway, he shifted from work mode, reminding him of the events from earlier. The dinner party. Jane Bennet hurting her back. When she refused the help of a doctor, Bing had taken her to one of the spare bedrooms.

Were they still here? Surely Bing would have ducked his head in the door to notify Darcy if they were leaving. Still, Jane had seemed uneasy at the thought of spending the night in the White House. Which would be just as well. Although Darcy had no objection to Jane, she reminded him too much of the first woman he'd encountered who made him wish he could pursue a relationship while in office.

For the hundredth time Darcy mused what made Elizabeth Bennet so special. She certainly was not the most beautiful woman he'd ever met. Movie stars and models always sought his company, and he had to send them on their way. However, Elizabeth was intriguing. Without a pressing need for a career, she still devoted herself to the unglamorous and sometimes dangerous labor of an aid worker in third-world countries. Of course, Darcy had met pretty, interesting, and compassionate women before. Hadn't he?

Caroline Bingley, Virginia Longworth, Camelia Cassidy…all smart, pretty, ambitious women with the "right" kind of family name. The kind his parents expected him to marry. However, their images didn't linger in his mind. He was ambivalent about ever seeing them again while eagerly anticipating the day he might encounter Elizabeth Bennet once more.

Oddly, what he remembered most from the state dinner was her silences. At first she had been nervous in his presence; then she had been angry and hadn't hesitated to let him know it—not just through her sarcasm and standoffish body language but also by her refusal to engage with him in conversation.

Even before he entered politics, Darcy had spent much of his life surrounded by people who sought to curry favor with him, who wanted something from him: jobs, money, approval, political alliances, friendship, even marriage. Elizabeth Bennet hadn't wanted anything from him. How refreshing. How…fascinating.

That's odd. A light was turned on in the Yellow Oval Room. His guests had congregated there for a while after dinner, but Darcy remembered switching off each table lamp when they left. Was Bing in there burning the midnight oil? Had Jane's crisis deepened? *I should have checked on them earlier.*

Nothing seemed out of order as Darcy took a cursory glance around the room. But as he turned to go, a faint rustle of clothing emanated from the sofa closest to the window. Darcy crept closer, as silently as possible. If Bing had fallen asleep on the sofa, Darcy didn't want to wake him.

But the form curled asleep on the sofa was not Bing. It was Elizabeth.

Darcy did a double take, but no, he wasn't hallucinating. The person on the sofa was definitely Elizabeth Bennet. He seized the opportunity to view her unobserved, eyes feasting on her slumbering form. It was simultaneously delightful and entirely inappropriate. His memory had not overestimated her beauty; if anything, he had underestimated it. He felt like a prince who had stumbled upon an enchanted princess. *What the hell am I thinking? I must be more sleep deprived than I thought.*

Elizabeth's head was propped on a cushion, and her sock-clad feet were curled together. The dark hair spread almost wantonly over the pillow was practically begging Darcy to touch it. Her lips were slightly parted, so lush and kissable. Her body was elegantly proportioned; the loose t-shirt and jeans did nothing to hide the shape of her breasts, her hips. Watching her, a soft smile curved his lips.

She was…so…unguarded. He should allow her to enjoy the sleep she so obviously needed, but he wished he could awaken her just to see her green eyes and wide smile.

His sleep-starved mind manufactured many possible reasons for her presence—mostly involving confessions of her attraction to him, which were followed by the removal of clothing. His imagination would never have run riot in such a way if he weren't so weary.

But of course. Elizabeth was here for Jane. Who had injured her back. He was a fool to think otherwise.

Darcy had no idea how much time passed as he watched Elizabeth's chest softly rise and fall. Every minute he promised himself that he would leave before she woke, but he always found reasons for delay. Then, inevitably, it happened. Her head lifted, her eyes opened, and she noticed him.

She shot to a standing position with the alacrity of a security guard found sleeping on his watch. Her face flushed a deep red. "M-Mr. P-President! I—Bing said—Jane's back—medicine—not sleeping—sorry!" With one hand she tried to smooth her hair into place, although it looked delightfully tousled. With the other she wiped her mouth. Had she drooled a little? Good Lord, Darcy even found that endearing.

Which he should not. It was unwise to find it—or anything having to do with Elizabeth Bennet—endearing. He needed to grow a spine and hurry her out of the Residence before someone discovered her and made assumptions about her presence.

In the face of his silence, she continued, albeit rather more coherently, "The S-Secret Service knows I-I'm here. B-Bing let me in." Her eyes blinked blearily.

"You came to see Jane?" She nodded with wary exhaustion. Darcy cleared his throat. "Can I call you a car to take you home?" *Wait, did that sound like I want her to leave?*

"N-no thank you," she stammered. "I-I brought my own car."

"Then why are you still here?" *Damn, that came out wrong.*

She drew herself up to her full height, her lips pressed tightly together. "I'll stay out of your way. I'm not snooping for state secrets or anything."

He'd offended her. Somehow he always managed to say the wrong thing in her presence. "No, no...I mean...it's no inconvenience. I just—I didn't want you to stay because you felt you were trapped." *Good Lord, I'm babbling now.*

Avoiding his gaze, Elizabeth rubbed her face as if trying to wake herself up. "I promised Jane I wouldn't leave her alone." Her voice was sharp.

Surely he could say something to her without messing up. *She's a guest. Maybe I could try for a reset.* "I beg your pardon. I'm being a terrible host. Would you like a bed?"

Her hands fell away from her face. "I'm sorry?"

"To sleep in," Darcy added quickly. "While Jane is here."

"Sleep, yes! But no." She shook her head. "I'd rather stay close to her room."

"Your devotion to your sister is quite commendable."

Jane.

He must seem like an insensitive lout. Or more of an insensitive lout than he already appeared. Why hadn't he asked about her sister first? "How is your sister—now? Is she any better?"

Elizabeth's eyes darted toward Jane's room. "I brought some of her pain medication. I think she's sleeping now. Bing is in with her."

He nodded, trying to let concern show on his face. *No insensitive lout here. No sir.* This seemed like a good, neutral topic of conversation. "Jane said she had a similar back injury before," he said casually.

Elizabeth regarded him warily as if his concern was somehow suspicious. "Yeah, two or three years ago. She was laid up for a while and in a lot of pain. It hurt to stand or walk. She missed close to a month of work. This doesn't seem quite as severe, but it's hard to tell."

"I can call for a doctor," Darcy said, trying to look solemn and presidential despite the fact that his inner teenager was cheering and high-fiving himself at the prospect of having Elizabeth in his house all night. *Calm the fuck down,* he told teenage Darcy. *Nothing will happen, and I need to ensure the press doesn't find out.* The admonishment did little to quiet his inner glee.

Elizabeth pursed her lips. "I don't think that's necessary at this point. Hopefully she'll be well enough in a few hours to sit in the car, and I can take her to see her doctor tomorrow." She paused and then added, "But thank you, Mr. President."

"Call me—" The words were out of his mouth before he thought them through. He barely knew her. If other people heard her using his first name, what would they think? "Er, Mr. President is fine," he finished lamely.

Her mouth twisted in a bitter smile, and no wonder. It probably sounded like a demand that she recognize his title. "Um…well, thank you for letting us stay, Mr. President," she said stiffly.

"Of course." Would she look askance at an offer to keep her company? She rubbed her eyes and stifled a yawn. No. Forced sleep deprivation was not the way to anyone's heart. *Not that I want to win her heart.* It would be progress if she thought of him more positively than as "the man who called me stupid and ugly."

He briefly allowed his eyes to linger on her, indulging his desire to admire her vivid green eyes. Unfortunately, they were narrowed and viewed him with suspicion. The situation was a bit...irregular...maybe even creepy... Damn. He would have gladly enjoyed her company all night, but there was no legitimate reason to remain.

"I'll be next door in the Treaty Room"—he pointed to the left—"if you need anything." Despite the heaviness in his body, Darcy knew sleep was an impossibility with Elizabeth in the Residence; he might as well work.

"You don't need to stay up on my account," she said.

"I'm not." *I totally am.* He gave her sour smile. "I'm trying to figure out what to do about Zavene."

"Because of the civil war?"

"Yes." *Huh.* The smallest country in Africa, Zavene was unknown to most Americans. Previous administrations had meddled in Zavenian politics, and Darcy believed the U.S. had a moral duty to try to stop the violence. Surely peace was achievable without involving the U.S. military, but Darcy didn't know how. The previous State Department had been understaffed, and they still didn't have an expert on Zavene.

"I served in the Peace Corps there for two years." Elizabeth stared down at her hands. "The people were wonderful. It's so distressing to think of them caught up in a war. Although I don't think the village I lived in has been affected yet."

"You lived there for *two years*....?" Darcy clasped his hands behind his back lest he frighten her with too much enthusiasm. "Could you explain to me the tribal differences that led to the war? The media portrayal seems too simplistic, and the State Department doesn't have a real expert."

Her eyebrows rose. "I'm not an expert, but I can tell you what I know. Do you have a map of the country? It would make it easier to explain."

"I have one in my study," he said, suppressing the broad grin that threatened to break out. He hesitated for just a second. *Would she perceive that as a bizarre proposition? Hello young woman, want to come upstairs and see my maps?* "I know that's not why you came to the White House—"

She was already striding toward the door. "Are you kidding?" She grinned impishly over her shoulder. "I love to show off how much I know. Now that I can flaunt it to the president, I'm in heaven!"

A slow smile crept over his face. "My pleasure."

***

Elizabeth stretched luxuriously, realizing too late that her feet had encountered an obstacle on the coffee table. Something clunked. Shit! Had she broken that swirly glass vase? It was probably a gift from the Sultan of Brunei that she'd have to sell her car to replace.

Tentatively she opened her eyes to examine the scene. Her feet *had* knocked over the remarkably ugly vase, but it appeared intact. Upon inspection, it revealed no cracks or nicks. *Whew.*

The sunlight streaming in through the windows suggested that it was morning—and further suggested that it was past time to wake up. She didn't know what the protocol was for having spent the night on the president's sofa, but she was sure it didn't involve sleeping in. Bathed in the sunlight, the Yellow Oval Room was far more cheerful and less forbidding with all the creams and golds in the upholstery brightening the decor, but she still couldn't imagine allowing a toddler or a dog within fifty feet of it.

The moment her brain registered "White House," adrenaline pumped through her body, waking her sluggish mind. The Zavene discussion had lasted at least two hours, so Elizabeth was functioning with only a couple hours of sleep, but it had been a surprisingly lively and enjoyable conversation.

She finger-combed her hair, wishing the room had a mirror since she had stupidly left her purse in Jane's room. On the other hand, she might be tempted to sneak out the back door if she could see herself.

Before going to bed—er, sofa—Elizabeth had checked on her sister, who appeared deeply asleep. Bing had sacked out in the overstuffed chair next to Jane's bed.

Elizabeth straightened the pillows she'd been using and folded the throw the president had given her. President William Darcy was an enigma. No one in her life had ever said such disparaging things, and he was disdainful of her family. At the same time, he had listened attentively to her description of Zavene. He had taken notes, asked intelligent questions, and thanked her without mansplaining or condescension.

At times she had even forgotten who she was speaking with. Her family was never interested in hearing about her experiences in foreign countries. And the president had the power to make a difference, unlike the coworkers with whom she occasionally traded stories.

If her information could have even a small impact on the fate of the Zavenian people, it was worth the effort of swallowing her anger. Although the effort hadn't been as great as she expected.

A loud gurgle reminded her how long it had been since dinner. An exit strategy was also necessary. Last night Elizabeth's priority had been remaining near Jane, but in the light of day it dawned on her that she had couch surfed in the *White House*. Either the president or his staff would need the Bennet sisters gone and soon.

She padded down the hallway toward the kitchen she'd passed the night before. Her brain desperately needed the boost a shot of caffeine would provide.

The thought that the president might be awake already hadn't crossed her mind, but there he was, sitting at the kitchen table with a cup of coffee and *The Washington Post*. The room was small and functional, with a plain oak set of table and chairs—the most ordinary thing she'd seen in the White House. The scene was simultaneously ordinary and bizarre: the president got bedhead just like everyone else.

"Ms. Bennet!" He set his coffee cup down with a loud thunk. "I didn't expect you so early." One hand reached the top of his head in an attempt to smooth his unruly locks.

"I'm afraid my brain doesn't come online until I have some coffee, so I was hoping—"

"I made a pot." He gestured to the coffeemaker over his shoulder. "Please help yourself." He gave her a genuinely warm smile. Which was odd. And a bit worrisome. Maybe he was just a morning person.

"You made it yourself? Don't you have staff for that?"

He stiffened, even though Elizabeth had meant it as a gentle tease. "I prefer not to have staff in the Residence when I'm here…It…feels less like a home."

"You're usually here by yourself?" she blurted out and then gave herself a mental kick. *Yes, it sounds lonely, but do not feel sorry for him. Do not. Even if he's alone, he's still the President of the United States, for God's sake! Not a homeless man.*

Maybe if he weren't so arrogant he'd have a wife and kids to share his home.

He combed his fingers through his hair, patting it in place. "Sometimes. Bing stays frequently. And my cousin Richard Fitzwilliam often stays here. He helps keep me on schedule, takes care of logistics, interfaces with the staff—that kind of thing. But he's away this week

visiting family. So it was nice having guests last night even by accident."
He gave her another enigmatic smile.

After a pause, she went to the counter to pour a cup of coffee. At least with her back to him she could escape the dark intensity of the eyes that followed her everywhere.

He cleared his throat. "I…um…if word gets out that you're here, it could be…problematic."

She stiffened but remained silent. *I should have expected this. The relaxed president who discussed Zavene so freely couldn't last forever.* She turned around, leaning her hips against the counter and holding the mug up near her face like a shield. He wanted them gone, and so did she. There was no reason to feel anger or regret.

"I'll check on Jane," she said. "With a night of rest and some more medicine, she might be able to walk to the car. We could be out within an hour."

He nodded briskly. "Good."

***

Elizabeth wasn't happy with him again, Darcy observed. They'd had such a delightful conversation in the Treaty Room last night, but somehow they'd lost that easiness in the light of the morning. Maybe she wished she'd seen more of the Residence. "I'm sorry I didn't have time to show you around."

She jerked her head back. "I didn't come here for a tour."

Really? What person isn't a little bit curious about the White House? "That wasn't even a little factor in your decision to stay?" he teased. "Few people have the chance to stay overnight at the White House."

Elizabeth's face went white. "Wow," she said slowly. "Not only am I ugly and stupid but apparently shallow as hell, too."

Shit. Instantly his chest tightened, constricting his breathing. He closed his eyes briefly, but when he opened them she was still glaring at him. Darcy would have happily lived the rest of his life without discussing that event again, but that wasn't an option. "I didn't intend to be insulting."

"It must be an inborn talent then."

Darcy's stomach coiled itself into a knot. Many people disliked what he said about them. They devoted hours of cable television time to discussing it. Gallons of ink had been used to describe his misjudgments. Why did he find *her* unhappiness so disturbing?

Still, damn it, he hadn't said it to her face. "Maybe you shouldn't eavesdrop. You might not like what you hear," he said.

"Maybe you shouldn't insult people," she retorted. "Then it wouldn't get tweeted."

Don't ever apologize. Hilliard's admonition echoed through his mind. But he had no hope of friendship with her otherwise. "I'm sorry about that," he blurted out. She frowned, and he rushed to explain. "I was tired and irritated with Hilliard. My comments had nothing to do with you."

She snorted. "How silly of me for taking comments about my attractiveness and intelligence personally."

Of all the women in the world, why did it have to be *this* one he insulted so thoroughly? "The truth is that I think you're"—he cleared his throat—"quite attractive and intelligent…"

She was silent for a moment. "Um…thank you." The rising inflection in her voice signaled her doubt. But she *had* to believe him.

He caught and held her eyes. "The fact is that you're one of the most attractive and intelligent women of my acquaintance."

Blinking rapidly, she swiftly averted her eyes. Had he said too much? Would she think he was propositioning her? Language was such an imprecise instrument for conveying thoughts, but maybe he could clarify his meaning. "My injudicious word choice was influenced by having recently met your family."

Her eyes darted back to his face. "My family?"

"Yes. Well…they're…you know…" He gestured, hoping she'd nod in understanding; instead she simply stared. "A bit much…over the top. You know," he finished helplessly.

"Nouveau riche?" she volunteered.

"Exactly!" Darcy said, relieved he hadn't been the one to say it. "Of course, *you're* not like that!" he added hastily.

"I'm honored you think so." Her lips were set in a flat line.

His apology should have decreased her anger. But it hadn't. He was pretty sure he had screwed up another conversation with her, but how? "Look, Ms. Bennet—"

His voice died when Caroline Bingley entered the kitchen.

Even on a Saturday, she was dressed in a designer suit and high heels. Sweeping into the room like she owned it, she brandished a sheaf of papers at Darcy. "You won't believe what ZNN—"

Caroline stopped short at the sight of Elizabeth leaning against the counter and feigned surprise. No doubt she had heard Elizabeth's voice as soon as she entered the Residence. Her posture positively bristled with territorialism. Slowly scanning Elizabeth from head to toe, Caroline eyed every crease in her rumpled clothes. Darcy loved this sleep-tousled version of Elizabeth, but she turned red under Caroline's scrutiny.

Caroline's lip curled as she reached the obvious, but incorrect, conclusion. Shit. How the hell did he set the record straight? He couldn't exactly introduce her as "Elizabeth Bennet, whom I did not sleep with last night, but I'd be good with it if she were interested."

A long silence followed. Darcy cleared his throat. "Uh...you remember Elizabeth Bennet?"

"I don't believe I've had that *pleasure*." Caroline's tone indicated that it was anything but. "Your family makes corn dogs or something, don't they?"

Elizabeth's lips twitched. At least she wasn't intimidated by Caroline. "Oh yeah. You have no idea how hard it is to get the corn kernels to stick to the dogs."

Caroline stared at the other woman blankly. Perhaps she didn't recognize Elizabeth's sarcasm.

"Elizabeth's family owns On-a-Stick, Inc.," Darcy said briskly. "They're a multimillion dollar company specializing in a variety of foods." Elizabeth's eyebrows shot up. Didn't she know he would have her family's company researched after their first encounter?

Caroline drew herself up and leveled her gaze at Darcy. "Will, honey, we need to get her out of here before the press finds out." Her tone very deliberately lacked energy, implying that finding strange women in the Residence was a regular occurrence. Darcy was torn between applauding the performance and tearing into her.

A quick glimpse of the murderous fury on Elizabeth's face determined that Darcy needed to clarify the situation. "Nothing happened—"

Caroline held up a hand. "I don't want to hear about it," she said frostily. "This"—she again surveyed Elizabeth from messy hair to shoeless feet—"is hardly helpful to your presidency."

"This isn't—she's not—!" Damn, why was public policy the only thing he could articulate well?

Caroline steamrolled right over his feeble objections as she crossed her arms and gave a dramatic sigh. "Will, it would be good if you could give us a heads up if you're going to pull something like *this*." She glared at Elizabeth like she was an inconvenient mess that Darcy had left on the floor of the kitchen.

Elizabeth moved away from the counter toward Caroline. "There is no 'this!'" she said heatedly. Despite the tension in the air, Darcy experienced a pang. Was the idea of spending the night with him so distasteful?

Ignoring Elizabeth, Caroline pulled out her phone, texting furiously. "The Secret Service has some experience with 'bimbo extraction' after your predecessor's divorce, but they're better if they don't have to do it on the fly."

Elizabeth got right up in Caroline's grill. "I am not a bimbo!"

Glancing up from her phone, Caroline fixed Elizabeth with a glare. "Bimbo is in the eye of the beholder, honey."

Shit. That did it. Storm clouds were practically visible over Elizabeth's head. "Why you—!" she spat at Caroline.

Darcy jumped between the two women, grabbing the phone from Caroline. She stared at her empty hand in shock. "There are no bimbos here," he said firmly to Caroline. "Elizabeth arrived late last night to help her sister Jane, who injured her back while here for dinner with Bing."

Caroline seemed mollified for only a second, then her eyes narrowed. "You're telling me we have *two* women to extract?"

"No! Okay…yes, but one spent the night with Bing—" Yeah, that sounded wrong, too. *Maybe everything sounded sordid when connected to the Residence—like you shouldn't even think of sex anywhere near the Lincoln Bedroom.*

"Jane was sedated with painkillers, and Bing watched over her," Elizabeth quickly clarified.

Caroline ignored Elizabeth, speaking directly to Darcy. "You know this will be a juicy story for the media. We need to get them both out before any reporters arrive."

Elizabeth shuddered, no doubt at the thought of becoming part of a media circus. "We can get her out of here—even if it's in a wheelchair."

Darcy didn't want her to leave, but that reaction was utterly nonsensical. "I'll contact the staff for a wheelchair," he said quickly. Elizabeth glanced at him out of the corner of her eye; did she think he was eager for her departure?

Before he could speak, Elizabeth turned toward the door. "I'll see if Jane is awake."

She can't leave like this. I need to find out why she is angry at me. I need to apologize for Caroline. I—

With an air of profound relief, Elizabeth hurried out of the kitchen. Darcy's eyes followed her, but he could do nothing to stop her. The moment she was gone, he rounded on Caroline. "You could have been nicer. Elizabeth was only here to help her sister."

Caroline regarded him coolly. "And somehow that translated into the need to spend the night at the Residence. How *convenient*."

Darcy flinched. Was it possible it had been a ruse? All that concern for her sister? The righteous indignation at his assumptions? She had a quick wit that could be construed as flirtatious. However, not once had she seemed particularly interested in him. Of course, she had stayed up with him for hours... Was it all part of an act? He should have been appalled at the idea. But his disgust at the thought was noticeably...weak.

Still, he couldn't allow Caroline to attribute such mercenary motives to Elizabeth. "I don't think that's what she's after."

Caroline laughed, a trill that ran up and down the scale. "You are so innocent sometimes, Will. I frequently wonder how you managed to wind up in the White House."

Darcy suppressed an urge to snap at her. Caroline and Bing were great additions to his team because they'd known him before he'd gone into politics. But sometimes he wished Caroline was a little more intimidated by his office.

"To a woman like that, you'd be the catch of a lifetime," she continued.

Darcy rolled his eyes. "Her family has plenty of money. She doesn't need my family's fortune."

Caroline huffed. "Very few people believe they have enough money, Will."

"Elizabeth's not like that," he insisted. Didn't Caroline think he could spot a gold digger by this point in his life?

She shrugged. "She might not be looking for a ring, just bragging rights."

Darcy had encountered plenty of women like that, too. "Funny, she seemed more interested in talking about Zavene than in seducing me." A fact that Darcy *should not* find disappointing.

"She could be playing a long game—concealing her true motives," Caroline said tartly. "In any case, we need to get both of them out of here as quickly as possible."

"You and Elizabeth seem united on that point." As much as he would love to have her stay for breakfast and a tour...

Caroline crossed her arms over her chest. "She's dangerous for you, Will. Stay away from her."

Chapter Seven

"Tell me about this guy," Elizabeth demanded.

"I don't know much." The phone muffled Jane's voice. "His name is Bill Collins. He's got brown hair…not very tall…I only spoke with him a little after the auction. Since then we've been emailing."

"What does he do?" Her high heels weren't designed for pacing, but Elizabeth had to burn off her nervous energy.

"I don't remember…" Jane sounded thoughtful. "Something in marketing maybe?"

"You will owe me big time." Elizabeth's sofa beckoned to her enticingly—soft and comfy, perfect for a night of sweat pants and binge watching. Hell, she'd even take a night of organizing the embarrassingly tall piles of paper on her desk. Instead she was trying not to breathe too deeply, or she'd risk popping a seam on her floor-length gown.

"You're not doing it for me," Jane reminded her sweetly. "You're doing it for the children, remember?"

Elizabeth sighed. Jane had her there. Months ago, Jane had participated in a "dream date" auction to benefit Help Our Children Eat. Of course, being beautiful and sweet, Jane's dream date had raised a lot of money. The winning bidder, Bill Collins, now wanted his date.

But Jane had a boyfriend.

Fearing the charity might have to refund the money, Jane had cast about for an alternative and asked Elizabeth to take her place. Elizabeth felt compelled to agree and had done her best to forget about it. After Jane sent Elizabeth's picture to Bill, he accepted the substitution. To sweeten the deal, Jane—through Bing—had acquired tickets to the very exclusive Carlisle Ball, an event that Bill was quite excited to attend. As a result, this evening would combine three of Elizabeth's least favorite things: a fancy, high-society event, high heels, and a blind date.

"I'm sure Bill won't be that bad," Jane reassured her.

Elizabeth ground her back teeth together. "He had to *buy* a date."

Jane switched tactics. "Bing and I will be there. Elizabeth was grateful for that. Jane's back trouble had fortunately proven less serious than before, and she had recovered after missing only a week of work.

"The rest of the family will be there too—they all received invitations," Jane continued brightly. *Doesn't she understand they're part of the problem?*

There was a knock at Elizabeth's door. "I think he's here."

"No matter what, it's just one short night," Jane said quickly before Elizabeth hung up.

Trudging across her hardwood floors, she noticed that they were dirty. Maybe she could stay home and clean them tonight instead.

Biting her lip, Elizabeth pulled the door open—and was momentarily struck dumb. No doubt Jane had instructed Bill to wear a tuxedo. However, Jane obviously hadn't specified that he should avoid wearing a plaid, crushed velvet tux. In retrospect, it was an unfortunate omission. Bill's ensemble made him look like a waiter crossed with a bagpipe player.

A short waiter. Elizabeth bested him by a couple of inches; she could have foregone the heels. A bad comb-over was his other most noticeable feature.

"Elizabeth?" He scrutinized her from head to foot until a reptilian smile bloomed on his lips. "Well, your picture didn't do you justice. I'm quite satisfied by the substitution."

It's for the children. It's for the children.

Puffing out his chest, he offered a hand. "I'm Bill." She shook it, resisting the urge to pull out of his warm, moist grip.

"Your chariot awaits, madam!" he announced with a grand sweeping gesture his arm. Lowering his voice, he added, "I'm joking. It's just a car, not a chariot."

"Um…okay."

"But it's a nice car. A really nice car." He held up his hand and whispered in her ear for some reason. "A BMW." Then he awaited her reaction.

When she gave none, he offered his arm. "Shall we go?"

After locking her apartment door, she congratulated herself for taking his arm without flinching. As they strolled down the hallway, they passed one of Elizabeth's neighbors. Bill nodded grandly as if to say, "Look who's on my arm!" Elizabeth considered whether she might die of embarrassment before they even reached the ball.

Waiting for the elevator, Bill asked, "What line of work are you in, Elizabeth?"

"International aid. I work for the Red Cross."

He sniffed. "I don't imagine there's much money in that." Without giving Elizabeth a chance to reply, he continued, "I'm in the staple industry."

"Staples?" *Did he mean household staples like bread and milk?*

He gazed into the distance and intoned portentously, "I am employed by De Bourgh Staplers and Office Supplies." For a moment he appeared about to salute. "The finest in the world."

They stepped into the elevator. "Oh." Elizabeth couldn't think of anything else to say.

However, it turned out that her input was not necessary for the conversation. "I always wanted to get into staplers," Bill continued. "I worked in erasers for a while, which was fine. And then hole punches, which I didn't like; it's not really a growing industry. But *then* I scored an interview at De Bourgh—the crème de la crème of the stapler world." He paused dramatically, awaiting her reaction.

"Um…how fortunate."

"Fortune had nothing to do with it," he asserted with a lift of his chin. "It was hard work and determination—and a dose of good luck."

Isn't that the same thing as fortune?

He gestured expansively as they exited the elevator. "Do you know how many kinds of staplers De Bourgh Staplers makes?"

"No."

"Take a guess," he said with a wink.

Ugh. "Twenty-three."

"You're way off," he chuckled. "Forty-nine. Forty-nine different kinds of staplers. I bet you didn't know that."

Didn't we just establish that? "No."

"And I'm vice president in charge of staples. It's a heavy responsibility. You wouldn't believe how many companies make inferior staples that don't close properly when they hit the strike plate…" After escorting her out of the building, he led her to his BMW. "The problem is they don't start with the proper materials…"

Jane was wrong. It would be a very *long* night.

***

Bill's soliloquy was still going strong by the time the car pulled up in front of Carlisle House. "Mrs. de Bourgh is such an excellent CEO. She frequently strolls among the cubicles and greets the employees, commenting on their work projects…or anything really. No detail is beneath her notice. Just Thursday she visited David Horvat for the sole purpose of relaying some child-rearing tips. How many other CEOs would be that involved in their employees' lives?

Hopefully none.

They emerged from the car, and Bill handed the keys to the valet parking attendant. Elizabeth settled her lightweight shawl around her shoulders, grateful for the mild May weather.

Jane—perhaps suffering from a guilty conscience—and Bing stood near the entrance, awaiting their arrival. Some of the tension drained from Elizabeth's shoulders; the right company could brighten the evening. After exchanging introductions, the two couples continued up a stone pathway that led to the house. Elizabeth stuck to Jane's side as they preceded the men. Falling in beside Bill, Bing inquired what he did for a living. The ensuing staple-filled monologue kept both men occupied for several minutes.

"On a scale of one to ten, how horrified are you?" Jane murmured from the side of her mouth.

"Thirty-eight."

Jane winced. "I'll help make it better. I can dance with him."

Elizabeth rolled her eyes. "Not nearly enough groveling. I'm planning to demand that you wash my car once a month—with a toothbrush." She grinned to show she was joking.

Jane squeezed Elizabeth's hand sympathetically. "Maybe you can leave early."

"I'll survive. Whoa!"

As they rounded a curve, Carlisle House finally came into view. "Palatial" was an inadequate word to describe it. French Château in style, the house's proportions would be better suited to a high school than a private residence. The front was ornamented with stone tracery and elaborately carved arches above the windows. A large stone arch soared over the double set of front doors.

Both women marveled at the house. "According to Bing, the Carlisles have the biggest private residence in the D.C. area," Jane said. "I guess it would have to be. How many houses have a ballroom anymore?"

As they approached the house, Bill broke off his office-supplies monologue to exclaim over the flowers, the chimney, the windows, and the staff—and loudly estimate the costs for each. The two couples entered the house through the ornately carved arch, which spilled them into a two-story front hallway decorated with a parade of six-foot-high floral arrangements. Here they were greeted by a phalanx of metal detectors and security guards. *There must be some bigwigs attending.*

Staff directed them to the ballroom at the back of the house. It was a baroque masterpiece, with shiny, gilded curlicues and an actual fresco on the ceiling that depicted a mythological scene.

"Wow!" Elizabeth exclaimed. "This is like a real English country house owned by Duke and Duchess So-and-So." *And I'm the poor relation.* "Just you wait. Any second now liveried servants will glide forward to inquire if we'd like to take tea with the lady of the house."

Jane giggled, as Elizabeth had intended, but Bill regarded her with an intense and somber expression. "Buying an English country house is on my bucket list. Yet another sign of our compatibility."

Elizabeth wondered how she had missed the others.

At one end of the enormous room, a big band played old standards for a crowd of enthusiastic dancers. The walls were lined with bars and tables groaning under the weight of a myriad of hors d'oeuvres.

Elizabeth was cataloging the emergency exits—in case of excessive groping—when Bill's arm snaked around her waist and pulled her against his body. The warm moisture of his hand radiated through the silk of her dress; Elizabeth imagined a damp handprint being left behind.

It's for the children. Still, there were limits. She glared at his lascivious smile and spoke with an even tone she didn't feel. "Bill, I don't think we know each other well enough for this."

He waggled his eyebrows at her. "I'd *like* to know you well enough."

Ugh. Shoot me now.

Rather than disappearing, his hand shifted to splay over her back. She smiled apologetically at him. "Sorry," she whispered, "I have an itchy rash there." The hand evaporated.

She put some distance between them, only then glimpsing a knot of people—socialites dressed to the nines, businessmen, and Secret Service agents—standing a few yards away. A man in the center of the group was staring at her. After a moment of disorientation, she recognized him. President Darcy.

Hundreds of people at the ball, and yet somehow his eyes had found her the instant she entered the room. Her stomach did a slow, sickening flip, and she could almost feel her sweat glands gearing up to work overtime. "You didn't tell me the president would be here!" Elizabeth hissed to her sister.

"You didn't know? I thought everyone knew the president attends the Carlisle Ball. It's the primary draw."

Panic urged her toward the nearest exit. The only thing worse than a blind date with Bill the stapler guy was a blind date with Bill the stapler guy while President Darcy watched. The last time she had encountered the commander in chief, he had labeled the Bennets nouveau riche, implied that she visited the White House for bragging rights, and eagerly agreed with Caroline Bingley that Elizabeth needed to be "extracted." His politics might be in the right place, but his heart certainly wasn't. Not that Elizabeth cared what he thought of her.

Still, it would have been nice to arrive at the soirée with a David Gandy lookalike. Instead she got a plaid tux, greasy comb-over, and smarmy smile—all of which had undoubtedly been catalogued by the president. The man himself was conversing with others in his group, but his eyes flickered back to her again and again.

His expression was unreadable, but no doubt he was laughing inside at her plight. Elizabeth's face was so hot that she wondered if she might spontaneously combust. *Is it too late to pretend I don't know Bill? Maybe I could slap him.*

Draped over Bing, Jane gave them both a sunshiny smile. "Would you two like to go dance—?"

Bill's eyes went wide. "OMG!" Elizabeth spun around, expecting to see a celebrity. "Open bar!" he crowed, throwing a fist in the air. "Score!"

Bing gave the other man a skeptical glance, but Bill only had eyes for the bar. "C'mon!" Grabbing Elizabeth's hand, he yanked her in that direction. Her eyes pleaded with Jane for a rescue, but her sister shrugged helplessly.

Bill dragged her toward the nearest bar like a kid pulling his mom toward a roller coaster. *Oh, God! Was the president watching this farce?*

At the bar, Bill shamelessly demanded the most expensive alcohol (a kind of scotch) and asked for a double shot. He ordered one for her, thrusting the glass into her hand as he sipped his appreciatively. "Ah, that's good stuff!"

Elizabeth happened to hate scotch. Discreetly faking a coughing fit, she turned around and poured most of her glass into the large fern behind her. Her date smacked his lips and was ready for a refill.

The conversation returned to the fascinating topic of Mrs. de Bourgh's genius in the stapler industry. Nodding absently at the appropriate moments, Elizabeth wondered whether appendicitis or gallstones would be more plausible for a woman her age. The scotch must have been top-notch; Bill was compelled to order another double.

The band struck up a rollicking song with a thudding bass line. "I love this song!" Bill exclaimed, now slurring his words slightly. "C'mon!" He tugged her arm, and Elizabeth soon found herself on the moderately packed dance floor.

The scotches did not improve Bill's coordination; his moves were less "getting down" than "having a seizure." Flailing his arms wildly, he threw his head back to howl out the lyrics, drawing both stares and a few discreetly raised phone cameras. Elizabeth gritted her teeth. *Hungry children. Remember the hungry children*, she reminded herself. At the same time, she contemplated how to fake an ankle injury; compassion could only trump humiliation for so long.

When the song finished, Elizabeth did an about-face and marched off the dance floor without looking back. Bill caught up to her at one of the bars, where she had just ordered a glass of white wine. She took several gulps before even glancing at the red, sweaty man; one strand of his comb-over drooped over his forehead. What the hell could she say to get out of this situation gracefully?

"Elizabeth?" Raising her head, she found Charlotte Lucas standing opposite. Tall, with a statuesque figure, Charlotte never took much time with her appearance. Tonight she wore a blindingly bright turquoise gown with orange shoes. The effect was…striking. But Charlotte had been a friend since childhood and Elizabeth was accustomed to her quirks. Elizabeth introduced Bill, relieved at the reprieve.

Charlotte repeated his name thoughtfully. "By any chance do you work for De Bourgh Staplers?"

Bill preened as if such recognition was his due. "As a matter of fact, I do."

"You've heard of him?" Elizabeth asked, not quite keeping the incredulity out of her voice.

Charlotte's eyes lit up with an excitement that couldn't possibly be feigned. "Of course! Haven't you?" She gestured deferentially to Bill. "He's like the crown prince of staplers! He'll probably take over when Catherine de Bourgh retires."

Bill smiled with false modesty. "That hasn't been decided."

Charlotte continued, "At Lucas and Lucas we've been following the office supplies industry avidly. It's going through so many upheavals, and it's so cutthroat."

"It does require a certain level of ruthlessness to survive, that's true." Now Bill's smile was smug.

Charlotte leaned closer and spoke in a lower voice as if corporate spies lurked in every corner. "What do you think about the merger between United Erasers and Best Pencils? Will it be good for the industry?"

That was all the encouragement Bill required. Soon the two were engrossed in a conversation about the market share for protractors and the best ways to advertise scotch tape.

"Maybe I'll go to the ladies' room," Elizabeth interjected during a break in the conversation. The others failed to react before launching into a spirited debate about number two pencils. As she made her getaway, Elizabeth wondered how long her reprieve could possibly last. Could Charlotte keep him talking all night?

A short search revealed Jane departing from the bar with a martini. "You sooo owe me!" she hissed in her sister's ear.

Jane's sympathetic expression confirmed that she had seen Bill dance. "Bing would be happy to dance with you," Jane offered.

Elizabeth choked back the sour taste in her mouth. "I'm not planning to dance again. I may need brain bleach to erase those memories."

"I'm sure someone decent would like to dance with you." Jane glanced meaningfully across the room. Following her eyes, Elizabeth discovered President Darcy watching them intently.

"Oh God!" Elizabeth blushed and turned her back to him. "Why is he always staring at me?"

"Maybe he likes you," Jane suggested.

"Yeah," Elizabeth scoffed. "He *likes* watching me suffer with a terrible date."

"Bing says he likes you."

"Sure, he can be friendly and charming." Elizabeth pursed her lips. "He's a politician. But he was eager to get rid of us that morning at the Residence."

"It was just awkward with Caroline there and everything. He has to be careful about the press."

Elizabeth gave her sister a level gaze. "You're suggesting the man who said I was ugly and stupid now likes me?"

Jane opened her mouth and closed it again.

"Precisely," Elizabeth said. "If he's watching me, it's to catalogue my faults."

Jane's brows drew down as if the thought saddened her. "He's been a very loyal friend to Bing."

"No doubt he's a terrific friend to his fellow old-money brats, but he's only been difficult and proud to me," Elizabeth spat. "He may expect everyone to defer to him, but that's not the way I'm built."

Jane frowned. "What if he's changed his mind—?"

Enough with this conversation. First a disastrous date with Bill, and now she should humor the jerk-in-chief? "It doesn't matter. I'll probably never see him again after tonight."

"Really? But you make such a cute couple!" The sound of her mother's voice ringing out from behind Elizabeth transformed her insides to ice. If Fanny thought the president liked Elizabeth, nothing would stop her, short of Elizabeth's joining a convent.

Elizabeth whirled around to find her mother, stuffed into a bright yellow dress with a hoop skirt, regarding her with a sorrowful expression. "Is it true that he's a bigwig in the stapler industry?" her mother asked. Elizabeth allowed her shoulders to sag with relief. Her mother meant Bill, not the president.

Fanny glared at Charlotte, who was laughing at one of Bill's jokes. Charlotte's turquoise dress contrasted garishly with his plaid tux. "He's going places, Lizzy! Don't let Charlotte monopolize him."

"I just met the guy," Elizabeth pointed out. "Why don't you ask Jane about how things are going with Bing? They've been together for months now." Elizabeth met Jane's poisonous glare with an innocent smile.

Before she could reply, Fanny's attention was caught by Betty Lucas, Charlotte's mother. She was one of Fanny's "best friends"; they weren't capable of a conversation without attempting to outdo each other.

"Betty!" They exchanged air kisses. Fanny presented Jane grandly. "Did you know that Jane is dating Charles Bingley, the president's chief of staff?"

"No!" Betty Lucas faked enthusiasm well. "How exciting."

Fanny leaned toward Betty as if imparting a great secret. "We hope to be hearing wedding bells soon."

"Mom!" Jane exclaimed. "We've been dating for three months!"

Betty made the appropriate noises of excitement but then tilted her head toward Charlotte and Bill. "Did you see Charlotte talking to the crown prince of staplers?"

"Jane met the president!" Fanny announced hurriedly.

"Bill works for Catherine de Bourgh," Betty parried.

"Bing's family is rich!"

"There's a lot of money in office supplies!"

"Jane visited the White House!" Fanny countered rather desperately.

When Betty failed to produce an adequate comeback, Fanny's head swiveled toward Jane expectantly.

Jane shrugged uncomfortably. "Just a dinner party."

"Kitty said you stayed overnight!" her mother sing-songed.

Jane's face suggested that she was thinking of ways to strangle Kitty. "Well…I did end up having to spend the night…" With an air of resignation, Jane described her back injury to Betty and how Bing had taken care of her at the White House, carefully leaving Elizabeth out of the story.

By the end of the tale, Mrs. Bennet was practically bursting with pride. "You didn't tell me the back injury happened at the White House! That was a very 'fortunate' turn of events!" She winked knowingly at Jane.

Jane rolled her eyes. "I was on painkillers for two weeks and missed five days of work."

Fanny Bennet waved away her eldest daughter's suffering. "You spent the night at the White House!" She clasped her hands together over her heart.

"Drugged and in pain," Jane objected.

"You are so clever!" Fanny eyed Elizabeth. "This is the kind of foresight you should exercise when you meet a good…prospect." Elizabeth closed her eyes and prayed for patience.

"Mom," Jane said through gritted teeth, "I didn't injure my back deliberately."

Fanny patted her daughter's hand with an understanding smile. "Of course you didn't, dear."

"I didn't—"

Jane's protest was interrupted by a loud exclamation from Betty. "Look at that! Charlotte is dancing with the stapler king." All eyes turned to the dance floor, where Bill was drunkenly grinding his pelvis up against

Charlotte's, although she didn't appear to mind. "How sweet!" Betty cooed, then turned to Elizabeth. "Isn't Bill Collins *your* date?"

Elizabeth fought back a smile. "He seems more compatible with Charlotte."

Betty gave Fanny a triumphant look.

"He arrived with you!" Fanny pointed an emphatic finger. "Go out there and get him back!"

Elizabeth glared. "I am not going to interrupt them while they're having a good time."

"You need to do something!" her mother wailed while Betty smirked. "Go!" She pushed Elizabeth toward the dance floor.

"I'll get a drink for Bill. He'll be thirsty when the song's over," Elizabeth said. Not that Bill needed more alcohol.

Her mother clapped her hands with glee. "That's a wonderful idea!"

Elizabeth grabbed Jane's hand. "I need your help."

Jane gave her a bewildered look. "What can I do?"

"Help me select a drink."

Their mother waved them away as if they were departing for a long trip. "Pick a good one, girls!"

A few steps away from their mother, Jane asked, "Are we actually getting a drink for Bill?"

Elizabeth snorted. "We're getting a drink for me. Bill doesn't need any more." Charlotte and Bill were still burning up the dance floor doing the nerds' version of dirty dancing. "Charlotte seems to like Bill. They're happy. I'm relieved. Mom doesn't get a vote," Elizabeth said.

The line to the closest bar was short, and they soon sauntered away with glasses of wine. Jane tugged on her elbow; Elizabeth looked up in time to see an entourage bearing down on them. She slid sideways to duck out of the way, but within seconds she and Jane were surrounded by Secret Service agents—and had become the objects of avid curiosity from nearby partygoers as Bing and President Darcy stepped forward to greet them. Great. I can't wait for snarky presidential comments about my date.

"Hi, Babe." Bing glided forward to give Jane a kiss that suggested they'd been apart for days rather than minutes. Elizabeth averted her gaze—and, naturally, wound up staring at the president.

"Ms. Bennet," the president shook her hand. "That is a lovely dress."

As before, the touch of his hand short-circuited her higher brain functions. He likes my dress! her brain screamed helplessly. Elizabeth struggled to reassert reason. Of course, he said nice things; being charming was one of the president's talents.

"Thank you." There had to be more she could say. Various possibilities flitted through her mind only to be immediately discarded. That tuxedo fits you like a second skin. That tuxedo makes you look edible. May I touch your hair? Why couldn't she think of anything appropriate? What was suitable small talk with the President of the United States? The weather? Sports? Politics? Ugh.

"So, how was your week?" she blurted out and immediately winced. His week had been all over the media. His transportation bill was likely to be defeated in the House, there had been a terrorist attack in Paris, and he faced a possible scandal involving the Secretary of Health and Human Services.

A corner of his mouth quirked up. "I've had better," he admitted. "How was yours?"

Elizabeth gulped wine, devoutly wishing her brain would come back online. Her week had been devoted to finding funding for a particular program that the federal government had declined to sponsor, but she could hardly say that to the president. "Good," she said. "A lot of meetings."

"I guess any week without a humanitarian disaster is good for you," he said.

"Yes, but I also like being out in the field." He quirked an eyebrow at her. "When I'm helping people…even under horrible circumstances, I feel…useful…alive. I don't have any time to worry about my petty concerns; I just focus on helping others get through the day. It's quite rewarding." She flushed. What had possessed her to babble like that to the president? No doubt he was plotting how to escape the conversation.

But he nodded slowly as if carefully considering her words. "I can understand that. As president, I have the opportunity to help a lot of people, but there's a special thrill when I can meet and help someone one-on-one." Her skin was growing hotter under the intensity of his gaze. Couldn't he turn his glare onto someone else?

Say something! "Yes…definitely…" Witty retort, Elizabeth. No doubt he's very impressed. Immediately she felt a flicker of irritation toward herself. Why should she care what he thought of her?

The band had finished a song, and people wandered off the dance floor. Finished canoodling, Bing and Jane were poised to go dance, but Bing was regarding President Darcy expectantly. Why?

His eyes remained focused on her as he stepped closer. "Ms. Bennet, would you join me for the next dance?"

Chapter Eight

Huh? Was he serious? Wasn't she too ugly and stupid? A flock of butterflies danced in her stomach. As much as the man's touch electrified her, she found his company too nerve-wracking to desire more, but could she actually refuse? "W-Wh—I—" she stammered. Wasn't her family nouveau riche? Hadn't he been dying to get her out of the Residence? "I-I—" Reasons to decline were legion, but not one of them would be acceptable to voice.

His head tilted to the side as he considered her. "Oh," he said suddenly, "unless your boyfriend would mind." His lip curled as if the idea were distasteful to him.

Jane choked on a laugh. Bill would be the perfect excuse, but the thought was too mortifying. "He's not my boyfriend," Elizabeth informed him frostily. "He's my...um"—*Oh God, how to explain him?*—"auction date," she finished lamely.

"You won an auction for him?" The president's expression was pained.

Surely her face was bright red by now. "I'm doing it for the hungry children..." she explained helplessly. Jane's lips were pressed together, holding back laughter. "In any case," Elizabeth said through gritted teeth, "he won't care who I dance with."

The president's gaze was disconcertingly focused. "Not a boyfriend?" She gave a definite shake of her head, and his shoulders relaxed. "So you can dance with me."

"I guess." She shrugged. Wait! No! He was the last man on earth she wanted to dance with! Wasn't he?

President Darcy eyed the band, which had acquired some stringed instruments. "I think they're about to play a waltz." He extended his hand and led her briskly to the dance floor. Heads turned and people whispered behind their hands as the Secret Service agents "encouraged" the crowds to give way.

Why couldn't I have managed a good excuse to decline? Thank you, I don't dance. I'm honored, but my old football injury is acting up. I'd like to dance, but I'm too ugly and stupid.

The dance floor was crowded with couples, but nobody infringed on the president's "personal space." One of his hands held hers in a firm grip, and his other rested on her waist. His hand warmed her skin through the thin silk of her dress—so different from the moist creepiness of Bill's grip. She was hyper-aware of his touch all over her body as if it had the power to travel through her bloodstream.

He cleared his throat as the opening notes of the waltz began. *Oh, I'm supposed to put my other hand on his shoulder!* The minute she did so, he swept her up into the dance.

Elizabeth's dancing experience was limited. Long-ago lessons had faded in her memory, but fortunately the waltz was easy to recall. They whirled about the dance floor, moving so fast that the room was a blur of colors. President Darcy was a marvelous partner, leading her effortlessly around the floor. She scarcely thought about her feet. Their bodies were perfectly in sync, moving as one—as if they'd been dancing together for years.

His eyes never left hers. The stormy blue was quite dark in the ballroom lighting. "You're very good," he said earnestly.

"Not really. I'm just following your lead."

"You're very good at responding to my cues." He licked his lips; her eyes followed every movement of his tongue. "Not every woman is so…responsive."

Surely that breathlessness was simply a result of the dancing, but the sudden weakness in her legs was harder to explain. *Did he mean his words to sound so…? Of course not. Find a safer topic of conversation.* "You must have had lots of practice," she said hastily.

"Cotillion classes," he chuckled.

"You're kidding!"

"Not at all," he said with a self-deprecating grin. "My mother required it. We learned to dance, escort a lady, walk properly, open doors for a date, and so on."

What a fascinating glimpse into his childhood. "How old were you?"

His eyes grew distant as he considered. "Fourth grade? Maybe fifth."

"I don't believe that's in your official biography," she teased.

"It better not be," he growled in mock anger. It was charming. This was a Darcy she could view as a friend.

"Are there pictures?" she asked.

"Yes. But they are safely stored in a box at Pemberley where no one can find them."

Elizabeth had heard of Pemberley, the Darcy family home in the Hamptons. Surely it wasn't as large as Carlisle House, but maybe it was just as opulent. "I bet you were very cute in a little suit and tie."

"Not at all. My ears stuck out, and I wore thick black glasses."

Their speed had not slowed. The ballroom continued to rush by in a smear of colors and faces. Cameras flashed constantly—a reminder that she wasn't dancing with just any guy. "I wore glasses at that age, too, and I had skinned knees all the time from rollerblading or climbing trees."

He grinned unexpectedly. "I'm not at all surprised."

His thumb was stroking the back of her hand in little circles, sparking shivers that raced down her spine. *Focus on the conversation.* "I was an awkward girl: all knees and elbows," she confessed.

There was an odd expression on his face. "Not many women would admit that."

"I'm sure most people try to impress you. But it's too late for me." Elizabeth shrugged, and the president winced. "It's rather interesting to speak the truth and see how you react."

His head tilted slightly. "Why is that?"

"I want to know what makes you tick," she responded promptly. "See the private man lurking beneath the public persona. The man behind the mask." She was beginning to suspect that man was rather intriguing.

He scowled. "I don't recommend that."

Huh. How had her light banter provoked this reaction? "Is this one of those 'I'd tell you but then I'd have to kill you' things?" she asked with a smile.

His lips twitched in amusement. "No. I just don't believe such an activity would reflect well on either you or me."

What an odd thing to say. What was he worried she would uncover? "If I don't figure you out now, I'm not likely to have another opportunity."

The last notes of the waltz were dying away, and around the dance floor couples were exchanging curtsies and bows. They slowed to a stop, but the president still held her hand, stroking it with his thumb. *Did he even know he was doing that?* "Do as you please," he said rather stiffly. "But don't be surprised if the results are not what you expect."

He gave her a nod and stalked away. Elizabeth stood at the edge of the dance floor, abandoned. *What the hell? Maybe he's just naturally prickly. Or maybe there's something about me that sets him off. But then why did he ask me to dance in the first place...?*

Of course. He wanted to be seen with her in public. If Elizabeth danced with him…she obviously had no hard feelings over the ugly and stupid comment. His apology had dispelled her lingering anger, but now she was feeling used. He had danced with her to repair damage to his reputation; once his task was accomplished, he was finished with her.

Anger surged through Elizabeth's veins. How dare he? Heels clicking on the wood, she practically sprinted from the dance floor. That was last time she would talk to William Darcy!

***

Darcy swept across the massive ballroom, two Secret Service agents clearing the way. There were only a couple of tables at the event, but one had been reserved for him. Darcy dropped into his chair and took out his phone, mostly so nobody would disturb him. In his current state, he might bite off someone's head.

What was it about Elizabeth Bennet? Why was he so disconcerted at the idea that she wanted to see the real William Darcy?

The obvious answer was that he didn't want her to know about his attraction to her, but it went deeper. Under her gaze he felt like everything had been stripped away, and he stood naked before her. He shuddered. That wasn't even the most unnerving part of the experience. No, the thing that had him most rattled was that he rather liked it. He seemed to enjoy the idea of being dissected for her amusement.

Maybe she could already discern the flaws in his character, and wasn't that a terrifying thought? At the same time he almost wanted her to get a glimpse of his secret fears and vices. Why on earth would he want something so torturous?

It's me, he decided. *I'm easier with her around. She makes jokes I laugh at.* It had taken all his willpower not to laugh aloud at her CIA-flavored jest. *She treats me with…not disrespect…more like irreverence.* He hadn't known that was something he needed.

What a relief to learn that the mega-dweeb she entered the room with wasn't her boyfriend! *She's a distraction. I should avoid events where she will be present. No…no…that would be rude…*

Darcy's chair jostled as Bing fell into the seat next to his. Jane gave her boyfriend a quick smile, laying her clutch on the table. "I need to find Lizzy."

"Hurry back," Bing said huskily. Darcy rolled his eyes.

After Jane disappeared, his best friend looked at Darcy. "I expected you to still be dancing with Elizabeth. I had to sit down because of my knee, but you could keep going." Bing had a high-school soccer injury that troubled him occasionally.

Oh, I wish.... Darcy shook his head. "One dance was enough."

"But—"

"There will be pictures of her on all the sites tomorrow. You know I only ever dance once with each woman." The words emerged more sharply than he intended.

"I thought you might make an exception for Elizabeth."

What was Bing getting at? Covering for his discomposure, Darcy gulped water from the glass in front of him. "Why would I do that?"

"Because you like her."

Darcy nearly choked on the water. "What?"

Bing was unrepentant. "You like her—more than anyone I've seen you with since college. In fact, you like her more than anyone. Period."

"I can't date while I'm in the White House."

"*I* didn't set up those rules," Bing countered.

"No. I—"

"Hello, gentlemen." Caroline Bingley's nasal voice broke into their conversation as she inserted herself beside Bing. Darcy hastily averted his eyes; he wasn't about to pursue that topic in Caroline's presence.

"What have we here?" Jane's cell phone had slid out of her clutch and rested on the table before Caroline.

Bing scowled and reached for the phone. "It's rude to read other people's texts."

Caroline deftly grabbed it before he did. "Rude?" She read the screen, giving Bing a triumphant look. "Wouldn't you like to know what the texts say about you?"

Bing hesitated but then shook his head. "No."

"I think you do." She smirked. "The text is from Fanny Bennet. I suppose that's her mother—what a name!" Caroline cleared her throat and read in a passable imitation of Fanny Bennet's screechy soprano. "Jane, very clever of you to find a way to stay overnight at the White House. Bing seems to like you so much. I'm sure we'll hear wedding bells soon."

She tossed the cell phone back on the table triumphantly. Bing had gone still and pale. Darcy's stomach churned; he had thought Jane—like

Elizabeth—was superior to her crass family. "Maybe it's not what it seems like," he suggested gently.

Bing gave a humorless laugh. "Or maybe it's exactly what it seems like: she faked a back injury to stay at the White House and solidify her hold over me."

The text from her mother was rather damning.

"It's the money," Caroline said.

"But they're rich!" Bing exclaimed.

"You never had them thoroughly vetted, did you?" Caroline shook her head impatiently and muttered "Amateurs!" under her breath. "I did a standard background check and was planning to tell you on Monday. The accountant for On-a-Stick, Inc. recently embezzled a lot of money from the company. They're teetering on the brink. Without a big infusion of cash, the company would have to sell out or risk bankruptcy."

Bing went even paler. "Jane never said anything…"

Caroline regarded him as if he were a small child. "Of course not. She's probably hoping to marry you quickly and then get Daddy's money to shore up her family's processed food empire. He's well-known for investing in troubled businesses."

All those mild looks Jane had given Bing…she'd never seemed as besotted with him as his friend believed. Certainly not as besotted as Bing. Why hadn't Darcy noticed that before?

Bing stared into space as though he were struggling to process the sight of a horrific car accident he had just witnessed.

"Bing?" Darcy asked.

"She …did ask me about how Dad chose the companies he invested in…and if I knew anyone who needed PR help from her friend Charlotte's firm. I didn't think anything of it." Darcy had to avert his gaze from Bing's crestfallen expression.

"Of course she did," Caroline crowed. Good Lord, was the woman capable of any empathy at all? Even for her own brother?

"There could be an innocent explanation—" Darcy offered.

"No, there couldn't!" Caroline cried.

Bing's expression was bleak. "Thanks, Darce, but you know this has happened before." Bing's heart had been broken by a gold digger in college. He had been head over heels, but she had only cared about what he could buy for her.

Darcy didn't want Jane to be like that. But Fanny Bennet's text left little room for ambiguity. Had the whole family been in on the scheme? Had Elizabeth's medicine delivery been part of the plan—a way to sneak into the White House? No, then she would have flattered and flirted with him, not exercised her acerbic wit.

Bing's face was gray and drawn. "Maybe you should talk to Jane about it," Darcy suggested.

"Yeah." Bing stared across the room, where his girlfriend was chatting with Elizabeth. "Yeah, I'll talk to her."

Darcy had no doubt that conversation would contain phrases like "this isn't working anymore." Maybe Bing was jumping to conclusions, but Darcy agreed with Caroline. It was unlikely there was an innocent explanation. *Thank goodness I didn't act on my disastrous feelings for Elizabeth Bennet! Her family is even worse than I thought.*

"I never trusted those Bennet women," Caroline said. "That Jane Bennet smiles too much. It isn't believable."

Darcy tried to catch Bing's gaze, but his friend was still staring forlornly at Jane.

***

From a discreet distance, Elizabeth watched a drunken Kitty laugh, hanging on the arm of some senator's son. So far Kitty's behavior had occasioned many winces but nothing egregious enough to warrant intervention. Why did her family have to be so mortifying? Kitty spilled champagne on her dress provoking louder laughter.

Elizabeth checked her phone. She hadn't even been at the ball for two hours, yet it already felt like the longest party of her life. The only saving grace was that Bill's continued interest in Charlotte relieved Elizabeth of those obligations. In the meantime, she had nothing to do except fume about the president's treatment of her.

"Lizzy!" Elizabeth had a one-second warning before her mother's hand clamped onto her upper arm. "How did you secure a dance with the president?" Her eyes were bright with excitement.

Elizabeth cringed. "He just asked me."

"He hasn't danced with anyone else. It must mean something!"

Elizabeth rolled her eyes. "It doesn't mean anything. He probably just felt bad about calling me stupid and ugly."

"Now, Lizzy, keep an open mind. Maybe he sees something in you that nobody else does." Before Elizabeth could reply to this backhanded insult, her mother rushed on to the next topic. "But it doesn't hurt to have more than one iron in the fire. Your eggs won't fertilize themselves!"

Elizabeth closed her eyes. *God, I hope nobody else heard that.*

"So I want you to meet this charming young man!" Without waiting for a response, Fanny dragged Elizabeth toward a knot of people.

"I'm here with Bill," Elizabeth said.

"Pfft! Who cares about staplers?" Mrs. Bennet leaned close and whispered in Elizabeth's ear. "He's a congressman, and his uncle does venture capital for troubled businesses. They might invest in our company. Be nice to him."

Elizabeth glanced at the group of partygoers. "Lydia is already 'being nice to him,'" she observed.

"She is quite good at charming young men." Mrs. Bennet gave a fond smile as her youngest daughter flashed her cleavage at the man next to her. "But I fear she may be too young for George Wickham. You're just the right age."

"I'm your go-to person for sarcastic quips," Elizabeth objected, "but I'm no good at charming men."

"If he's not the right guy, you don't need to go on a date with him," her mother hissed in her ear as they approached the others. "Just be nice to him, chat him up."

When Elizabeth balked again, her mother ordered, "Do it for the company!"

Damn. Elizabeth's shoulders slumped. That was a plea she couldn't ignore.

The potential egg fertilizer was obligingly chatting up John Bennet while Lydia hung on the poor man's arm like it was the last life preserver on the Titanic. George Wickham was tall, with well-defined cheekbones and a sensual mouth. His sandy brown hair was longish, nearly touching his collar, and slicked back from his face. It was a style Elizabeth didn't particularly care for, but many women swooned over it. Apparently, Lydia was one of them; she tossed her head in annoyance as Elizabeth joined the group.

Fanny brazenly interrupted the ongoing conversation. "This is George Wickham," she trilled to Elizabeth. "Mr. Wickham, this is my second oldest daughter, Elizabeth."

Elizabeth gritted her teeth and managed to meet the man's gaze. Her mother's matchmaking was about as subtle as a falling anvil.

As he took Elizabeth's hand, Mr. Wickham treated her to a blinding smile. No doubt he paid a fortune for teeth whitening. "Ms. Bennet." Instead of shaking her hand, he turned the palm down and kissed the back.

"Ooh," Lydia gasped.

Yes, he was attractive and gallant, but he was not the first congressman Elizabeth had met. "Who do you represent in Congress, Mr. Wickham?"

"Please call me George." He again flashed that impossibly white smile. "And I represent the 12th congressional district: New York City."

"Oh, *New York*," Lydia echoed in awe. "So you're a congressman." He nodded placidly. "What do you do in your free time when you're not making laws and stuff? Do you go shopping? There's this little boutique on—"

Mrs. Bennet jabbed her youngest daughter in the ribs. "Ow! Mom, why'd you do that?"

Their mother glanced away airily. "I have no idea what you're talking about."

"I don't have much time to shop." George smiled ingratiatingly. "Crafting legislation and meeting with constituents is pretty time-consuming."

"Oh." Lydia pouted.

There was an awkward pause. Finally, Elizabeth's father cleared his throat. "I was just telling George about On-a-Stick," he said to Elizabeth.

"I am a big fan of the company's products," George said smoothly. "My favorite is Jerky On-a-Stick."

At least he deigned to eat On-a-Stick products. Unlike a certain president. "That's good." *Damn, what a lame thing to say.* Usually she could hold up her end of a conversation with no problem, but maybe she was still rattled by her encounter with President Darcy. "They're great products."

"Indeed."

Elizabeth didn't know why George wasn't nodding off to sleep given the boredom level in the conversation.

"Dear?" Fanny fluttered her eyelashes at John. "Would you like to dance?" Elizabeth's dad stared blankly as his wife gave him a *meaningful look.* Elizabeth restrained an eyeroll; they were about as subtle as a runaway train. "This is my *favorite* song," Fanny said.

George raised his eyebrows. While the band was on break, the DJ was playing a pretty hardcore rap song.

"It is?" John gave his wife a puzzled look, but when she gestured impatiently, he gamely took his wife's arm and escorted her to the dance floor.

Lydia took the opportunity to edge closer to George like a spider luring a fly into its web. *Oh God, I am such an awful sister.* "Isn't it cute how they still want to touch each other at their age?" She smirked at the congressman.

George looked slightly uncomfortable. "Er, yes."

George's uncle would never rescue the Bennets' company if Lydia served as the family representative. Elizabeth would have to step in.

She felt the weight of someone's gaze on her; President Darcy was staring at her again. Wait, no, he was watching *George* with narrowed eyes, and the congressman was smirking back. Maybe they were political rivals. George Wickham wasn't a prominent name mentioned in political conversations, but he might be up-and-coming.

So the president didn't want her talking to George? Maybe he shouldn't have used Elizabeth to score political points. Elizabeth gave George a bright smile. "Would you like to dance?"

He glanced in President Darcy's direction. "I'd love to. But I have two left feet." He leaned closer to her. "I was actually thinking of touring the grounds. The music is rather loud."

The silence outside would be a balm for her ears. "That would be wonderful."

With a pleased grin, George held out his right arm—Lydia still had possession of the left—for Elizabeth to take. They promenaded awkwardly, three abreast, toward the exit as Lydia cozied up to the congressman, allowing her breast to brush his arm.

Elizabeth didn't need to compete with Lydia over George, but she found her sister's brazenness to be embarrassing and more than a little disturbing. Her parents had never tried to curb Lydia's more wanton impulses, and it was probably too late now.

When they swept into the front hallway, the temperature dropped at least five degrees; Elizabeth sighed gratefully. They continued through the hallway and the metal detectors to the front of the house.

It was night, of course, but the Secret Service had brought in lights that illuminated the sides of the house. Fortunately, it was warm for

May, and Elizabeth was quite comfortable with a shawl around her shoulders. George led the two women toward a path curving toward the back of the house and into a garden. The ornamental shrubs were early-spring green, and the azaleas were bursting with pinks, but the rose bushes and other plants were still rather bare.

George removed his tuxedo jacket and rolled up his sleeves. He had a build that was more likely to be found on an athlete than a congressman.

As their feet crunched along the gravel path, both Lydia and Elizabeth wobbled in their high heels. Lydia clutched George's arm. "Don't abandon me! I can't make it without you," she teased. Elizabeth snorted.

"I wouldn't dream of it," George said, his eyes darting to Elizabeth. "Are you all right?"

"I will be." Elizabeth rested her hand on a low stone wall to balance herself while she removed her shoes and stepped barefoot onto the gravel, made from rounded river stones. Her feet reacted like Medieval prisoners that had been released from the rack. "Ahh… much better." George grinned at her.

They continued their perambulations. Much of the garden was in silhouette, but the light revealed clusters of daffodils and tulips. Everything was exquisitely maintained; the gardening budget must be huge.

"I'm afraid I don't know much about Congress. Which party do you belong to?" Elizabeth asked him.

"I'm a Republican," he replied with an easy grin. "But I'm a pretty progressive Republican. You have to be to represent New York City."

"I'm in favor of progress, too," Lydia said.

George lifted one corner of his mouth. "Yes, unfortunately, in Washington one learns all too quickly the truth of the saying, 'If the opposite of pro is con, what's the opposite of progress?'"

Lydia thought for a moment. "Congress?" She guffawed. "That's a scream!"

"Do you work with the president much?" Elizabeth asked.

He hesitated for a moment. "Not professionally, but I know Will personally."

"Who's Will?" Lydia asked. "Oh! The *president*! You know him? That is *so* cool!" She edged closer to George, invading even more of his personal space.

"We grew up together," George said in a humble-brag way.

"You grew up with the *president*?" Lydia's eyes were wide and sparkling.

Huh. That was odd. "I've read a fair amount about President Darcy. I haven't seen you mentioned in anything about his childhood."

"Yeah, you wouldn't." George's mouth flattened to a thin line. "We had a...falling out a while ago, and his staff has tried to erase me from the official record." He kicked a stone in the pathway.

"Really?" Lydia could scent juicy gossip like a dog smelled a steak.

Evidently being difficult and proud weren't the president's only offenses. Why would he pretend an old childhood friend didn't exist? "Was it over political differences?" she asked. The president might have felt betrayed when George joined the other party.

George blew out a breath. "No, not at all."

Now Elizabeth was even more curious. "What happened?" Lydia asked. "I mean, if you don't mind telling us."

George's eyes glittered, reflecting the floodlights. He hesitated; a pained expression ghosted over his face, but he also seemed about to burst with suppressed energy. "It's a difficult part of my past, but sometimes it helps to talk about it."

Lydia nodded sympathetically, rubbing his arm with her hand. "You can unburden yourself to us. It's an important part of the healing process." Elizabeth suppressed a laugh.

"But you can't share it with anybody else," George said. "The story is rather..."—he swallowed hard—"personal."

Elizabeth felt a sudden rush of sympathy. George might be overly dramatic in his presentation of the facts, but the memories seemed to genuinely pain him. "Of course, we won't say anything," she promised gently.

"Thank you," George said.

"We're trustworthy," Lydia added.

George patted Lydia's hand. "You're a very kind soul." Lydia beamed.

He led them into a more secluded part of the garden. "We can't let anyone overhear."

George perched himself on a boulder while Lydia and Elizabeth took seats on an opposite bench. He lowered his voice. "Will and I practically grew up together. My father was the chief operating officer of his father's business. We played together as kids, went to the same school, had double dates." George stared out into space, lost in the memories. "But then Darcy Industries went into a slump. My father was fired and lost everything. Somehow Mr. Darcy managed to hold on to most of his wealth and rebound." George's smile twisted bitterly. "My father always thought he paid off some people at the Securities and Exchange Commission."

Elizabeth gasped. That would be a federal crime.

"My father died a broken and disillusioned man. However, when Mr. Darcy died seven years ago, I found out that he had left me a hundred thousand dollars in his will. I think he was trying to make amends to my family."

Lydia was hanging on every word. "Yay!" She clapped her hands in glee.

George's lip curled. "Will wouldn't give it to me."

Wow, this was worse than anything Elizabeth could have imagined, completely unbalancing her. She knew the president could be cold and abrupt and proud, but...

"Did you ask him for it?" Lydia asked.

George gave a harsh laugh. "Of course. But by then he had destroyed the original will, and he denied that it ever contained such a provision."

Elizabeth's hand flew up to her mouth. "How horrible! Can't you sue him?"

"I could, but he warned me that I'd be going up against the best lawyers money could buy, and my legal fees could easily eat up any money I won as part of the case."

What a shabby way to treat a childhood friend! Now Elizabeth regretted acquiescing—even grudgingly—to dance with the president. *I should have stepped on his feet.* "B-But you deserve that money! It's yours."

"Yeah." George looked down at his hands. "But I'm proud of what I've accomplished on my own. I've bootstrapped myself to where I am through hard work in my uncle's company."

Lydia's eyes were shining. "That's so admirable."

He gave her a brief smile. "My mother says adversity builds strength of character."

Elizabeth was still trying to wrap her mind around the depths of the president's treachery. *Why does it bother me so much? I knew he was a jerk and we'd never be buddies.* "Have you ever considered going to the press about it?" she asked.

"Sure." He shoved his hands into his pockets. "But we belong to opposing parties, and the press loves Will. They'd just think I was making it up, and I don't have a shred of proof."

Lydia made a sympathetic noise, dabbing her eye with a tissue.

George looked up at the moon, the cool light illuminating his fine features. "If I spoke out now, it would only hurt the country."

"How good you are…to put the needs of the country ahead of yours." Lydia sighed.

He shrugged. "I can only pray that Will is behaving just as admirably. He's very good about looking like a boy scout, but he's ruthless when he wants to be. I worry…what's actually happening at the White House that we'll find out later?"

Elizabeth shivered. She had never thought President Darcy as bad as all that! Such a lack of honor could be devastating for the country, particularly after his predecessor's egregious behavior.

George slid off the boulder. "He *is* doing some good things for the country, but someday the country will see the real William Darcy. I just have to wait." His gaze landed on Elizabeth. "I saw you dancing with him and wanted to warn you." He crept a little closer to her. "I wouldn't want you to fall into his trap." He held her eyes. "You seem like a nice girl, and he's good-looking, powerful, rich. But he's bad news."

Elizabeth laughed softly. "Thank you. A warning is quite unnecessary. I don't know why he asked me to dance, but he doesn't really like me. And I'm certainly not establishing a Washington, D.C. chapter of the William Darcy fan club anytime soon."

Wickham's mouth opened slightly. "Oh, I thought…the way he looked at you…" He abruptly closed his mouth.

Lydia snorted. "You think he *likes* Lizzy?"

Did Lydia have to be quite so incredulous? "My family isn't nearly old enough money for him," Elizabeth told George.

"He *is* a snob," George said quickly. "The whole family is. His sister is even worse, but"—he smiled smoothly and took another step toward her —"I can't imagine any man not finding you fascinating."

Elizabeth chuckled. His flirting was outrageous.

Lydia cleared her throat. "My mother says I'm fascinating, too. I took a philosophy class last semester." George frowned at this apparent non-sequitur, but his gaze stayed fixed on Elizabeth, especially her lips.

What is wrong with me? A cute guy is flirting with me, and I can only feel hurt at the revelation of the president's perfidy. Despite herself, she had begun to like him, but George's story was a timely warning that she couldn't trust the man; he was a politician and looked after his own best interests. In the future, she vowed she would avoid him altogether.

Lydia's phone chirped, and she pulled it out of her clutch, giggling at whatever she read. "OMG! I need to go meet Maria in the ladies' room!" she announced. "She just found out why Olga broke up with Jared." Within seconds Lydia had disappeared, her attraction to George not nearly as acute as her need for gossip.

In Lydia's absence, the garden was very dark and very isolated. Elizabeth cleared her throat. "I should be getting back—"

George laid his hand on her forearm. "Forgive me if I'm being too forward, but I feel very drawn to you..." They were nearly chest to chest.

Elizabeth was momentarily stunned. The man moved so quickly. His hand traced along her jaw. "I think we have real chemistry," he said huskily.

"Uh..." Her brain was formulating a response when he kissed her. It was a gentle kiss, soft and tentative. Not demanding. Nice in its own way.

But it did nothing for her. The president's touch to her fingertips was far more thrilling. Damn it. Why did her libido have to be such a poor judge of character? Why couldn't she be attracted to a nice, charming guy like George instead of a jerk like President Darcy?

He pulled away from her and smiled. "I knew we had chemistry!" Apparently, he didn't recognize the taste of chemistry.

He intertwined his fingers with hers. "Maybe we could—"

Elizabeth took a step back. "George, I'm flattered, b-but...this is moving a little fast..."

"I didn't mean to rush you." He held up a placating hand. "I'm just so attracted to you...."

Elizabeth's phone buzzed. Pulling it out of her clutch, she saw a text from Jane: "Call me." She made an apologetic face. "I should go and—"

"Could I at least give you my number?" George's eyes pleaded with her. "Then I can call you for a proper date."

Elizabeth managed a smile; she'd find a way to let him down easy. "Of course." She rattled off her number.

"All right." He pumped his fist, grinning broadly as he punched it into his phone.

Elizabeth said goodbye, smiling absently as her thoughts focused on Jane. Turning without a backward glance, she hurried toward the front of the house—as fast as she could on bare feet—while calling up Jane's number on speed dial.

"Lizzy, where are you?" Jane's strained voice sent a thrill of fear down Elizabeth's spine.

"Outside getting some air. Is something wrong?"

"I want to go. Can you meet me at the valet stand?" Jane's voice broke on the last word.

"Sure." Elizabeth picked up her pace. "What's wrong, honey?"

"Bing—" Jane's voice wobbled, and she started over. "Bing broke up with me."

Chapter Nine

"How are you?" Elizabeth asked.

"I'd be a lot better if everyone stopped asking me that," Jane sighed on the other end of the phone.

"I guess you get sick of it," Elizabeth said, cradling the phone against her shoulder as she unpacked her suitcase and hung clothes in the hotel closet. "Everyone's just worried."

"Yeah." Jane sighed again. "I know everyone wants to help, but I'm really fine. It's been two months since B-Bing—" Her voice stuttered over the name and crackled over the international line. "Since then. I'm doing better."

"Yeah, you are," Elizabeth said softly. Even though Bing and Jane hadn't been together for very long, their affair had grown intense quickly; Bing's rejection, without an adequate explanation, had badly shaken the sensitive woman's self-confidence.

Silently she cursed Charles Bingley for about the thousandth time for having broken up with her sister in that manner. According to Jane, their relationship had been smooth sailing—until he broke it off during the ball with the feeble excuse that his job didn't allow time to date. Elizabeth had believed Bing might be "The One" for Jane. Boy, had she been wrong.

"The name 'Bing' just sounds way too fun for a guy who turned out to be such an ass," she joked. "Maybe we should call him something else, like Jerkwad or Crapface."

Jane laughed. "Yeah, call the chief of staff Crapface; that'll score points with the administration." She hesitated. "He's going to be at the summit, isn't he?" Her voice was a mere whisper.

Elizabeth perused the conference booklet detailing all the activities for the First International Paris Disaster Relief Summit. "The president will be giving a speech tomorrow night. I suppose it's possible Bing came as well, but I'm not likely to run into them."

"You do know them."

Elizabeth snorted. "I've had a couple of close encounters, but I doubt anyone in the White House wants to renew our acquaintance." *And after George Wickham's tale, I'll avoid President Darcy like the plague.*

She experienced a dull pang of guilt over owing George a call. They had been on two pleasant dates that had only confirmed Elizabeth's lack of interest in anything romantic, though George was convinced they were soulmates. She had given him the "let's be friends" speech, but he seemed likely to push for more.

"There are a lot of important people here," she told Jane. "I can't imagine that I'm a priority."

She turned the page to a picture of the president. Elizabeth's heartbeat accelerated. *This is stupid. I see pictures of the president every day. Yeah, and this happens every time you see one*, jeered the cynical voice at the back of her head. *Okay, so the president is an attractive man*, she admitted to herself. *So what? It doesn't mean anything to me.* She turned the page.

"But what if—?"

"I'm going to do my best to avoid them," Elizabeth said firmly. *If I see the president, I'm going to be sorely tempted to give him a piece of my mind about his treatment of George Wickham. And that would not be advisable.*

"I guess there's no reason for Bing or the president to seek you out," Jane said.

"I'm sure they don't even know I'm here."

***

"You want me to what?" Elizabeth must have misheard. Out of the blue, Margot, her boss, had summoned Elizabeth to the hotel suite that served as the Red Cross headquarters at the summit. It was a spacious room, dominated by a large conference table and accompanying swivel chairs.

Margot repeated her words more slowly. "I want you to brief the president and some of his staff about the Red Cross programs for refugees."

"Why me?" Elizabeth winced when her voice squeaked.

Flipping her short, dark hair out of her eyes, Margot leaned back against the conference table and folded her arms. "You are well-versed in the policies and have had extensive field experience. You know that we need to get our name in front of the administration whenever we can. And we still haven't heard whether we got the State Department grant."

Bewildered, Elizabeth took a deep breath. Of course, she understood how important an opportunity it was, but the thought of seeing President Darcy... Her stomach churned sickeningly. "Craig has almost as much experience," Elizabeth countered.

John, one of her more abrasive coworkers, drawled from across the room, "Most people jump at the chance to do a presentation for the president."

Elizabeth ignored him, focusing on Margot. "I won't be a good representative for the Red Cross. I'll get all tongue-tied and incoherent."

Margot lifted one eyebrow. "You yelled at the mayor of Pen na Nol and made him back down when he threatened the villagers in the church. There's a much smaller chance of being shot here."

"Don't you want someone higher up the food chain?" Elizabeth asked. "There have to be five people here with more impressive titles." *Why me?*

Margot shifted in her chair. "The truth is…the president's staff requested you specifically."

"What?" Alarm spiked down Elizabeth's spine. "Why?" Knees suddenly weak, she sank into one of the chairs.

"I thought you might know."

"But you've met the president. Haven't you?" John asked. That's how you ended up being Presidential Dis Girl

Elizabeth shrugged uneasily. "Well, yeah, but…I don't even think he likes me."

"He did call you ugly and stupid," John pointed out. Elizabeth was in no danger of forgetting that.

Margot sighed. "Maybe he's trying to apologize." Elizabeth gave her a blank stare. "Look, you don't need to chat him up. Just go in, brief him, and leave."

This was the man who had cheated George Wickham out of his inheritance. Whose best friend had callously dumped her sister. After examining the conference schedule, Elizabeth had a carefully crafted a plan to avoid him for the entire summit.

Margot stood up straight, her tall, gaunt figure looming over Elizabeth. "The White House wants *you* specifically. We have no reason to turn down their request, and need I remind you, this *is part of your job*." Her eyes bored into Elizabeth's until the younger woman averted her eyes.

Damn. Elizabeth slumped into her chair. It *was* part of her job. The Red Cross and their mission had benefited from having William Darcy in the White House, no matter what Elizabeth thought of him personally. He was a good president. The grant could potentially help thousands of people. There was no reason for the organization to piss off the president unnecessarily. Hell, she might not even have a chance to meet him at the meeting.

Surely she could give the presentation and leave—all without speaking directly to the president. He probably wouldn't even pay attention. Her shoulders drooped. "I'll do it, but I'm going to need you to buy me drinks afterward."

Delighted, Margot clapped her on the shoulder. "You've got it."

Elizabeth managed a wan smile just as a new thought struck her: *Why did the White House staff request* me?

***

4:05 p.m.

Darcy watched as the minute hand hit the five. Secretary of State Gus Callahan was still describing the refugee crisis in Myanmar. Darcy didn't need all the details, although he was glad the State Department was paying attention to the situation. And it was 4:05.

He leaned over and mumbled in the ear of the man next to him. "Are you sure she's coming?"

Richard Fitzwilliam's eyes widened. Probably because Darcy had asked that question four times in one hour. He wouldn't have allowed most White House staff to notice his impatience, but Fitz was a cousin and a friend from childhood. He wouldn't blab to the media—or gossip with the staff—about the president's obsession with a certain dark-haired aid worker. As the president's primary assistant, Fitz had been the best person to discreetly ask the Red Cross to send Elizabeth Bennet for the refugee briefing—and make it sound like a random White House preference. The fewer people who knew it was Darcy's specific request, the better.

"She's probably already here," Fitz whispered back. "The staff will hold her outside until we're ready."

That's right. That was the procedure. Her absence didn't mean she wasn't coming. God damn it! This Bennet woman had Darcy so rattled that he forgot basic operating procedures.

But what if she was sick? What if the Red Cross decided to send someone else after all? What if—?

Darcy savagely cut off that line of thought. He needed to concentrate on the report about refugees in Myanmar, not moon over some woman he hadn't seen in two months. Although it seemed longer than two months. What if she had cut her hair? Would she be wearing a suit for this occasion? He'd never seen her in a suit.

Maybe she had a boyfriend now. *Oh, Lord.* Somehow, over their relatively brief acquaintance, Darcy had grown accustomed to encountering her occasionally. When Bing had broken up with Jane Bennet, Darcy hadn't anticipated the loss of being cut off from Elizabeth.

Almost equally unbearable was the need to keep his feelings contained. During one late-night phone call, he'd unburdened himself to his sister Georgiana, who had been very sympathetic but equally horrified by the tales of Elizabeth's family.

When Darcy had learned that Elizabeth was attending the summit, he'd been unable to resist the impulse to contrive a meeting. Perhaps she'd been hoping to see him as well; the thought gave him a secret thrill.

It had been a rare indulgence to request her personally, but the alternative had been taking the risk that he might not see her at all. He would only say a few words to her and content himself with the rare treat of watching her do a presentation.

Finally, Callahan's droning voice petered out. "Thank you, Gus," Darcy said. He peered around the crowded, dark-paneled conference room. "What's next on the agenda?" As if he didn't know already.

Fitz gave him an amused look before responding, "Elizabeth Bennet from the Red Cross to brief you on African refugees." A staffer opened the door to admit Elizabeth.

She hadn't cut her hair. It was up in a loose bun that should have enhanced her professional image but inspired naughty thoughts of fingering each dark tendril. Her trim black suit and blue blouse were very appropriate, but the skirt skimmed the top of her knees. Darcy hastily yanked his gaze up to her face before he was caught staring at her legs. She did not grant him a smile; no doubt she was nervous.

As he stood to shake her hand, Darcy tried to radiate reassurance. "Ms. Bennet, thank you for coming. Let me introduce you." He named the men and women around the table, ending the recitation with the staff closest to him. "And this is my cousin and primary assistant, Richard Fitzwilliam." Fitz's eyebrows shot up, and no wonder: Darcy almost never mentioned their blood connection.

Darcy indicated the older woman on his other side. "And this is my aunt, Catherine de Bourgh, director of the De Bourgh Foundation." Elizabeth would be aware of the foundation's work in international disaster relief. Impeccably dressed as always, Aunt Catherine greeted Elizabeth with her customary glower. Unfazed, Elizabeth gave Darcy's aunt a brief, courteous nod as if she met billionaire philanthropists every day. *Where does she get such sangfroid?*

Striving for a casualness he never felt in her presence, Darcy said, "So I understand you will brief us on disaster relief in Africa?"

"That's right, Mr. President," she responded crisply. Nothing in her tone indicated they had ever met personally—or that he had waltzed with his arms wrapped around her. Resting her laptop on the conference table, she began hooking it up to the projector. "I have a fifteen-minute PowerPoint presentation, and then I'd be happy to take questions," she announced to the room at large. Darcy gestured for her to proceed.

The moment she spoke, he regretted the professional setting. He longed for her playful smile and sparkling eyes. On the other hand, this confident, take-charge Elizabeth gave Darcy an illicit thrill.

Bing used to tease Darcy that he found intelligence to be an aphrodisiac, and Darcy was forced to admit that he found her knowledgeability and poise very...alluring. Every part of the presentation was mesmerizing. Even the way her hands pointed to something on the screen was fascinating. Her posture was competent, professional, and yet she charmed the listeners with off-the-cuff remarks...African refugees had never been so interesting.

Thirty minutes into the presentation, Darcy realized he was in love. An undistinguished meeting room of a random hotel in Paris was an odd setting for such a momentous revelation, but it was inescapable. Her presentation had been well organized, clear, and persuasive—the best one he'd seen all day. She had answered all the questions competently and deflected the hostile ones. She'd even made a couple of jokes that had the entire room roaring with laughter. The hardened policy wonks and career bureaucrats at the table were practically eating out of her hand. Even Callahan's face lacked its habitual scowl.

She was brilliant. She was beautiful. She was everything he had ever wanted in a woman.

Except he'd always assumed the right woman for him would come from a similarly well-heeled family. A family with taste and a sense of decorum.

Oh God, I'm in love with her. What am I going to do about it?

Letting her go again no longer seemed like a feasible alternative. The very thought produced sweaty palms and a rapid heartbeat—not to mention a withering sense of despair. The alternative was surrendering to the attraction. Upon his return to Washington, he could discreetly call her for a date. *Yes, that's what I'll do.* A wave of relief caused him to sag into his chair, momentarily giddy.

Elizabeth scanned the table. "If there aren't any other questions—"

He should thank her and dismiss her. He'd had half an hour to indulge his obsession—and he should focus on the summit. Still, his entire body basked in the glow of her presence like a plant growing toward the sunlight. He wanted more smiles. More laughter. More time with her. More *Elizabeth*.

Darcy cleared his throat. "Ms. Bennet, would you be available to join us for dinner tonight? It's sponsored by the De Bourgh Foundation, but I'll be there, as well as others from the administration." From the corner of his eye, Darcy saw his aunt's head jerk in his direction. She could object all she wanted; he didn't care.

Elizabeth's lips parted slightly as she regarded him. Her mouth closed, then opened again. Perhaps she suspected the ulterior motive behind his invitation. "O-Of course, Mr. P-President. I'd be delighted to join you. Thank you."

Darcy beamed at her. "Tom, over by the door, can give you further information."

As Elizabeth wound her way toward the exit, Darcy leaned back in his chair. This summit was going pretty well.

***

What a mess!

Elizabeth twitched her shoulders, trying to get her jacket to settle more comfortably, but one side had a tendency to ride up. She pulled at the collar of her blouse. The mirror outside the door to the banquet hall showed that the collar was not choking her, but her neck seemed to feel otherwise. Deep down, however, she knew the suit wasn't the problem. By all rights she should be done with suits for the day. She should be enjoying overpriced red wine and cheese at a local restaurant with her coworkers and other friends from the aid community.

Instead she was dithering in the corridor, sweating inside her suit and trying to remember all the talking points Margot and John had drilled into her head. "If you see anyone from the State Department, tell them how valuable the grant could be" had been Margot's parting words as Elizabeth left the suite.

Their excitement had scuttled Elizabeth's faint hope of avoiding the dinner by claiming a fit of hysterical blindness or sudden-onset amnesia. She wasn't the kind of person who hobnobbed with politicians; her job usually involved emergency rations and muddy roads, not cocktail parties and conversation about budgets. Of course, she would be genuinely happy if she could secure the funding for them, but what if she scuttled the plan by accident?

She paced the corridor outside the banquet hall door trying to dismiss the series of niggling doubts that had attacked as soon as she exited the elevator—and causing the Secret Service agent at the door to eye her warily. The primary doubt had to do with why the president had invited her to this shindig in the first place.

She didn't have a good answer.

He had been cordial during the presentation, but they weren't friends; he didn't even like her. Bing hadn't accompanied the president on the trip, so Jane's ex hadn't wanted to reminisce about "good times." And her family was still as vulgar and nouveau riche as ever.

Maybe he was still compensating for having called her stupid and ugly. Or maybe he wanted more information about Zavene. Or was he setting her up to fail? Perhaps it was all some Machiavellian plot. He was a politician; who knows what kind of long game he was playing? Maybe she was a pawn in a complicated political strategy to get even with George Wickham. Elizabeth took a deep breath, abruptly feeling dizzy and leaning against the wall.

It isn't likely. President Darcy had a reputation for being a straight shooter. Of course, she didn't know him that well. The man who had shafted George Wickham would probably be capable of all sorts of manipulation.

Her stomach churned with each glance at the banquet hall door. Every muscle in her body screamed with the need to flee, but that might hurt the Red Cross. This was even worse than the Carlisle Ball—where nothing had been at stake except her reputation.

Half an hour, she promised herself, knowing it was probably a lie. *I'll go in, chat up the Red Cross's latest projects to some of the administration's staff, eat some food, and leave. An hour tops.* Taking a deep breath to settle her nerves, she strode through the metal detectors and into the banquet hall as if she belonged there. *I am such an imposter.*

The room wasn't particularly large, nor was the crowd. This must be an exclusive dinner. Elizabeth didn't know anybody in the room personally, although she recognized faces she'd seen on television. The

Secretary of State. The Director of Homeland Security. Two generals. The U.N. Secretary General. All *way* above her pay grade.

Then there were the old money philanthropic types like Felix Webster and Catherine de Bourgh. *Don't be intimidated*, she reminded herself. *My family owns On a Stick, Inc. I belong here too.* That only recalled the president's "nouveau riche" comment.

Guests milled about, talking, drinking wine, and nibbling on hors d'oeuvres; some gathered around tables at the other end of the room. Nobody had noticed her. Maybe she could linger by the bar and then slip off to the ladies' room until dinner was served. She edged her way to the bar and ordered a glass of white wine.

She took a gulp as she surveyed the room. It was lavishly appointed with ornate plasterwork. The ceilings, with crystal chandeliers straining against the velvet cords holding them in place, were so high that Elizabeth felt small in comparison. There weren't a lot of buildings in the U.S. that boasted such baroque grandeur. Elizabeth had the heady sensation that she should be there as a tourist rather than an invited guest.

Then she spied someone she recognized—and immediately wished she hadn't. Holding a drink, Bill Collins hovered at Catherine de Bourgh's impeccably clad elbow, perhaps awaiting the opportunity to be sent on some kind of meaningless errand. His eyes lit up when he noticed Elizabeth, and he scurried over to her.

"Elizabeth!" Greeting her like an old friend, he placed his hands on her shoulders. "Allow me to greet you in the French style! I've been practicing." He air kissed both of her cheeks.

"There!" he exclaimed. "How did I do?" He took a generous swallow from his drink. *Oh yeah, open bar.*

"Um…" Elizabeth had never been called upon to judge air kisses before. "Quite good."

He gave her a ghastly grimace. "I hope there are no hard feelings over our last date."

Elizabeth had been surprised that Charlotte had started dating Bill, and shocked when she had confessed deep and abiding feelings for the man. "No, I—"

"My passion for Charlotte simply swept me away." He clasped both hands over his heart. "I was helpless to resist. United by our love of office products, we are true soulmates—with but one heart and one mind."

Elizabeth choked on a mouthful of wine.

Bill continued, oblivious to her frantic coughing. "She is my rose petal. My peony. My sunrise. My moonset."

Moonset? "I'm very happy for you," Elizabeth gasped out between coughs.

He eyed her disbelievingly. "I know you regret never tasting a piece of this." He slapped himself on the butt. Elizabeth managed to cover her wince. "But my heart and my body belong to Charlotte."

Pressing her lips together to catch any errant laughs, Elizabeth nodded. "Of course. I will respect that."

Sidling closer to her, Bill lowered his voice. "In fact, I got that tattooed for Charlotte's birthday."

"Got what tattooed?" *Wait, do I want to know?*

He gave her a sly, secretive smile. "'Property of Charlotte'— tastefully done, of course—in a very nice cursive script tattooed right here on my—" He raised his hand to slap his butt again.

Elizabeth responded swiftly before receiving more details. "You don't say!"

He nodded with a self-satisfied smile. "But don't tell Charlotte. It's a surprise."

"I won't tell her," Elizabeth reassured him. *Or anyone else. In fact, I'm hoping they'll invent a brain bleach to erase that image.*

Elizabeth groped around for a more innocuous topic of conversation. "Um…has Mrs. de Bourgh met Charlotte?"

Bill's face was rapturous. "Yes. They got along swimmingly. I was concerned at first that Mrs. de Bourgh would think Charlotte's family too"—he dropped his voice as if he were about to confess his beloved had a terrible disease—"bourgeois. But she believes the Lucases are an eminently suitable family for someone of my station in life."

"How fortunate," Elizabeth managed to choke out.

"I am hoping someday Charlotte will make me the happiest of men." Bill gazed rapturously into the distance.

"Um, great." Elizabeth wondered if they made stapler-themed wedding décor.

"And to think," Bill waxed on, "none of this would have happened if I'd found you remotely attractive."

Elizabeth managed not to spray her white wine over everything. "Yeah…that's very…fortunate." She eyed the wine in her glass. Was it too soon to claim the need for a refill?

"Ms. Bennet?" A young brown-haired man in an impeccably tailored suit approached. He had been at the meeting earlier. Oh, the president's cousin. Shit. Out of the frying pan… He stuck out his hand. "Richard Fitzwilliam. Please call me Fitz." His easy grin instantly helped her tight muscles relax. "I wanted to take the opportunity to—"

Bill had already seized the other man's hand. "Nice to meet you, Fitz. Bill Collins. I work with your aunt at De Bourgh Enterprises."

Fitz tilted his head to the side. "My condolences."

Bill continued obliviously, "I supervise the stapler division—"

Fitz must have sensed an impending soliloquy. He turned to Elizabeth. "I enjoyed your presentation today."

Elizabeth raised an eyebrow. "Enjoyed?"

"Yes!" Fitz grinned broadly. "Do you know how many briefings I sit through every day? To have one that's lively, informative, and with a sense of humor? Well, that's like manna from heaven."

Was he serious? "Oh, I'm glad you thought so. I was so nervous!" *Damn. Why did I admit that?*

"Mrs. de Bourgh has a great remedy for nerves," Bill weighed in. "It involves rubbing raw onion on your hands and swallowing a pinch of saffron."

"Well, at least it doesn't require live chickens…unlike her cure for eczema," Fitz murmured. *Was he serious?* Movement from the other end of the room caught his eye. "Aunt Catherine is glancing this way. Perhaps she needs you."

Bill wrenched his stricken face toward his employer. "I'm coming, Mrs. de Bourgh! I'm coming!" he cried as he hurried away.

Fitz watched him go, somewhat bemused. Elizabeth cleared her throat. "Bill is extremely grateful for your aunt's…patronage."

A smile played about Fitz's lips. "I'm sure she's grateful for his…attentiveness." He took a sip from his drink. "I'm pleased to finally meet you. I've heard so much."

"From Bing?" she asked. *That might not be good.*

Fitz blinked rapidly. "No. Darcy sings your praises." He gestured expansively with a drink in one hand. "I'm sure you know he's not easily impressed."

Wait. What? "The president mentioned me?" What would he say about her except that she was the sister of the woman Bing dumped?

Fitz gave a matter-of-fact nod. "He greatly admires you…your work." When she didn't respond, he rubbed his chin and regarded her quizzically. "You didn't—he didn't tell you?"

"No!" Elizabeth was too shocked to dissemble.

"Hmm." Fitz's eyes focused on his wine glass. "Well, he's not always forthcoming."

"That's an understatement." Her phone pinged, and she pulled it out of her purse. "Please excuse me for a second." She frowned at the screen and tucked the phone away.

"Bad news?" Fitz inquired with a look of polite interest.

She shrugged. "It's not that big a deal. I've been trying to get an earlier flight back to the U.S. Right now, I'm scheduled for Thursday, and that'll make me miss my mom's birthday. I'd been hoping for a place on a Wednesday flight."

"That's a shame." He seemed to genuinely sympathize with Elizabeth—so much more amiable than his cousin. She might even be friends with a guy like this. "The summit was a bigger success than the organizers expected," he said. "A lot of people must be leaving on Wednesday after the closing speeches."

Elizabeth nodded, happy to be on a more neutral topic of conversation. "I hope they make this an annual event."

"I'm sure they will." His attention was caught by something off to his right. "I'm going for a refill," he said abruptly, holding up his empty glass. "Can I get you something?"

Yeah, a good stiff drink. But that would be a spectacularly bad idea with her empty stomach. "Another glass of white wine would be lovely. Thank you."

He bobbed his head and hurried to the bar.

"Elizabeth!" Whirling at the sound of her name, she found President Darcy approaching with determined, ground-eating strides. He had been impressive in a tux, but this perfectly tailored blue suit was devastating. The dark cobalt hue magnified the blueness of his eyes, crinkling with a welcoming smile. Sensuous lips curved in a grin that made Elizabeth's knees weak. She double-checked to make sure her mouth wasn't hanging open.

The president took her hand in both of his in a gesture that was more a clasp than a handshake. "I'm so happy you came. And you had a chance to speak with Fitz—"

"There you are, William!" Catherine de Bourgh bore down on them like an ocean liner approaching a dinghy, and Elizabeth quelled an impulse to back away. The woman's foundation was well known for donating millions to worthy causes, but at the moment she looked like she had sucked on a lemon. She appeared to be in her early seventies, despite having had a fair amount of "work" done to her face. Holding herself in a very upright posture, she tilted up her chin and contemplated Elizabeth coolly.

The president hesitated. Was he ashamed of Elizabeth? Then he swallowed. "Elizabeth Bennet, this is my aunt, Catherine de Bourgh." Shaking the woman's hand was like squeezing a wet washrag. "Aunt Catherine is actually the host of tonight's dinner."

The older woman narrowed her eyes at her nephew. "Which William feels entitled to invite everyone to," she said with a sniff.

The woman obviously wasn't happy about Elizabeth's presence. Perhaps the words were intended to intimidate her, but they had the opposite effect. Elizabeth gave the woman a smile full of teeth. "He's the president. Does he need to ask permission?"

Mrs. de Bourgh was clearly unaccustomed to being challenged. "Well, naturally—"

Elizabeth continued, "Of course, he needs Congress's permission to declare war or pass a budget. But for something as simple as a dinner invitation, I would think it's one of the privileges of the office." Mrs. de Bourgh goggled at Elizabeth. Taking advantage of the momentary silence, Elizabeth addressed President Darcy. "Do you do it often? Benefit from your aunt's hospitality?"

He had a faint smile on his face. "Not often, no. But occasionally I find her events useful." *How often did he invite* women *to such occasions?*

Mrs. de Bourgh recovered her voice. "You were always like that, even before you were elected to the Senate."

"Always like what?" Fitz asked, returning with a glass of white wine, which he handed to Elizabeth, and a gin and tonic for himself.

"Inviting random people to my dinners," the older woman said.

Fitz gave her a rakish grin. "That's because Darcy is just trying to liven them up."

"It's a dreadful habit," the older woman sniffed. "Very MC."

Fitz and the president both froze, although their aunt seemed oblivious to the sudden tension. Elizabeth wasn't familiar with that acronym, but the others reacted like the older woman had uttered a curse.

Ah, who cares if I appear ignorant. The president doesn't like me anyway. "What's MC?" she asked. Fitz shifted uneasily while President Darcy appeared fascinated by something on the other side of the room. Then comprehension dawned. "Middle class? You actually say things like that?" *Wow, talk about pretentious.* Shaking with suppressed laughter, Elizabeth nearly spilled her wine.

The president had the grace to look embarrassed. "Aunt Catherine is rather old fashioned—"

The woman in question interrupted ruthlessly, struck by a sudden need to question Elizabeth. "Bennett, hmm? Are you related to the Connecticut Bennetts?"

"Not that I know of."

"Or Kevin Bennett? He runs a hedge fund."

"I don't think so."

"Ms. Bennet's family spells it with one 't,'" the president explained.

"One 't'? Whoever heard of such a thing? Why on earth would anyone spell Bennett with one 't'?"

The woman was so rude that it was almost comical. Elizabeth shrugged. "I honestly don't know. They didn't consult me."

The president shoved his hands in his pockets and looked away while Fitz's twitching lips suggested repressed laughter.

The older woman regarded Elizabeth like an interesting puzzle. "What does your family do?"

"Do?" There were very few things her family did as a group. Elizabeth very much doubted Mrs. de Bourgh wanted an account of making Thanksgiving dinners or fights on family trips.

The woman gestured impatiently. "Where does your family's money originate from?"

"We own On-a-Stick, Inc." Unsurprisingly, Elizabeth received a blank look. "Doughnut On-a-Stick. Cheese On-a-Stick? That sort of thing."

Now Mrs. de Bourgh looked like she had sucked on a roomful of lemons. "You don't say."

Elizabeth squeezed her wine glass harder. The woman's attitude had triggered a perverse desire to shock her. Her snobbishness actually exceeded her nephew's. "My father says that food on a stick is the wave of the future," Elizabeth said, pasting on a blithe smile. "It's becoming quite popular here in France. The company has received inquiries from some of the top chefs of Europe. I would imagine that the next time you visit France, there will be some food on a stick options on every menu."

Fitz's hand covered his mouth, but Elizabeth heard a faint snort of laughter. The president's expression was harder to read. Mrs. de Bourgh appeared slightly nauseated. "No. Certainly not—"

Irritation made Elizabeth a little reckless. "And I believe that my father spoke to President Darcy about Zucchini On-a-Stick for the White House."

All eyes turned to the president; would he call her bluff? "We did have that discussion," he said in a neutral tone.

"I didn't realize you were from *that* family," Mrs. de Bourgh sneered.

Elizabeth was on a roll now, and nobody was safe. "It's a distinguished family tradition. My great-great-grandfather sold mutton on a stick from a street cart in the Victorian era, and a very distant ancestor sold salted pork on a stick during the Revolutionary War. My father's company merely elaborated on the concept."

Elizabeth kept a straight face as the older woman glared. Abruptly, she turned to Fitz. "I believe I'd like a martini. Will you escort me to the bar?" Fitz offered his arm to his aunt and led her away, but not before winking at Elizabeth.

Elizabeth wished she could sag into the nearest chair. Her anger had ebbed, and now she worried that her rant would have consequences. What had possessed her to say such things? The president cleared his throat. Shit. Did he think she'd been taunting his aunt? What if her sarcasm cost the Red Cross its grant? *I should have thought about that before shooting off my mouth.* She started composing an apology in her head.

A smile played about his lips. "Salted pork on a stick?"

She shrugged helplessly. "Our family legacy is sadly neglected in the history books."

"Along with sarcasm?" he asked dryly.

Was he angry? Well, she could hardly deny the truth. "I seem to have gotten more than my fair share of that."

"I noticed." He wasn't quite smiling, but his eyes were alive—a clearer blue, with only a hint of gray.

An awkward pause followed; Elizabeth sipped her wine. Should she ask him about the grant? She had planned to buttonhole a lower-level State Department staffer on the topic. Discussing it with the president seemed a bit like bringing in a tank to kill a spider.

He cleared his throat. "You seem to be the only one in your family who's not in the family business."

"I love my family, but I'm very different from them. Lydia says I'm a compulsive do-gooder. What I do for a living needs to have meaning for me, or I get bored and depressed."

"Huh," he said slowly, "I understand that completely."

"You do?"

"Done right, politics is all about public service. Of course, some politicians just want the power, but many want to make the world a better place."

Elizabeth's eyebrows climbed her forehead. Those had to be the least cynical words she had ever heard uttered by a politician. Did he truly believe them? "Is that why you do it?" she asked, aware that she was violating her vow not to engage with the man. "You certainly could have stayed home and watched your stock shares multiply."

"I would imagine people say the same thing about you. You don't have to dig wells in Africa when you could live a life of constant manicures and cocktail parties."

He had been quite deft at wrestling the conversation back to her, but she would not allow it. "I seem to recall we were talking about you," she said in a teasing voice, "and why you felt the need to serve your country."

He stared at the ice cubes in his drink. "I could have lived like a playboy. But that lifestyle makes me…cranky, as my sister says." He gave her a wry grin. "Although some days when all I do is pose for photographs and fight with Congress, I'm not sure what I do has any meaning at all."

Wow, he sounded almost human. "It must be the most stressful job in the world." *Wait, am I feeling sorry for the president?*

He stared into space. "It can be. Fortunately, I have a good staff. That helps a lot." His eyes met hers, and he grinned. "Plus, there are a lot of perks. I don't have to buy my own groceries or take my car in for repairs."

Given his family's wealth, Elizabeth rather doubted that he'd *ever* purchased his own food or darkened the door of a car garage.

He rubbed his hands together like an excited little boy. "And, hey, Air Force One is pretty cool!"

Did President Darcy just make a joke? Laughter bubbled up without her permission. "So you're in it for the fun toys?" *Damn it. This is the man who ruined George Wickham's life*, she reminded herself. Polite, but distant: that was the plan. "Amused" was not an option.

He quirked an eyebrow at her. "The presidential limo is full of neat gadgets. I'll have to show you sometime."

In what universe would she be hitching a ride with the president? She didn't know why he even bothered to talk to her. Maybe he said those kinds of things to everyone, making them believe they were part of his inner circle.

During the silence that followed, the president sobered. "I thought your presentation today was very cogent," he said finally.

There's a word I don't hear every day. "Thank you." She cursed herself for blushing. "I'm glad you found it interesting."

"I hope it didn't cause problems for the Red Cross that I requested you to give the talk."

The hairs on the back of Elizabeth's neck rose. *He* was the one who had requested her! Why? She struggled to keep her tone even. "Not at all. They were excited about the opportunity."

He had requested her, so she might as well ask him. *Tank meet spider.* "Um…we're hoping to get a State Department grant to fund our projects in Africa. It's pretty crucial funding for us." His expression was blank. *Well, Margot and John will be happy I mentioned it.*

"When did you apply?"

Elizabeth was caught off guard. "I-In April. We were supposed to hear two weeks ago."

"Hmm." President Darcy stroked his chin thoughtfully, drawing her attention to the light sprinkling of stubble. It suited him. "I'll have Fitz investigate."

"Thank you." Mission accomplished. The tension drained from every muscle in her body, leaving her limp with relief. Now she could leave. Except it would be terribly rude, particularly after he'd agreed to do her a favor. No use imagining her quiet hotel room and soft, welcoming bed.

Another awkward pause. Evidently the president felt no urgent need to speak with anyone else; in fact, he regarded her quite intently. Perhaps something in her manner or dress secretly amused him. Sweat dampened the back of her neck, making her collar stick to her skin, and the wine in her glass sloshed as her hands shook. Maybe he and Fitz would return to the presidential suite that evening and laugh over her faux pas.

He still watched her expectantly. *Think, Elizabeth. There must be some way to make small talk with a president.*

"So, um, have you finished writing the speech you're giving tomorrow?" she asked. *Lame, lame, lame!*

He cleared his throat. "The speechwriters finished it back in D.C." *Of course. Why didn't I think of that?* "I hope I do a good job. The topic is so important."

"You always do a good job," Elizabeth said without thinking.

"Thank you."

Oh God! Had that sounded like...flirting? Did he think she was coming on to him? "I mean, that's something the press always talks about, right?" she said hastily. "How you're good at public speaking."

His shoulders slumped a bit. "I suppose. But the speech is rather dry. Maybe I should borrow some of your jokes."

She tapped a finger on her chin. "Hmm. That does run into some copyright issues. I might need to charge a fee..."

He laughed, lighting up his entire face. *Why does he have to be so attractive?*

"Although it might be useful as a marketing gimmick." She held up her hands like an advertising marquee. "Actual jokes used by the President of the United States."

When he laughed, dark strands of hair fell across his forehead—practically begging to be touched. "If the international aid worker thing doesn't pan out, you could try writing comedy."

She made a face. "If the international aid worker thing doesn't pan out, I'll be stuck marketing On-a-Stick products for the rest of my life."

"Would that be so bad?"

She shrugged. "Compared to what? Compared to slinging fries at McDonald's? Yeah, it's better. But I spent all my adulthood trying to separate myself from the family business."

"You love your family, but you don't necessarily want to follow in their footsteps." His eyes were fixed on his aunt, where she fussed at Fitz near the bar.

Perhaps a career in politics was his way to separate himself from an overbearing family. His parents had died when he was young, but if

Catherine de Bourgh exemplified his family, the need for some distance
was understandable.

"Fitz seems nice," she said.

"Yeah, he's a great guy. Not just my cousin, but a good friend."

"Fitz and Bing. Your friends have such interesting names. Like
the sounds a can of soda makes when you open it. Or maybe a store that
sells magical items from Harry Potter."

He guffawed, startling her and drawing eyes from around the
room. "I'll have to tell that to Fitz; he'll love that!"

"Oh God!" Elizabeth covered her face with her hands. "Don't tell
him I said it."

"Are you giving me an order?" His tone was light. "You know, I'm
commander in chief of the military."

Who was she to tell the president what to do—even in jest? "Oh
shit," she muttered. "I mean, oh crap, I mean—okay, I'm shutting up
now."

His face was solemn, but a corner of his mouth quirked upward.
"It's okay to fucking curse in front of the president. We already
established that I won't have you audited or drafted."

His delivery was so deadpan that Elizabeth couldn't help laughing.
They were drawing curious looks from around the room; maybe the
president wasn't usually this amusing. She'd never read anything that
suggested he had a good sense of humor. "But arresting me is still on the
table?" With her hands on her hips, she gave him a mock frown. "Does
Bing know you talk to constituents this way?"

President Darcy stepped back and glanced away self-consciously.
"It doesn't happen very often. You must have caught me on a good day."

This abrupt shift in mood took Elizabeth off guard. Was he always
so mercurial? *It doesn't matter.* In the ensuing silence, she allowed her
smile to melt away. She had no business enjoying this man's company.
He might be occasionally charming. He might be a good president, but he
was a horrible man. And his best friend had broken her sister's heart.
Perhaps she did find him a little attractive, but Rodney the jerk who
captained her high school football team had been attractive, too, and
Elizabeth had no trouble resisting him.

Jane and George would be appalled at Elizabeth's behavior. The
thought was like a bucket of cold water. Whatever else Elizabeth was, she
wasn't a hypocrite.

"Thank you for investigating the grant." She infused her voice with a note of finality. "I don't want to take up any more of your valuable time. I'm sure you have a hundred things requiring your attention."

His head jerked back. "Um…yes…"

She held up her empty wine glass. "And I'll get some more of this sauvignon blanc."

A smooth, professional mask settled over his features. *Of course: the real Darcy. Funny and charismatic when he wants, but he's still a politician. An extremely successful politician.* His smile was stiff and practiced.

"I hope we have a chance to talk again before the end of the summit," he said.

I hope we don't. Just before she turned toward the bar, Fitz slipped up to the president, having finally escaped his aunt's clutches. "Elizabeth, could you hold up a minute, please?"

"Okay." She watched, baffled, as Fitz pulled the president away and murmured something in his ear. No doubt the subject was of national importance, but why should Elizabeth linger?

When President Darcy turned back to her, his eyes were stormy and his face determined. Another lock of dark hair had fallen over his forehead, but Elizabeth pointedly ignored it. *I refuse to be attracted to this man.* "I hear you need a lift?" he asked.

Elizabeth regarded him blankly for a moment before recalling her conversation with Fitz. "T-There's n-no need to bother you. I have a flight on Thursday," she stammered. Maybe Fitz thought he was doing Elizabeth a favor by bringing her dilemma to the president's attention, but she would have preferred to avoid his scrutiny.

"You shouldn't miss your mother's birthday," he said with a twinkle in his eye. *When did his eyes start to twinkle?*

She brushed damp hair from her forehead. Why was the room so hot and stuffy? "It's okay. I mean, this isn't a president-level crisis. It's not even a cabinet-level crisis." The president chuckled. "This is the kind of thing you would fob off on a minor aide—an intern even…if it *were* your problem, which it isn't."

"I see what you mean," the president muttered over his shoulder at Fitz. To Elizabeth he said, "Fitz told me you're a hard person to help."

Elizabeth's eyes shot daggers at Fitz. "I don't need help."

President Darcy stuck his hands in his jacket pockets. "Well, the thing is, I have this airplane called Air Force One—you might have heard of it—and it's got lots of room. I don't have many guests on this trip."

Air Force One. Suddenly Elizabeth couldn't breathe. He wanted to give her a ride on Air Force One... She could practically hear Lydia's squeals of excitement. *But I'm not Lydia.* "I don't need special help, sir." Accepting the favor would definitely not help her avoid the man.

He rolled his eyes. "This is silly. You need a ride, and I have eleven empty seats on the most luxurious aircraft the U.S. government possesses. Why are we even debating it?"

Put that way, her resistance did seem rather...unnecessary. And potentially offensive to the man whose government may be giving her employer a grant. "Won't the Secret Service object to a random civilian riding along?" she asked.

He waved away that objection. "They'll do a quick background check on you. It'll be fine." His eyes were imploring her earnestly as if her acceptance were absolutely essential to him, although she couldn't fathom why. By now, other people at the party were edging closer with the hopes of eavesdropping. The last thing Elizabeth wanted was for this to become a topic of gossip or the subject of speculation on some website. She just wanted the business concluded.

And refusing a plea from your own country's chief executive seemed...unpatriotic or something. She sighed. "Of course, I'd be thrilled to accept a seat on Air Force One. Thank you, Mr. President."

Chapter Ten

Elizabeth texted her parents and sisters the news right before she departed for the airport on Wednesday. Phoning with the news would have provoked a level of squealing that she wasn't prepared to handle.

Lydia sent dozens of emojis—each more excited than the last—and demands for pictures. Her mother reminded her to keep her eyes open for rich men. Jane only asked if Bing was on the plane, and Elizabeth was happy to text back a negative answer, although she did arrange for Jane to pick her up when they landed.

The sun was setting when Fitz called her hotel room with an invitation to join him for a limo ride to the airport. Elizabeth expected they'd be sharing the limo with other White House staffers, but somehow they ended up alone in the back of the cavernous vehicle.

Fitz was good company, with easy manners and no shortage of lively discussions about the summit and their stay in Paris. Elizabeth's ears pricked up when he mentioned her conversation with Mrs. de Bourgh.

"Do you think the president was upset that I was so sarcastic toward her?" Elizabeth finally asked the question that had been bothering her for days. "I said the first things that came into my head. I wouldn't want him to think I enjoy being offensive to his relatives."

"Trust me, Darcy thought it was hilarious," Fitz drawled.

"He was barely smiling."

"That's the equivalent of a hearty laugh for Darce. He loved seeing Aunt Catherine at a loss for words. She's a bit of a thorn in his side, constantly expecting special treatment as the president's aunt."

Fitz shifted in his seat, which had the effect of bringing him slightly closer to her, setting her nerves on edge. Was he interested in her? Was that the reason for the empty limo? Maybe he used his proximity to the president to facilitate his social life. Elizabeth's stomach lurched. Despite Fitz's easy demeanor and good looks, she felt no spark of attraction. Accepting the ride had been a mistake.

She leaned away from him, wondering when the spacious vehicle had grown so hot and stuffy.

"Elizabeth?" Fitz reached out to touch her knee.

She flinched. *Well, this is awkward.*

He chuckled softly. "Don't worry. You're a very attractive woman, but you're not remotely my type."

"What's 'your type'?" Elizabeth asked waspishly.

"Tall, dark, and with XY chromosomes," Fitz answered instantly.

"Oh. *Oh.*" Now Elizabeth had to laugh, too. "I definitely don't meet that criteria."

Fitz waved his hand negligently. "Plus, you're practically taken. I'd never do that."

What the hell did that mean?

Before she had a chance to ask, Fitz launched into a childhood anecdote about the president and his sister Georgiana at the Darcy family estate in the Hamptons. "—So we ran off and left Darce to take the blame!" Fitz laughed.

"Did he tell on you?"

"No. He took the blame *and* the punishment and never ratted us out," Fitz said. "He was—and is—a great guy."

Why is he so intent on making that point? I already voted for him.

"He's also an incredibly loyal friend," Fitz volunteered. "You've met Bing, right?" Elizabeth nodded, not trusting herself to venture an opinion of his character. "Bing and Caroline's mother died when they were still young, and Darcy's mother and father were like a second set of parents to them. Darcy has always felt a little protective of Bing, even though he's only a few years younger."

Elizabeth gritted her teeth. "Does Bing need that much protecting?"

Fitz shrugged. "He's a bit of an idealist—a real romantic at heart. He's always in search of 'The One' and always in danger of having his heart broken." Elizabeth bit her tongue before she forcefully contradicted her host. "Recently, in fact, Bing thought he'd found her—the love of his life—but it turned out she was only interested in his father's money."

Elizabeth's chest tightened. Could he possibly be talking about Jane? No. Nobody would perceive Jane as a gold digger. But surely Bing hadn't met and broken up with someone else since dating Jane.

Fitz rattled on, oblivious to Elizabeth's consternation. "Supposedly she acted as if her family had money, but they were just keeping up appearances." Oh. Elizabeth felt queasy. Her family's financial problems had torpedoed Jane's chances with Bing.

Fortunately, Fitz's eyes were focused on the passing scenery. "Even after they found out, Bing still wasn't sure he could break up with her, but Darcy stiffened his backbone. He wouldn't let his friend fall for a gold digger."

The nausea hardened into a pit of anger as Elizabeth's nails bit into her clenched fists. Swallowing, she strove to keep her voice level. "And how did they know this woman didn't actually love Bing?"

Fitz shrugged. "I don't know. There are women like that who have a string of rich boyfriends until one of them coughs up a ring."

Elizabeth clasped her hands together to disguise their violent shaking. It was true that Jane's past two boyfriends had been from wealthy families, but those were the people with whom the Bennets had socialized.

There was no doubt that Fitz was talking about Jane. And the president had encouraged Bing to break her heart! That high-handed, arrogant bastard! Making such appalling assumptions about Jane, whose heart was so bruised that she still refused to date. Maybe Elizabeth should order Fitz to stop the limo so she could disembark and find another way home. The alternative was eight hours in an airplane with that vile man.

Adrenaline buzzed uselessly through her veins; neither fight nor flight were particularly useful in this situation. Although if William Darcy appeared in front of her at that moment, she might be tempted to punch him.

"Are you all right?" Fitz watched her closely.

This was her chance. Elizabeth could claim a sudden illness and take a cab back to the hotel. But she would miss her mother's birthday, and she had canceled her other flight.

Air Force One was a big plane, with a lot of people. Chances were that the president would be busy working with his staff, and she wouldn't even see him. If she did see him…

It would be tempting to tell him what she thought of his character. She took a deep breath, willing her heartbeat to slow. He was a jerk, but he was also the president. She couldn't let her anger rule her behavior no matter how satisfying it would be to berate him in front of his staff one thousand feet up in the air. Elizabeth leaned back against the soft limousine seat, envisioning herself being calm and polite as she shook President Darcy's hand; however, the image was instantly shattered by a fiery fantasy of hurling accusatory words at him.

Fitz peered out the window. "Oh, we're at the airport." As soon as the limo came to a stop he opened the door.

She fixed a smile on her face as they climbed up the gangway and received the crew's effusive welcomes while they entered the aircraft.

Elizabeth had expected to be given a seat at the back of the press section, somewhere she would be forgotten as she slept away the trip to D.C.

However, the president hurried up to her only a minute after she arrived, taking her hand with a wide grin and welcoming words. Elizabeth merely offered a tight smile.

"We need to put on seat belts for takeoff," he said, "but after that, I hope you'll let me show you around the plane."

Unable to gracefully decline before a host of witnesses, Elizabeth was as neatly entrapped as she had been when he asked her to dance. "Um, sure," she murmured, inwardly seething. Just being in his presence felt like a betrayal of her sister.

Giving her a brisk nod, he strode toward the front of the plane. *Maybe this is normal. Maybe he offers a tour to every visitor.*

Fitz showed her to one of the "guest seats" in the middle of the plane and left for his own seat. The two rows were mostly occupied by staff, although Mrs. de Bourgh and Bill were behind her, deeply engrossed in a task on the computer—and fortunately too far away for conversation.

Sinking gratefully into the seat—which was wider and softer than any airplane seat she had ever encountered—Elizabeth couldn't resist glancing around curiously. In some ways, the plane was like any other, with curved white walls, tiny windows, and industrial carpeting. However, the front appeared to be divided into a set of rooms where the president and his staff could work during the flight.

The takeoff was smooth and fast, but Elizabeth's hopes that the president would forget her were immediately dashed. As soon as the seatbelt sign winked off, the president was at her side. "Ready for the tour?" The occupants of the surrounding seats gave Elizabeth curious glances as she stood to receive the undivided attention of the nation's commander in chief.

Without waiting for a response, President Darcy walked her toward the back of the plane. *Typical.* He gestured to a closed door. "That is the press area, which we usually keep closed off so we can conduct our business up here in private. Sometimes I do go back there to chat up the reporters."

He ushered her toward the front of the plane with a hand on the small of her back. "The front of the plane is the interesting part—lots of features you don't find on a regular 747. We have six bathrooms and two kitchens, which are capable of producing some pretty good meals." His eyes focused intently on her face as if her opinion was of great importance to him. *Why should he care?* The attention was beginning to make her uncomfortable. It's not like she was a politician he needed to impress.

He opened a door. "This is the meeting room, although we also use it for a dining room." The large table, office chairs, and white board were standard but incongruous on an airplane.

As they continued along the corridor, he gestured to the doors they passed. "The rooms along here serve as the galley, the senior staff room, and the medical office—I always have to travel with a doctor. Fortunately, she usually doesn't have much to do."

A female staffer walking in the other direction did a double take as they passed, which the president ignored. He opened another door. "This is my study."

The room wouldn't be considered spacious by most standards, but it was impressively appointed for a space on an airplane. A large wooden desk, completely empty, dominated one side while a few chairs lined the opposite wall.

He gestured to the desk with a rueful smile. "It's nice to have a desk, but it's a bit of a pain, too. If I leave anything on it, the stuff rolls off whenever the plane banks."

She followed him back into the corridor. At some point, he had changed into a dark blue t-shirt and jeans that hugged his butt...which was definitely worth watching as he walked ahead of her.

What the hell am I doing? I can't be jonesing after the guy who hurt Jane and George. And, oh yeah, he's the fucking president! She hastily averted her eyes. The walls were quite interesting. How did they get that exact shade of off-white?

But she had to admit it was difficult to maintain her indignation in the face of such friendliness—the polar opposite of the man who had denigrated her at the state dinner. What's with the Jekyll/Hyde routine?

An awful suspicion was creeping up on her. When a bachelor president had taken office, there had been plenty of rumors about his love life, but no reputable source had confirmed hanky panky in the White House. Elizabeth believed in his presidency and thought the rumors were just rumors. But what if some of the rumors were true? What if his staff was simply good at covering up his sexual escapades? A new woman every night?

The air temperature was suddenly much cooler. Elizabeth shivered. They crossed over into a new corridor, and he indicated an exterior door. "So that's the special presidential entrance for the plane." He looked almost embarrassed. "Just for me and a wife—if I had one."

How should she respond to that? "Oh."

Taking her elbow, he navigated her to the final door at the end of the corridor. "This is the presidential suite, such as it is." He opened the door and gestured for her to enter. "If I had a family traveling with me, this is where they'd hang out. But, of course, it's just me."

The triangular space was sparsely furnished with two sofas—one attached to each wall—a coffee table, and a small desk that held nothing but a phone. There was a mural of a mountain scene on the far wall between the sofas. Despite her reservations, it was a fascinating glimpse into the world of presidential privilege. "Are we up at the front of the plane?"

The president nodded. "Right in the nose."

She tilted her head to the side, regarding the space. "But where did they put the cockpit?"

He pointed upward. "There's an upper story. The cockpit and crew quarters are up there." Oh, of course. Elizabeth had forgotten that 747s were two stories.

Closing the door behind them, he guided her toward one of the sofas. "Air Force One isn't very luxuriously appointed compared to some privately owned jets, but this room can seat eight comfortably. And each of these sofas converts into a bed, although they're pretty small." His hand patted the cushion as they sat.

"I don't use the suite much since I'm usually working in the office, but sometimes I nap in here. Fortunately, national crises are scarce today, so we can rest a bit before arriving in Washington."

Elizabeth had noticed the dim lighting throughout the plane and that passengers were getting comfortable for the night.

"Would you like something to eat?" he asked. "I assure you that the food is several steps above the usual airplane fare."

"No, thanks. I had dinner." *What the hell is happening here?*

"I asked them to stash some sauvignon blanc in here," he said, standing and opening the cabinets over the desk. "I know it's your favorite." *When had he noticed that?*

As odd as it was to get a personal tour of Air Force One from the president, now things were downright Twilight Zone. She was alone with President Darcy in a room with two beds, and he planned on pouring a bottle of her favorite wine. This was beginning to feel like a date.

An unexpected and totally bizarre date.

Damn. Fitz had said I was "practically taken." Why didn't I figure it out earlier? Apparently, the president thought that all he needed to do was crook his finger and she'd come running. What the hell?

Hadn't anyone thought to consult her on whether she'd like to be "taken" by the president? This wasn't the Middle Ages, when the king could order a woman into his bed. But maybe that's the way things worked in this administration. She shivered again.

The president had a reputation for being a straight shooter, respectful of women, and a staunch proponent of women's rights. She wouldn't have expected him to be a player. But he also had an extremely loyal staff. They wouldn't be the first White House staffers to cover up indiscretions.

How many other women had received a "personal" tour of Air Force One that ended in the presidential suite? What a sweet set up for a seduction. No wonder the staffer in the corridor had done a double take.

And Fitz? Oh-so-helpful. Was he the go-between, lining up suitable women? Damn it! Elizabeth had liked him.

Her hand flew to her mouth. Maybe she had done or said something that suggested she was amenable to a dalliance with the president. That would explain his friendliness at the dinner and insistence on giving her a ride. Her breathing sped up. Oh God, what had she gotten herself into?

Her hands began to shake so violently that she had to clasp them together to conceal the tremors. Her gaze bounced all over the room; every muscle in her body readied itself for fight or flight. Fortunately, the president—distracted by the missing wine—remained oblivious to her nerves.

His voice broke into her racing thoughts. "Okay, here are the glasses." Her eyes followed the glasses rather than the man as he set them on the coffee table. "But I think they forgot the wine." He winked at her. *Winked!* "I'll be back in a minute."

Oh my God. Oh my God. Oh my God. What am I going to do? She shot to her feet, her ragged breaths echoing in the empty room.

Elizabeth wasn't a Puritan and wasn't opposed to a little fooling around on principle. But she'd only slept with guys she was dating. Under other circumstances—with a guy she found attractive…and smart…and articulate—she would consider dating him. Hell, in a lot of ways he was exactly the kind of guy she liked.

But those were the key words, weren't they? "Under other circumstances." Attractive, smart, and articulate were worthless without a good character or personal moral principles. Not only was he proud and difficult, but he also had encouraged his friend to dump her sister and had robbed George Wickham of his inheritance.

And now he had brought her to his suite and maybe expected her to put out. Another violent shiver caused Elizabeth to wrap her arms around herself. *I'm alone in this tiny room with him and a thousand feet up in the air. Maybe I should leave before he gets back.* She took a stumbling step toward the door. *But what if I'm wrong? What if he's just being friendly? He's Bing's friend. I'm Jane's sister. Maybe the president is just catching up...kicking back. He hasn't done anything inappropriate...*

The decision was made for her when President Darcy strolled through the door, triumphantly brandishing a bottle of wine. "I knew we had it!"

He set the bottle next to the glasses as Elizabeth sank back into her seat. Maybe she was being paranoid, misjudging the man. He seemed genuinely happy to have her here. Maybe he just wanted to be friends.

And it's not like I'm supermodel material. He could seduce anyone—like real supermodels. Why would he want me?

Settling rather close to her on the sofa, the president opened the bottle of wine, splashing some into each glass. The label showed it to be something very good—and very expensive.

The president raised his glass in a toast, and Elizabeth followed suit, a little apprehensive about what he would say. "To friends," he said simply. Elizabeth's shoulders relaxed as she clinked her glass with his. That was a toast she could get behind.

After taking a sip, she set her glass on the coffee table. The wine was excellent, dry and crisp, but she had no intention of drinking much more. Her eyes surveyed the room, examining the windows, the mural, the sofas—everything except the other inhabitant. "This is exciting," she said. "Very few people get to see this. I feel very privileged. My sisters will be so jealous. My parents will be so excited to tell their friends." *You're babbling, Elizabeth. Stop it.* She took a breath. "Thank you for showing me around."

"My pleasure," he said in a low voice.

It wasn't her imagination. He was leaning closer to her. His warm breath brushed her neck. A hint of spicy aftershave teased her nose.

"There is something I need to tell you, Elizabeth." His voice was husky.

Oh no. "Y-Yes?" She stared at the wine glass, not wanting to look at him when their faces were inches apart.

"I am very attracted to you—since we first met." His voice sunk to a lower register. "*Very* attracted to you."

Shit. It was happening. The man who had ruined George and torpedoed Jane's relationship was hitting on her. Clearly, he expected her to be on the same page.

Her eyes fixed on the far wall. "Oh. I…um…didn't know." She swallowed hard.

"Of course you did. You've been flirting with me." He chuckled softly.

I have?

He put soft fingers on her chin and gently turned her face toward his. She inhaled his spicy scent. Why did he have to smell so edible? "I've wanted to do this for a very long time," he breathed. And then his lips were on hers. Elizabeth's resistance dissolved instantly. He could kiss!

It started with soft, velvety strokes of lips meeting lips. But then he increased the intensity, licking at the seam of her lips until her mouth opened without a second thought. She had to know what he could do with that tongue. She wasn't disappointed. His tongue swept in, dueling and entwining with hers. He tasted of white wine and an undefinable flavor that resembled his scent. The taste of William Darcy.

Elizabeth hadn't given any thought—well, perhaps she had occasionally imagined—to how the president might kiss, but she wouldn't have expected this…passion. Searing. Overwhelming. Shattering. Speaking the intensity of his attraction without words.

The rest of the world fell away; Elizabeth could only feel. Her whole world narrowed to a single point of focus, a solitary part of her body. Bill and George had both spoken to her about chemistry, imagining a connection that hadn't existed. But *this* was chemistry. Whatever she thought of William Darcy, her body was completely on board with kissing him. Craving his kisses—and more. *I want more. I want more…*

She moaned, a needy, greedy sound. His hands roamed over her back and upper arms, caressing, pulling her closer, and crushing her against his body. One hand traveled up her neck, into her hair.

Out in the hallway, someone laughed. The sound was enough to
re-engage the rational part of her brain. Someone might enter the room
and see them. *What am I doing? This is the president. This is the*
PRESIDENT!

She pulled away so quickly he flinched.

Every cell in her body urged her to close the small distance
between them and enjoy more touches, more caresses, more kisses. They
were so close, so connected; it seemed impossible that such a thing could
be wrong.

No. Panting, Elizabeth tried to restart her higher brain functions
despite the tumult her senses. She reached deep for that well of fury that
had powered her since Fitz's words in the limo, conjuring up the image of
Jane's stricken, tear-stained face. *Why would the man who had treated*
Jane and George so cavalierly care about me? It was an act. It was all an
act.

He had brought her in here with the idea of putting those beds to
use. Here she was, thousands of miles up in the sky with nobody around
except the president's staff. Okay, so the kisses were amazing.
Phenomenal. Life changing. But the man's character was rotten. *Don't*
forget who this guy is.

"I can't tell you how long I've been waiting to do that," he
crooned, allowing his fingers to play along the skin revealed by the V of
her blouse. "I wanted to stay away. I've been trying to
avoid...entanglements. But every time I see you..."

Despite her misgivings, part of her soul drank up the words like
water in a desert; what an honor to have *this* man say them to her.

But how many other women had he said them to? How many
women had he said them to in *this room*? She couldn't be blinded by the
mask of his charisma or fooled into believing he experienced genuine
feelings. He was a politician. Charm was the primary weapon in his
arsenal, and every word was suspect.

The president was still speaking. "Those two months when we
were apart...God, I thought about you all the time..." He closed in for
another kiss, and Elizabeth felt the pull, the desire. But she forced herself
to scramble backward, sliding off the sofa and stumbling to her feet. His
hand grabbed empty air.

"I-I don't think this is a good idea, Mr. President."

A crease formed between his eyebrows. More puzzled than put
out. "Please call me Will."

"Okay. I don't think this is a good idea, *Will*."

"I don't understand." He stood as well.

"I-I'm sorry if I misled you by kissing you back. I was just so startled…"

He scowled. "Startled? You knew where this was going!"

Elizabeth barked a laugh. "Yeah, maybe I should have. Maybe I'm the only person on this plane who *didn't* know, but I didn't have a clue that you were interested in me."

His mouth opened in shock, but he shut it with an abrupt snap. "Now you know," he snapped. Closing his eyes briefly, he took a deep breath and spoke in a gentler tone. "You don't have a boyfriend, do you?" She shook her head mutely. "So is it a problem?"

"Is it a problem?" *Where to begin?* She gave a slightly hysterical laugh. "You called me ugly and stupid. You've been rude to me and my family in just about every way possible. Do the words 'nouveau riche' ring a bell?"

He couldn't have been more startled if she'd hit him on the head with a frying pan. "But I apologized! You're *still* upset about that?"

Laughter bubbled out of her. "Of course I am! You may be a snob who apologized, but you're still a snob!"

"A snob?" His head jerked back. "To be fair, your family is sort of—"

She didn't wait for him to dig his hole deeper. Anger simmered in her veins, demanding release. "You interfered in Jane's relationship with Bing—and she's still not over it!"

"How did you know—? Never mind, I—" He didn't even bother to deny it.

Nothing would stop Elizabeth now. "And you deprived George Wickham of his inheritance!"

Darcy looked like he was chewing on something bitter. "Wickham!" he spat.

Elizabeth drew herself to her full height, delivering the coup de grace in a shaky voice. "And then you bring me to Air Force One, all high and mighty, Mr. President, to put the moves on me! Thinking that I'd be so awed by your power that I'd put out for you!"

He staggered back a step as if she had punched him. "That wasn't what I—I wasn't going to—I wanted to ask you out on a date, damn it! A date! Not some sort of tawdry affair!"

She scoffed. "Sure you did! Because that's what old-money scions like you do with nouveau-riche 'sluts' like me."

A pained expression rolled over his face. "I *never* thought of you that way! I swear. I'm…very interested in you. In *dating* you. I've never felt like this about any other woman." His hands, balled into fists, were pressed against his thighs. "Just give me a chance. Let me prove it—I really care about you." His eyes pleaded with her.

It was a good act. Elizabeth snorted. "You've been proud and difficult since I first met you. All you do is belittle me and my family. Why in the world would I want to date you?"

His mouth worked, but no sound escaped.

"Just as I thought. You don't have a single good reason." Elizabeth stomped to the door, threw it open, and slammed it closed behind her.

***

That could have gone better. Darcy stared at the door, which still quivered slightly from the force of Elizabeth's slam. Fortunately, he was usually alone at this end of the plane so it was unlikely anyone would come to investigate. Wouldn't that be the icing on the clusterfuck cake?

Sinking onto the sofa, he drank the rest of his wine. Then he poured a full glass with shaky hands and drank that. Leaning forward, he rested his arms on his knees and hung his head. His field of vision filled with the dull industrial gray carpeting. The sight blurred and swam. "Shit." He blinked rapidly to clear it.

Of course, other women had rejected him—albeit not recently—but his interest had never provoked blind fury. He winced again at the memory of her angry red face. He had blown his chances with Elizabeth quite spectacularly. Slumping back into the sofa, Darcy massaged his forehead with one hand. Maybe he was destined to remain single. Maybe there was something inherently defective in his character. Elizabeth certainly seemed to think so.

She hadn't even been particularly gentle or polite in her rejection. How had he read her so completely wrong?

He had been certain she liked him. She had teased him. Flirted. It had been flirting, hadn't it? The smiles, the jokes, the coy looks—each one carefully stowed in his memory—flashed through his mind. No, he must have misinterpreted her behavior. Based on her reaction, she hadn't been flirting. In fact, she barely tolerated him. Darcy had just grossly misread her signals. He groaned aloud. *No wonder I'm still single. I should stick to public policy.*

Georgiana had teased him that someone so socially inept should never run for public office. He thought he'd improved. Through the years in Congress and the Senate, he'd learned to read people and figure out what they wanted so he could work out mutually beneficial arrangements. He could supervise staff. Inspire voters. Get world leaders on board with his plans. His election to the highest office in the land proved that he wasn't a complete failure.

However, he remained hopeless when it came to romantic cues. His ineptitude had helped to destroy his two long-term relationships. He still wasn't sure what he had done wrong with those women, which was probably a sign he was hopelessly out of touch. And now this one was DOA.

Romance just isn't part of my DNA. Gah. What a farce. He rubbed both hands over his face, staring at the bottle of wine—the label and year he'd selected so carefully. It would help him start getting trashed. Oblivious, floaty disassociation from reality would be far preferable to this gnawing ache.

But presidents didn't have the luxury of inebriation, particularly not on Air Force One when it was crawling with press. The fundamental unfairness struck him forcefully. Everyone else in the world could get drunk as needed. When life handed them lemons, they could have a scotch on the rocks. But constant sobriety was one of the "privileges" of his office.

Damn the press. Damn the presidency. Damn it all! He didn't want any of it.

In one motion, he shot to his feet, grabbed the wine glass and threw it at the opposite bulkhead where it shattered into a million pieces. He threw the other glass, relishing the energy of the throw and the loud crash of glass on metal. *It wasn't enough.* His muscles itched for more destruction, and his hands moved restlessly until he grabbed the wine bottle and hurled it with all possible force. It crashed into the wall with a deeper and more satisfying sound, splattering wine and shards of glass all over the cushions of the other sofa.

Darcy stared at the wreckage as the scent of the wine permeated the room. *That didn't accomplish anything. I don't even feel better.*

All his energy suddenly drained away, and he slouched into the sofa cushions. God, he was a mess. A proud, difficult, socially inept mess. No wonder Elizabeth didn't want to have anything to do with him.

How had he fooled himself into believing she could have feelings for him? After their first encounter he had uttered the blasphemous lie that she was stupid and unattractive—and then had insulted her family. It was the height of arrogance to think he could overcome such an inauspicious beginning. What were her words? "Proud and difficult." Right on the money.

Of course, some of her dislike for Darcy was Wickham's fault. Goddamn Wickham. Darcy hadn't spoken to the man in two years, and he still managed to ruin Darcy's life. Although to be fair, Darcy had done most of the ruining without any assistance. How had he misinterpreted her feelings toward him so thoroughly?

He stared at the door, which failed to provide any answers. Idly he wondered where Elizabeth had gone. Most of the guest seats were taken up by his staff as well as Aunt Catherine and her staff—people Elizabeth would no doubt wish to avoid. That only left...

Shit! He needed to tell Fitz!

Darcy lunged across the sofa for the white intra-plane phone, knocking the receiver off. Scrambling for it with clumsy hands, he finally got it up to his ear and pressed the right button. His cousin picked up on the first ring with a sleepy greeting. "Fitz," Darcy said quickly, "I've got a problem. Can you come to the suite? And"—Darcy exhaled heavily—"you better bring Hilliard with you."

Twenty minutes later he had finished explaining the whole thing to his press secretary and his cousin, whose mouths were hanging open so widely that it was almost comical. "You did what?" Hilliard yelled.

"He made a pass at her." Fitz's eyes were closed, and his shoulders slumped forward.

"I did not make a pass at her," Darcy ground out through clenched teeth. "I *kissed* her."

Hilliard tugged at the few hairs remaining on the top of his head. "Sir, that could be interpreted as a sexual assault."

"She wasn't unwilling!" he exploded. "She kissed me back."

Hilliard rolled his eyes. "Yeah, try proving *that* in a court of law."

Darcy dropped his head into his hands. How had things gone south so quickly? He'd been elated to finally get Elizabeth alone...and now, half an hour later, he was discussing possible accusations of assault. The bottle of scotch was more and more appealing, to hell with the press.

"I wanted to ask her on a date," he moaned. "I just got…enthusiastic and kissed her first."

Pacing as much as the small space would allow, Hilliard scribbled notes in his spiral-bound notebook. "Okay. Did she slap you or push you away?"

"No!" he insisted. "I wouldn't—I thought she liked me."

"What did she say?" Hilliard's voice had a slightly hysterical edge.

"I don't know." Her words were the last thing he wanted to remember. "She made it clear she didn't like me."

The press secretary regarded Darcy blankly. "I could have been an accountant," Hilliard said.

"What?" Darcy asked, turning to Fitz, who seemed equally confused by the non-sequitur.

Hilliard wasn't looking at Darcy, and he almost seemed to be talking to himself. "Mom wanted me to be an accountant. I have a good head for numbers. And it's low stress. But no, *I* wanted the *excitement* of politics. I just had to—"

"Bob?" Darcy tried to catch his eye.

Hilliard shook himself. "Never mind, sir."

Fitz frowned briefly at Hilliard, but then his eyes came to rest on Darcy. "Why doesn't she like you, Darce? I don't get it."

"Well, I called her ugly and stupid."

Both men gaped at him. "Not to her face!" he added hastily. "And not in public! It was just that—well, her sister overheard…and so did she. Then her sister put it on Twitter. Okay, it sounds bad when I put it that way."

"She's *that* woman? I thought her name sounded familiar." Hilliard paused his pacing long enough to make another note.

"I can't believe she agreed to *speak* with you after that!" Fitz exclaimed.

"I apologized to her! Months ago."

Fitz shook his head. "Still, you're lucky you got anything more than a polite grin out of her."

Darcy supposed that was true; he'd never thought of it that way. "She said a snob with an apology was still a snob," he murmured.

Fitz chuckled. "I like her."

Hilliard made an impatient gesture. "What else did she say? What else did she object to?"

"I was rude to her family and called them nouveau riche."

Both men stared at him with wide eyes. "What?" Darcy asked.

"Are you sure she didn't slap you?" Fitz asked.

"I would've," Hilliard said under his breath as he returned his attention to his notepad.

"Very funny," Darcy mumbled.

"No wonder you're still single," Fitz said.

Darcy massaged the back of his neck in a futile attempt to loosen tense muscles. "Um…there's more…Somehow she found out that I also encouraged Bing to break up with her sister."

"Shit!" Fitz snapped his fingers. "That was her sis— I'm sorry, Darce, I didn't know."

One mystery solved. Darcy waved it away. What was one more disaster in a whole string of them?

"Is there anything else?" Hilliard asked a bit desperately.

"Yeah." Darcy gritted his teeth when Hilliard made the sign of the cross. "She also got a load about me from our friend Wickham."

"Damnit!" Fitz punched the bulkhead.

"That is…not good," Hilliard said slowly. Knowing Wickham might attempt to sabotage Darcy, they had discussed him at the beginning of the campaign.

"He told her I cheated him out of his inheritance," Darcy spat.

In the ensuing silence, Darcy realized that Hilliard's eyes had gone unfocused again. "Or I could have been a math teacher. They're in high demand…"

Fitz watched the press secretary with concern. "Bob, maybe you should be thinking about a vacation."

"Bob, focus!" Darcy said sharply.

"Sorry, sir." Hilliard grimaced and made another note. "Okay…so we need to be…concerned about the media."

"Understatement of the year," Fitz muttered. Darcy glared at him. "When did she meet Wickham?" Fitz asked.

Darcy dug his hands into his pockets and slumped against the back of the sofa. "I don't know for sure. I saw them talking at the Carlisle Ball." The image of how Wickham had stood waaaaay too close to Elizabeth was branded in his memory.

A chill raced down his spine. "What if Wickham got his hooks into her? What if she's *dating* him?" His skin crawled. *Just when I thought it couldn't get worse….* "No. No. She said she didn't have a boyfriend. But maybe it's a casual thing…" Darcy grabbed the arm of the sofa against the impulse to race through the door and ask her.

Fitz clasped Darcy's shoulder. "She's smart. I'm sure she'll see through him."

Darcy gave Fitz a level stare. "Like she did with the story of the inheritance?"

"That isn't relevant," Hilliard snapped. "We need to focus on damage control. How did she come to be on Air Force One in the first place? She didn't fly to Paris with us."

Now Fitz stood and started pacing. Noticing the broken glass on the opposite sofa, he gave Darcy a speculative glance, which he ignored. Fitz leaned against the bulkhead. "Her flight was canceled."

"So you offered her a lift?" Hilliard sighed.

Fitz shrugged. "I knew Darcy liked her, so I got *him* to invite her. I gave her a ride to the airport."

"You procured a woman for your boss," Hilliard said flatly.

Fitz stood up straight. "I wouldn't put it that way."

Hilliard shook his head slowly, staring at his notebook. "I'm going to be subpoenaed one day, aren't I? And I'll have to testify in front of a congressional hearing. I should have become a fireman. When I was seven, I loved firetrucks. I never should have given up on my dreams."

"It wasn't like that!" Fitz protested. "There hasn't been a woman who caught Darcy's eye in ages. He's been talking about Elizabeth Bennet for months but wouldn't make a move because of the president thing."

"With good reason," Hilliard said, frantically scribbling on his pad.

"I thought I'd help him out," Fitz finished.

"Big help." Hilliard glowered at him. "Fitz, did he ask you to go out and get him a woman?"

Fitz rolled his eyes. "Darcy didn't even tell me he *liked* the woman. I just guessed by how he talked about her."

Hilliard looked up from his notepad. "Where is she now?"

Fitz's head shot up in alarm. "Please tell me you got her a nice seat in the guest area," he implored his cousin.

Darcy pinched the bridge of his nose; they wouldn't like the answer. "She stormed out. I don't know where she went."

Fitz pushed off from the bulkhead. Hilliard was already hurrying to the exit. "She could be speaking to the press right now! Why didn't you start with that?"

Fitz gave Darcy a reproving look before both men disappeared through the door.

Chapter Eleven

Why hadn't he warned them immediately that Elizabeth might be taking a damaging story to the press? After all, he'd summoned them for damage control. They could have visited Elizabeth immediately and persuaded her to stay quiet. Now the damage might already be done. He could imagine the headlines: "President Accused of Sexual Assault." "Air Force One Love Nest." "President Darcy: Awkward Loner or Sexual Menace?"

Why hadn't he sent them to stop her half an hour ago?

He wanted to claim that he didn't know. But he did. It was because he didn't care anymore. It was hard to care about anything at all. Darcy hadn't moved when Hilliard and Fitz returned to the suite, quite a bit less panicked. Good.

"Where is she?" Darcy asked.

"In the press area," Fitz responded.

Icy fingers of fear crept up Darcy's spine. Maybe he did care after all. The only thing worse than crashing and burning with the only woman who'd caught his interest in years was performing said crashing and burning in the full view of the media.

"But we don't think she talked to anyone," Hilliard said. "Most of the reporters are asleep; nobody seemed to be writing up an urgent story."

"Did you talk to her?" Darcy asked.

Fitz shook his head. "She was curled up, fast asleep in the last row of the press section. I didn't want to have that conversation with the press around."

"Which is probably why she decided to sit there," Hilliard observed.

Darcy sighed. "Nobody accused her of being stupid."

"If you like her, I'm sure she's very smart," Fitz said. Darcy raised his eyebrows. "What?" Fitz asked. "You like intelligent women. It's your thing."

"We'll have to talk to her in the morning," Hilliard said.

Darcy scowled. "Just leave the poor woman alone."

"Sir, we need to know if she's likely to go to the press."

"She's not the type to do that sort of thing."

Hilliard took a deep breath as if summoning his patience. "With all due respect, Mr. President, I'm not sure you're the best judge of what this woman would do. You thought she'd like being kissed by you."

That was a depressingly accurate statement. Darcy waved an irritated hand at Hilliard. "All right, but you have no tact. Send Fitz to talk with her, and let's hammer out a media strategy."

***

A hard bump woke Elizabeth. Peering out the window, she was shocked to discover they had landed. The unfamiliar airport was characterized by low-slung red brick buildings and lots of people in military uniforms; presumably it was Andrews Air Force Base, where Air Force One traditionally landed.

The reporters around her were gathering their stuff, chatting softly. A few gave her curious glances, but she studiously avoided meeting anyone's gaze. Hopefully nobody had noticed her panicked state upon entering the press area the previous night.

Sitting up, Elizabeth stretched, scrubbed her eyes with her hands, and checked the time. 8:32 a.m. She'd planned to fake sleep so nobody would question her; at some point it had become the real thing. However, every time she shifted position, she would wake enough to remember why she was hiding, and her stomach would tense into a hard knot. Fleeing his suite had been the right choice, but she had allowed anger to guide some of her words to him. *I definitely could have handled that better.*

Was it true that Will had planned to invite her on a date? Had she assumed he was making a pass when he was actually trying to romance her? Her initial impression of him was of an honorable—if tactless—man. Maybe that had been right. Maybe she had horribly misjudged him the previous night.

No. His actions toward George and Jane attested to his character. As did his snide comments about her family. Even if she had been wrong about his intentions, she hadn't been wrong about their compatibility. Nothing would work between them.

She regretted her manner of rejecting him, but not the fact of it.

It was time to get off the damned airplane and meet Jane's car. *I hope he doesn't try to talk to me again.* What would she say? Just the thought made her whole body twitchy.

The door to the press area finally opened, and the reporters started filing out. However, before Elizabeth could follow suit, Fitz pushed his way into the compartment and pulled her into the front row of seats with him.

He waited until they were alone. "We need to talk."

She shook her head wearily. "Fitz, I just want to go home. I don't want to talk to him."

Fitz blinked. "He's already gone. The president always gets off first."

Of course he did. Why hadn't she thought of that? She stood. "Then I want to go."

He grabbed her elbow, and she gave him a hard stare. "Are you keeping me here?"

Fitz released her arm like it had burned him. "Of course not; you're not under arrest." As Elizabeth edged toward the door, Fitz spoke faster. "But I do want to tell you about Wickham—"

"I don't want to hear it."

"But—"

She held up a hand. "I don't want to hear anything about Will or George or anyone connected to the White House. I just want to go home."

Fitz stared at her for a long moment and then nodded. "All right. But can you tell me one thing? Are you going to the media with this?"

Huh? Maybe she was more tired than she thought. Why would she involve the media in one of the most mortifying experiences of her life? She turned his question over again in her head, but it still didn't make any sense. "The media?" she repeated.

Fitz shifted uneasily, lowering his voice even though they were alone. "Darcy said he kissed you."

She cringed. "He told you about that?"

Fitz shrugged. "He didn't have a choice. We need to know if you'll approach the media with the tale." She gaped at him. "You know"—he pitched his voice higher—"'the president grabbed me and kissed me'—"

"It wasn't like that!" she said indignantly. "I mean, I don't want— I don't like the—I don't want to be his girlfriend, okay? But I didn't mind the kiss." Actually, she wouldn't mind reenacting the kiss. Yeah, she would have fond memories of it—if not the rest of the farce.

"Uh…you're smiling," Fitz said, rubbing his chin.

"It was a good kiss," she sighed. Fitz stared at her quizzically. "Can I go now?" she asked.

He sat up straighter in his seat. "Sure, but who are you planning to share this story with?"

Elizabeth stared at the ceiling as she considered. "Maybe Jane, but I can't tell anyone else...definitely not the rest of my family. The president doesn't need that much squealing in his life."

"Good." Tension leaked from Fitz's body.

She ran both hands through her disheveled hair. All she wanted was a shower and a nap—far away from anything presidential. "I don't want to hurt the president. I mean, I believe in what he stands for, and the last thing I want is to be at the center of some sex-fueled controversy—especially when nothing happened."

Fitz grinned. "He'll be relieved to hear that."

"I just don't want to see him ever again," she said firmly.

Fitz flinched as if she'd punched him. "Elizabeth, he's a really good guy." He reached out to touch her arm.

The last of her patience evaporated, leaving behind a bundle of raw, exposed nerve endings. Fitz had obtained the reassurance he needed, and now *she* needed to be left alone. She yanked her arm away. "No. You don't know me, and you don't know what happened between us. I don't need your input."

He exhaled, eyes focused on the floor. "Fair enough."

"Is that it?" she snapped.

"Yeah. There's a porter at the foot of the stairs who will help you obtain your luggage, and we have a limo to—"

Elizabeth interrupted. "No, thanks. My sister is on her way to pick me up." Without waiting for a reply, she stood and hurried through the door. Hopefully she would never see Air Force One again.

***

During the half-hour wait for Jane, Elizabeth contemplated whether she should have accepted the offer of the limo. The White House staff and press were long gone; Elizabeth stood in front of a red-brick building in the blazing July heat watching the flight crew and various Air Force officers service the airplane.

Finally, Jane's Prius pulled up in front of her. Shading her eyes with her hand, Elizabeth couldn't stifle a groan when she saw Lydia in the passenger's seat. Of course, she loved her younger sister, but she wouldn't have a high tolerance for Lydia's particular brand of crazy today.

Jane hopped out of the car to open the trunk and help Elizabeth load her luggage, giving her a quick hug. "I'm sorry it took so long. This place is like Fort Knox. I was worried they wouldn't admit me at all."

Elizabeth swung her laptop bag into the back of the Prius. "What is Lydia doing here?" she asked under her breath.

Jane rolled her eyes. "Sorry about that. She locked herself out of her dorm last night."

"Again?"

"I wasn't planning to bring her this morning, but she was so excited about Air Force One." Jane gazed at the plane. "Plus she wanted a chance to 'ogle cute guys in uniform.'"

Elizabeth exchanged eye rolls with her sister. "At least my misfortunes provide an opportunity for my sister to drool over some beefcake."

Jane climbed into the car while Elizabeth slid into the back seat. Jane turned to Lydia. "Honey, do you think you could let Lizzy have the front seat? She had a long flight."

Lydia screwed up her face. "I'll get carsick in the back seat." Jane sighed audibly. "I will! If I so much as look at my phone *one time* I'll be in danger of puking."

"It's fine," Elizabeth said wearily.

Jane pursed her lips but said nothing as she steered the car toward the exit. Elizabeth considered the range of neutral topics. "I'm grateful I made it back in time for Mom's birthday."

"She'll be happy," Jane said.

"Yeah." Lydia twisted around in her seat so she could meet Elizabeth's eyes. "So does Air Force One have gold-plated bathrooms and barf bags with the presidential seal?"

Elizabeth managed to restrain an eye roll. "It wasn't as luxurious as I expected—and more crowded. It was actually a lot like a regular airplane, but with more security."

Lydia bounced in her seat. "Did the president chat you up? Did he ask you to dance again?"

"There's nowhere to dance on an airplane."

Lydia gestured impatiently. "You know what I mean! He totally wants to do you."

"Lydia!" Jane exclaimed at the same time Elizabeth screeched, "What?"

"C'mon, Lizzy." Lydia smirked. "He was totally checking you out during that ball thing."

Warning klaxons sounded in Elizabeth's head. She had to throw Lydia off the scent. "What are you smoking? This is the man who called me stupid and ugly."

"He can change his mind. Did he make a pass at you?"

"Of course not. Don't be silly, Lydia." Elizabeth winced as her voice squeaked into higher registers. Everyone in her family agreed that she was a lousy liar.

"I don't believe you!" Lydia sing-songed.

"This the president we're talking about!" Jane scoffed. "On Air Force One!"

Elizabeth struggled to piece together her disjointed thoughts. "Nothing happened. I barely saw him."

"Hmm." Lydia made a moue of disappointment. "Although I guess it's just as well. After he stole George's inheritance like that."

Oh no. "What about George? You met him *once* at a ball."

"Yeah, sure," Lydia agreed hastily.

Elizabeth recognized that tone of voice. "Lydia, have you been hanging around—?"

"Lizzy's jealous!" her younger sister chorused.

"No, I'm not. But he's a lot older than you are."

Lydia snorted inelegantly. "Like anyone cares about that sort of thing nowadays. Besides, he's cute. Double besides, we're just friends." She crossed her arms over her chest. "Happy?"

She should pursue it, but instead she sank back into her seat. Nothing Elizabeth said would affect Lydia.

Double besides?

***

It was an ordinary white business envelope, with an ordinary flag stamp in the corner and hand addressed to her. That alone was enough to make it stand out. Most of the mail Elizabeth received was bills, credit card solicitations, and advertisements. However, it was even more extraordinary because of the return address: 1600 Pennsylvania Avenue, Washington D.C.

Everyone knew that was the address of the White House, and there was only one person who would write to her from there. Unless Fitz had sent her a customer satisfaction survey about her trip on Air Force One.

Elizabeth stood by the mailboxes in her apartment building's lobby for a long time—staring at the envelope, not sure if she wanted to open it.

It had been a week since her ill-fated trip on Air Force One, and she'd been aggressively trying to avoid any thoughts about it. About him. The efficacy of the avoidance strategy was…limited, however. She zombied her way through the workday, her mind caught up in debating whether she should have behaved differently in the presidential suite. At night, she stared at the ceiling for hours before falling into a restless sleep.

I was right to reject him. I was. The guy was proud and difficult, seemingly incapable of navigating a conversation without insulting her family. Still, it was hard to forget the way he moved through the corridors of Air Force One…in those jeans…or that kiss…

He is pretty damn hot. But that is just a superficial attraction. And that hardly mattered since medical science still hadn't found a way to do personality transplants.

But maybe her words had been unnecessarily harsh and unpleasant. Some nights she figured she was just one of a line of women parading through that suite. Other nights she was haunted by the wounded expression on his face and his protestations that he wanted to date her. Which William Darcy was the real one?

Every night she wished she'd listened to what Fitz had to say about George Wickham. If Elizabeth hadn't been so angrily desperate to get off the airplane, Fitz might have said something revelatory. Of course, it wouldn't have changed anything, but…. she couldn't help wondering…

Chastising herself under her breath, Elizabeth took the elevator to the ninth floor and let herself into her apartment. Sitting at the kitchen table, she regarded the letter from the White House like a ticking time bomb.

Finally, she took a deep breath and tore open the envelope with trembling fingers. The letter inside was handwritten in the same scrawl as the address on the envelope. Elizabeth's hands shook so hard that she had to lay it flat on the table to read.

Dear Ms. Bennet,

Please forgive me for contacting you this way, but a letter is harder to delete or ignore than a text or email. Do not fear that this is a renewed attempt to change your mind. You made your opinion of my character perfectly clear, and I respect your decision. I merely wanted to defend myself against some of the accusations you leveled at me on Air Force One. I am distressed at the thought that you are laboring under a delusion, and—at least for my own peace of mind—I believe it is important that you know the truth. For this reason, I implore you to read the rest of this letter.

I don't know exactly what Wickham told you regarding his relationship with my family, but I can relay to you the truth of the matter. He is the son of my father's business manager, and we played together as children. However, his parents indulged him as a child, and he grew up without much discipline or direction in life. His father paid for the very best private schools and colleges, but he never applied himself to his studies and left college after six years of wasting his parents' money.

My father had always been fond of Wickham and blind to his faults. When my father passed away, he left a substantial sum of money to Wickham in his will. Naturally, I was inclined to follow his instructions despite my reservations about Wickham's character. I was prepared to write him a check, but Wickham requested instead that I give him a property in Manhattan that my family owned. He claimed that he had fond memories of it from our childhood days. I consulted my sister Georgiana, and we agreed to give it to him even though its value far exceeded the amount my father had bequeathed him. At the time, we hoped the stability of a home in New York would help him establish himself in a career.

Wickham promptly sold the property for an enormous profit and then proceeded to indulge in years of dissolution: drinking, gambling, and other unsavory activities—supported by the proceeds of the sale. Needless to say, I was unhappy about this turn of events but felt we had done what we could for him. We were simply grateful that Wickham was banished from our lives.

Unfortunately, that was not the last encounter we had with him. Two years later, having wasted all his money, Wickham showed up at my sister's apartment in New York City. He tried to seduce her—no doubt hoping that he could somehow get his hands on her inheritance. Georgiana resisted his advances, but he said some horrible things to her that left her quite shaken. After that incident, I threatened him with a restraining order if he should ever come near Georgiana again. Since he was considering involvement in politics, he decided not to risk legal repercussions.

I wanted to reveal Wickham for who he is, but I was in the process of gearing up for my senatorial bid, and Georgiana felt that the story would my hurt my candidacy. Although we were undoubtedly the victims *of Wickham's schemes, she had no desire to draw attention to his past association with our family or, truth be told, to herself. She's very shy and doesn't particularly like the scrutiny that comes from being a presidential sister. So I let the matter drop, which perhaps I should not have done. It allowed Wickham to later insinuate himself into the Republican party and use his supposed "inside knowledge" of me as a springboard to secure the nomination for a New York City congressional district.*

Although Wickham and I have often been at the same events, he has not attempted to speak with me over the past few years. Hilliard believes he is waiting for a good opportunity to attack me, so I was understandably disturbed when he sought you out for conversation at the Carlisle Ball. I wish I had inquired of you what he had said, but a penchant for gossip is not an attractive trait in a president.

I swear to you that this is the whole and truthful story of my relationship with Wickham. Fitz can verify all the particulars should you wish to inquire.

As to the business with Bing, I do not wish to violate his confidence. However, I can say that he was under the strong impression that your mother had pressured Jane into pursuing a relationship with him. Caroline's discovery that your family's company is struggling seemed to support this conclusion. In addition, your sister's interest in Bing seemed rather tepid; I never had the impression that deeper feelings were engaged.

Bing, on the other hand, was on the verge of becoming emotionally invested in your sister. I did not encourage him to break up with her; that was his decision. But I did not dissuade him from the course either. It seemed highly probable that he would be badly hurt if your sister was primarily interested in his money. Of course, you know your sister better than I do, and perhaps I was wrong about her degree of emotional engagement.

I cannot deny the other accusations you leveled at me. I have said intemperate things I later regretted. My disparaging comments at the state dinner were patently false. Nothing could be further from the truth.

However, you cannot deny that your family displays a certain...exuberance that isn't often exhibited at the kind of formal events we have attended together. While you and Jane are the souls of tact and propriety, the same cannot be said for the rest of your family. Unfortunately, as president, I must consider such things. Since I had considered asking you to date me, I was concerned about how your family's behavior would reflect on my presidency. Perhaps it was wrong of me, but I feared that your family would not perform well with the spotlight of the media shining on them.

It may not be fair, but in politics, perception matters. Even such trivial things as a girlfriend's family can make a difference in how congressmen view me and whether they adhere to my legislative agenda. I did overcome such reservations, however, and grew most eager to pursue a relationship with you. Of course, all that debate hardly matters now. Our paths are unlikely to cross again.

I thank you for reading this letter and have only one request: please do not share it with anyone, particularly not the media. It contains information that could be injurious to many people other than myself.

Please accept my best wishes for your future happiness.

William Darcy

For a long time, Elizabeth stared at the letter where it rested on her kitchen table. She had been right that it was a time bomb, and it had exploded all over her life—shattering many things she thought she knew.

She read it again, trying to absorb all the information despite feeling that her brain cells were scattered all over the kitchen floor. Of course, it was conceivable that the whole letter was a lie, but everything in it was entirely consistent with Will's behavior and the events she had witnessed. Little things he had done and said now made sense.

Oddly, the revelations about George Wickham were the least surprising aspect of the letter. In hindsight, the congressman's tale had been full of inconsistencies that she should have noticed. He'd been eager to badmouth the Darcys and vague about the details. Perhaps Elizabeth would have noticed if she hadn't already been predisposed to dislike the subject of his gossip. *I was so confident about my powers of discernment, and that lulled me into believing George's pack of lies.* Her throat was tight and thick. *What a fool I was.*

Elizabeth's heart grew heavy over the revelations about Jane and Bing's relationship. No doubt Fanny Bennet had said something that suggested she was encouraging Jane to date Bing for his money. How was Bing to know that Jane and Elizabeth laughed at their mother's obsession? Nor had it ever occurred to Elizabeth that Jane's serene demeanor would lead anyone to doubt the depth of her love. Evidently, Jane and Bing hadn't had a frank discussion about their feelings and the future of their relationship. That could hardly be blamed on Will.

As for the rest of it…Elizabeth was forced to concede that she had not sufficiently considered to what extent his role as the president would circumscribe his life. Of course, he was concerned about how the Bennets' impropriety would reflect on him. Even Elizabeth cringed at Fanny's and Lydia's antics, and she wasn't in the media spotlight. Yet he had overcome these reservations and had wanted a relationship with her despite the risk of public humiliation.

He must really care for me.

This was the letter's most shocking revelation: the depth of Will's feelings. He had not been attempting to seduce her; he had been expressing a desire for a deeper relationship.

And I ruined it.

"You may be the most attractive, interesting woman of my acquaintance." When he had uttered those words, Elizabeth had viewed them as run-of-the-mill flattery. But every woman wanted to hear a man speak such words about her. *I heard them from the President of the United States—and didn't take it seriously.*

With 20/20 hindsight, his behavior was entirely consistent. He had demonstrated his growing interest by seeking her out at the ball and the summit…inviting her to the dinner and offering a ride on his plane. Only her preconceptions about his personality had led her to misinterpret every gesture…and reject him as cruelly as possible.

If someone had plunged a knife into her breastbone, it could hardly have been less excruciating. It was difficult to breathe around the pain in her chest. He had every right to experience bitterness, but instead he had written a gracious, even-handed letter, demonstrating quite some strength of character.

All this time her perceptions had been backward. She thought the funny, charismatic side of Darcy was an act—a mask he used to charm her just like he charmed voters. He was rarely that relaxed in public but was notoriously reserved. Perhaps the proud, reserved man was the true mask—which Will dropped when he was with her.

Groaning, she covered her face with her hands. Few other women had been offered that gift. And she'd thrown it in the dirt and stomped on it with both feet. Almost certainly he wanted nothing more to do with her, and yet he risked exposure to the media by sending a letter that wished her future happiness.

He would never know that Elizabeth shared his attraction—an attraction that could have bloomed into something even greater if she hadn't actively attempted to stifle it. That kiss...

A hot tear splashed onto the table. Followed by another one. She didn't even really know why she was crying. Over the missed opportunity of a relationship with the president? The embarrassment at how badly she had misinterpreted the situation? Or was she sorry about the harsh way she had rejected him? There were so many regrets to choose from.

Elizabeth stared at the clock on the opposite wall, weighed down by the decisions that had led her to this point. But ultimately it didn't matter; it was too late to change anything.

Chapter Twelve

After a day of reading and re-reading the letter from Will, Elizabeth reluctantly concluded the words wouldn't reveal much more about the man's thoughts. However, the exercise wasn't a total loss. With each re-reading she found fresh evidence of how she had misjudged the man and made false assumptions.

The next day she called and confessed everything to Jane—except the part that involved Bing. After listening sympathetically to Elizabeth's word vomit, Jane asked only one question: "Do you believe him?"

Elizabeth didn't hesitate. "Yeah. Do you think I should?"

"It's unlikely someone would invent all of that, and a lot of the letter doesn't show him in a good light."

Elizabeth blinked, trying to keep the tears at bay. "Not only did I misjudge him, but I yelled at the President of the United States!"

"I'll come over and cheer you up," Jane said immediately.

"Thanks, but I don't think they make Hallmark cards for this."

"I'll be right over."

During the intervening time, Elizabeth re-read the letter only twice. To distract herself, she straightened an already tidy apartment. It wasn't large by Washington standards, and the building was on the old side. But at least she had a separate bedroom and a well-appointed kitchen, which shared space with the living/dining room.

Finally, there was a knock at the door. She opened it to reveal Jane holding up a 7-Eleven bag containing several pints of Ben and Jerry's. "Want to drown your sorrows?"

Elizabeth smiled wanly. "You know me so well."

Twenty minutes later, they were sprawled on Elizabeth's couch, the ice cream on the coffee table along with several bowls so they could scoop as they pleased.

Elizabeth licked her spoon, dwelling on the delicious flavor so as not to think about the calories. It was never beneficial to think about calories in such a situation. "I don't think there's a single flavor of Ben and Jerry's I don't like. They are like ice cream geniuses. Gods among men. Ice cream gods."

Jane scraped the bottom of her bowl. "Mmm," she agreed.

"I mean…can you imagine life without Chunky Monkey or Cookie Dough or Phish Food?" Elizabeth eyed the pints, planning her next assault. "It wouldn't be worth living." She scooped some Brownie Batter into her bowl and took a big bite, swooning against Jane's shoulder. "You are my favorite sister, did you know that?" She took another bite of ice cream. "You're kind and you listen to me whine, and you'd give me a kidney if I needed one."

Jane grinned. "I totally would."

"But most of all…you bring me Ben and Jerry's. That gets you the best sister prize right there." Elizabeth swallowed another spoonful, savoring it as it went down.

"Are you drunk?"

"Yeah, drunk on Ben and Jerry's."

"So now is the time for some sage sisterly advice."

"Okay," Elizabeth sighed, setting her bowl on the table. "Lay it on me."

Jane stared at her for a moment, and then her eyes fell to the floor. "I got nothing, actually. Pretty sure they don't make I-called-the-president-a-jerk-and-now-I-regret-it cards." Elizabeth stuck out her tongue at her older sister. "And I'm not even sure that's what you're so unhappy about."

"Yeah. Sorta. My judgment was so skewed. I thought George Wickham was a good guy and the president was a jerk." Elizabeth hugged a throw cushion to her chest. "I said some terrible things to him, Jane. Hurled all kinds of accusations."

"If that's the biggest problem, then you should apologize to him— and move on."

She squeezed the cushion harder as her body tensed. "It's not that easy. How do I get in touch with him? A letter or email would almost certainly be read by someone else. I don't have his cell phone number, and the White House operator isn't likely to patch me through."

"Yeah, that's true…" Jane said thoughtfully.

Elizabeth's eyes lit up. "But you have Bing's number! Maybe I could get Bing to relay a message somehow."

Jane shook her head. "I deleted it. I didn't want to call him in a fit of weakness." Elizabeth hated the shadow of sorrow in her sister's eyes. "It's a shame you can't call the president; who knows what might happen?" Jane grinned lasciviously.

Elizabeth chuckled as she scooped more ice cream. "I guess few women have the chance for sex in the White House China Room."

"You do seem to be attracted to him."

"Attracted? To President McDreamy? With his stormy blue eyes and soft dark hair and his sensual lips? I have no idea what you're talking about." Both sisters giggled.

"You've given this more than a passing thought," Jane said.

"Maybe," Elizabeth said primly, popping a spoonful of ice cream in her mouth. Jane snorted. Elizabeth slowly lowered the bowl to her lap. She sighed. "Not really. He's still proud and difficult…it wouldn't have worked anyway."

"You don't know that," Jane, ever the optimist, said.

Elizabeth slumped against the back of the sofa. "I'll probably never see him again. So it doesn't matter if he's madly in love with me or just thought I'd make a good booty call."

Jane bit a fingernail. "There's got to be some way you can apologize to him."

"If you think of one let me know. In the meantime, I plan to brood and mope about my apartment."

"Yeah, most therapists consider that the best way to get over the blues." Jane's sarcasm was thick enough to cut with a knife. "Maybe I'll buy some stock in Ben and Jerry's."

Elizabeth threw the cushion at her sister.

"At least I have a vacation coming up," she pointed out. "Aunt Madeline and Uncle Thomas rented that place in the Hamptons again."

"Awesome. You can mope in style."

Elizabeth ignored this. "Why aren't you coming this year?"

"I wish, but work is crazy." Jane's expression brightened. "We got a new contract."

At last some good news. It should ease some of the financial pressures that had her family so stressed lately. "From where?" Elizabeth asked.

"That USDA contract. We'll be supplying school lunches for hundreds of schools! We just found out yesterday. Dad cracked a smile for the first time in months."

At the sound of a knock on the door, Elizabeth frowned. "I'm not expecting anyone." She padded over to the door and peered through the peephole. "It's Lydia," she groaned to Jane. No doubt there was some "crisis" that involved a lot of complaining and very little common sense.

Elizabeth turned the knob. "Lyds, what are you doing here?"

Lydia flounced into the apartment. "My life is crazy! I needed someone to talk to!" she moaned dramatically.

Elizabeth sighed. "Sure."

"Oh, hi, Jane," Lydia said in a colorless voice. Then her eyes fell on the coffee table. "Ben and Jerry's!" She practically tripped over her own feet racing to the table, where she surveyed the containers. "You ate all the Chunky Monkey! Why didn't you save any for me?"

"We didn't know you were coming," Jane said reasonably.

"But you do know that it's my favorite," Lydia pouted. "God, nobody ever takes my needs into consideration." Sulking didn't prevent Lydia from filling her bowl with several scoops and flopping onto the sofa. She tasted a spoonful. "This is good, but it's a little soft. You should have put it back in the freezer before I got here."

Elizabeth and Jane exchanged eye rolls over Lydia's head.

The sooner they discussed the "crisis," the sooner they would be done. "So why are you so upset?" Elizabeth asked.

"Oh, there's all this shit going down with Miso and Olga. I told Olga she was my BFF, and that was like, you know, months ago. Then on Tuesday, I told Miso that she was my BFF, because I've been hanging around with her more than Olga lately. So, of course, Olga hears about it and comes to me and she's all like, 'I thought I was your BFF.' And I'm like, 'You were, but now you're not.' And Olga says, 'Best friends *forever*. That's what it means. So you can't just up and decide we're not best friends because you promised forever.' And I said…"

Elizabeth tuned out Lydia's monologue, peppered with sentiments that were far better suited to middle school than college. She despaired that her sister would ever grow up. As it often did, her mind turned to thoughts of Will's letter and George Wickham.

Wickham!

"Lydia!" she said. Lydia huffed at the interruption, but Elizabeth continued. "You haven't been seeing George Wickham, have you?"

Lydia's eyes slid sideways. "You mean dating him? No, of course not."

"Good. That's good." Elizabeth said, relieved. "He's not trustworthy. A lot of what he told us about the president isn't true."

Lydia's eyes narrowed. "Who said so?"

Elizabeth immediately saw the problem with her assertion. "Well, er, the president did. In confidence. I can't explain it all. But believe me when I say George didn't tell us everything."

"How do you know the president is telling the truth?"

"He's the president!" Elizabeth exclaimed.

"The last one lied like a rug." Lydia crossed her arms over her chest.

Elizabeth exhaled deeply. "Will is known for his honesty—for bringing integrity back to the White House."

"Will? *Will?*" Lydia screeched. Elizabeth winced at her stupid mistake. "Who calls the president 'Will'?" Elizabeth stared at her sister blankly; surely there was a plausible excuse for calling the president by his first name—but inspiration did not strike.

"I knew it!" Lydia crowed. "Something *did* happen on Air Force One! You looked so strange when we picked you up. What base did you get to? Second? Third? All the way home?"

"It's not like that!" Elizabeth lowered her voice as if members of the press lurked in her curtains. "I don't even like him."

Lydia gave her a disbelieving look. "Right. Sure. Admit it: you think he's hot."

"I don't think he's hot." *I should be crossing my fingers behind my back.*

"C'mon! You totally flirted with him and made a play for him." Lydia pointed the spoon accusingly at Elizabeth. "Did he shoot you down?"

"You don't know what you're talking about, Lydia." The Twitter queen of Washington D.C. would be the worst person to know the truth. "He's proud and difficult. He called me stupid and ugly. I don't want to have anything to do with him."

Lydia put her hands on her hips. "You. Think. He's. Hot. Case closed."

"He's the one who thinks Elizabeth's hot!" Jane blurted out and then slapped a hand over her mouth with a horrified expression on her face.

Lydia whirled toward Elizabeth. "*He* likes *you*? Oh my God! The president likes *you*?" She clapped her hands as if she'd received the best birthday present in the world.

"No, he doesn't," Elizabeth replied briskly. "Jane is just joking, right, Jane?"

Lydia glanced over her shoulder at Jane, who was still frozen with her hand over her mouth. "Then why does she look like she just betrayed a state secret?"

She had to throw Lydia off the scent. "Um…she realized the joke was in bad taste," Elizabeth said. "It hurt my feelings."

Lydia's eyes lit up. "OMG! He *hit* on you when you were on Air Force One!"

Why did Lydia's primary talent have to be sniffing out secrets? She continued with a gleeful air, "And you don't like him, so you were upset—when every other woman in the world would be thrilled. What happened? Did the Secret Service have to intervene to save your virtue?"

"No, no, no!" Elizabeth cried. "You are way, way off base! You don't know what you're talking about."

Lydia folded her arms and gave Elizabeth a piercing look. "I hope you don't plan a career as a professional poker player."

Elizabeth gave Jane a despairing look. "I hope someday Lydia will use her powers for good," Jane murmured as her shoulders slumped.

"Okay, something happened," Elizabeth conceded. "But I can't tell you about it, and it's not going to happen again."

Lydia grinned triumphantly. "I knew it!"

"You can't say anything about what you know," Elizabeth implored her. "Or what you *think* you know. There's nothing going on, and I don't want any rumors to start."

Lydia was all wounded innocence. "Of course not. I am a vault. I am a Fort Knox of information."

Somehow Elizabeth was not reassured.

***

"Rise and shine! Rise and shine!" Fitz put on his best Southern belle voice as he burst into Darcy's bedroom. Darcy groaned.

Fitz prodded him with a hand on his arm, shaking Darcy's entire body. "C'mon, sleepyhead. Time to get up."

"Who let you in here?" Darcy groaned without opening his eyes. He usually wasn't plagued by visitors until breakfast.

"I did." That voice undoubtedly belonged to Bing.

Darcy rolled onto his back, keeping his arm over his eyes. "Who let *you* in?"

"I stayed overnight at the Residence. We both did."

"Whyzat?" Darcy cleared his throat. "Why is that?" The night before was a complete blank, and apparently a small rodent had died in his mouth.

"You asked us to," Fitz said, far too happily for this early in the morning. "To get you up in time for the flight to Pemberley."

Pemberley. They were going to Pemberley. That was the first good news Darcy had heard since waking. Maybe that was a reason to open his eyes. They tentatively peeled open just a crack.

Damn! Someone had obviously installed klieg lights in his bedroom while he was asleep. Darcy blinked furiously. "Why is it so bright?"

With a grin, Fitz pulled a pair of aviator sunglasses from his shirt pocket and handed them to Darcy, who was not too proud to put them on. Bing regarded him more soberly as he provided a water bottle and two Advils.

The night before was returning to Darcy in bits and pieces. "How many bourbons did I have?"

Fitz shrugged. "Four? Before you switched to beer."

"No wonder I feel like a tank ran me over." Darcy sat up and rested his back against the headboard of the impressive canopy bed. It was noticeable how having a hangover in the lap of presidential luxury was no better than having a hangover anywhere else. "Why did you let me do it?"

Fitz laughed. "You are such a kidder! I tried to stop you before the third bourbon, but you said, and I quote, 'I'm the leader of the free world, you can't tell me what to do.'"

"And then later on, you said 'the world can manage without me for one night,'" Bing added.

Those words did sound vaguely familiar. "Damn," Darcy winced. He and Bing had occasionally gotten smashed at college, but it wasn't something he did very often. "I don't remember it ever feeling quite this awful."

"It's a good thing there wasn't an international crisis, or I would have had to call the vice president," Bing said with a smirk.

Darcy waved nonchalantly. "She'd be able to handle it." *She's happily married.* He finished off the bottle of water, which Bing took as he handed him another one. Darcy frowned at it mulishly. "Drink up," Bing ordered. "You need to be presentable before we pour you into the limo."

"Hilliard would kill me if the press got a picture of you in your current state," Fitz added.

Darcy let his head fall back and bump against the headboard, wincing when the movement caused his brain to slosh around in his skull. "If I look half as bad as I feel, you're probably right."

Fitz gestured to the water bottle. "Finish that up, and your reward is a cup of coffee."

The magic words. "I'd kill for some coffee."

"I'll get some started." Fitz hurried from the room.

While Darcy drank, Bing settled into a chair by the bed with a sheaf of papers in his lap: the usual summary of world events that had transpired during the night. But instead of diving into them, Bing sat still, watching Darcy intently.

"What?" Self-consciously, Darcy tried to flatten down some of his unruly hair.

"Darce, it's not like you to…" He trailed off as he tried to find a way to put it delicately.

"Get smashed?" Darcy chuckled. "You can say that to the president, you know."

"I was going to say 'shit-faced.'" Bing grinned.

Of course, his chief of staff was concerned. "It won't happen again."

"Good, but that's not my biggest concern. What triggered it? I haven't seen you that lit since college."

When Darcy hesitated, Bing glanced across the room at Fitz, who had just returned with a cup of coffee. His cousin shrugged. "Don't look at me. One minute he was fine, watching some talking heads on ZNN. The next he was diving into the bottle of bourbon."

Darcy shoved both hands through his unruly hair, not caring about the pain when his fingers caught on snags. "I'll be fine."

"What was he watching?" Bing asked Fitz.

"Give it a rest," Darcy snarled at them.

Fitz ignored him. "Wiley Montrose and crew were discussing 'what is wrong with the president?'"

"They've done that a thousand times." Bing waved this away. "Why was this different?"

Fitz crossed his arms over his chest. "Greg Parese suggested that the president just needed to get laid. That's when the bourbon came out."

"Well…shit," Bing said.

"It doesn't matter," Darcy snapped. "Where's the coffee?"

"Why does that bother you so much?" Bing watched him with narrowed eyes.

"You are not my shrink," Darcy ground out, staring at the opposite wall.

"I think the isolation is getting to him," Fitz said to Bing.

Bing nodded as he rubbed his chin. "I'm surprised it took this long."

"Do you think we should hire someone for him?" Fitz asked.

Darcy flew out of bed, sending covers flying. "What the fuck?" he asked Fitz.

Fitz smirked at Bing. "Well, that got a reaction."

Shooting a glare at Fitz, Darcy went to collect the coffee on his dresser. His cousin knew him too damn well. The coffee was still hot, and the first sip was ambrosia.

"Does this have something to do with Elizabeth?" Fitz asked him.

"Elizabeth?" Bing's eyebrows drew together.

"Bennet," Darcy added.

"Jane's sister? What does she have to do with Wiley Montrose?"

"She has more to do with the getting laid part," Fitz drawled.

"What!"

I should explain everything to Bing, Darcy told himself, but just the thought exhausted him. "It's complicated," he said, closing his eyes as he massaged tight neck muscles.

"Darcy tried to kiss her on Air Force One, and she didn't like it," Fitz said.

"Well, maybe it's not that complicated," Darcy conceded.

"You tried to kiss Jane's sister? When was she on Air Force One?" Bing's voice rose higher and higher.

"We gave her a ride back from the Paris summit," Fitz explained. "Apparently, Mr. Suave here had been nursing a crush for a while."

"Not a crush," Darcy mumbled. "I'm not a fifteen-year-old girl."

"I stand corrected." Fitz's voice was tinged with amusement. "Darcy had been nursing a grand passion for Ms. Bennet. He kissed her and said he wanted to date her."

"And she turned you down?" Bing said incredulously.

"Ran screaming from the room," Fitz chuckled.

"No screaming," Darcy corrected.

"But there was running?" Bing asked.

"There was running," Fitz confirmed.

"It was more of a fast walk," Darcy said.

"Oh God." Bing massaged his forehead. "Does Hilliard know?"

"Yeah," Fitz said. "Elizabeth promised she wouldn't go to the press. And it's been around a month since it happened. We're probably in the clear."

Darcy shook his head but stopped when the brain sloshing resumed. "I really liked her and wanted to take her on a proper date."

"What happened?" Bing inquired.

Darcy sighed. "According to her, I insulted her family, ridiculed her, cheated Wickham out of his inheritance, and was overall proud and difficult."

Bing gave a low whistle. "With mad skills like those, it's amazing you're still single."

"I didn't...I mean, I thought..." He cleared his throat. "In retrospect, I can see that I made...some mistakes." Fitz didn't bother to hide his smirk. "I just wish I could apologize." He didn't say anything about the letter. Who knows if she'd even read it—and Bing would be apoplectic worrying she might take it to the media.

"That would be good."

Darcy snorted. "Yeah, but how? I can't exactly land Marine One on her lawn."

"There's this newfangled thing called the telephone. I've heard it's very effective," Fitz said.

"I don't have her number." Darcy gulped some more coffee.

"If only you had a network of intelligence agencies full of highly trained operatives who could sniff out even the most publicly available information...."

"Yeah, that's not overkill at all." Fitz opened his mouth to retort, but Darcy cut him off. "She'd probably hang up on me if I called. And what would be the point anyway? I've shot any chance I had with her."

"You don't know that," Bing said.

"Oh?" Darcy raised an eyebrow at his friend. "You want to call Jane while I call Elizabeth?"

Bing's shoulders slumped. "Point taken."

"Elizabeth hates me."

"I'm sure that's not true," Bing said.

"She told me she never wanted to see him again," Fitz volunteered.

Bing glared at the other man. "You're not helping."

In the long silence that followed, Darcy tried to concentrate on the sensation of caffeine coursing through his blood. "I'm sure someone else will catch your eye eventually," Fitz said.

"Yeah," Darcy said without conviction. The last thing he wanted was to return to escorting around women like Caroline Bingley. "Elizabeth was just different…"

His friends regarded him quizzically.

"It's her eyes."

"Her eyes?" Bing echoed dubiously.

"It's like she really sees me…and knows who I am—really knows. She even teases me. Teases me! Nobody does that except you guys."

They stared at him with their mouths agape. Why? He hadn't said anything earth-shattering.

"Shit," Bing whispered, "you're in love with her."

Of course. I've known that for months.

"Don't be ridiculous," Darcy said.

Great. Now it was obvious even to his friends.

"I'm with Bing on this one, Darce," Fitz said. "You sound like a man in love."

I need to choose my words more carefully.

"I'm not in love with her," he said firmly. "This will pass."

I'm so screwed.

"Well, it hardly matters." Fitz shrugged.

What the hell? It totally matters!

Fitz continued, "She never wants to see you again, so the point is moot."

I'll never see her again, but I'm still screwed. Totally screwed.

His stomach lurched with nausea that had nothing to do with the hangover. He lifted the coffee cup to his lips, but it was empty. Drunkenness had a lot to recommend it; last night he had effectively drowned his memories of Elizabeth in bourbon, but the hangover wasn't proving as effective. Damn it.

It didn't prevent him from fantasizing about how he would behave differently if he did encounter Elizabeth. *I can be sensitive and kind, can't I? I could show her I care about her and respect her—and her family. Right? Demonstrate that she's not one in a string of imaginary women parading through my bedroom.*

Darcy was immediately distracted by a vision of Elizabeth in his bedroom. He shook his head quickly to dispel the image. There was no point fantasizing about something that would never come to pass. *Focus on the present, Darcy.* He smiled grimly at his friends. "All right, time to leave for Pemberley."

***

Elizabeth squinted into the bright sun and surveyed all the other people crowded around Pemberley's gates, not at all sure she should be there. It was a bit surreal; she'd never expected to go near the president's estate.

The wheels had been set in motion the night before when Elizabeth's Uncle Thomas folded down the front page of the newspaper and announced to the room at large, "The president is coming to the Hamptons."

Elizabeth had been stretched out on the sofa of the little living room in their rented cabin. After dinner, they had taken a long walk on the beach—all the exertion she was capable of on her first day of vacation. But her uncle's words dashed away all her drowsiness in an instant.

Aunt Madeline lifted her eyes from her mystery novel, but whatever she had intended to say was drowned out by Elizabeth's undignified squawk. "What? Here? Now?"

Uncle Thomas raised his bushy eyebrows. "Yes. Tomorrow, in fact."

"He has a house right on the water," Aunt Madeline chimed in. "Called Pemberley. It's been in his family for three generations. I hear it's gorgeous, but I haven't been out that way myself." She gave a little laugh. "That's not exactly our part of the Hamptons." The Gardiners' cozy rented cabin was very nice, but it was a far cry from Billionaire's Row.

Her uncle folded the newspaper in his lap. "I would imagine there will be quite a crowd gathered to see him arrive."

"Can we go?" The words were out of Elizabeth's mouth before she had a chance to take them back—or think them through.

"I didn't know you were so interested in politics," her uncle said.

Elizabeth squirmed in her seat. "Well, I'm not usually, but…you know…President Darcy has done some good things.…He's brought dignity back to the office. And his legislative achievements…" *God, I sound like a* New York Times *editorial.* "I really admire him," she finished lamely.

Yeah, I admire his butt and his eyes and his kisses…

"Hmm. I wouldn't mind going." With a little shrug, Uncle Thomas returned to his paper.

Aunt Madeline—the more perceptive of the two—eyed Elizabeth with interest. With good reason. Elizabeth was hardly the type to get excited at the chance to meet a celebrity. "Your mother said Jane had dated the president's chief of staff. Did you have a chance to meet the president?"

Elizabeth ran both hands through her hair. How much should she tell her aunt? "Um…yeah. I met him. He's"—how could you describe a man who was so complicated and infuriating and attractive all at once?—"intense…"

"I would think you wouldn't care about seeing his limo if you already met the man," her uncle observed from behind his newspaper.

Here was her chance to change her mind, to explain it had been a momentary whim that she had reconsidered. Elizabeth swallowed hard. "I…um…want to show my support. He's done so much for the environment. And he's supportive of refugees"—she gestured vaguely—"and there might be protesters, so people should be there to show support."

Aunt Madeline regarded her with pursed lips. "We do support his policies, and it would be interesting. I've never seen a sitting president." She shrugged, pulling out her iPad. "Maybe I can find out approximately what time he'll be arriving."

Elizabeth opened her mouth to tell her aunt to forget the whole idea but then closed it again. She needed to apologize. Will probably thought she never wanted to see him again. If he saw her—even just in passing—he might understand that she was sorry for misjudging him. Of course, he might not see her at all, but it was better than doing nothing.

And now they were here—outside Pemberley in a crowd of people who had come to greet the president's limo upon his arrival in the Hamptons. Many of the locals were reminiscing about other presidential arrivals. Others had obviously traveled from long distances merely to glimpse the president through a car window and possibly see him wave. Some had hand-painted signs with messages of support while others had signs objecting to the president's actions in the Middle East, economic decisions, or other policies.

The police had erected barriers along both sides of Pemberley's driveway so that the crowds of people wouldn't block the entrance. The property was surrounded by a tall iron fence and a variety of vegetation; the house wasn't even visible from the road. The gate stretching across the entrance was patrolled by unsmiling Secret Service officers toting big guns.

Elizabeth and the Gardiners had been standing in the crowd for an hour and remained unsure how much longer they would have to wait. The president didn't need to keep a tight schedule on his vacation. Absent any shade, the sun shone mercilessly on Elizabeth's head, and sweat trickled between her shoulder blades under her yellow sundress. The dress was a bit of an indulgence. Will would likely get only a fleeting glimpse of her—if he noticed her at all—but hopefully she would stand out among all the shorts-and-t-shirt-clad onlookers.

Standing out was essential; they were pretty far back in the crowd. Elizabeth thought she would glimpse the cars in the motorcade, but would she see the president inside one? More than once she'd considered just giving up and leaving, but if there was even the slightest chance she might show him how sorry she was for misjudging him...

That hope kept her standing in the hot sun.

Her aunt and uncle hadn't complained once about the heat or the long wait. They seemed to regard it as an adventure, as if seeing the presidential motorcade was one of the perks of their vacation. Her uncle had struck up a conversation about fishing with another man in the crowd, but her aunt had been giving Elizabeth curious glances all morning.

"Why the sudden interest in presidential motorcades?" Aunt Madeline finally asked.

"I find the president's limousine fascinating," Elizabeth said hurriedly. "Did you know that it's custom made with bullet-proof glass and armor plating so that it could withstand a bomb blast? The doors are nearly a foot thick."

Aunt Madeline was skeptical. "Mm-hmm. You did extensive research, did you?"

"I looked it up on the Internet last night," Elizabeth conceded.

Her aunt gave a dry chuckle. "What's actually going on?"

Elizabeth shrugged with attempted nonchalance. "It's not every day you get to see the presidential motorcade. It's kind of cool."

The other woman squinted at Elizabeth. "Didn't you meet the president at the state dinner?"

"Sort of?" Elizabeth shrank back from her aunt's scrutiny.

"Mm-hmm. *And* you danced with him at a ball?"

Elizabeth swallowed hard. "You're very well informed."

"I would imagine that your mother has told everyone she's ever met."

I should have expected that. "Is there a problem if I want to see him again?" *God, I sound like a girl with a crush.*

Aunt Madeline's lips pressed flat. "Why would you spend hours in the sun for a five-second glimpse of the man when you've already waltzed with him?"

It was a good question. An excellent question. A completely reasonable and innocuous explanation probably lurked somewhere, but Elizabeth had no idea where. "Um." Her mind was blank. "Um." Elizabeth scrutinized the people closest to them, but nobody was paying the least bit of attention to their conversation. She blew out a breath. "I owe him an apology."

"The president?" she said faintly. You owe *the President of the United States* an apology?" Elizabeth nodded miserably. "What the hell for?" Her aunt lowered her voice. "Did you vote for the other guy? Set fire to the Oval Office? Drop the nuclear launch codes down a drain?"

Elizabeth cleared her throat. "I…um…made some…assumptions about him that turned out to be untrue, and said some rather unpleasant things to his face." *Oh Lord.* She squeezed her eyes tightly closed, not wanting to think about it, let alone discuss it.

"When was this?" her aunt asked.

"A month ago, on Air Force One."

Her aunt yelped. "Air Force—!" Elizabeth slapped her hand over the other woman's mouth.

"Nobody can know," Elizabeth whispered before removing her hand. "I swore the family to secrecy."

Aunt Madeline's eyes sparkled. "You were on *Air Force One?*" she hissed. "Lizzy, when were you planning to tell me? Deathbed confession?"

Elizabeth bit down a smile. "It was just a fluke. The president offered me a ride back from Paris."

Uh-oh. Her aunt's curiosity was provoked. The older woman pushed up her glasses and fixed Elizabeth with a penetrating stare. "Do you have a crush on the president?"

"Of course not," Elizabeth scoffed. "He's a jerk! He's proud and difficult—and he called my family nouveau riche."

He also wrote this heartbreakingly sincere letter that I've read so many times it's in danger of falling apart. Yeah, maybe I have some feelings for him.

Aunt Madeline regarded Elizabeth over the rim of her glasses. "But you still owe him an apology."

This was hard to explain. How had her life grown so complicated? Elizabeth sighed. "It's just that…I'm not—he's not quite as big a jerk as I thought. I misjudged him, and it's difficult to contact him without a lot of other people knowing. I thought if he sees me here and I wave and smile, then he'll know that I'm sorry."

Aunt Madeline surveyed the crowd. "You could hold up a sign that says 'I'm sorry.'"

Elizabeth grimaced. "I thought about it, but that might prompt questions I don't want to answer. Hopefully he'll get the message just by seeing me." *If he sees me.* There were masses of people between her and the driveway.

As if reading Elizabeth's mind, her aunt observed tartly, "He'll never see you stuck way back here."

Elizabeth bowed her head sadly. "I should have arrived earlier, but I didn't realize how big the crowd would be." She felt the burn of sudden tears. What if he didn't see her? What if her plan didn't work?

Aunt Madeline pursed her lips. "There has to be something we can do about that."

Alarm set Elizabeth's insides to quivering. Her aunt could be a force of nature when she got ahold of an idea. "The crowd is packed pretty tightly," Elizabeth said.

Her aunt's eyes lit up. Oh no, Madeline Gardiner perceived a challenge. "You leave that to me." Before Elizabeth could object, a cry went up from the crowd: the front of the motorcade had been spotted.

While everyone's attention was focused on the road, Aunt Madeline grabbed Elizabeth's arm and started pushing forward into the crowd. Ruthlessly leaving her husband behind, the five-foot-two, sixty-two-year-old woman shouldered people out of her path. "Excuse me, we need to get closer. Excuse me!" A plump lady gave her aunt a disgruntled look. "My niece has an incurable disease, and it's always been her dream to see the president in person," Aunt Madeline explained. The woman's mouth dropped open as she gestured for them to go in front of her.

"Excuse me! Coming through!" Aunt Madeline barked. "My niece is writing her dissertation on presidential motorcades. She needs a good view." They received some perplexed expressions, but people gave way. Elizabeth's face burned. Hopefully nobody would ask the discipline of this supposed dissertation.

They were drawing closer to the front of the crowd as the first car in the motorcade—a local Hamptons police car—turned into the driveway, passing the first rows. The car behind it was an SUV that likely contained Secret Service agents.

Aunt Madeline hadn't given up. "Excuse us! My niece is the official White House artist and needs to compose a painting for this occasion!" Some people frowned as they gave way, but Elizabeth and her aunt were making progress. She could see the front row and the police officers holding back the crowds.

"Coming through!" her aunt yelled. "Woman with an urgent petition who needs to see the president!"

Now they were right behind the front row, but it was packed tightly, everyone shoulder to shoulder. Undaunted, Aunt Madeline gave Elizabeth a hard shove between her shoulder blades, causing her to stumble and push between two people—a tall, tattooed man and a plump middle-aged woman—in the front row. They barely noticed, their attention fixed on an enormous black limousine now turning into the driveway.

The crowd cheered and whistled. People screamed and jumped up and down. Parents held up their children for a look. This was it: the president's limo. As it pulled closer, Elizabeth squinted her eyes and angled her head, trying to get a glimpse of his face despite the car's darkened windows.

There he was! Smiling and waving at the crowd. But he hadn't seen her. As the car slowly drew closer to where she stood, Elizabeth started smiling and waving frantically. Hopefully, somehow, she'd stand out from the crowd, and he'd recognize her presence for the apology she intended.

The moment he recognized her, his eyes grew wide. And she realized all over again that he actually had the power to make her heart stop and steal her breath from her body—even from behind tinted glass. She grinned like an idiot, but her hand fell to her side. All her attention was focused on the president.

He was no longer smiling. Instead his forehead was creased, and his lips were slightly open as he followed her with his eyes. Was he unhappy at her presence? Maybe he never wanted to see her again. That would be understandable after all the unforgivable things she'd said. Tears pricked the back of her eyes, and she pressed her lips together. *You came to deliver a message, nothing more*, she reminded herself. Only now did she realize that she had secretly hoped for something else.

Their eyes remained locked as the car glided past Elizabeth's position. He even turned his head to keep his gaze fixed on hers as long as possible. Others in the crowd stared at her, pointing and murmuring.

Then he was gone. She could only see the back of the limo while another black SUV prepared to turn into the driveway. The crowd started to loosen up as people chatted and sought the easiest ways to disperse. Elizabeth's whole body felt weighted down and incapable of the slightest movement. *I accomplished what I set out to do. He noticed me. Nothing else was ever possible.*

Exclamations of surprise suddenly drew Elizabeth's attention. People in the crowd pointed and yelled. The limo had stopped. Right before reaching Pemberley's gates, it had come to a complete standstill.

Then it began backing up.

"What the hell?" someone behind Elizabeth exclaimed.

"Maybe they're going out for a gallon of milk," the woman next to Elizabeth joked to her friend.

Elizabeth couldn't move. Couldn't speak. Her thoughts were scattered. Above all, she tried not to hope this had anything to do with her. It was probably some security thing. She remained frozen in place as the limo reversed until its rearmost door was directly in front of her.

The door opened to reveal the president. He was not smiling, but his eyes sparkled as he extended a hand to her. He looked utterly delectable in black jeans and a close-fitting blue t-shirt the same shade as his eyes. "C'mon," he said to her. "Get in!"

Chapter Thirteen

She hesitated. Was he talking to her? Shock had even stolen away her voice. Her eyes fixed on his hand, trembling slightly as it offered her a second chance.

Will's face softened. "Please, come."

Game over. She could no more have refused that entreaty than she could have commanded her heart to stop beating. She placed her hand in his, relishing the warmth as his fingers curved around hers. People in the crowd around her yelled and cheered—and filmed with their phones.

Will pulled her gently into the interior of the limo, bringing her from bright sunshine into abrupt dimness. He gestured to the seat next to him, and she fell onto it gratefully. A man in a suit—a Secret Service agent?—swung the door shut behind her and then spoke into his phone; the limo lurched forward.

Will turned toward her, giving her a slight smile for the first time. "Hello, Elizabeth. What brings you here?"

***

Darcy's day had not improved. The short flight to New York had been uneventful, but that hadn't eased his throbbing head. Bing had briefed him on the latest threat to nuclear non-proliferation, and Darcy had spent much of the plane flight wrangling on the phone with two difficult congressmen who seemed determined not to support the administration's position. By the time he finished the second call, he was nauseated, irritable, and tired.

The presidential limo, nicknamed "the Beast," was extremely secure but, surprisingly, rather cramped on the inside—with only two seats facing forward and three seats facing back. Today the close quarters irritated him more than usual. Perhaps sensing this, Bing and Fitz had tried to lighten his mood with jokes and banter, but Darcy had growled at them until they fell silent. Now, half listening to Bing's report on flooding in Mississippi, Darcy kept his temper in check by dreaming about a cool, dark room at Pemberley.

When the gates of Pemberley loomed into sight, Darcy had been overwhelmed with relief. He just wanted the sanctuary of his private suite and a respite from the scrutiny—even the well-meaning concern of his friends.

The only thing between him and his sanctuary was the usual crowd of gawkers clustered at the gate, baking in the July sun and holding signs either cheering or condemning him. Darcy steeled himself, knowing he would need to wave and smile at the crowds; if he didn't, a local paper or cable news station would report how he was unfriendly to the voters, or it might launch rumors that he appeared ill. Never in his life had Darcy felt less like greeting random strangers, but he plastered on a grin and managed a feeble wave.

When he first saw her, he dismissed her as a hangover-induced hallucination. "Elizabeths" had popped up all over Washington for weeks; upon a second glance, they were always revealed to be women with dark hair who bore almost no other resemblance to the actual Elizabeth Bennet.

But the resemblance didn't fade upon a second look; it grew stronger. Another second of staring confirmed that he was, in fact, viewing the actual Elizabeth Bennet. She met his eyes unflinchingly and with a wide smile, but her blush suggested an endearing touch of embarrassment.

What the hell is she doing here? What did her presence mean?

Taken off guard, Darcy's smile and wave faded. He could only gape at her, twisting his head to keep her face in view until she was out of sight. Everything he'd dreamed of saying to her—the apologies and explanations—flashed through his mind. How could he leave them unsaid when she was so close?

Elizabeth wouldn't have trekked all the way to Pemberley if she still cursed his name. She had smiled and waved, hadn't she? If he didn't talk to her now, he might not get another opportunity.

Darcy hit the intercom button. "Tucker, stop the car," he ordered the Secret Service officer who was driving. As the limo abruptly halted, Kinski, the head of his security detail—who sat opposite Darcy in the back of the limo—was instantly on alert. "Is there a problem, sir?" His hand was already reaching under his suit jacket for his shoulder holster.

Shit. How did he explain this? Darcy held up his hands. "No, nothing like that. I…um…recognized someone in the crowd…"

Kinski hadn't removed his hand from the butt of his gun. "Someone who's been in other crowds?" The Secret Service was always alarmed when people showed up too frequently at presidential events, fearing a potential assassin awaiting an opportunity.

Darcy sighed. "No, no. It's Ms. Bennet, the woman who hitched a ride on Air Force One back from Paris."

Beside Kinski, Bing sat up straighter. "Elizabeth is out there? Is Jane with her?"

"I didn't see her."

Now both Fitz and Bing were craning their necks to catch a glimpse of Elizabeth out of the rear window. Kinski murmured into his phone, no doubt explaining to the rest of the detail why the presidential limo had stopped so unexpectedly. He lowered the phone. "There's probably a reasonable explanation for Ms. Bennet's presence," he said in a clipped voice. "I'll send an agent to question her."

Darcy waved his hand impatiently. "Good Lord, no! She's not a *suspect*! I just want…I want…" Bing, Fitz, and Kinski gawked at him, awaiting the end of the sentence. *What do I want?* "I just want to talk with her."

This is that chance I said I wanted. I can apologize. Show her that I'm not proud and difficult—at least not always. Demonstrate my affection…

Kinski's scowl deepened.

Darcy could continue on as if nothing had happened, maybe calling her later. But the very thought was utterly intolerable. His eyes met Fitz's, recalling the multiple bourbons from the previous night. He would do almost anything to avoid that feeling again.

"Back up. I want to give her a ride," he told Kinski.

The agent nearly fell out of his seat in shock. "Sir, we can't—the presidential limo doesn't pick up hitchhikers!"

"Back. Up," Darcy said firmly.

Kinski was still bug-eyed. "She hasn't been cleared—!"

"She's wearing a sundress." *A quite fetching sundress.* "There's no place for a concealed weapon."

Kinski shook his head emphatically. "Sir, you don't know—shoes, purses, weapons could be anywhere."

Darcy rolled his eyes. "She doesn't want to kill me." *Shout at me, perhaps. Kill me, no.*

"I can send an agent to collect her—"

That would be logical…but she might refuse to go with an agent. Then Darcy would lose track of her again. He might be setting himself up for heartache once more, but it was better than certain despair. "No," Darcy didn't raise his voice, but he was very firm, "I want her in the limo. Now."

Kinski's face was quite red, and he appeared on the verge of a stroke. Bing had gone bug-eyed at Darcy's uncharacteristic behavior, but Fitz's eyes danced with merriment.

"Sir, you cannot simply—"

"Reverse. The. Car. Now," Darcy said in his best leader-of-the-free-world voice.

They locked eyes for a moment; then Kinski, muttering curses under his breath, took out his phone and gave the order.

The car reversed. When it stopped, Kinski pulled out his gun, ready to jump out of the vehicle if necessary. But Darcy only had eyes for Elizabeth—and her shocked expression as they opened the limo door. He extended a hand to her. "C'mon. Get in!" Her mouth hung open, and her hand was at her throat. She didn't move. Had he misinterpreted her presence at the gate?

Oh God, he didn't want her to refuse. He needed her in the limo beside him, teasing him about being stiff. "Please, come." He didn't even care that the words sounded completely desperate.

Then—with excruciating slowness—she placed her hand in his and gave him a tentative smile. Darcy's heart melted, followed by the rest of his body. He pulled her into the limo with an arm as limp as a wet noodle. Once inside the vehicle, Elizabeth glanced around dazedly. Fitz quickly vacated the seat next to Darcy, and she slid into it just as Kinski slammed the door shut and the limo started moving again, gliding past the gates of Pemberley.

Only then did Darcy allow his gaze to linger over her. She was here. She was actually in his limousine. "Hello, Elizabeth," he said. "What brings you here?"

She didn't answer immediately. Her mouth fell open as she perused the inside of the Beast.

Kinski scrutinized her from head to foot, but her thin sundress and flip-flops didn't leave a lot of options for concealed weapons. The agent reached over and gently pulled Elizabeth's small purse from her hands; she surrendered it with only a slight widening of her eyes.

As the agent examined the contents, Elizabeth noticed the other occupants of the limo. "Hello, Elizabeth!" Fitz waved cheerfully to her.

"Um, hi, Fitz," she said slowly, blinking.

Bing stretched his arm across the space between them to shake her hand. "Good to see you again."

Her jaw tightened as she shook his hand. Darcy couldn't help remembering what she had said about her sister.

Kinski returned the purse to her, evidently having failed to discover any pipe bombs or Uzis.

What now?

Darcy hadn't thought much beyond getting her into the car. To be honest, he hadn't thought much beyond "Elizabeth. Want. Now." His lips itched to kiss her silly; they hadn't done nearly enough kissing. But, he recognized reluctantly, that might not be her plan, particularly in front of an audience.

Now he could conceive a hundred reasons this might be a bad idea. Maybe she'd come to Pemberley because she was still angry. Maybe she hadn't read Darcy's letter at all and still believed Wickham's lies. Maybe she *had* read Darcy's letter and still believed Wickham's lies. Maybe she was dating Wickham. *Shudder.*

Maybe she was traveling with a friend who wanted to show support for the administration's environmental policies, and she hadn't wanted to come to Pemberley at all.

He took a deep breath to slow his racing thoughts. He could only learn her thinking by talking to her. *Earlier today I was pining away for an opportunity to apologize to her and set things right. Now is my chance. And damn the audience.*

Their eyes locked. "I'm sorry," he said.

"I'm sorry," Elizabeth said simultaneously.

He blinked in confusion while Elizabeth jerked her head back.

"*You're* sorry?" he asked. "What are you sorry for?"

"I believed George Wickham's lies. I misjudged you. I made assumptions that weren't true," she said in a simple, matter-of-fact tone.

He shrugged; her sins were nothing compared to his. "I'm sorry I was arrogant and condescending and rude. I was so certain you would leap at the opportunity to date me that I made assumptions and started kissing you without—"

"It's okay," Elizabeth said hastily.

Darcy was acutely aware of the limo's other inhabitants. Staring intently at his phone, Bing was doing a good imitation of someone who wasn't overhearing a painfully intimate conversation. On the other hand, Fitz was watching them frankly, his arms crossed over his chest and a smirk on his face. Kinski stared out the window—as his job demanded—but he was clearly fighting a smile.

"You weren't that bad," Elizabeth demurred.

"Yes, I was," Darcy insisted.

"No, really, you weren't. I wasn't that offended."

"Yes, I was." He wasn't about to let himself off the hook.

Her eyebrows knit together. "No, you weren't."

"Yes, I was." Why couldn't she acknowledge it so they could move on?

"No, you weren't—"

Fitz gave an exasperated sigh. "For crying out loud! Will you two get over it already?"

Elizabeth laughed. "I suppose we'll have to agree to disagree on that point."

The limo had stopped in front of Pemberley's main entrance, but no one had exited the vehicle. They were waiting for Darcy. Perhaps they should continue the conversation in a more private setting. "Elizabeth, can I give you a tour of Pemberley?" he asked.

"I would love that."

Darcy had won the election as President of the United States. Why was *today* the day he felt like he'd won the lottery?

***

Nowhere did the gap between Elizabeth's childhood and Will's become more evident than in Pemberley. The Bennets were in the upper echelons now, but her upbringing had been solidly middle class. That had never been true for the Darcy family.

The estate was lovely, of course. Pemberley was far enough from the road that it was a world away from the crowd at the gate. Elizabeth knew the Hamptons weren't that big and the real estate wasn't cheap. How many acres did the Darcy family own here? As they climbed out of the limo, she could see another house not too far away, so the property couldn't be too large.

"Who are your neighbors?" she asked Will, pointing to the house. "Anyone I know?"

He coughed. "Um…that's the estate's guest house."

Well…shit, it was big enough to be another mansion.

The initial exhilaration of being with Will again was beginning to fade, and a kind of queasiness was replacing it. Everything at Pemberley was tasteful, beautiful, perfect…and completely overwhelming. The exterior of the house was weathered shingles, giving it a seaside New

England appearance. But the size was far beyond any fisherman's house. The circular drive had deposited them at a white-columned portico that easily accommodated three additional cars from the motorcade. More columns adorned a porch that ran the length of the house. The house appeared to be three stories and stretched dauntingly in both directions.

Elizabeth glanced at Will's patrician profile as they approached the front door. Maybe she could get a tour, stay for an hour or so, and then discreetly depart.

The double doors were tall enough to admit any small-to-medium giants who happened to be in the neighborhood. As they approached, someone—a waiting servant perhaps?—opened one side so Will and Elizabeth could enter, followed by Bing and Fitz. The two-story, marble-clad foyer featured twin staircases and an understated yet elegant chandelier. The paneling was exquisite, a light-colored wood that Elizabeth couldn't identify, which contrasted nicely with the gray marble of the floors. "How old is the house?" she asked.

"A little more than one hundred years," Will replied. "It was designed by the renowned architect Stanford White, and I had it renovated and modernized ten years ago, not long after my parents' death."

"They did a very nice job." *That was a stupid understatement.* "It's exquisite."

"Thank you," he said simply.

People flowed into the house around them. Secret Service agents bustled into different rooms to secure the building. One agent appeared to be setting up communication equipment in a corner of the foyer. Staffers carried luggage up to the second floor. Bing hurried up the stairs, with Fitz following more slowly. No doubt they had visited many times before.

Will led her through the doorway between the two staircases. "Let me show you my favorite room."

Elizabeth gasped. Two stories tall, the room boasted windows—well, not really windows so much as a wall made from glass panels—that provided a stunning view of the ocean. Tearing her eyes from the scenery, she noticed that the room had dual conversational areas with all-white chairs and sofas grouped around two antique stone fireplaces. Her parents had a large living room but nothing on this scale. Balconies crafted from simple ironwork ran halfway up three of the walls, revealing entrances to second-story rooms. As if reading her mind, Will said, "That door leads to the master bedroom suite"—he pointed—"and the other side has doors to two of the bedrooms."

Elizabeth drank in all the details so she would be able to describe them later to Jane. The décor wasn't at all ostentatious; in fact, it was the very simplicity and understated elegance of the room that made it so appealing. It was big, but not nearly as grand or formal as the White House—and consequently it felt much more like a home.

Will observed her intently as if her reaction to the house was terribly important. "It's…um… magnificent," she said in awe. The word was completely inadequate, but he appeared very pleased nonetheless. "It just—it takes my breath away, Mr. President."

His brow furrowed. "I thought we were past the 'Mr. President' stage."

"Are we?" He'd said something to that effect on Air Force One, but she hadn't taken it seriously.

"I just picked you up by the side of the road. Surely that counts for something." His lips twitched. "I would like to believe you don't get into cars with strangers."

She laughed. "I don't. I turned down the previous two presidential limos that happened by."

This sally provoked a broad grin—the equivalent of a full-belly laugh for this man. "Would you like to see more?" he asked.

"Of course." His posture was still painfully straight, but his pride in the house was so sweet she couldn't help but find it charming.

The next stop was a kitchen Elizabeth's mother would drool over, with a "breakfast nook" bigger than her parents' dining room (which itself was not small). The nook had another spectacular water view. "How big is the house?" she asked Will.

"The main house is eighteen thousand square feet, and the property is twenty-eight acres. I'm very grateful for every acre right now since it provides some much-needed privacy."

Elizabeth tried to wrap her mind around such scale. "I would guess so," she said.

He led her into another room. Wait, when had he started holding her hand? Her hand felt so comfortable in his that she hadn't noticed.

The sight of the next room pushed all other thoughts from her mind. It was a two-story library filled with thousands of books. "Wow. I could stay here for days and never leave."

Will gave her a relaxed smile. "A woman after my own heart. I holed up here frequently as a child."

Elizabeth imagined a serious, dark-haired boy curled up in one of the armchairs near the huge limestone fireplace. It was a cozy image but also rather isolated. "Did your family live here in the winter?"

Will fondly surveyed the room. "Technically Pemberley is a summer house, but my mother didn't care much for New York City, so we usually lived here year-round, venturing into the city frequently to stay with my father in our penthouse. Georgiana and I had tutors until we were old enough to attend boarding school."

Tutors. Boarding schools. Penthouses. His experience was so alien to her that he might as well have been from another country. By the time Mary, Kitty, and Lydia had been in high school, their parents had been able to afford a local private day school, but Elizabeth and Jane had gone to public school. Pemberley was lovely to admire, but every room reminded her that she didn't belong here.

It would be best for her own emotional well-being if she simply thanked Will and left, but the very thought hurt her heart. His every look in her direction gave her goosebumps. If she left now, she felt strongly that she'd be missing out on something vital and important.

Darcy brought them back to the grand foyer, which was now empty except for a somber Secret Service agent posted near the front door. Darcy glanced up the stairs. "Would you like to go upstairs and select a bedroom?" he asked. "I'm afraid Bing has the one with the best view and Fitz has the one with the biggest bed, but there are twelve others to choose from. And each has its own bathroom."

She regarded him blankly.

"Or would you prefer to stay at the guest house?" he asked hurriedly. "Some of the Secret Service agents are staying there, but plenty of rooms are unoccupied. And it houses the pool table and home theater."

She swallowed. "I'm staying here?" Her heart pounded against her ribs, but she didn't know whether from fear or anger.

A line formed between his brows. "Yes, of course...I thought..."

"Were you planning to consult me on your plans for my day? Or did you just assume that once I got in your limo I'd put out for you?" She said it with a smile, but a brittle edge of sarcasm in her voice.

The agent near the door made a choking noise. Will glared at him, and the man swiftly averted his eyes.

"I climbed into your limo for the sole purpose of apologizing to you," she continued, pointing her finger at Will. "I received your letter and regretted misjudging you. This visit is not about becoming your love toy!"

The agent snorted.

Will ignored him. "I'm sorry, Elizabeth. It appears I made another assumption." He rubbed his hand over his face, taking a deep breath. "I was hoping you could stay tonight so that you could have dinner with us—and meet my sister, who is arriving in the morning." He crossed his arms over his chest. "My intentions were not...dishonorable. I didn't expect you to—I mean, I thought you'd stay in a guest room. There's a lock on the door and everything."

The energy drained from Elizabeth's body, leaving her feeling weak and more than a little ridiculous. He had offered a guest room or even the guest house. Certainly, he wouldn't plan to seduce a woman ensconced in another building surrounded by federal agents. *Why do I always jump to the worst conclusions with Will?*

It was all so implausible—the idea that he just wanted her company and conversation. "Why me?" The words burst out before she could censor them. "I'm just an aid worker from an annoying nouveau-riche family."

Will gaped at her. "Why you? I-I"—he pushed a hand through already unruly, dark locks—"God, I wish you could see yourself through my eyes." He shook his head in wonderment. "You're the woman I've been waiting for: smart, beautiful, funny, well-spoken...the whole package."

The Secret Service agent was assiduously studying the flower arrangement in the corner.

Elizabeth took some time to absorb these words. Her hand went to her throat in surprise. "W-Wow." Her voice trembled. "I-I didn't know." His admission was so much more than she had expected.

Taking both her hands in his, he drew them to his chest, pulling her closer. "Do you believe me?"

How could she disbelieve such a declaration? She swallowed thickly. "Oh, yeah." Now her hands shook for an entirely different reason. She forced herself to examine her feelings unflinchingly; there was no denying she viewed him differently from anyone else she had ever met. Even when compared to men she had dated. And didn't that give her pause?

Will stepped closer, his eyes on her mouth. He must have resolved to ignore the Secret Service agent. *He wants to kiss me again.* Her lips tingled at the thought.

But just as he bent his head to hers, the sound of rapid footsteps echoed across the marble floor. Will raised his head, dropped his hands, and stepped away from her as Bing skidded to a stop beside him. "What is it?" he demanded, his eyes still fixed on Elizabeth.

Bing cleared his throat. "Um…we got a call from the agent down at the gate. There's…there's a woman who—well, she claims the President of the United States kidnapped her niece."

***

I'm having the strangest day.

After clarifying the Gardiners' identity to Will, Elizabeth— mortified that she hadn't thought of them in her whirlwind tour of Pemberley—spoke to her aunt on the phone. Aunt Madeline's late-60s radical consciousness had been reignited by her encounter with the Secret Service agents, whom she referred to as "jack-booted thugs." However, a five-minute conversation with Elizabeth allayed the older woman's fears that her niece was being held in a secure government facility. And the Gardiners readily accepted Will's invitation to visit Pemberley, which Elizabeth relayed.

The lead Secret Service agent, a stone-faced guy named Kinski, had opposed the idea. Elizabeth was a known quantity, having attended previous events with the president and traveled on Air Force One. But Kinski had insisted he would need at least 24 hours to thoroughly vet her relatives.

Will, who'd never struck her as particularly spontaneous, surprised Elizabeth by firmly informing Kinski that the Secret Service had an hour to check out the Gardiners before he had them admitted. Will might have been influenced by Aunt Madeline's threats to apprise the lurking reporters that her niece had been kidnapped by the president.

The whole situation made Elizabeth squirm. She was loath to cause Will any more trouble, particularly after making such egregious assumptions about his intentions. Relations between them were proceeding smoothly for once, and she was eager to enjoy more of his company.

Will's condescending, abrupt side hadn't appeared at all, except when the Secret Service agent had pushed him too far. Being on vacation in familiar surroundings made even the most type-A president more mellow. Experiencing this side of him was revelatory; this was the Will who had written the letter that made her regret her anger on Air Force One.

Of course, all that friendliness might dissipate when the Gardiners arrived. Will hadn't been particularly patient or understanding with Elizabeth's immediate family. Although the Gardiners had far better manners than the Bennets, they were solidly middle class. Their encounter with Will might yield stilted conversation and snide remarks that would quickly send Elizabeth scurrying back to the Gardiners' rented cabin.

Elizabeth paced the living room floor, watched the front door, and tried not to bite her nails as she awaited her aunt and uncle. When the doorbell finally sounded, the Secret Service agent admitted the Gardiners, and Elizabeth rushed into the foyer to receive relieved hugs.

"I thought you were past the age where we had to worry about you getting into cars with strangers," Aunt Madeline joked.

Elizabeth's cheeks heated. "I'm sorry! My mind was...elsewhere, and I didn't think about how worried you would be." Truthfully, she'd been so wrapped up in Will she hadn't given her relatives a thought.

Aunt Madeline gave her a cheeky grin. "I can't be too upset. I'd be distracted, too, in your place."

Her uncle shook his head at Elizabeth. "Next time, don't leave the house without your phone."

She nodded sheepishly; leaving her phone behind plugged into the wall charger was a particularly bad habit.

As Elizabeth led the Gardiners into the living room, her aunt gaped at the majestic view through the windows. Fitz, Bing, and Will had just emerged from a meeting in the study, so Elizabeth made introductions. Fortunately, the Gardiners handled the august company with far more aplomb than had the Bennets.

Uncle Thomas shook Will's hand. "Thank you for inviting us, Mr. President. It's an honor. This is indeed a beautiful house."

Will smiled genially. "Thank you. I'm pleased to have the opportunity to demonstrate that your niece is safe."

Aunt Madeline laughed nervously, and Uncle Thomas patted her hand. "Maddie worries, you know. We don't have our own children, so our nieces are very dear to us."

Her face heating again, Elizabeth stared at her feet.

Will was unfazed. "Your concern for your niece is admirable. Would you join us for lunch?" He gestured toward French doors opening onto a flagstone patio.

The Gardiners immediately accepted the invitation, and soon everyone was settled on the elegantly appointed patio. As with the interior of the house, all the patio furniture was white. Elizabeth couldn't help wondering what they would do if children visited. Cover everything with plastic? White upholstery was practically guaranteed to draw tomato sauce, apple juice, or grubby fingers.

A casually dressed maid appeared out of nowhere to serve everyone iced tea and sandwiches. The hot, late morning weather had given way to cooler temperatures and a mild sea breeze. It was the kind of day that could make a person vow never to return inside again. Although Elizabeth usually preferred southern beaches, she understood how someone could fall in love with this place.

Conversation had been desultory, mostly limited to comments on the food and weather. But once everyone was settled, Will turned his attention to the Gardiners.

"Where are you folks from?" he asked.

Uh-oh, this is where the wheels fall off. She didn't know how Will would handle the information that the Gardiners weren't any kind of riche—nouveau or otherwise.

Uncle Thomas answered, "We're originally from Virginia, but now we live in New York City."

Will nodded pleasantly. "And what do you do for a living?"

Elizabeth managed not to wince. The typical D.C. question: the most important thing about anyone was their occupation.

"Maddie and I own and operate a beer distributorship," her uncle replied.

Elizabeth watched Will's face closely. If he thought food on a stick was declasse, selling beer had to be practically criminal. Although the Gardiners were successful, their world was decidedly more blue-collar than anything Will had likely encountered in his life.

"Really," Will said, exchanging a glance with Fitz.

Here it comes. She was surprised at a touch of regret. Against all reason, she had hoped that Will would like the Gardiners. Why? Had she actually fooled herself into believing they could have something together?

"Do you sell microbrews?" Will asked.

Huh?

"Indeed we do!" Uncle Thomas smiled expansively. "I love to help small businesses get off the ground. We supply 23 percent of the restaurants in the city, so our distribution can make a big difference to some of the craft breweries."

Both Will and Fitz leaned forward with avid interest. What the hell?

"My cousin, Fitz's brother, has started a microbrewery," Will said, "but he's having trouble finding a distributor in New York City." They had her uncle's complete attention now. "Would you consider it?" Will asked.

Uncle Thomas regarded the president for a long moment. "Do you have any beer that I could sample?"

Will frowned, but Fitz laughed and slapped his thigh. "Good man! My brother wouldn't want to do business with someone who would sell just any beer."

"We have plenty." Will gestured to Fitz. "Can you find whatever we have on ice?"

Soon everyone was sampling five kinds of One Eye Jack microbrew and debating the merits of the different varieties. Fitz and Uncle Thomas were deep in a discussion of hops and yeast while Will talked to Aunt Madeline about branding and marketing strategies. Elizabeth had another dizzying moment when it felt like a bizarre dream.

Bing leaned toward Elizabeth, the only other person not involved in a conversation. "Er…how is Jane?" He finished off the beer in his glass.

Sudden dryness in her mouth caused Elizabeth to gulp her beer. She didn't want to have this conversation with Bing. Or, indeed, any conversation with Bing. Will had made some wrongheaded and hurtful assumptions about Jane, and his opinion had no doubt influenced his friend's, but Bing was a grown man and responsible for his own decisions. "Fine…she's doing well," Elizabeth muttered. Inwardly she cursed herself. Could she have sounded less convincing?

"Good…that's good…" Bing squeezed his glass so tightly Elizabeth feared it might shatter. "I-Is she…er…seeing anyone?"

"I don't think that's any of your business," Elizabeth said through gritted teeth.

Setting his glass on the coffee table, Bing leveled his gaze at her. "You're right. It isn't my business, but I still want to know." His voice shook. "Is she seeing anyone?"

Perhaps now was the time to describe Jane's torrid affair with a race car driver or international spy, but Elizabeth's eyes were drawn to the trembling of Bing's hands. She sighed. "Jane's had a few dates. But I don't know that there's anyone special."

Bing blew out a breath and sagged back into his chair. Maybe I shouldn't have told him that. Would Jane be angry? Bing rubbed the back of his neck. "Do you think she'd…answer if…I called her?"

Elizabeth answered without thinking. "She deleted your number from her phone, so she probably wouldn't know it was you."

"Shit." Bing winced. "You don't pull any punches."

"Why should I?" Elizabeth asked. "You hurt her, dumping her like that without any warning. At a party! I don't know why she would give you a second chance. I don't know that she should."

Bing shot a glance at Will. "You're giving Darcy another chance."

What the hell? "I am?" she spluttered. "I don't know what you're thinking, but we had an argument. I wanted to apologize. So did he. That's the reason I'm here." Had Will implied something else to his friend?

Bing raised one perfect blond eyebrow. "You apologized in the limo. So why did you stick around? I doubt it's so you could score some free microbrew."

Elizabeth's gaze dropped down to her mostly empty glass. Why was she still at Pemberley? She'd lived her whole life without William Darcy, but then a month without him had felt interminable. It could be months until she saw him again—if ever—and some impulse she preferred not to examine too closely demanded that she soak up every moment in his presence. The feelings were deeply unsettling, which should have prompted an intense desire to leave Pemberley. Yet she felt the opposite.

How could one man be so confusing?

When Will concluded his conversation and stood, he naturally drew the eyes of everyone on the patio. "I have to say the ocean looks awfully appealing," he said to Elizabeth with a relaxed grin. "Would you like to join me for a swim?"

Elizabeth exchanged glances with her aunt. "We don't have swimsuits."

Will waved a negligent hand. "I can send an agent to the Gardiners' rental house to fetch them. You'll need some things for tonight in any case."

"You're spending the night?" Uncle Thomas asked Elizabeth.

She folded her arms over her chest and glared at Will. "It's customary to invite someone before planning on their acceptance."

"You're not staying the night?" Will appeared so crestfallen she almost felt guilty.

Fitz laughed. "What my socially inept cousin is trying to say is that we would love the honor of your company at dinner tonight and would be thrilled if you could stay overnight."

"What he said." Will pointed to his cousin. "I would like to introduce you to Georgie tomorrow." His eyes pleaded with Elizabeth. Why in the world was it so important to him? "Of course, I'd love to have your aunt and uncle stay as well," he added hastily.

"We have plans," Elizabeth said quickly. Her aunt regarded her skeptically. "But we might be able to change them," she added.

Aunt Madeline gave the group a somewhat frozen smile. "Please excuse us for a minute."

She pulled Elizabeth from the patio and into the glorious living room; Uncle Thomas trailed after them and closed the French doors. "We have plans for this evening?" Aunt Madeline asked Elizabeth. "Did it slip my mind?"

Elizabeth stared at her flip-flops. "We discussed trying that new restaurant that was reviewed in the paper."

"The one where we didn't even get reservations?" Her aunt snorted. "I think we can forgo that pleasure for an opportunity when the President of the United States invites us to his house for dinner."

"Of course. It's fine," Elizabeth said hastily. She was half appalled and half thrilled at the idea of remaining at Pemberley.

Uncle Thomas stepped toward Elizabeth until they were face-to-face. "Lizzy, has something happened with the president? Has he made you feel uncomfortable? We won't stay if you think he's a creep."

"It's nothing like that." The words tumbled out of Elizabeth's mouth. "I...he...he and I..." She blew out a frustrated breath and started again. "We never seem to be on the same wavelength. He's so proud and acted like such a snob when he talked to my family, but at times like these he's trying so hard to be pleasant. I don't understand why his behavior changed."

"I can guess a reason or two why," Aunt Madeline said with a small smile. Elizabeth was certain she didn't want to know what her aunt was thinking. "I would like to stay. Goodness knows we won't get an opportunity like this again."

"I wouldn't be so sure of that, my dear," Uncle Thomas said enigmatically.

Elizabeth returned to the patio and informed Will that they'd rearranged their plans so they could stay for the night. She didn't believe she'd ever seen him smile so broadly.

Afterward, things happened quickly—which probably wasn't unusual around the president. He had an agent drive Aunt Madeline to their rental house to pack up clothing for everyone. Elizabeth chatted with Fitz and her uncle while Bing and Will attended to some presidential duties. By the time her aunt returned, everyone was more than ready for a couple of hours at the beach.

***

The beach at Pemberley was one of Darcy's favorite places in the world, and he was thrilled to share it with Elizabeth. Her aunt and uncle were very pleasant company and a great addition to the party.

Darcy had been eagerly anticipating the sight of Elizabeth in a swimsuit, but his own reaction overwhelmed him. Her bikini was blue and covered more skin than many such suits. Still, it left little to the imagination, and Darcy had spent many hours imagining what he was now able to see. Time and again he resolved to sit back in his beach chair and enjoy the vast cloudless sky and rhythmic sounds of the waves, but his eyes were drawn back to Elizabeth's bikini; he was helpless in the face of such an alluring sight.

It wasn't just her incredible hotness in the bikini that drew his attention. She was so clearly enjoying herself, alternately floating in an inner tube or splashing with her aunt and uncle. Her eyes sparkled, and she laughed with abandon. When she swam, she cut through the water with a blithe lack of self-consciousness. If he joined her in the water, could she teach him that kind of spontaneity? Could spontaneity even be learned?

Darcy's board shorts were not loose enough to completely conceal his…reaction to her presence. He was compelled to place a towel over his lap—and still couldn't avert his eyes from her form. Hopefully her aunt and uncle were enjoying the beach too much to notice his stares; otherwise, they might worry the danger of kidnapping hadn't passed.

Caroline had arrived a couple of hours ago and was stretched out on the beach chair next to his. Her designer bathing suit consisted of a complicated set of straps that would surely become hopelessly tangled if she actually attempted to swim. Of course, the suit's true purpose was to show off her slender figure, which it did very well. Nevertheless, Darcy's gaze was never drawn to her.

Behind her oversized sunglasses, Caroline observed Elizabeth frolic in the surf as well. "You would think her family could afford a more flattering swimsuit for her," she sniffed.

"I think it's quite flattering," Darcy said mildly.

Caroline rolled her eyes. "Puh-leeze! It's at least two years out of date. And look how brown she is; I bet her skin will be dry and wrinkly before she's forty."

"It's just a light tan. I think it gives her a healthy glow, don't you, Bing?"

On Darcy's other side, Bing glared at his friend, not happy to be dragged into the discussion. "I suppose," he replied noncommittally.

Caroline settled back into her chair with a moue of displeasure. "I don't see why you invited them to spend the night," she complained. "They're nice enough people, but we don't know *anyone* in common. Her family has *some* money I suppose; the danger of bankruptcy seems to have passed for now. But they all went to *public school*, for heaven's sake. What on earth will we find to talk about at dinner?"

Darcy managed to hide a grin. "I'm sure we'll muddle through."

"I don't see the appeal." She regarded Darcy over the rim of her sunglasses.

Darcy gritted his teeth. "You don't need to. They're *my* guests, Caroline."

She huffed and shook her hair back from her face. "Maybe I'll see if Fitz would like to go for a walk." Rising gracefully from the chair, she stalked over to the towel where Fitz had fallen asleep while sunbathing and prodded the man with her toe. Soon the pair was strolling down the beach.

Naturally, Darcy's attention returned to Elizabeth like a homing pigeon. Bing chuckled and Darcy sighed, watching her push her aunt around on the inner tube. "I can't help it."

"She is very attractive."

Darcy deliberately misunderstood his friend. "Bing, she's married and at least twice your age."

"Ha, ha," Bing said. "Even Caroline noticed your...attraction."

Darcy's fists clenched on his thighs. "Yes, Elizabeth is attractive. Too damn attractive."

"Why's that?" Bing asked. "Does she have a boyfriend?"

What a horrifying thought. "I don't think so, but she…I just don't think she's into me."

Bing leaned closer to Darcy. "Why do you say that?"

"There's the whole ran-screaming-from-me thing."

Bing raised an eyebrow. "I thought she didn't scream, and it was a fast walk."

"Whatever you call it, she fled my presence."

"But she sought you out today."

"To apologize."

"That might not be the only reason," Bing said. "You wanted to apologize to her, but that's not all you want."

"Hmm." Darcy was mesmerized as he watched Elizabeth playfully splash her uncle.

"She blushes when you look at her."

"She does?" Darcy gave Bing a sharp look. "But she argues with everything I say."

Bing chuckled. "Isn't that part of her appeal?"

"Huh," Darcy considered. "Maybe."

Bing squinted at his friend. "You like the woman. She's on your beach. Why are you sitting here like a dead horseshoe crab? She keeps glancing this way."

"She does?"

"Yeah." Bing chuckled. "Why don't you go play in the water with her?"

Darcy snorted. "Do you know how long it's been since I 'played' in the water?"

"I'm guessing you could have counted your age in single digits."

Darcy nodded. Why had he wasted his time going to college and learning about politics? Obviously playing in the water was a vital life skill he had grievously neglected.

"I bet it's like riding a bicycle," Bing said, clasping Darcy's shoulder. "You'll remember once you get started."

Darcy eyed Elizabeth wistfully. It did look like fun. Could he simply wade into the ocean and join in the splashing? *Oh Lord, I'd probably look like an idiot.*

Darcy slid down in his beach chair. "Maybe later."

Bing gave him a long look. "You know," he said slowly, "I think what you need is a strategy."

"A strategy to play in the ocean," Darcy echoed.

His friend's eyes glittered. "You need the proper tools…and I happen to have water guns in my beach bag…"

Hmm. It *would* be easier to join the fun with a water gun in hand, although it wouldn't be exactly dignified.

"It's a high-powered gun…with pump action and a scope for accuracy…" Bing's voice tantalized him.

Elizabeth's musical laughter traveled over the waves. *Ah, screw dignity.*

"Yeah," he heard himself replying, "I want to borrow it."

Chapter Fourteen

Elizabeth regarded herself critically in the mirror. She adjusted the strap on her dress. Fortunately, her aunt had the foresight to pick up the only semi-nice piece of clothing Elizabeth had packed—a summery cotton dress with purple flowers. With no plans to socialize, Elizabeth had left her fancier dresses at home. It was the best she could do on short notice. Naturally, Caroline Bingley would appear in a designer frock that cost more than Elizabeth's monthly rent. Elizabeth bit her lip. *Maybe I shouldn't have agreed to stay; there's no doubt the Gardiners and I are out of our element.*

No. Pushing away the negative thoughts, Elizabeth smiled at her reflection, and her eyes brightened. No matter what the other woman thought, Elizabeth was not at Pemberley to compete with Caroline. *Will invited me. If he'd wanted to date Caroline, he would have done so long ago.*

Her stomach growled. She had developed an appetite during her time on the beach—which had become particularly energetic after Will had joined in with his high-powered water gun. He'd had surprisingly good aim, but Elizabeth had retaliated once Bing gave her another gun. Her muscles were sore from running around the beach, and her stomach hurt from laughing so much, but it had been a long time since she'd had so much fun. *I don't think I ever heard Will laugh before.*

Her phone trilled, and Elizabeth glanced at the caller ID. Lydia. Damn it. She was very tempted not to answer and ruin her good mood, but Lydia would just keep calling. Might as well get it over with. "Hello?"

"OMG!" Lydia squealed. "There are pictures of you on the news! You're like marginally famous."

"What?" Elizabeth sank onto the edge of the bed before her knees gave out. "Pictures?"

"It's some shot of you getting into the president's limo. I guess he isn't too proud and rude after all, huh?"

"Shit." Elizabeth buried her head in her palm. Of course, she'd seen people taking pictures but hadn't considered that they would be newsworthy. In retrospect, it was a rather naïve assumption; the presidential limo surely never picked up people by the side of the road.

"It's really not a very flattering picture," Lydia prattled on. "It's blurry, and only part of your face is showing. You look constipated."

Elizabeth groaned. "Great. I've always wanted to look constipated getting into the presidential limo."

"Now you can check that off your bucket list," Lydia chirped.

Did Lydia even get sarcasm?

"Did they know my name?" Elizabeth asked.

"No. They called you 'unidentified woman.' I might not have recognized you, but I know that puke-yellow dress you're wearing. I was jumping up and down over at Tanya's house and pointing at the TV yelling 'I know that dress! I told her not to buy that dress!'"

I'm on national television, and all my sister can do is diss the color of my dress.

"However, I'm a big enough person to admit that I was wrong. Obviously that color works for you. 'Cause it's going to get you *laaaaid*!" Lydia drew out the last word with a flourish.

Oh Good Lord, I hope she doesn't put that on Twitter. "It is not. I'm not getting laid. There is no laying going on," Elizabeth insisted. "I am staying completely upright."

"Has it already happened?" Lydia adopted a knowing tone. "That was quick work. But I shouldn't be surprised after the Air Force One incid—"

"Nothing has happened, and nothing will happen," Elizabeth said through gritted teeth. If she couldn't convince her sister of that, how could she hope to convince the rest of the world?

"Riiiight. You get in a limo with a gorgeous guy to play pinochle, whatever that is."

"Aunt Maddie and Uncle Thomas are here, too, you know."

"Like they're going to stop you?"

"We're just having a fun day at the president's beach house."

"But then comes the night. They have to sleep sometime!" Lydia sing-songed.

Elizabeth ground her teeth, wishing she hadn't answered the phone. "Nothing is going to happen between me and the president," she said in a low, firm voice. "He invited us for dinner and to spend the night, and we'll go back to the Gardiners' cabin tomorrow." She peeked at the clock on the bedside table—already five minutes late to dinner. Damn.

"If you say so."

Why did it have to be *Lydia* who put all these pieces together? "Just. Don't. Say. Anything. To. Anyone," Elizabeth ordered.

"Aye, captain, whatever you say, captain." Lydia's eye roll was practically audible.

"Just please keep this quiet. Don't start any rumors. It's important for a lot of reasons."

Lydia sighed heavily. "How long can you keep it hidden anyway with those pictures out there?"

"There's nothing to hide. We're friends. I'm visiting Pemberley with my aunt and uncle. There's nothing more to it than that."

"Yeah, the media will buy that." Lydia's tone suggested that she *did* understand sarcasm. She hung up before Elizabeth could get in another plea.

***

Despite her hunger, Elizabeth only ate part of her dinner. The food was delicious: salmon on a bed of risotto with a red bell pepper sauce. However, she was unsettled by her conversation with Lydia and all too aware of Will's eyes on her, dark and intent. They had apologized to each other, but what happened next?

In the foyer, he had appeared quite interested in pursuing some sort of relationship, although she wondered if he could actually get past all the accusations she had hurled at him. He was far more relaxed and friendlier—and he hadn't blinked at making the Gardiners' acquaintance. Had he toned down the arrogance because he still harbored a passion for her? And if he did, was it what Elizabeth wanted?

As a small dinner party, they ate in the "breakfast nook" off the kitchen rather than the formal dining room, which could have accommodated a small village. Self-conscious, Elizabeth spoke little during the meal, and the conversation was carried mainly by the Gardiners, Fitz, and Bing. Caroline made sneering comments about other women's fashion choices; Elizabeth ignored the implications. Will answered direct questions but avoided getting drawn into any discussions. The conversation mostly centered around the weather and what to do in the Hamptons, yet the atmosphere was decidedly strained.

Dessert was a mouthwatering mocha cheesecake, but Elizabeth declined a piece as her stomach was a churning mess by then.

After dinner, everyone gathered for drinks in the living room. With the French doors open, they could hear the distant sounds of the waves on the beach. A gentle breeze brought a faint scent of salt water into the room. Elizabeth sunk gratefully into a white sofa, unable to remain tense in such an environment.

Will had loosened up after a few drinks. Although his eyes still lingered on her, he was chattier with everyone. When foreign travel became a topic of conversation, Fitz asked Elizabeth about her work in Africa. To her shock, Will rattled off a list of every place she'd been posted during her tenure with the organization.

"How did you know all that?" she asked.

He lowered his eyebrows mysteriously. "I have a finely tuned intelligence apparatus at my disposal."

"And Google," Fitz chimed in.

Will chuckled. "Busted!"

Elizabeth joined in the laughter, but she wondered: How much time had he spent on Google? All that information could hardly be found in one place. "I don't know whether to be creeped out or flattered," she said with a grin.

"I would prefer flattered," Will said, a corner of his mouth quirking upward. "Creepy isn't the vibe I was hoping for."

Fitz nodded knowingly. "Especially not in the eyes of the woman he—" Will coughed loudly. "—Not in the eyes of a pretty woman," Fitz finished.

What had Fitz been planning to say? Elizabeth wondered even as she grinned at Fitz to acknowledge the compliment.

Will leaned forward, elbows on his knees. "It's quite impressive." His words were addressed to Fitz, but his eyes were on Elizabeth. "Most field officers have racked up only half the amount of field time by that point in their career."

"How do you know that?" Elizabeth blurted out. If the Red Cross kept such statistics, they certainly didn't publish them.

"Um…" Will's gaze fell to the glass in his hand. "I did a little research."

"Fitz," Elizabeth asked with a smile, "would now be a good time to be creeped out?"

Everybody laughed.

Before long, Bing announced that he was calling it a night, which prompted a wave of similar proclamations from most of the other guests. Elizabeth considered staying downstairs so she could have a frank talk with Will, but she shuddered at the thought of the knowing looks she'd receive. She didn't want anyone to believe she was taking advantage of the situation. Lydia's insinuations had reminded Elizabeth that it was best to put some distance between herself and Will. But a voice at the back of her head asked if she was avoiding the conversation.

When she stood to follow the Gardiners toward the stairs, Will's face seemed to darken. But by the time Elizabeth reached her room, she had convinced herself it was simply her imagination.

***

The guest room Elizabeth had picked had a nautical theme as well as white beadboard wainscoting, dark blue linens, and dormer windows. Everything was of the highest quality, but it didn't feel like part of a billionaire's home. The room itself was comfortable, almost cozy, and not at all pretentious. So far she'd seen no gold-plated faucets or throne-like chairs. But as she climbed into the four-poster bed, she wondered if she'd ever before slept on sheets with such a high thread count.

After hours of tossing and turning, she was just as awake as she had been when she'd stretched out on the mattress. Her mind replayed things her day with Darcy: his apology in the limo, the words in the front hallway, his smile in the library. Maybe she should have stayed downstairs to speak with him. Maybe she shouldn't have accepted the invitation to stay overnight. Then there were the images: memories of his laughter on the beach and his haunting stare at dinner.

One minute she was convinced that he was still interested in her, and goosebumps would form all over her body. The next minute she knew that he could never forgive the awful things she had said to him, and her mood would grow heavy and black. Perhaps he simply wanted them to be better friends. But then there was the conversation in the foyer. She had never looked at a friend that way…

Surely the President of the United States didn't lack for company; he was constantly surrounded by people. On the other hand, spending most of the day with him had demonstrated how isolated his life was. When every movement required a seven-car motorcade, you weren't going to drop by the nearest diner to chat up the locals or meet your buddies for some wings. Aside from Fitz and Bing, he didn't seem to have many friends. Even Caroline was more like a hanger-on than a true companion.

What did Elizabeth even want from him? The thought of a relationship provoked shivers of excitement but also prickles of apprehension. He had been affable and charming today, but everyone was relaxed on vacation. Was the cold and distant William Darcy waiting in the wings, ready to rip out her heart the moment she opened it up to him?

Wait a minute. My heart? What the hell am I thinking? When did my heart become involved?

Elizabeth bolted upright in bed, staring at the opposite wall. She couldn't possibly feel anything that deep for Will. Why, compared to her last boyfriend...or the one before him...

Oh.

There was no comparison. Will left the others in the dust. She'd loved her previous boyfriends, but never with such intensity, and their breakups had been fairly smooth. There had never before been a guy who had consumed her thoughts from morning to night. At times he filled her mind so completely that there was no room left for anything else.

Oh, God. She embraced her blanket-clad legs and rested her face on her knees. *I'm in love with the President of the United States.*

Suddenly her heart pounded so violently that it shook her whole body. Her breathing sounded like she had completed a marathon. She laughed humorlessly, the sound muffled by her knees. This would be a disaster. Even if he did want a relationship, so many things stood in the way: his security, his staff, the press, public opinion... Not to mention that he might revert to the proud and difficult President Darcy at any moment.

None of that matters. The die had already been cast. I already gave away my heart. The only question is: What will I do about it?

There was no chance this would end well. His job would someday inevitably divide them. Her heart would be broken. Knowing that, she should run as fast and as far from him as possible. The only problem was she didn't want to go.

She stared at the wall for a long time, her thoughts tumbling over each other but always running in the same circles. Then her stomach rumbled. *I could barely swallow a bite at dinner, and now I'm famished.* Ignoring the feelings didn't work; with every passing minute, her stomach grew more growly. *Maybe if I ate something then I could sleep.*

The digital clock on the bedside table read 2:08 a.m. It had been more than two hours since everyone had retired for the night, so the downstairs was likely to be empty. Will had said the Secret Service agents remained outside the house at night, and the staff lived offsite. Maybe she could slip downstairs and snatch a sliver of that decadent-looking cheesecake.

At that thought her stomach grumbled loudly. "All right, all right," she muttered as she pushed the covers aside and slid to the floor. Pausing at the door, she considered pulling her sweatshirt over her tank top and pajama bottoms, but the house was rather stuffy, and she wouldn't be downstairs very long.

She crept through her door onto the balcony that overlooked the living room. The interior of the house was completely dark; the only illumination was from floodlamps outside shining in through the glass—bright enough to light the way down the curved staircase and into the foyer.

Instinctively she moved quietly as she padded to the kitchen. It was rather silly; nobody slept on this floor, but the quest for food seemed illicit enough that she wanted to disturb as little as possible.

In the kitchen, she switched on the overhead lights. The room was like something out of a contemporary version of Downton Abbey with its gleaming appliances and copious counter space. There were two refrigerators, one so large it had to be designed for restaurants. She found the cheesecake in the smaller unit, and a little searching yielded a plate and utensils. Within a minute she was perched on a stool beside the marble-topped island, savoring a slice of mocha cheesecake that was just as delectable as she had imagined. Elizabeth couldn't hold back a soft moan.

"Are you all right?"

Elizabeth's fork clattered to the floor. She whirled around to find Will standing in the doorway, softly illuminated in the yellow glow of the overhead lights. He was wearing long pajama bottoms and a t-shirt that she couldn't help noticing fit snugly over a chest that was more muscular than a politician's chest had any right to be. He looked...delicious. Far better than the cheesecake.

His presence had always unsettled her, but her recent realizations had completely stripped away her defenses. She could practically feel the weight of his gaze on her skin. Her cheeks immediately heated. *Oh God, I'm blushing. Can he guess what I was thinking about him?* She hastily averted her eyes.

He watched her expectantly. Oh, right. He had asked a question. "I'm f-fine—I-I just—" She gestured helplessly at the cheesecake.

"I'm sorry, I didn't mean to startle you." Will crossed the room in long, elegant strides until he stood directly in front of her stool. Close enough that she could smell the faint scent of sandalwood. Elizabeth's breath caught. What would he do?

His eyes dropped to the floor, and he bent to retrieve her fork. Strolling to the far counter, he dropped her fork in the sink and unerringly opening the correct drawer to retrieve another one.

Her eyes were incapable of focusing on anything else in the room as he returned to her stool. She accepted the new fork automatically. "Um," Elizabeth mumbled, "I-I'm having cheesecake." *Thanks for the update, Captain Obvious.*

A slight smile curved up one corner of his mouth. "When you didn't eat any at dinner, I thought maybe you didn't care for cheesecake."

He had noticed? "I love cheesecake. I just didn't—I wasn't hungry for it then." She gave a little laugh that sounded fake to her ears. "But up in my room I could hear it calling my name."

He chuckled. "Yeah, me, too. I couldn't forget how good it was. Do you mind if I join you?"

A chill raced down her spine. "Not at all."

He poured himself a glass of milk and then pulled the cheesecake from the refrigerator. "I always like milk with dessert," he said. What a ridiculously ordinary fact to know about the leader of the free world.

For some reason, every gesture he made was inordinately fascinating. His hands deftly, competently cut a slice and transferred it to the plate. The cheesecake was smoothly returned to the refrigerator. *You know you've lost it when watching someone serve cake turns you on.*

As Will settled on the stool next to hers, Elizabeth could only stare at his hands. So strong and competent. How would they feel stroking her skin?

"Good," Will said.

Had he read her mind? "Sorry?"

"The cake is good," he explained as he chewed. "Very rich."

Cake. He was talking about cake! Not her skin. Was she beginning to obsess? Did she even need to ask? This was definitely obsession territory.

Elizabeth's head angled down as she kept her attention on the cake. *Yeah, okay, I'm in love with the guy, but maybe it's just a crush. A crush would be better, easier to recover from when things don't work out. Stop obsessing. Focus on something else.* Taking another forkful, she savored the rich mocha flavor, the smooth texture.

I can do this; I can clear out the obsessive thoughts. Obsessive thoughts about the President of the United States. Where the hell had her common sense gone? China?

Will cleared his throat, drawing her attention back to his impossibly handsome face. He seemed to be blushing, but it must have been a trick of the light. "Um…when we get back to D.C…." He swallowed. "Would you have dinner with me one night?"

Did he mean a date? Safer to assume he didn't. "You mean to talk about refugee issues? Sure. Although I might not be the best-qualified person for a policy discussion—"

"Not to discuss policy." He cut her off. "Although," he added hastily, "I mean, we can talk about whatever you want." Will dropped his head into his hands. "God, I'm babbling." His nervousness was reassuring.

His head rose, and stormy blue eyes met hers. "Elizabeth, will you go on a date with me?"

"Oh." *Impossible to misinterpret that.* At the same time, the world had grown slightly surreal. *Is this really happening?*

His words rekindled all her internal debates, recalling all the logical reasons why opening her heart was a terrible idea. But he was standing before her, somber gray-blue eyes watching her as if she were the most precious thing in the world. At the moment logic seemed like an alien concept.

Her entire body was vibrating at a very high frequency. She could see the uncertainty in his eyes. Hear the hitch in his breathing. Feel the warmth from his body. As if her every sense had been magnified. Really, there was only one possible response. "Um, sure, I'd love that," she heard herself say.

His smile started as a mere quirk of the lips and grew into a broad grin. "I'll try not to be too proud and difficult."

She winced. "I never should have said that."

Darcy shook his head, his lips pressed together. "I deserved it. My parents told me to be compassionate to others…but taught me, through their words and actions, to be proud and judgmental."

She couldn't stand one more second of not touching him. Reaching out her hand, she stroked Will's jawline. "When I said that, I didn't understand you. You have no improper pride…and I was the one being difficult."

He held his breath, lips slightly opened, completely immobile as if worried about scaring her away. "Wow," he said softly.

A second later he slid off his stool, and his lips were on hers.

This kiss wasn't as good as the one on the airplane. It was better. Much better.

She let go of the reservations, the what-ifs, and focused on the moment. Her mouth opened instantly and his tongue stroked hers, tasting of mocha and milk and the faintest hint of mint. Inhaling deeply, she breathed in the scent of sandalwood and the unique smell that was Will Darcy. He made a sound, deep in the back of his throat, that signaled his desire…and stoked hers.

His hands flowed around her body; one settled on her upper back while the other caressed her lower back teasingly under the edge of her tank top. The slide of skin against skin was addictive. She craved more. And Will obliged. He inched closer to plunder her mouth more thoroughly. She pulled him closer still by wrapping her legs around his hips and drawing him to her body. He hissed out a breath and embraced her more tightly, the force of his passion pushing Elizabeth's stool until she bumped against the island.

One of his hands caressed her knee and then skimmed up her leg until his fingers were just under the edge of her shorts. Tingles erupted all over her body. Then his lips slid away from hers, and he trailed a series of small kisses down the side of her neck to her collarbone, nudging the strap of her tank top to the side with his nose so he could nuzzle the soft skin of her shoulder. Elizabeth arched her back, pressing her breasts into his chest where they met firm muscles. A moan erupted from deep in Will's throat.

Finally, he twisted his lips away from her shoulder and rested his forehead against hers, panting hard. "Oh my God, Elizabeth."

Elizabeth thought she knew how good kissing could be, but she had been sadly misinformed. There was no comparison. It was as if she were kissing for the first time. "If that's my reward for agreeing to a date, I can't imagine what my post-date prize will be," she whispered, her lips teasing his ear.

"There's no need to wait," he said in a rather strangled voice. "We could declare this"—with one hand he gestured to the kitchen and empty cake plates—"to be our first official date."

"Goodness, Mr. President, you move rather fast," she murmured.

Grinning wickedly, he stroked her cheek with his fingertips. "A good president is decisive. He decides on a goal and initiates a course of action to attain it."

She nuzzled his hand, inhaling his delicious scent. "And what is your goal for the evening?" she asked. Her fingers skimmed the length of his spine, provoking shivers from him.

His eyes locked onto hers, dark and intense. "My goal for tonight is to get you into my bed," he said in a husky voice. "And I am prepared to take any action to achieve that goal. Any action." His hand traveled more boldly under her shirt even as he watched her with some caution in his eyes. "I hope that coincides with your goals."

Elizabeth nearly laughed. Did he doubt her interest? Didn't he know that he was just about irresistible when he was so tender and sweet and unbelievably sexy?

The hand stroking the skin of her back made it difficult to concentrate. "That coincides admirably with my goals," she murmured, stroking her hand along his biceps.

"We never did complete the house tour," he said.

She leaned toward him. "I am rather curious to see the master bedroom."

He kissed his way up her neck. "It is"—kiss—"lovely. I think"—kiss—"you'll particularly appreciate"—kiss—"the hand-carved mantelpiece."

She tilted her head back to give him better access. "Mm-hmm...I do love a good mantelpiece."

"And the slanted beadboard ceiling..." He kissed the soft skin under her jaw.

"Oh, I hope I get a good look at the ceiling..."

His words were emerging in ragged gasps. "And...uh...the bathroom has a tub...carved from a...single piece of marble."

"Wow..." His lips finally found hers, and for a long moment there were no sounds save for moans of pleasure.

When he pulled away, his eyes were focused on her lips. "And...there's a...lovely view...out the window...in the morning...when the s-sun rises..." He seemed to be having trouble forming words.

"Maybe I should join you now so I won't miss it," she whispered.

He swallowed hard. "How wonderful that our goals coincide."

Will took her hand and led her to the stairs.

Chapter Fifteen

"Cowabunga!"

Elizabeth was startled from a deep sleep by a shout that only gave a second's warning before someone landed on the bed, sprawling all over her drowsing form.

The bed. Will's bed. In Will's bedroom. Where I spent the night. After...

Everything came back to her in a rush. Every detail of the night. Whatever other obstacles she and Will might encounter, a lack of chemistry wasn't one of them. It had been off the charts.

Pemberley's master bedroom was enormous, with a vaulted ceiling and huge windows overlooking the ocean. Weak, early morning sunshine peeked in around crisp linen curtains. The enormous canopy bed was of a scale with the room, dwarfing Elizabeth and the bed's other inhabitant.

I actually slept with the President of the United States.

The thought made her a little lightheaded.

Who just jumped on top of me?

A slight blonde woman squawked at the sight of Elizabeth and quickly scrambled off the end of the bed. Will sat up and brushed hair from his eyes. The sheet fell to his waist, providing such a sufficiently distracting sight that Elizabeth momentarily forgot everything else.

"Oh! Oh! Oh!" The young woman's panicked noises drew Elizabeth's attention. She had turned pink from her face, down her chest, and onto her arms and legs. "Oh my God, Will! I'm so sorry! I thought you were alone—you never—! I didn't think—oh my God! I'm so, so sorry!

Will ran a hand through his delightfully disheveled hair and gave a bemused chuckle. "Elizabeth, this is my sister Georgiana. Georgie, this is Elizabeth Bennet."

Georgiana's mouth formed a perfect "o." "I thought you said Elizabeth Bennet would never speak to you again. Although I guess you didn't do a lot of speaking last night." She immediately clapped both hands over her mouth. "Oh shit, did I say that out loud?"

Will rolled his eyes but gave his sister a fond smile. "Have I mentioned that there's a reason Georgie doesn't speak to the press? She was born without a filter. It's a genetic condition. So sad. The doctors can't do anything for her."

Georgiana stuck out her tongue at Will. "You may be president, but you're still a jerk."

"Hey! That's what I said," Elizabeth chuckled.

She gave Elizabeth an arch look. "I think you and I will get along very well."

Before Elizabeth could respond, Georgiana held out her hands imploringly. "That is, if I haven't blown it all with the way I barged in like that. I got here early, and I thought I would surprise Will and...well, he's usually alone. So I didn't think—we have this thing, you know, from when I was little where I'd jump on the bed and yell 'Cowabunga!' Not that I do it anymore."

Will cleared his throat meaningfully.

"Not much anymore. And I thought it would be a funny way to wake him up. But the Secret Service didn't tell me that you weren't alone." She frowned at Will. "Why didn't they warn me you have company? Anyway, that's how I ended up sneaking into your room and jumping on you. I'm sorry, Elizabeth, I'm not usually this flaky. Although it's true that I frequently talk too much." She stopped to catch her breath.

"It's a pleasure to meet you, Georgiana." Elizabeth gave Will a sidelong glance. "Maybe I should return to my room before the others wake up." He nodded reluctantly.

"Oh, is it a secret? No wonder the Secret Service didn't warn me. Ha! The Secret Service isn't in on the secret!" Georgiana giggled at her own joke. "I won't say anything, I promise! Not even to Bethany, who is my best friend. We're both on crew together. Oh Will, did you see the video I sent you of the last regatta? Wasn't it epic?"

"Very epic," Will said with a smile. "Georgie, why don't you get settled in your room, and I'll see you at breakfast."

Georgiana backed toward the door. "Yeah...I'll do that...right now...I'm so, so sorry..."

Will rubbed his face with his hands. "Just go."

"But I want Elizabeth to know that I'm really, really sorry..." Will threw a pillow at her. She fled, closing the door behind her.

Elizabeth and Will exchanged glances before bursting into laughter. "I suppose that gets the morning-after awkwardness out of the way," Elizabeth said.

"I'm sorry about Georgie," he said with a rueful grin.

Elizabeth waved away the apology. "Georgiana is endearing, and she brought out a different side of you."

"I'm glad you're not angry." He touched his fingers lightly to her cheek. He held her gaze for several long moments until Will lowered his eyes to the bed. "Um…we didn't…" He cleared his throat. "Last night, we didn't have much of a chance to talk about this—" He gestured to the space between the two of them.

"We didn't have much of a chance to talk about anything last night," Elizabeth observed.

"Is that a complaint Ms. Bennet?" he teased.

"Not at all." She gave him a quick kiss.

He sighed. "Oh God, Elizabeth, you'll make me lose my train of thought." He swallowed hard. "I want to figure this out…establish parameters."

"Parameters," she echoed. What a clinical word for a relationship. Was it a relationship? She had assumed…but maybe he just wanted the one night, which would probably be for the best… "What kind?"

"I would like it to be a real relationship. I want to date you, Elizabeth."

She sucked in her breath. He didn't deal in small change. "Are you sure? It could be complicated."

He scowled. "Screw complicated. I don't have much in my life that's for me and me alone. I want to grab it with both hands." He watched her with shining eyes.

Oh. Of course, a real relationship with the president was impossible, but maybe knowing it was doomed would keep it from hurting so much when it ended. It was a theory—or at least an excuse. In any case, she no longer had the willpower to resist him.

His shoulders tightened, and the tendons stood out from his neck as she remained silent. He lowered his head. "If you don't want to deal with the complications, I could hardly blame you. We might conceal a relationship for a while, but eventually the media will know, and your life will become a zoo."

She was unable to shake the sensation of preparing to jump into icy water from a great height. "I know…I've thought about that…but I've tried *not* dating you"—she swallowed hard—"and I've found I don't enjoy it …I think it's time to give the other option a try."

Will's face lit up like a boy watching fireworks as he stretched out his arms and gathered her to his chest. "Are you sure you want to attempt a relationship with me? It's not going to be easy."

She snuggled closer, enjoying the firm hold. At that moment her body was so light and weightless it seemed like it could float off the bed. "I don't want easy. I want you."

When she lifted her face, his mouth engulfed hers. Soft velvety lips stroked hers, and her whole body responded; desire raced through her veins. He drew back slightly, meeting her eyes. "If we're late for breakfast, people might guess the truth."

Elizabeth smiled against his mouth. "Let's be late to breakfast…"

***

Darcy swore he could hear birds singing in the shower. At one point, he realized he was whistling. Whistling! He hadn't even known he could whistle.

All the reasons why he avoided relationships still lurked at the back of his mind, but it was a simple matter to drown such concerns in showers of happiness. Something that felt so right surely couldn't be wrong. Surely any new obstacles could be overcome. What a fool he had been to resist for so long.

Elizabeth had returned to her room to preserve the illusion that she had spent the night there. Although he would see her at breakfast, it seemed like an eternity—and they would be surrounded by other people.

Unable to stay away, Darcy dressed quickly and stationed himself in the hallway outside Elizabeth's door. It wasn't long before she emerged wearing a slim-fitting purple shirt and shorts that had just the right amount of short.

Grabbing her by the hands, he swung her against the wall, pressed his body against hers, and kissed her. She melted…boneless against his body until it was impossible to know where he ended and she began. Their kisses, their bodies were perfectly in sync, partners in an intricate dance—just like the previous night when she had somehow anticipated his every move and reacted with such ardor. Every cell in his body hummed in satisfaction and clamored for more contact.

After a minute he reluctantly pulled back, peering down at her shining eyes and flushed cheeks. I did that to her. Darcy had won the majority of votes throughout the United States, yet having won the affection of this woman felt like his greatest accomplishment.

He didn't want to let her go down to breakfast without him, let alone leave Pemberley today, but it would be difficult to justify adding days—and nights—to her visit. *If only I needed an emergency briefing on Zavene.*

Their relationship was so new that he had an intense desire to keep it private—even from those closest to him. The more openly they shared their affection, the more likely word would leak to the media. The Pemberley staff's complete discretion could not be guaranteed.

And yet…when they returned to Washington, seeing each other would be even more difficult. *To hell with it.* Darcy refused to live without her for the rest of his vacation; they would find a way to make it work. "Will you stay tonight?" he whispered in her ear.

Her gaze flickered downward. "I thought you wanted to be discreet."

Praying that none of the other guests happened by, Darcy pressed her against the wall again. "If discretion means I can't see you tonight, then it's overrated."

Her body relaxed under his. "I want to see you tonight, too," she murmured. "Is there a way to sneak me in without alerting the press?"

Darcy couldn't prevent the broad grin from spreading over his face. "I'm sure. I'll talk to Bing and Kinski about it."

Her fingers curled around the back of his head, and she drew him down for another kiss. "I can't wait."

***

The cook had outdone herself with brunch. It was a feast of omelets, French toast, fruit salad, and mimosas. The water outside the windows reflected sunlight into the room, making it bright and cheery. Acting as if they had simply encountered each other on the stairs, Darcy and Elizabeth were the last to arrive. Darcy officially introduced Elizabeth to Georgiana, who did an admirable job of pretending they hadn't already met under vastly more embarrassing circumstances.

Darcy cadged a seat next to Elizabeth, where he allowed his thigh to rest against hers. Throughout the meal, they often shared a secret smile but said very little. Conversation revolved around the day's plans. Bing favored a boating excursion to do some fishing while Georgiana and Caroline expressed more interest in a day at the beach. Thomas Gardiner was talking with great animation to Fitz about John's microbrewery.

Darcy's thoughts were preoccupied with figuring out when he and Elizabeth could sneak away without anyone noticing—and how he could slip her into Pemberley that evening.

Fitz stared at him with one eyebrow raised, and Caroline glared at Elizabeth. And it was no wonder…Darcy was beaming at Elizabeth like a fool. They couldn't conceal this relationship from their nearest and dearest for very long. Darcy didn't mind, as long as they could keep it from the press for now. Media scrutiny at this point might send her running.

When Elizabeth's hand clasped his knee, Darcy started and then had to stifle a laugh. A corner of her mouth curved upward as well, but she deliberately stared out the window. Slowly he lowered his hand under the table, skimming over the top of her leg and teasing the inside of her thigh with his forefinger. Elizabeth squirmed, murmuring out of the side of her mouth, "You are an evil man."

Darcy just grinned. *There must be some way we can make a relationship work. This is too good to lose without a fight.*

Bing cleared his throat, drawing Darcy's attention. "I'd like to give you the daily briefing after breakfast." His expression was a bit perplexed as if he noticed Darcy's distraction.

"Anything urgent?" Darcy asked. Bing shook his head. "That's what I like to hear."

Darcy turned to Elizabeth. "Would you like to take a walk after my briefing?"

"I'd love that. I haven't seen most of the grounds yet."

Elizabeth's aunt regarded them warily. Did she worry he would break Elizabeth's heart?

All conversation ceased at the sound of faint but rapid knocking on the front door.

"Shit," Fitz swore.

Bing shrugged. "It's probably just a messenger with papers for Darce to sign. It happens."

It could also be bad news about some domestic or foreign emergency. That happens, too.

Everyone was silent as the Secret Service agent in the front hall opened the door. The voices were too low to discern any words. Brisk footfalls echoed in the front hallway as the new visitor approached the kitchen and breakfast room.

Hilliard appeared in the doorway, red in the face and out of breath. Darcy's chest tightened. Shit. The press secretary wouldn't have made an unannounced trip to Pemberley unless it was serious. Darcy dropped Elizabeth's hand and stood.

Hilliard's eyes swept over the breakfast table, and he frowned slightly when he noticed Elizabeth. Damn it! Was Hilliard going to object to their relationship? To hell with him. The man's gaze focused on Darcy. "Sir, we have a situation." His expression was grave but revealed nothing.

Darcy inclined his head toward the hallway. "All right. We can discuss it in my office." Fitz and Bing had already rushed to their feet.

Hilliard's eyes found Caroline. "We'll need you, too." She nodded and stood immediately.

Darcy surveyed his guests. "Please excuse us." He met Elizabeth's eyes, wishing he could give her a goodbye kiss, which was ridiculous; he'd probably return in half an hour.

She gave him a rueful smile. "I'll see you later."

Steeling himself against the impulse to kiss her, Darcy turned and led the way to his office. His gut churned, and he made a conscious effort to slow his breathing as he considered the possible problems. It wasn't a domestic or international crisis because then it would be the National Security Council staff coming to him. This had to be some kind of PR nightmare—the thing he hated most about his job.

The study was usually a refuge for Darcy, but today it felt like a dungeon. The huge stone fireplace yawned empty and cold. Blinds drawn to secure his privacy shut out the sunshine of the beautiful beach day. Darcy settled behind his desk while the others took chairs facing him. "Okay," he sighed, "what's the bad news, Bob?"

Hilliard set his laptop up on the desk. "It's easier if I show you," he said as everyone crowded around. "This was broadcast early this morning."

The screen filled with a familiar Grant News frame surrounding the head of one of their anchors. The crawl at the bottom read: "Exclusive Breaking News." Darcy suppressed a groan.

"We have just learned some disturbing new information about President Darcy and his behavior toward a vulnerable young woman," the well-coifed blonde said crisply. "I'll let Grant News reporter Blake Rhodes explain."

The screen shifted to the fleshy face of Blake Rhodes. "Thank you, Tina. Earlier today I sat down for an interview with Lydia Bennet, the youngest daughter of Thomas Bennet, founder and CEO of On-a-Stick, Inc. Her family has recently been running in elite Democratic circles, and they have met the president numerous times. However, in the interview, she had some rather disturbing things to say."

Darcy was already grinding his back teeth. He didn't know what Lydia Bennet could possibly say about him, but Hilliard's unscheduled trip to Pemberley promised it would be bad. Very bad.

The view on the screen switched to a studio set, with Rhodes and Lydia occupying two of the chairs; the third seated…Wickham. God damn it! The situation had just gone from possibly very bad to possibly catastrophic.

"Also joining us," Rhodes continued, "is Congressman George Wickham, representing the 12th district of New York. Congressman Wickham first brought Miss Bennet to our attention. Thank you for being here, Congressman.'"

"My pleasure, Blake." Wickham flashed his cat-that-ate-the-canary grin. If only Darcy could reach into the computer screen and strangle the man.

Rhodes's eyes focused on Lydia. "You said you were concerned about your sister; can you explain to me why?" He leaned forward, affecting a concerned expression.

The college student's conservative blouse and skirt lent her an undeserved air of age and maturity. Without a fidget or smirk, her face registered only anxious concern. Idly, Darcy wondered how the producers had managed to wring such solemn behavior from her. "My second oldest sister, Elizabeth, has met the president a number of times…well, we all have." Lydia giggled, and for a moment, the vain teenager surfaced, but she quickly sobered. "She really doesn't like him. She said he was"—Lydia used air quotes—"proud, rude, and condescending.'"

Only his awareness of being observed allowed Darcy to control his flinch. Elizabeth might have said such a thing after the Air Force One incident, but he was confident that she had since changed her mind.

Rhodes wasn't trying very hard to suppress his smile. "I see. Why is this of particular concern now?"

"She hates him, but now all of sudden I find out that she's staying at his mansion in the Hamptons. It doesn't make sense." Lydia bit her lip and knitted her eyebrows together. "Something else is going on. She'd never be happy hanging out with him."

"You don't think she simply changed her mind?" Rhodes asked.

Now Lydia's lower lip was quivering. *Damn, she is good at this.* "No. Especially not after I saw that picture from yesterday."

Rhodes turned to the camera. "Here is the image Miss Bennet is referring to."

The picture on the screen showed Elizabeth about to climb into the presidential limo as Darcy held her hand, drawing her in. The camera captured her expression at a moment when it seemed almost bleak. Her eyes were downcast, her lips pressed into a thin line. She looked like she was being drawn into the limo against her will.

Rhodes's plummy voice described the picture. "This was taken right outside President Darcy's estate of Pemberley in the Hamptons. Witnesses say the presidential limo was about to enter the Pemberley gates when it backed up. The door opened, and the president beckoned Ms. Bennet inside. Although she seemed hesitant at first, he took her hand and pulled her into the car."

Darcy's hands clenched into fists, but he resisted the urge to punch something.

When the Grant News studio returned to the screen, Wickham was shaking his head slowly as if terribly concerned about Elizabeth's "plight." "Lydia and I questioned whether Elizabeth Bennet truly wished to get into the presidential limousine of her own free will, or if she felt she had no choice." The congressman's oily insinuation left no doubt which option he believed.

"Elizabeth Bennet has not emerged from Pemberley since," Rhodes intoned ominously.

"But the thing that got me really worried was the recording," Lydia said, right on cue.

Nails bit into Darcy's palms. He knew Lydia was a dupe here, but he still felt betrayed by how readily she had taken to the role of his accuser.

Rhodes nodded sympathetically. "I can understand why." He turned to the camera. "We have an audio recording that was captured by witnesses a few minutes after Elizabeth Bennet entered the limo. It records a conversation between an older woman and the Secret Service agent at the gate."

Darcy winced, knowing what they would hear.

A scratchy audio recording played while the transcribed words appeared on the screen. "You need to help me! My niece went into Pemberley with the president and hasn't come out. We haven't been able to get in touch with her. Her name is Elizabeth Bennet..."

The muscles in Darcy's jaw hurt, and he wanted very badly to throw something. They were taking the most wonderful night of his life and portraying it as something tawdry and sinister.

Rhodes appeared onscreen again. "Lydia Bennet has identified the woman on the recording as her aunt, sixty-two-year-old Madeline Gardiner. She and her husband, Thomas Gardiner, had accompanied Ms. Bennet to greet the presidential limo as it arrived at Pemberley. Shortly after that recording was made, Mr. and Mrs. Gardiner entered Pemberley and—like their niece—haven't been seen since."

Only Rhodes could make a day at the beach sound ominous. Darcy gripped the arms of his chair, fighting the impulse to pound his fists on the desk. They were implying that he was some sort of serial kidnapper. It was a ridiculous suggestion. However, experience had taught Darcy that many people would swallow the insinuations whole.

"You can't possibly be suggesting that the president kidnapped your sister," Rhodes said to Lydia.

Lydia shrugged expressively. "I don't know what's going on. But I do know that Lizzy doesn't like the guy. He insulted her at a state dinner a few months ago. It was all over Twitter. And now suddenly, she's spending the night with him? That doesn't make sense to me."

Darcy closed his eyes, wanting to shut out the spectacle of people using his love life for political purposes. It was an excellent strategy on Wickham's part. He didn't need to make them believe the kidnapping accusation; he just needed to muddy the waters enough so that the voters didn't know what to believe. No doubt he hoped to use the subsequent loss of confidence in Darcy to fuel his own political ascendency.

Wickham cleared his throat, drawing attention to himself. "And then there was the information about the Bennet family's company."

"Yes." Rhodes looked at the camera again. "Congressman Wickham brought us some very interesting information." He turned back to Lydia. "Did you know that your family's company, On-a-Stick, Inc., recently received a contract from the USDA worth more than $5 million?"

Lydia grinned with every appearance of guilelessness. "Yeah, Dad was so happy about it. The company wasn't doing so well, so the contract really made a difference."

Darcy suppressed a groan. Lydia's filter was even less effective than Georgiana's.

Rhodes had a concerned expression on his face, but no doubt he was jumping with glee inside. "Do you think your sister's sudden interest in the president might have something to do with the contract?"

Lydia's mouth dropped open; she was an excellent actress. "You mean President Darcy gave my family's company the contract in exchange for her—?" She clapped both hands over her mouth. "OMG! That would be terrible."

Darcy hadn't thought it was possible for his muscles to grow tenser, but he felt like a tautly stretched rubber band ready to snap. While the rational part of his brain dispassionately observed the clever political maneuvering behind the scheme, the rest of him seethed at the insinuations and insults. He had an uncharacteristic desire to wrap his hands around Wickham's neck—and squeeze.

Wickham shook his head in a grotesque parody of reluctant concern. "I didn't want to believe it either, Blake, when I first made the connection, but the evidence is hard to deny."

What evidence? It's two pieces of unrelated information.

"Indeed," Rhodes intoned, "but I'm afraid we have some more disturbing footage to add to it. We were looking through our archives and found this footage shot by Grant News outside President Darcy's private quarters on Air Force One."

The screen shifted to grainy footage of the door to the presidential suite. It opened with a jerk. The image of Elizabeth stumbling out was a little blurry, but Darcy could see that her hair was disordered and her expression was distraught. She slammed the door behind her, rushing down the hallway and out of the camera frame.

A news cameraman would never have been allowed in that location; the network must have hidden a camera outside the presidential suite. "Shit," Darcy breathed, fear was beginning to crowd out his annoyance. That shot did appear pretty damning.

"What the fuck?" Caroline squawked from behind him.

The screen shifted back to Rhodes. "The woman has been identified as Elizabeth Bennet. This incident occurred on Air Force One two months ago when the president was returning from Paris." He turned back to Lydia. "Her behavior in that footage certainly supports the idea that she doesn't like the president."

Lydia tossed her head. "Of course, she doesn't like him. He said she was ugly and stupid!"

If Darcy never heard those two words again, he would be a very happy man.

"We have confirmed that Ms. Bennet was alone with the president in the suite and that he had requested a bottle of white wine," Rhodes told the camera. "However, she was only in the suite about fifteen minutes before she exited looking, as you can see, rather disheveled. Afterward she escaped to the press area of Air Force One, where she spent the night. That isn't the usual protocol for guests of the president's; customarily they stay in a separate guest area."

Wickham's eyes widened with faux outrage. "What did he do to that poor girl?"

Lydia slapped her thigh. "I *thought* the president made a pass at her! She denied it, but the way she acted—"

Darcy rubbed his chest as if that would somehow ease the iron bands constricting his breathing. He couldn't imagine what Elizabeth might have said to Lydia after that fateful encounter. It was a minor miracle Darcy had quelled that anger after bungling the scene on Air Force One—and now his job was about to plunge her into a very public spectacle.

Rhodes shook his head. "Terrible, taking advantage of a defenseless young woman like that."

Despite his anger, Darcy snorted. "Defenseless" was not the way to describe the Elizabeth he had encountered on Air Force One.

"What did he do to make her change her mind about him so suddenly?" Lydia asked in a horrified whisper.

Wickham took Lydia's hand in a comforting manner. "It may be that he used the USDA contract to 'persuade' her." Lydia shuddered. Darcy winced, knowing that some voters would buy this scandalmongering.

"We will continue to investigate," Rhodes promised Lydia. He arranged his features into an expression of grave concern as he faced the camera. "We've contacted the White House to inquire about the incident but have received no reply. We'll keep you informed as we receive more information."

As Hilliard switched off the recording, he glared at Darcy. "What the hell have you been up to?" Bing cradled his head in his hands while

Fitz cursed colorfully and continuously. Caroline stared at Darcy with icy disdain.

"Nothing, Bob," Darcy growled. "I haven't hurt or abducted the woman. She's out there having French toast." He gestured to the kitchen.

"Yes, I saw her." Hilliard stood and started pacing. "I'm sure you've guessed how quickly the rest of the media has picked up on this. Reporters are gathering at Pemberley's gates. Lydia Bennet and Wickham are making appearances on other cable news shows. Mainstream newspapers are calling me for comments. And do you know what's trending on Twitter now? #Investigate PemberleyNow. #WhereIsElizabethBennet. #FreeElizabethBennet."

Darcy slumped back in his chair. "Shit."

"You really screwed the pooch this time, Will," Caroline said, her expression far more vindicated than concerned.

Bing's head jerked up. "It's not Darcy's fault. Wickham has always sought ways to use him to advance his political career."

Fitz sighed. "He knew he couldn't make that old story about the inheritance stand up to scrutiny."

"So what's our next move?" Bing asked.

"Can't we just have Elizabeth go out there and make a statement?" Fitz asked.

Hilliard sighed. "It's not that simple. She hasn't had media training. You know how easy it is for the media to trip you up and twist your words. She might say something that's construed the wrong way and make the whole situation worse."

"I wouldn't ask her to do it anyway," Darcy asserted. "She didn't create this mess, and she wouldn't be in this situation if it weren't for me." His shoulders drooped as he imagined her reaction to this news. *Not only has she been dragged into this farce but so has her family. She'll probably never speak to me again.*

Fitz drummed his fingers on his desk while he thought. "Can't she at least tell everyone she wasn't kidnapped?"

"That wouldn't do anything to address the rumors of coercion," Hilliard said. "If everyone believes she's sleeping with the president to preserve her family's USDA contract, they'll think the president told her what to say."

Bing bounced from one foot to the other as he stood with his back to the fireplace. "At the very least Elizabeth and her relatives need to leave

Pemberley. When the media films them buying groceries and eating dinner, it'll restore a sense of normalcy."

"Yeah, except..." Hilliard ran both hands through his sparse hair.

"What?" Darcy snapped, his patience at low ebb.

"Do we know what Elizabeth will say if she's questioned?"

"She's not going to throw me under the bus!" Darcy exclaimed.

"Are we sure of that?"

"Yes," Darcy growled.

Hilliard's dubious expression irritated Darcy even more. "Do we know how the company got the USDA contract?" he asked.

"I didn't even know they had such a contract until five minutes ago!" Darcy yelled.

"Chances are that they were awarded it through the regular bidding process," Fitz said soothingly. "I'll investigate."

Caroline smiled sourly. "Even if it was all above board, a lot of people won't believe it."

Bing put his head in his hands. "This sucks! We've tried so hard to avoid this kind of thing."

"Yeah," Darcy sighed. After his predecessor's attempts to use the office of president to enrich himself and his family, Darcy had made a special point of ensuring his administration avoided any hint of impropriety. An incident like this could paint him as hypocritical—a bandwagon the press would jump onto very quickly.

Bing slammed his fist on the fireplace mantel. "This is crazy! They're just friends. Her aunt and uncle were with her, and she spent the night in her own guest room alone. We can at least get those facts out there, even if a lot of people won't believe it."

Hilliard gave Darcy a sharp look. "Is that true?"

Darcy rubbed his face with his hands, wishing for just a moment that he could issue such a denial. But then he wouldn't wish away the previous night for the world. Nor was he about to start lying to the American people. "No," he said to Hilliard.

Bing's head jerked back. "But she went to *her* room, and you went to—!"

"It doesn't matter," Fitz said with a sympathetic glance at Darcy. "If Darcy can't deny they slept together, then the details are irrelevant to you and me and the American people. That's between Darcy and Elizabeth."

Bing nodded, but Caroline looked like she had smelled something disgusting.

Hilliard sighed. "Unfortunately, it's not. Not when you're president."

Darcy stared at the nautical painting over the fireplace. How had things gone so wrong so quickly? "It was *one night*," he said to himself. "Just one night." Couldn't the universe grant him one night to call his own with a woman he cared about? "Was that too much to ask?"

Hilliard stared at him blankly. "You're the president," he said as if that answered the question.

Darcy muttered curses under his breath. He'd been right all along. He couldn't date in the White House. Only a fool would think otherwise.

"Can we release some kind of statement in response?" Bing asked.

Hilliard settled back into his chair. "We'll have to eventually, but I don't think we're quite ready. I've got Preston back at the White House monitoring the press coverage. We'll see what the other networks and papers say." He turned to Darcy. "And, sir, you'll need to sit down with me and give me the history of your interactions with Ms. Bennet."

Darcy massaged his forehead, wondering how much detail he would have to go into. "Yeah, okay."

Hilliard nodded briskly. "And we'll need to fly more staff out here, unless you'd like to return to Washington...?"

"No." He'd just arrived at Pemberley!

"All right. We can set up a crisis team in the guest house." He glanced down to scribble in a notebook.

A crisis team. I need a crisis team to handle my love life. Kind of an apt metaphor, actually.

Caroline was examining her nails. "What you really need is a team to take out the trash." Everyone ignored her.

"How bad do you think it'll get?" Fitz asked.

Hilliard scrunched up his face. "It's hard to say. We'll try to spin it; hopefully the press will pick up on our version of events. But with the allegations of an improperly awarded contract and coercion..." He shook his head. "That's the kind of juicy story the media loves. Even if they don't think all the allegations are credible, they'll hop on the bandwagon because those headlines bring in viewers." He blew out a breath. "We really won't know the extent of the damage until the weekly approval polls."

Bing continued to pace, twisting his watch on his wrist. "We've been able to turn other attacks to our advantage. There's got to be a bright side to this."

There was a long silence before Hilliard cleared his throat. "Well, fewer people will think the president is gay." Darcy glared at him. "Okay, it's a dim bright side, but still…"

"At least being seen as cold and aloof will no longer be your biggest public perception issue." Fitz gave a sour smile.

"They won't still be asking 'What's wrong with the president?'" Caroline said with a sneer. "Now they'll know."

Bing gave his sister a quelling look before turning to Darcy. "I hate to state the obvious again, but we need to get Elizabeth and her relatives out of Pemberley."

Darcy climbed to his feet on legs that were suddenly shaky. He didn't know how he would break such awful news. It would devastate her. What could he possibly say to her that would comfort her at such a time? He inhaled deeply, but it did nothing to calm him. "I'll go talk to her—"

Hilliard grabbed his arm. "No. I need you. First, you need to explain to me what you did with her, and then we need to make some decisions."

"But—"

"It's best if you aren't seen with her—even here. Someone will talk." The look in Hilliard's eyes was uncompromising.

Damn it. Hilliard was right. An unscrupulous staff member could have taken pictures of them at dinner or brunch or at the beach—or an "unnamed source" could leak information about anything they did. But, still…Elizabeth would need him when she got this news.

He pulled his arm away. "No, I—"

"Mr. President, you need to concentrate on your *job*. If you want to be an effective president, there's a lot of clean up to be done; you need to focus on that."

His presidency came first; the country came first. Darcy had never resented that fact more than at that moment. He sagged back into his chair, rubbing his eyes. "All right."

"I'll go escort Elizabeth and the Gardiners out," Bing volunteered.

Elizabeth would leave Pemberley without another chance to talk with her. Their first night would be their only night. As Bing strode toward the door, he took Darcy's heart with him.

"Bing," he called. His friend stopped and glanced back. "Tell her..." What the hell could Darcy say to compensate for unceremoniously booting her from his home? Or for the way she would be hounded by the media? How did you apologize for destroying someone's life? He didn't have the words. "Tell her...I'm sorry." He grimaced at the woeful inadequacy of his words.

Bing nodded sympathetically and continued out the door. Darcy did nothing to stop him.

Chapter Sixteen

Elizabeth stared down at the mob of reporters in front of her apartment building. The landlord had requested police officers, who did prevent the press from harassing most residents. However, if Elizabeth were to set a foot outside the door, it would be like waving a steak in front of a pack of hungry dogs. Even when she just pushed her curtains aside to gaze out the window, cameras pointed up, shooting her with telephoto lenses. Trapped in her apartment, she felt like an out-of-favor queen fearing that the peasants would seize her and drag her to the guillotine.

Surely the visit to Pemberley had taken place more than a week ago; it felt like months. Time dragged when you were a media sensation.

Everyone in the world wanted to speak with her. Her voicemail was so full of interview requests that she had stopped using her landline. Yet there was no word from the one person whose voice she most needed to hear.

Allowing the curtains to fall over the window, Elizabeth reflected that she could hardly blame him for not calling. Lydia's interview had spawned a whirlwind of consequences, including nonstop coverage by every cable station in the country. As a result, Elizabeth had stopped watching television altogether and avoided using her laptop.

Elizabeth wiped away the moisture at the corner of her eye. Without communication from Will, she had no idea what he was thinking. Did he know that Elizabeth had no hand in fostering Lydia's accusations? That watching the video had ripped her apart? That she had screamed at her sister over the phone until she was hoarse, and they were no longer speaking?

The familiar queasiness roiled her stomach. Elizabeth had told Bing that Lydia had reached her own conclusions—or Wickham's conclusions—without any encouragement from her. But that didn't mean Bing—or Will—believed her. *If only I could get a message to him. Of course, I'd probably mess that up, too.* She slumped onto her sofa and stared at the darkened television screen.

It was painful to realize that Will's first impulse had been right: her family was ill-mannered and nouveau riche. He would have been better off if he had steered clear of the Bennets altogether. His wariness of them had been proven to be prescient while Elizabeth had been a fool to think she could escape that family legacy. Her one consolation was that the rest of her family had closed ranks and refused to speak with the press about her. Every time someone shoved a microphone in her father's face, he regarded it as an opportunity to promote jerky on-a-stick; after a while, the reporters had left him alone.

It shouldn't matter what he thought of her. She'd never see him or speak to him or breathe the same air as him ever again. Being subpoenaed to testify in front of Congress was the closest she might ever come. God forbid. Another tear rolled down her cheek, and she dashed it away impatiently with her palm. Hadn't she done enough crying over him?

She sat on the sofa for several long minutes, unable to summon the energy to move—or even care.

Although she was anticipating it, the knock at the door still startled her. Elizabeth trudged across the living room to admit Jane and Kitty. Before Elizabeth could blink, Kitty shot through the doorway and plastered herself against the adjacent wall as if fearing enemy fire. Charlotte and Bill Collins swept into the apartment after her. Jane, with a hood around her face, was last, and Elizabeth locked the door behind them.

Elizabeth got her first good look at Kitty and gaped. Her sister was wearing an oversized men's blazer over a turtleneck and black jeans. Her hair was stuffed under a bowler hat, and an enormous black mustache was plastered on her upper lip.

Elizabeth laughed, gesturing to Kitty. "What's with the getup?"

Busily scanning the room, Kitty didn't bother to glance at Elizabeth. "It's a disguise. Duh."

"I understand that it's a disguise," Elizabeth said patiently. "My question is: why?"

"The press knows what your sisters look like," Kitty answered in hushed tones. "They'd be merciless if they recognized us."

Elizabeth blinked at her. "And you think that dressing like Charlie Chaplin is *less* noticeable?"

Charlotte stifled a giggled.

"Well, nobody asked me about you," Kitty said tartly, "so it must have worked."

Pulling down her hood, Jane brandished a 7-Eleven bag. "I got Chunky Monkey, Cookie Dough, and a couple other flavors."

The thought of food made Elizabeth slightly nauseated. "You can eat it. I'm not hungry," she sighed as she flopped onto the sofa. Company had sounded appealing when Jane had called, but now that her visitors were here, talking with them seemed to demand more energy than she possessed.

"Elizabeth Bennet turns down Ben and Jerry's? Alert the media!" Jane laughed, but it failed to elicit a smile from her sister. "Did you have lunch? Or dinner?"

Did I? Elizabeth couldn't remember.

"We're not going to let you do this to yourself." Marching over to the coffee table, Jane plunked several containers of ice cream in front of Elizabeth.

Elizabeth crossed her arms over her chest, not caring that she resembled a sulky teenager. "This isn't your business."

Kitty took a position next to Jane, and they eyed Elizabeth with identical glares. "Of course, this is our business! This is an interruption!"

A what?

"An intervention," Jane hissed at Kitty.

"An intervention!" Kitty corrected herself.

Charlotte rolled her eyes. "The point is that you've been holed up in this apartment for three days in your pajamas. It's not healthy! You need to put on real clothes tomorrow and go into work. Working at home isn't good for you."

"I can't," Elizabeth said flatly.

Jane sank onto the sofa beside her sister and put a comforting arm around her shoulders. "You can! I know it'll be tough getting through the crowd of reporters, but you're a strong, confident woman." Jane's grin was so energetic it was practically manic.

Elizabeth brushed bits of hair from her eyes. "I've been suspended from work."

"Oh." The smile slid off Jane's face.

Charlotte slid into a chair opposite them. "Was it too much for them—the media and everything?" Every time the story about Elizabeth and Will had died down, George Wickham had appeared on a cable news show to toss around more accusations. He had been extremely effective at keeping the scandal—and his name—in the news.

Elizabeth hunched her shoulders, staring at the carpet. "No. It was the notification that their latest grant is being reviewed by the inspector general over allegations of impropriety."

"Shit!" Jane immediately clapped her hand over her mouth. Elizabeth's eyebrows shot up. Jane never cursed.

"They think the Red Cross got the grant because of you and the president?" Charlotte asked.

Elizabeth nodded. "I didn't even like him back when the grant was awarded," she said with a laugh that sounded bitter even to her ears. "I just hope the staff can convince the inspector that the Red Cross won it fair and square. If not, my job is toast." A familiar sensation burned behind her eyes, but she blinked it back. She'd shed enough tears today.

"That's so unfair," Jane said.

The awkward silence following Jane's declaration provided Bill with an opportunity; he planted himself on Elizabeth's other side. "I would encourage you to give up all hopes of winning the president's affection," he said earnestly.

"Oh?"

He grinned broadly as if delivering good news. "His aunt does not view your acquaintance favorably."

He actually believed she should concede any hopes of a relationship with Will because of Mrs. de Bourgh's opinion. "I don't particularly care what his aunt thinks."

Bill drew back, a horrified look on his face. "You don't?" She might as well have confessed to murdering kittens.

Charlotte perched on the arm of the sofa and patted Bill's shoulder soothingly. "Lizzy has always been a bit of a free spirit."

Elizabeth didn't know whether to laugh or cry.

Bill shook his head disapprovingly. "I live my life by the motto 'What would Mrs. de Bourgh do?' It does simplify things."

"You should put that on a bracelet," Kitty said.

Charlotte continued speaking as she absently stroked Bill's hair. "Elizabeth knows that there are many other reasons not to date the president." She gave Elizabeth a meaningful look.

Elizabeth sighed, unsure if she was more irritated at Charlotte or herself. She had known that dating Will would be difficult and likely end in heartbreak, but they hadn't even gotten to the dating part. They'd had one night, and she was left with nothing except a bruised heart and wall-to-wall media coverage of every trip to buy shampoo.

"You need to get out of the apartment," Jane said. "You can at least go to a coffee shop or the mall or something."

Elizabeth slouched further into the sofa. "I went to the grocery store a couple of days ago. So many reporters followed me that the manager eventually asked me to leave."

"No shit!" Kitty's eyes went wide.

Jane patted Elizabeth's hand. "I'm sure it won't always be that way." Kitty pulled a pint of ice cream out of the bag and peeled off the lid before handing it to Jane. "In the meantime, you need to eat," Jane continued. "You're losing weight." She waved the container under Elizabeth's nose. "I brought Chocolate Chip Cookie Dough. Doesn't it smell divine?"

Elizabeth groaned. "Jane…"

Jane's tone would have been best suited to a cheerleader. "Eat something, take a shower, and then we can go to Mom and Dad's. At least it'll get you out of the house."

Elizabeth pushed the container away. "I'm not hungry, and I'm not inflicting the press on Mom and Dad again—especially now that the reporters are finally leaving them alone. I've caused them enough trouble." She cringed at the memory of reporters trampling her mother's flower beds and harassing Mary as she left for work.

Jane smiled even more broadly. "They're doing better, Lizzy. Mom is a lot calmer; she's resting a lot."

"Thank God for Xanax," Kitty interjected.

Jane glared at Kitty for a moment before continuing. "Dad's buried himself in work. You know how he is."

"His lawyers are trying to get the USDA to reinstitute the contract," Kitty added. "On-a-Stick already manufactured a lot of the food. If the government doesn't proceed with the contract, it could bankrupt us."

Elizabeth ground her teeth. Not only had she ruined her life but also her family's business. Maybe for an encore she could set fire to the White House.

"Kitty," Jane whispered, "Lizzy doesn't need to hear that now."

"I'm being the bad cop," Kitty explained. "You're the good cop."

"This isn't an interrogation," Jane said.

"Damn it!" Elizabeth's exclamation cut short the debate. She pushed off the sofa and walked the length of the room, wishing she could jog or jump, anything to absorb her excess of energy. "I'm ruining everybody's lives." Tears threatened to return.

"It's not your fault!" Charlotte said fiercely. "If anything, it's Lydia's."

Elizabeth rubbed her face. "I guess." Although she was hardly blameless.

Bill cleared his throat. "On the drive over here, Charlotte and I were debating the nature of Lydia's evil...er...nature."

Elizabeth's eyes widened. Was Bill actually saying what she thought he was saying?

Bill continued, "Charlotte was inclined to believe it was the result of your parents' lax oversight as Lydia matured, but I think she must be naturally bad."

Jane's mouth fell open while Charlotte turned bright red. "Bill," she murmured out of the side of her mouth, "you know how we talked about keeping some things private between the two of us...?"

Bill was perplexed. "But this isn't about sex."

Just pretend that didn't happen, Elizabeth told herself. "I don't think Lydia's evil," she said. "Misguided perhaps. George Wickham is using her, although I told her not to trust him."

Kitty shook her head. "Nobody's been able to reach her for the past week. She hasn't been at her apartment."

"It would be best if Lydia were silenced," Bill said meaningfully.

Elizabeth's eyes narrowed. "Have you ever tried to 'silence' Lydia? The girl talks like there's a two-for-one special on words."

Bill drew himself up to his full height—which wasn't very full. "No, I mean, *silenced*." He drew his finger across his neck.

"Bill!" Charlotte laughed nervously as if it were all a joke.

"Oh my God," Jane said faintly.

"Maybe I can sell the story of my life to Hollywood," Kitty thought aloud.

"You're not serious!" Elizabeth exclaimed.

Bill regarded her disdainfully. "I assure you I am. The office products business is very rough and tumble."

Elizabeth screwed her eyes shut, deciding that it was best not to pursue that line of inquiry. "I don't want Lydia 'silenced.' She's my sister, and I love her."

"The president would probably prefer to have the Secret Service do it anyway." Bill nodded sagaciously.

Elizabeth threw her hands up in the air. The idea was so absurd that it wasn't worth debating.

"The real problem is the press," Jane interjected somewhat desperately.

No, the real problem is my sister screwed over the man I love. But there was no point in debating that. "They're not going to leave me alone even if I ask nicely," Elizabeth sighed.

"You could do an interview or a prepared statement or a press conference. Or even strategic leaks," Charlotte suggested. The gears of a seasoned PR pro were practically visible as they turned in her head.

Why didn't I ask Charlotte for advice earlier? Because I thought nothing could be done.

"That's a good idea," Jane said. "The media is waiting for you to say something. Then some of them might leave you alone."

Elizabeth considered this for a moment, chewing on her lip. *What would be most helpful to Will?* No, it was too risky. "I might say something that makes this worse—that hurts Will's presidency."

"Screw Darcy!" Charlotte said viciously.

"I'm not sure Mrs. de Bourgh would like that," Bill said slowly.

Charlotte ignored him. "The president has left you twisting in the wind even though he professes to care for you. This happens all the time in Washington: allies turn on each other when someone runs afoul of the media. Don't think he has your back. You're on your own, honey."

Elizabeth shuddered; Charlotte had expressed the thoughts she hadn't allowed herself to think all week. She wanted to deny Charlotte's assertion but couldn't find the words.

When Bing had hustled Elizabeth and the Gardiners out of Pemberley—with a rushed and garbled explanation about Lydia and negative press coverage—he had assured her that Will would call. But it had been a week, and Elizabeth had heard nothing.

Elizabeth cleared her throat, finally finding her voice. "It's a shit storm out there. He's really busy."

Charlotte snorted. "You still think you're going to hear from him?"

"Char, I think he really cares about Lizzy," Jane said. At Charlotte's glare, she shrugged apologetically. "Well…it's possible he cares…maybe."

Kitty made a dubious face. "It kind of sounds like a one-night thing to me. The media just blew it up into this big thing."

Elizabeth pounded her fist against the wall, startling Kitty. "A one-night stand? I wouldn't do that. Especially with the president."

Kitty withstood her narrow-eyed stare for seconds before shrugging and glancing away. "I would. Especially with the president."

He wanted a relationship with me. He did. Even if a relationship was now impossible, it was important that she cling to that conviction.

Charlotte dismissed it all with a wave. "Maybe he did intend for it to be more than a one-night thing." Her expression showed how likely she thought that was. "But Lydia's interview torpedoed any chance of something more." Elizabeth forced herself not to shrink away from Charlotte's words. "He can't call you. Can't be seen with you," Charlotte continued. "You're the third rail right now. Touch you and he dies."

Jane gasped. "That's a little harsh."

"I know how PR works, and image is everything to a president." As Charlotte gazed at Elizabeth, her eyes softened a bit. "He's not going to call you," she said regretfully.

Elizabeth stared down at her hands with a self-deprecating laugh. "He said he would call and then he didn't. It's the oldest story in the world. I was just too thick to get the message." Her eyes burned with unshed tears.

Jane turned to Charlotte, her hands on her hips. "He defended Lizzy in that statement to the press and in the interview with NBC."

"He has to defend her. He doesn't want to give any weight to the accusations," Charlotte pointed out. Why did Charlotte need to voice Elizabeth's worst fears? Her shoulders slumped as she suddenly felt weighed down by the whole discussion.

Kitty looked chagrined. "I hate to say it, but I think Charlotte's right."

Bill puffed out his chest. "Well, I'm happy to say I think Charlotte is right." His expression clouded. "Although I'm not sure if Mrs. de Bourgh would approve."

"When the press asks Will if we're dating, he won't answer. And Hilliard just says, 'the president's private life is private,'" Elizabeth said slowly as she sank into her blue recliner. "Charlotte is right. The White House wants to avoid the perception of a one-night stand, but a relationship would be career suicide at this point—if that's what Will ever wanted."

Maybe he never intended to pursue a relationship; maybe all those words were meant to get her into bed, and the media storm was a convenient reason to cut her loose. The very thought was like pressing on a bruise. At Pemberley she had believed him with a deep visceral understanding, but could she trust that sensation? Maybe it was just a combination of hope, willful blindness, and afterglow.

"He might be trying to avoid throwing you under the bus, but that's about all he can do." Charlotte's mouth was a thin, white line. "His hands are tied."

Any affection Will had felt for Elizabeth had undoubtedly been killed by Lydia's betrayal. There was nothing left to salvage; Elizabeth could only hope to repair the damage to his presidency. She owed him that much. Her lips trembled, and she pressed them together. *I will fall apart later; not here in front of everyone.*

Everyone's expressions were so full of sympathy that Elizabeth had to lower her eyes. "How could talking to the media help me?" she asked Charlotte.

Charlotte tapped a finger to her lips thoughtfully. "Your story will lend the president's account credibility. If nobody hears from you, it'll be easier to believe the idea of coercion."

Elizabeth nodded. "And that hurts Will."

Charlotte shrugged. "If that's your chief concern. His poll numbers *have* taken a hit, and it's just the beginning of the scandal."

Scandal. Great. I've become a Washington scandal; what a proud legacy.

"This is just the beginning?" Jane asked incredulously, no doubt wondering how much worse it could get.

"They're talking about congressional hearings," Charlotte said. "Lizzy would have to testify about whether the president coerced her."

Elizabeth shuddered. She couldn't think of anything more humiliating than testifying about her intimate relationships in front of twenty hostile congressmen and a roomful of reporters.

If a statement might help prevent that, it was probably the best strategy. "Okay," she said to Charlotte, "I'd like to write a statement. Will you read it to the press for me?"

***

Hilliard burst into the Oval Office, not even apologizing for interrupting Darcy's strategy session with Bing and Secretary of Energy Kurt Abbott over the renewable energy bill. Darcy's heart plummeted into his stomach. Nothing good ever came from Hilliard's unexpected appearances.

"Excuse me, sir." Hilliard didn't sound very apologetic. "We have a situation." Without missing a beat, he strode to the television in the corner of the room and switched it on. Darcy's stomach roiled. Another public relations nightmare. It had to be.

Everyone stood hastily. Darcy shook Abbott's hand. "Kurt, we'll have to finish this another time. See if you can get some room on my schedule next week."

"Sure," Abbott said. "Thank you, Mr. President."

But Darcy's attention was already riveted on Hilliard and the television, which was on a commercial break. "What is it?" he asked once the door closed softly behind Abbott.

"ZNN announced that Elizabeth Bennet has released a statement," Hilliard said curtly.

Darcy's heart went into overdrive, crashing against his ribs like it was trying to escape. His mouth opened, but no words emerged. *What will Elizabeth say? Is she angry? Vindictive?*

"Do we think it's authentic?" Bing asked.

"I'm assuming ZNN vetted the statement. It's coming from Walter Lucas's PR firm." Hilliard's expression was grim.

Bing nodded. "The Lucases are family friends of the Bennets."

Hilliard focused on Darcy with laser-like intensity. "What did Ms. Bennet say when you spoke to her? What was her frame of mind?"

Darcy hesitated. "Darce?" Bing asked.

"I...um...didn't call her yet," he mumbled, suddenly finding the carpet very interesting.

"I told her you would!" Bing said sharply.

Darcy didn't meet his friend's eyes. "I didn't know what to say." He'd lain awake nights staring at the canopy of his bed and trying to find words to apologize for having her unceremoniously removed from Pemberley. To express his regret for throwing her life into chaos. Wondering if she could forgive him for ruining her life after just one night...

Then he'd chastise himself for not calling her earlier. Of course, the longer he delayed, the more he had to apologize for and the harder it was to imagine facing her.

"You didn't call her?" Hilliard gasped. "After she experienced the world's worst morning after, you didn't even call?"

Things were bad when Hilliard was lecturing him on how to treat a woman. Of course, he was right; Darcy should have called Elizabeth. But what if she said she never wanted to see him again? She'd said that once; Darcy was certain that she was capable of saying it again.

And then there was the fact that he was responsible for bringing Wickham into her family's life. The man was probably debauching Elizabeth's youngest sister and had brought media scrutiny to every corner of the Bennet family's lives. They'd even interviewed Elizabeth's senior prom date. He massaged the back of his neck. They must hate him. And to think he'd once been convinced that he was such a better person than the Bennets.

"Are you trying to make me lose my remaining hair?" A muscle twitched under Hilliard's eye.

"This isn't about you, Bob," Darcy growled.

Hilliard ignored him. "So we have no insight into Ms. Bennet's state of mind except that she's been ghosted by the guy who thrust her life into complete chaos?"

"The guy who spent one night with her and then didn't call her," Bing added helpfully.

Darcy flopped onto one of the sofas, making himself as small as possible as though it could keep him from becoming a target. "When you put it that way, it doesn't sound good."

"It's *not* good!" Hilliard hissed. "We don't have a fucking clue what this statement will say. What if Elizabeth supports her sister's account? She might say that from spite alone. The Republicans are speculating that you used government funds to get a woman in your bed. That's an impeachable offense!"

What is wrong with me? Darcy wondered. *Hilliard is right. I could be impeached, and all I can think about is Elizabeth—and whether she'll forgive me. Why the hell didn't I call her?*

He pushed away the persistent fear that she *did* feel coerced by him. She had turned him down once. What had prompted her change of heart? Undoubtedly, she knew about the USDA deal. Maybe she'd believed he expected a quid pro quo? Such thoughts gnawed at him in the dark and the silence of the empty Residence.

With his eyes riveted to the television, Bing shushed them. "It's on!" Darcy clutched the arm of the sofa until his fingers turned white. In the still moments before the press conference started, his own ragged breaths were inordinately loud.

A woman Darcy vaguely recognized as Charlotte Lucas was walking to a podium in a small room crammed with reporters and photographers. There must have been at least one hundred people pressed together in the space. When she reached the podium, a hush fell over the room like a cloak.

Darcy was accustomed to his life's frequent ventures into the surreal, but a press conference about his love life was a level of grotesque he had never reached before. Anxiety prickled all over his body. The next few minutes would determine his fate.

Although Ms. Lucas couldn't be much older than Elizabeth, she was quite self-possessed, wearing a high-end designer suit as she gazed unflinchingly at the reporters. "I will read a prepared statement from Elizabeth Bennet," she said crisply. "I will take no questions afterward." Opening a piece of paper, she placed it on the podium.

Realizing he was holding his breath, Darcy released it, reeling with sudden dizziness.

Ms. Lucas read, "'I am aware that there have been many rumors circulating regarding my relationship with President Darcy and the contract given to my family's business. I would like to lay out the facts as I know them.

"'My family received the USDA contract through the regular bidding process. I am not part of the family business and played no part in procuring the contract. I do not believe the president knew that On-a-Stick, Inc. was bidding for the contract, but at no time did he discuss the matter with me or with any member of my family.

"'At no time did the president state or imply that the contract or any other matter relied on a romantic or sexual relationship with him. We were and are friends—a relationship based on similar interests and mutual admiration. The time I have spent with him has been solely for the purpose of enjoying his company.

"'I ask that the media respect my privacy and the privacy of my family during this time. I have nothing further to add. Signed, Elizabeth Bennet.'"

True to her word, Charlotte Lucas folded up the statement and walked from the room, ignoring the reporters shouting questions at her. Hilliard used the remote to switch off the set.

Darcy expelled a long breath as Hilliard jumped from his seat and high-fived Bing. "Yes!" he exulted. "You were right about her," Hilliard told Darcy.

"You're not out of the woods, but at least she confirmed your story." Bing sagged against the fireplace mantel. "Thank God!"

Darcy nodded, unsure why he didn't share their sense of relief.

"Now we'll have to see if the press believes her assertions, or if they think you coerced her into making the statement," Hilliard said as he made notes on a legal pad.

Leaning forward in his seat, Darcy dropped his head into his hands. "Why did she say we were *friends*?" he asked nobody in particular. When he lifted his head, the others were staring at him.

"Sorry?" Hilliard asked. "Did you want her to say you were enemies?"

"No." Darcy laughed without mirth. "But friends—gah!" Perhaps that was how she viewed their relationship now, but the word just felt wrong.

"Actually," Hilliard said, "if you notice, she didn't deny you had a romantic relationship." Both Bing and Darcy looked at him. "She said you were friends, but she never said you were just friends. She left a lot of wiggle room there."

Darcy's heart leapt. "So you think there's hope?"

Hilliard nodded. "Yeah, as long as she sticks to that statement, we might be able to avoid congressional hearings."

There was a long pause during which Darcy said nothing.

Hilliard jerked his head up. "Oh, that wasn't the kind of hope you meant." He sat up straighter and cleared his throat. "Well, of course there's hope. Isn't there always hope? Unless she marries someone else. But what do I know? I've been married three times. More importantly…"

Darcy tuned Hilliard out. Elizabeth *had* defended him; she seemed to care about him. Maybe he should call her, but what if that muddied the waters? What if she hung up on him?

Darcy's phone rang. Everyone's eyes were drawn to the pocket where he kept it. Few people had his private cell phone number, but the group included the Joint Chiefs of Staff and the Secretary of State. Darcy always answered it. He pulled it from his pocket, and his eyes widened at the name on the screen. "Georgie? What's up?"

"I just saw Elizabeth's statement," his sister said. "Have you called her, or are you foxholing?"

"Sort of the latter," Darcy mumbled.

Georgiana groaned in frustration. "You left her twisting in the wind? She's the best thing that ever happened to you. Call her. Call her now!"

Georgie was right. Darcy had never felt like this with any other woman. Elizabeth's statement had signaled that she didn't blame him for the fiasco. Maybe there was something to salvage.

"All right," he sighed.

"Good," Georgiana grunted and hung up.

Darcy stood, striding toward his desk. "I'm calling Elizabeth."

Hilliard jumped to his feet. "But first we must organize our press strategy—well, re-organize it."

Darcy waved his hand. "You can do it. I've got a phone call to make."

"But—"

"Bob, line up some media training for her. I'll pay for it. So she can prepare to speak with the press and go on talk shows if...needed."

Hilliard scribbled in his notebook. "You mean, if she agrees to talk to you..."

Bing frowned and stroked his chin. "Darce, are you sure about this? Being seen with her will stir up more rumors and accusations—and make congressional hearings more likely."

"Did you hear what she said?" Darcy gestured toward the television. "I'm not giving up hope without talking to her first."

Bing leaned over the desk, getting right in Darcy's face. "You could be setting yourself up for more heartbreak. And it's not like you have a lot of time to devote to a relationship, with the big push for the renewable energy bill—"

"I can do both," Darcy snapped at his friend. Then he turned to Hilliard. "I want you to work up a media strategy to help us avoid congressional hearings."

"Yes, sir," Hilliard said. "But—"

"Now, if you'll excuse me, gentlemen, I need to make a call." He gave the two men pointed looks until they both hurried toward the door. After taking a deep breath, he picked up his phone.

Chapter Seventeen

Elizabeth had been in motion the entire time Charlotte read the statement. The adrenaline fizzing in her blood compelled her to pace in front of the television in her parents' family room, forcing everyone on the sofa to peer around her. Miraculously, nobody complained. It helped that her mother was upstairs sleeping off another Xanax, and Lydia was still MIA.

For the fifteenth time she reached for her cell phone for some distraction and again recalled that—overwhelmed by calls from the media, friends, and acquaintances she barely knew— she had left it behind in her apartment. When the press conference was over, her father clicked off the television from his easy chair.

"I think Charlotte did a good job," Jane said stoutly.

"Yes, and that was a well-written statement," Elizabeth's father said.

"Thank you. Of course, Charlotte helped me write it," Elizabeth said. "I just hope it's enough."

Jane gave Elizabeth an encouraging smile. "Hopefully it will change some minds."

Mary folded her arms and scowled. "I doubt everyone will believe it. Some people are determined to think the worst of the president, and the rumors play right into that idea."

Elizabeth sighed and sank onto a recliner. Writing the statement, getting the language just right, organizing the press conference, and handling all the questions had been an enormous effort. Now that it was over, her adrenaline had abandoned her, and she was ready for a nap.

"Don't worry, my dear," her father smiled at her, "all of this will blow over eventually."

Kitty nodded enthusiastically. "In five years nobody will be talking about it." Elizabeth wasn't comforted.

At the sound of the doorbell, her father frowned. "I'm not expecting anyone."

Mary stood. "It might be the press. They'd kill to get a quote from Lizzy."

Her father grunted. "If those reporters don't agree to get off the property, I'm calling the police." He and Mary marched toward the front hall like street toughs ready for a fight.

"Just give them the sales pitch for cookies on-a-stick," Kitty called after them. "They won't be able to run away fast enough!"

Elizabeth huddled in the recliner, imagining all kinds of miscreants who might lurk behind the door. She strained her ears, but heard no sounds of shouting or pitched battle. Her father soon returned looking rather baffled. He was followed by a vaguely familiar older woman whose gaze raked the room disdainfully.

"Lizzy," her father said, "this is Catherine de Bourgh, President Darcy's aunt. She said you met before."

What the hell was *she* doing here? Elizabeth gaped at the woman, who was eying her mother's collection of unicorn figurines with a curl in her lip. Elizabeth's shoulders tensed, feeling like they were hunched around her ears. Nevertheless, she gestured to the sofa. "Please, take a seat."

Mrs. de Bourgh gave the sofa a sidelong glance as if she suspected it might harbor Ebola. "I don't believe I'll be staying that long." The older woman sniffed. "Your house is quite a bit smaller than I expected."

"Yes, well," said Elizabeth's father with a shrug, "we thought about buying a new one, but we are rather attached to the neighborhood."

"I don't see why you don't tear down this house and build a new one then," Mrs. de Bourgh drawled. "How in the world can your family make do with anything less than eight thousand square feet? Especially with such an excessive number of daughters."

Apparently, she hadn't expected a response because she continued, "And, if you tore down, you could rid yourselves of those hideous lion statues at the end of the drive."

John Bennet looked stricken. "But they're covered in real fake gold leaf!"

Mrs. de Bourgh regarded him like a particularly stupid kindergarten student. "Yes. You have identified the precise problem. And those turrets"—she gestured to the top of the house —"so gaudy!"

"But the style and color of the turrets were designed specifically to match the lions." Her father sounded bewildered by the criticism.

"Good. Now you're beginning to see the problem," Mrs. de Bourgh said in a slow, patient voice.

Her father gaped like a fish but said nothing.

The older woman turned to Elizabeth. "There seemed to be a garden of sorts in your backyard, accessible through the room with all the framed teddy bear paintings." Her voice dripped with contempt. "Might I have a word with you out there?"

What could the woman possibly want with me? Did it have something to do with her foundation? Elizabeth exchanged a brief, perplexed glance with Jane before following Mrs. de Bourgh into the hall and through their mother's "work room," which was littered with abandoned craft projects.

Both women were silent as they emerged through the back door into the yard, which consisted mostly of mud, clumps of grass, and the overgrown remains of Fanny Bennet's last attempts at gardening. Mrs. de Bourgh surveyed the yard. "While I commend your parents' desire to save money on landscaping, I'm afraid the results are a crime against nature." She glided down the pathway and seated herself on a stone bench with great ceremony.

Elizabeth bit back an angry retort; the other woman might be tactless, but the nonexistent landscaping could not be defended. After taking a leisurely stroll to the opposite bench, she took more time than strictly necessary to arrange herself on it.

"I cannot imagine my visit comes as a surprise to you," the older woman intoned solemnly.

Elizabeth saw no reason to dissemble. "Actually, I have no idea why you're here."

Mrs. de Bourgh pursed her lips in disapproval. "You might wish to play games, Ms. Bennet, but I will not play along." She sat a little straighter on the bench. "You must know that I am here to say you can never see my nephew, William Darcy, again."

"I don't believe that's your decision." Elizabeth gave her a blatantly false smile.

Mrs. de Bourgh toyed with one of the bracelets on her wrist. "My nephew is an intelligent man, but he does not always know what is best for him. It is up to those of us who care for him to watch out for his best interests."

"He's the President of the United States; I would say he's very capable of taking care of himself," Elizabeth said in a careful and controlled tone.

Mrs. de Bourgh waved away that objection. "In personal matters, he does not always know what is best. And what is best for him is a woman of his own station in life. Someone who travels in the same circles, and who can be a *help* in his political career." Tilting her head back slightly, she looked down at Elizabeth. "Not a hindrance."

What was an adequate response to such a statement? She hadn't set out to create problems for Will; that had been Lydia.

It probably doesn't matter anyway, said a voice in the back of her head. *The man hasn't called in nearly a week.* Still, Elizabeth's pride was piqued. "If I were to date your nephew, I would not consider myself to be a hindrance to his career." She didn't bother keeping the frostiness out of her tone.

"I beg to differ. A president's private life is not private. He belongs to the whole country. If William were to marry you, it would be detrimental to his presidency and therefore to the whole country."

Marry? Elizabeth felt suddenly faint. *Who said anything about marriage?*

Pull yourself together. Don't let that old bat see how the idea has shaken you. Instead she laughed grimly. "You think my relationship with your nephew could bring about the end of western civilization?" Elizabeth raised a skeptical eyebrow.

Mrs. de Bourgh sniffed. "No need to be overly dramatic. I am simply pointing out the humiliation he would suffer."

Now Elizabeth's pulse was racing, and her body was hot all over. "There would be nothing shameful in dating me."

Mrs. de Bourgh stood swiftly, advancing across the pathway. "Nothing shameful! Don't you understand the shame you have already visited upon his administration? Are the shades of the White House to be thus polluted?"

Elizabeth re-examined this sentence in her head, but it still didn't make sense. "I don't think the White House has shades. I've only seen curtains and Venetian blinds."

"Wretched girl!" The older woman shook a bony finger at Elizabeth. "Will you at least promise me that you will exit William's life and bother him no more?"

Elizabeth shot to her feet, facing her across a narrow gap. "No, I will not. I only promise to make decisions based on what is best for myself and my family."

Mrs. de Bourgh had grown quite red in the face. "I will cut you! I will never speak to you again!"

Elizabeth smiled at her. "Promise?"

The older woman's eyes grew wide with fury as she drew in a breath. Elizabeth didn't linger to discover what additional invective she planned to hurl, ducking around her and retreating hastily into the house. Mrs. de Bourgh's voice followed her. "You ungrateful wretch! Gold digger! I will ruin you and your family!" Elizabeth slammed the back door, shutting out the sound of the woman's imprecations.

Her father was standing in the back hallway, a bemused expression on his face. "So, it went well?"

Elizabeth gave him a small smile. "I think we're off her Christmas card list."

Her father chuckled as he ambled away.

***

It was ridiculously difficult for the president to go anywhere given logistics, scheduling, security, transportation, traffic disruption, and Secret Service protocols. It was almost impossible for the president to go anywhere *secretly*. Yet they appeared to have pulled it off.

Nobody expected the president to slip out of the White House at 10 p.m. through the back gate. The press had gone home, and the tourists were in bed. Evidently, no one had noticed the Beast surrounded by the slimmest of motorcades, only five vehicles, roll on the D.C. streets. Fortunately, Washington teemed with motorcades; there was no reason to suspect this one was special—unless someone scrutinized the limo closely.

Darcy prayed this gambit would be successful. It had been difficult enough to arrange the rendezvous with Elizabeth. He'd left three messages on her voicemail before she'd even returned his call—with many apologies. Unfortunately, they hadn't spoken in person. An unexpected crisis with NATO funding had tied up all of Darcy's time, and Bing had ultimately made most of the arrangements.

Darcy, Bing, Fitz, and the head of the presidential Secret Service detail had spent many hours selecting a location secure enough and private enough for the meeting. Secure not only from would-be assassins but also from the media. Kinski had asked more than once why Elizabeth couldn't come to the White House, and Bing had reiterated all the public relations dangers if the media discovered it.

Finally, they agreed on Fitz's condo. His building had an underground parking garage, and its location overlooking Rock Creek Park meant it was somewhat sheltered from prying eyes. The Secret

Service's planning had been tight; nevertheless, Darcy breathed a sigh of relief when he arrived at Fitz's place undiscovered.

The elevator opened onto the foyer—Fitz owned the whole floor—and his cousin immediately opened the door to admit him. Despite his nerves, Darcy remembered to compliment Fitz on the apartment, which he had never seen, and thank him. It had a beautiful view of the park illuminated in the moonlight, with the twinkling lights of the city in the distance. The furnishings were minimalist and modern—sleek, efficient, calming—although nothing about them screamed "romantic rendezvous."

Darcy told himself that was appropriate. *We'll have a calm, rational discussion. Too much romantic ambiance would be distracting, wouldn't it?*

If only there were some candles I could light.

Fitz clasped Darcy briefly on the shoulder and gave him an encouraging smile before leaving. The resulting sense of privacy was completely illusory. The Secret Service had reluctantly agreed to leave Darcy alone inside the condo, but there were agents stationed in the elevator lobby, the building's entrances, and in the units above and below Fitz's. Goodness knows what they'd said to Fitz's neighbors as an incentive to vacate. At least the conversation would be private.

Darcy mixed himself a gin and tonic at the bar. Drank it. Mixed another. Drank half of it before he worried about becoming too tipsy and poured the rest down the sink. When he noticed his hands were shaking, he made himself another.

Perched on Fitz's ultra-contemporary cream-colored sofa, Darcy tried to quiet the flock of butterflies invading his stomach. He stood to stretch his legs. Admired the view again. Sat on the sofa. Reviewed what he planned to say. Said a silent prayer that he would get the response he wanted. Rinse. Repeat.

The Secret Service agent in charge of collecting Elizabeth had warned Darcy that the process of getting her secretly and securely into the building might take time. But Darcy was unaccustomed to free time. Every minute was scheduled with decisions and documents and briefing books he needed to read. A few unoccupied minutes just felt odd and wrong. The president never had to wait; other people waited for him.

Finally, the door opened, and Elizabeth edged through, closing it behind her. She hovered near the entrance, her mouth curved in a fragile smile.

It took Darcy's breath away. He had forgotten her effect on him.

Her light blue dress somehow made her eyes even greener, and although the sandals had a low heel, they somehow rendered her legs impossibly long. A sweater was loosely draped over her shoulders to ward off the late-night September chill, but as they stared at each other, it slipped from her body and puddled on the floor. She did not pick it up.

What a relief to see her whole and in the flesh. Weeks of anxiety fell away in an instant. However, Darcy noticed fresh signs of strain. She had lost weight, her cheeks were hollowed out, and there were dark circles under her eyes. No doubt she didn't sleep well with the paparazzi camped outside her building. Guilt gnawed his stomach. No other man in the United States would have made her endure that media circus. Still, he was pathetically grateful she had chosen him and selfishly hopeful she would want to continue.

"Will," she whispered, still not moving.

"Elizabeth." He crossed the room in three strides. All his carefully chosen and rehearsed words had melted out of his brain. He had only one mission: getting his arms around her as quickly as possible.

He was kissing her without having made the conscious decision to do so. But it was impossible *not* to kiss her. What he had intended to be a quick peck turned into a gloriously prolonged duel of tongues and lips in which both were the winners. She tasted of chocolate and white wine and smelled like…happiness…home…all the things his life was lacking.

When they finally separated, they were both panting. The iron bands around Darcy's chest had eased, and he could breathe freely for the first time in weeks. *How did I breathe at all while we were apart?*

"Elizabeth, it's—God, it's good to see you…I-I don't have the words to express…."

She blinked rapidly, a suspicious sheen in her eyes. "I know. I don't either."

He pulled her close to his body, where she fit perfectly. "I'm sorry I needed to sound so…businesslike in my voicemails. We don't know how secure your phone is. I hope you didn't mind talking to Bing."

Her head rested on his chest, a warm weight. "Of course not. Bing did a great job making the arrangements," she assured him. "He mostly coordinated with Jane, actually. I think she enjoyed talking to him once she overcame the shock of the initial call." Darcy could practically hear the smile in her voice.

"Bing said he asked her out to dinner."

"Yes. Jane was happy. Maybe they can work out their differences."

But Darcy didn't want to discuss Jane and Bing. He slid his hand down her arm and into her palm, intertwining their fingers. "Thank you for agreeing to meet me—especially after I threw you out of my house and neglected to call you."

When she didn't respond, Darcy drew back to get a glimpse of her face, but her eyes were downcast. "That...um..." She swallowed hard. "That hurt...a lot."

The bands tightened around his chest again. "I'm so, so...sorry." His voice was husky with emotion. "Hilliard was apoplectic...and then with the allegations of coercion...."

She sighed heavily. "I understand. With the things Lydia said...and now it looks like there will be hearings....Of course, you don't want to be associated with me..."

What?

He placed his hands on both of her shoulders, waiting until she glanced up at him. "Elizabeth, I do not hold you responsible for something your sister did. She's just a pawn in Wickham's twisted vendetta against me."

"But she wouldn't have been a useful pawn if you and I hadn't—" Her voice broke off. She swallowed and continued. "If I hadn't told her just enough to give them a weapon against you."

Darcy caught and held her eyes. "If it hadn't been that, Wickham would have found something else to use against me. I can't express how sorry I am that my relationship with your family brought Wickham into your orbit. If it weren't for me, he never would have learned of Lydia's existence."

Elizabeth's lips twisted. "They're living together now."

Shit. Darcy closed his eyes briefly. "I'm so sorry."

Elizabeth shrugged. "She never did have the best judgment."

"I'm still sorry." Darcy smoothed back hair from her eyes.

"You don't blame me for this mess?"

"Of course not. Although I wish to hell it hadn't ended like that, I wouldn't have traded that night for anything."

She stared at him for a moment. "Wow."

He gave a little chuckle. "Do you think chemistry like this happens to me all the time? That was the best night of my life."

She peered up at him through her lashes. "The best night of your—really?"

Inching closer, he took her hand, kissing her fingertips. "Really. It was spectacular and lovely, and I can't wait to do it again."

Her eyes fell to the floor, and she shook her head. "Will…"

He needed to be sitting down for this. Grasping her hand, he led Elizabeth to the sofa.

But once they were seated side by side, rational thoughts dribbled out of his mind, and resolve flew out the window. Misgivings were forgotten. Reservations melted away. All supplanted by the overwhelming need to touch her. It was bliss. She nestled against him, relaxing into his touch as he stroked her hair, her shoulder, her neck. Each touch reassured him that she was real, and her presence wasn't a dream.

Her hand traced his knee, his bicep with feathery, soft touches. Tantalizing feelings teased his senses, prompting a desire for more…more. A shudder ran up his spine, and goosebumps rose all over his skin. Her touch stimulated every nerve in his body so that every part of him was coming alive.

Unable to bear more teasing, he covered her mouth with his and pressed her into the sofa. Her body was warm and pliable beneath his as her lips parted. He was drowning in her taste, her scent, every sensation from his tongue…his fingers…every inch of skin pressed against her. She moaned, exciting him even further. His hands reached around, tugging at the zipper on the back of her dress.

Elizabeth sat up, pushing him back. His hands reached out, but only caught empty air. "Will, we can't—w-we need to talk." Every line of her body had stiffened; her hands shook as if they were suddenly very cold.

Darcy righted himself, gripping the sofa cushions to avoid reaching for her. "I can't apologize enough for the cameras, the reporters, everything. That's why I avoided dat—hooking up in office."

Her lips pinched together. "Was it just a hook up for you?"

"God, no!" She couldn't believe that. "I-I—If I weren't the president, we'd be on our tenth date by now." He hesitated. "At least as far as I'm concerned."

"Yeah, I'd like that," she said softly, staring down at her hands folded in her lap.

"Unfortunately, I am the president." He laughed ruefully. "I had resolved not to date during my presidency; it's just too messy. But then I met you, and you made me want to break all my rules."

Her body curved toward his. "That may be the sweetest thing anyone has ever said to me."

The sweep of her neck was so soft...so tempting.... "I've broken so many of my rules since I met you..." He nuzzled her neck, inhaling the sweet fragrance of her skin.

"Will..." she breathed.

He pressed her against the back of the sofa for another kiss.

Putting her hands between them, she shook her head sadly. "You need to sit over there." She gestured to the other end of the sofa and gave him a little push. "Every time you come near me, my brain starts screaming 'Kiss Will, touch Will,' and my higher reasoning shuts off."

"I have problems with incoherency when I'm with you, too." He slid to the end of the sofa. At that moment he would have gladly traded the presidency and all its privileges to be Joe Smith, accountant.

Taking a deep breath, he dug around for his higher brain functions and the coherent words he planned to say. He cleared his throat. "I greatly appreciate your statement through Lucas and Lucas. It was well written and thoroughly supported my account."

Elizabeth sighed. "Lot of good it did. I thought it might derail the movement toward hearings and help my family get that contract back."

Darcy pressed his lips together. Hilliard and Bing had not been very successful in their efforts to forestall the inquiry. Wickham and other political enemies had too much to gain by dragging Darcy's name through the mud. "That might have been too much to expect."

"At least the State Department cleared the Red Cross grant, so I'm back at work," she said.

"Thank God," he said fervently.

"But still, everyone just seems to think I'm coerced, lying, or brainwashed—as if it's not possible that I'm genuinely attached to you." She smiled sourly.

He leaned closer, drinking in her faint lavender scent. "Are you?"

She was breathing rapidly. "Am I what?"

"Genuinely attached to me?"

"Oh yes."

That called for another kiss. The distance between them was crossed in an eyeblink. After a long silence, he pulled away, giving her a tentative smile. "I heard what you said to my aunt."

She grinned. "That's not the kind of sweet nothing I expected you to whisper in my ear."

Darcy laughed. "She called and gave me an earful about what you said. The conversation had the opposite of its intended effect. It gave me hope that I hadn't lost you altogether."

"I'm not lost, b—"

He didn't allow her to finish. "Thank God!" He clasped both of her hands in his, realizing what she needed to hear. "Elizabeth, I have to tell you something." Her eyes, dark, mossy green, watched him somberly. "I think...no, I know...I'm in love with you."

She swallowed, looking down at her hands. For a moment Darcy feared she was about to cry. "Will, oh God...I-I love you, too." Her expression was unreadable. It certainly wasn't happiness at their mutual declaration.

He would simply have to change her mind. His hands squeezed hers gently. "Then I want to pursue this and see where it goes. You know, date. Go out. Whatever the kids are calling it these days." He pulled her into his arms. "I don't ever want to let you go again."

She frowned. "How is that even possible?"

"Well, my dating options are limited, but we can still order out for pizza and watch a movie on the couch. Or did you know the White House has its own bowling alley? Complete with shoes."

She was silent, staring into space. The ticking of a clock behind them was overly loud in the quiet of the condo.

His palms grew sweaty. What if she wasn't willing to make the sacrifices? "I realize I'm asking a lot," he said finally. "The reporters will never leave you alone...You'd have to surrender a lot of privacy. But I can make sure you have security."

She still wouldn't look at him. Darcy's heart pounded against his ribs. *She can't say no. Please, don't say no.*

"I'm not...I can deal with the media." She swallowed. "It's...your poll numbers."

Okay, those words just didn't make sense. "What?"

"You've seen it. Since this whole thing broke, your poll numbers have taken a nosedive. The media's been questioning your honesty.

Congressmen are going on television and implying that you're immoral. And your approval ratings have plummeted."

"I don't care," Darcy said. "The only person whose opinion counts is yours."

She ran her fingertips along his cheek. "That's sweet...and totally unrealistic. You have a tough vote coming up in Congress over the renewable energy and environment bill. You need bipartisan support, or it won't go anywhere—"

Darcy shook his head. "I don't need anything—"

"Will." Her eyes were dark and solemn. "That bill is so much bigger than you and me. It's about the future of the United States—the future of the world. If we're dating, it will pull everyone's attention from what's important and fuel more speculation. Maybe prompt a congressional investigation."

"There's nothing for them to find," Darcy said sharply.

"That won't stop them. The congressmen who oppose the bill will use the allegations of coercion to kill it. You can't afford to be weakened by a scandal. If we date, it'll keep the whole thing in everyone's mind; if we don't, it might blow over." He thrust his chin out stubbornly, and she sighed. "You need all your political capital to get the American people behind your initiatives."

The future he had envisioned was disintegrating like a sandcastle in the surf. He closed his eyes as though that could shut out reality. "Yeah, okay, things are bad now, but it'll settle down."

"Do you really think it'll settle down if I'm visiting the White House regularly for sleepovers, reminding everyone how you 'took advantage' of me?" she asked incredulously. "If I'm around it'll keep the whole thing in the forefront of everyone's mind. It'll be a huge distraction from your agenda."

"Surely there's a way to—"

She shook her head. "I can go on every news show and talk until I'm blue in the face about not being coerced, but your opponents can too easily use the scandal to demonize you."

Darcy didn't care that her arguments were almost identical to Hilliard's. "But—"

"Dating me lowers your approval ratings nearly twenty points," she said softly.

Darcy cursed under his breath. Bing must have told her the results of the poll they had secretly commissioned. "Bing has enough trouble with his own love life; he should stay out of mine."

"He's not worried about your love life," Elizabeth said. "He's worried about your political life—which he should be. You need to concentrate all your energy on repairing the damage that Lydia and George created. And so should I." He opened his mouth to object, but she kept speaking. "I know you don't hold me responsible, but I want to ameliorate the damage my family caused."

He scowled but could not meet her eyes.

"There's damage," she continued doggedly. "Otherwise this rendezvous wouldn't have required so much cloak and dagger. If I'm wrong, go ahead and tell me."

For a moment Darcy couldn't choke out anything past the lump in his throat. "I don't care," he finally said through gritted teeth.

"I do! I believe in your presidency and the things you want to accomplish." Elizabeth waved her hands around in her enthusiasm. "I know you can make this country a better place. It's not just the environmental bill. It's also the refugee program and improving foreign relations—and a hundred other things. I don't want you to be a one-term president; you have too much to do."

Darcy closed his eyes and tipped his head against the back of the sofa. "I believe you're exaggerating the effect that our relationship would have on my presidency."

"Maybe." Elizabeth bit off her words. "But can you afford to take the chance?"

Darcy couldn't help picturing the thousands of people who had helped to get him elected. Who believed in him. The millions of voters who were counting on him to address the problems he had pledged to fix. The hundreds of government workers who had uprooted their jobs and brought their families to Washington to help Darcy build a better tomorrow. If you put them on one side of the scale and Elizabeth on the other, it was no contest. But why did he have to sacrifice *her*? He'd gladly give up something else. An arm or a leg. Not Elizabeth.

Turning toward her, he smoothed her hair away from her face. "Maybe in a few months this will all have died down and—"

"And we can convince them that I actually love you and that you're not forcing me to do your evil bidding?" Her lips trembled. "How likely do you think that is? Scandals like this never die. As long as I'm around, it'll always prompt rumors and innuendo that you have some hold over me. They're always suggesting I'm secretly visiting the White House. That we had a clandestine wedding. That I'm pregnant. It'll never stop."

A tear rolled down her cheek. "Which is why"—she took a deep breath as if steeling herself—"I accepted a two-year assignment with the Red Cross in Indonesia."

A powerful force sucked all the oxygen from Darcy's lungs. The tiniest inhale caused a stabbing pain in his chest. *No. No. No...*

Now he could identify that look in her eyes. It was goodbye.

He gaped at her, not wanting to believe the truth in her words. "No!" She nodded slowly, sadly. "No. You can't!"

"I thought you were finished with telling me what to do," she teased gently.

Something inside his chest cracked in two. Nothing else could explain the pain. Glancing down at his shirt, he expected to see blood seeping through the front, but there was nothing. "Don't do this..."

She managed a tremulous smile that quickly disappeared. "It's a great opportunity. I'll be helping people..." Evidently alarmed by what she saw in his face, she murmured, "Maybe we can be together after you leave office."

"In six and half years?" He laughed bitterly. "If you're not married to someone else then?" He pushed himself off the sofa and stalked to the big picture window. The bright twinkling lights of Washington D.C. mocked him. "God damn it!" He slammed his fist against the window, which vibrated in response.

Why couldn't I have met her before I ran for office? Despite his initial reservations he knew she'd make an excellent First Lady. Pedigree was nothing compared to her compassion, her intelligence, the light she brought to his life. *If the electorate had been presented with her as my wife, they would have loved her.*

A hand skimmed down his back. Whirling around, Darcy pulled her into his arms, hugging her as if he would never let her go. If only he *could* hold her forever. The front of his shirt grew damp with her tears.

He closed his eyes. All his inner clamoring ceased. *God damn it! She's right.*

He hated that she was right. Hated that she was more aware of his duty than he was. Hated that she was the first one ready to make the sacrifice. But he owed the country his best. He had to clean up his predecessor's messes and restore confidence—and he couldn't do that if he put himself and his needs first.

His shoulders slumped. "All right," he whispered in her ear. Elizabeth emitted a little sob. "But I'm coming after you in six years. Husband or no husband." This elicited a little laugh.

Drawing back, he peered at her tear-stained face, still the most beautiful sight he had ever seen, and admitted to himself that this was goodbye. He touched a finger to her lips. The last time he would ever do so.

He peeked at the clock over her shoulder. "It's eleven thirty, and I don't want to send you home just yet." Fitz had told Darcy the condo was his for the night. Barring a national crisis, nobody would disturb them. A new song started playing over the stereo system, something slow and full of longing. "We have tonight."

She gazed up at him, sorrow and love in her eyes. "You want me to stay?"

"We have tonight," he repeated. "I don't want to waste it. Will you dance with me?"

She gave him a tiny smile. "Of course."

Chapter Eighteen

Darcy poured some brandy into the crystal glass. More than he should, but he didn't care. He set the stopper back in the decanter with a clink. The television was already on. Usually he didn't get to the Residence until late into the night, but today he'd called it an early day. He couldn't stand the thought of watching the press conference in the Oval Office with all his staff making surreptitious glances at him. Better to be alone.

The front door opened and closed. Who was that? There weren't many with a key to the Residence. Fitz was traveling, and Bing was doing damage control in the West Wing.

"Will?" Georgiana's figure appeared in the doorway to the Treaty Room.

He stood and hurried to give her a hug. "Why are you here? Aren't you supposed to be in school?"

She bit her lip. "Fitz called and said you might need some company, so I flew down this morning." Her gaze flicked over the brandy glass in his hand. "He wouldn't say why."

Darcy nodded slowly; his head felt ten pounds heavier than usual. Being alone suddenly didn't seem so appealing. "Thanks for coming." He and Georgiana had a different relationship than many siblings. Their parents' untimely death had required Darcy to usher Georgiana into adulthood; but it had also forced his sister to grow up quickly, and she had begun mothering him when she was in high school. Darcy grumbled about it, but secretly loved to know that someone was watching out for him.

He gestured her to the room's other leather armchair. "I was just sitting down to watch Hilliard's press briefing."

She sat, a bemused expression on her face.

"It'll explain everything." *So I won't have to.* He sipped his brandy and fidgeted with a paperclip as the briefing started, and Hilliard answered a series of policy questions. What was the White House's reaction to the latest election in Italy? Did the president plan to do anything about the famine in Central Africa? Was the administration concerned about the most recent unemployment report?

Darcy wasn't even aware of tuning it out, or that he was imagining fine eyes and a dark tumble of curls, until a question jarred him into awareness.

It was a standard question the media asked at every recent briefing. "What is the nature of the president's relationship with Ms. Elizabeth Bennet?" The question came from Ron Rodriguez, a reporter from *The Washington Post*.

Hilliard had been giving a curt "no comment" in response to the question for weeks. Today was the day it would change.

Georgiana's eyes darted to Darcy. He clutched the arm of the chair. Hilliard's expression didn't change except for a tightening around the mouth. "The president and Ms. Bennet have discontinued their relationship," he said matter-of-factly.

Georgiana gasped.

Darcy knew what Hilliard would say; still, the words cut through him like a sword stroke. He'd always harbored the impossible hope that some twist of fate would somehow intervene, but the public announcement was like a shovelful of dirt on the coffin.

"That can't be true!" Georgiana's eyes begged him.

Onscreen, the press room broke into a frenzy as reporters disregarded protocol and called out questions, each trying to be louder than the next. Hilliard called on Cara Schultz from ZNN. "When did they break off their relationship? And was it because of the accusations of coercion?"

The press secretary took a deep breath. "The reasons for the breakup, like the relationship itself, are private. The president steadfastly denies any allegations of coercion, as has Ms. Bennet."

Another reporter: "Will the president continue to socialize with Elizabeth Bennet?"

"Ms. Bennet has accepted an overseas assignment with the Red Cross in Indonesia. In fact, she just landed in Jakarta an hour ago." That was why they'd waited nearly two weeks for the briefing. Not many news organizations would bother to send reporters halfway around the world. At least Elizabeth would get some peace. "However, the president and Ms. Bennet remain friends," Hilliard added.

Darcy averted his eyes from his sister's woebegone expression. "It was her decision, Georgie," he said.

Other reporters started shouting out questions, some of them frankly intrusive. Since he had been authorized to share very little information, Hilliard repeated "no comment" many times. Finally, he said firmly, "I will not answer any more questions on this topic." As the briefing moved on to other subjects, Darcy muted the television.

"Why?" Georgiana's brows knitted together. "You said she was the best thing that ever happened to you."

Darcy stared down into his empty glass. "She doesn't want me, Georgie. She doesn't want a relationship with me."

"Was it all the press scrutiny?"

"It's not that simple," Darcy muttered. "There were a lot of reasons. She thought the relationship was hurting my presidency."

Georgiana's expression was heart-wrenching. "So she still loves you?"

Answering that question would break him. He scrubbed his face with both hands. "Hell, I don't know that I have what it takes to make a long-term relationship work." During the silence that followed, Georgiana regarded him with a sympathetic tilt to her head.

Onscreen, Hilliard was still talking. Darcy hated the sight of him. With a quick jab on the remote, he turned the television off and stared at the black screen without seeing it.

It's not like I have the time to devote to a real relationship. Now nothing would distract him from his legislative priorities. Nothing to focus on except his presidency. It would be business as usual.

It was a good development. An improvement.

It was.

***

"Will? Will!"

Darcy's head snapped toward Bing. Had his attention drifted off *again*? How long this time?

"Peter asked your opinion on the Republicans' proposed changes to the bill." Darcy hated that too-patient tone, the one that sounded like Bing was coaxing a wild animal into its cage with soft words and a piece of meat. Darcy had been hearing it more and more.

He wanted to rub the bleariness from his eyes, but he couldn't look like he'd been sleeping. In fact, he'd been daydreaming—imagining a future with Elizabeth in six years. If she'd still talk to him then. If she wasn't married to someone else. It had been more than five months since he'd seen her in Fitz's apartment. It seemed like an eternity.

Bing continued to date Jane; Darcy was happy for his friend and only a little jealous. Well, maybe more than a little. Although Bing received some media scrutiny, he didn't realize what a gift his comparative lack of fame was.

Bing never mentioned anything he learned about Elizabeth from Jane, and Darcy never asked. An old college friend of Darcy's at the Red Cross gave him occasional updates on Elizabeth's progress in Indonesia, which wasn't terribly satisfying. The reports focused on the program she was running and didn't provide crucial information like whether she was dating someone. The thought made every muscle in his body tense.

With an effort of will, Darcy drew his attention back to the meeting. At least this one was in the small Residence meeting room with senior staff rather than an official West Wing meeting with junior staffers who were prone to gossiping. Darcy took a sip from his glass, grateful he had switched from wine at dinner to scotch. It probably contributed to his tendency to lose focus, but Darcy needed it.

"I'm sorry." He straightened up in his chair, widening his eyes: the picture of alertness. "Cynthia, could you read the changes off again?"

"Of course, Mr. President."

As Cynthia read, Darcy tried to focus his attention on the admittedly dry material. It was important, worthy of his concentration, but lately his thoughts were like heavy, sticky mud. They moved slowly and resisted changing direction. He was so, so damn tired all the time. When this odd fatigue had first crept over him around four months ago, Darcy had thought he was getting sick, but no other symptoms had materialized. Maybe it was the lack of sleep, but that usually didn't faze him. Was there a difference because this bout of sleeplessness was brought on by insomnia rather than too much work?

Cynthia had fallen quiet.

"Thank you," Darcy said automatically, mentally kicking himself when he realized he couldn't remember what she said. These changes were important; accepting some of the Republican amendments could help them gain the votes they needed to pass the renewable energy bill.

Bing watched him with a stony stare. Yeah, he knew Darcy's mind had been otherwise occupied.

"What do you think, Mr. President?" Peter regarded him expectantly.

Darcy had been in this position before and knew how to cover for his ignorance. "I'm not sure." He turned to his director of legislative affairs. "Sarah, what's your opinion?"

As Sarah launched into a complicated discussion of the advantages and disadvantages of the Republicans' revisions, Darcy attempted to follow her argument. But he was well aware of the weight of Bing's gaze: narrowed eyes, thinned lips. Yeah, he wasn't fooling Bing.

That was the problem with hiring old friends, Darcy thought ruefully. Damn. He would hear about it later.

***

Bing slammed a pile of papers on the end of Darcy's desk, startling him. "What the hell, Bing?" Darcy glared. Sometimes the best defense was a good offense.

"What the hell were *you* doing in the meeting today?" Bing demanded as he stalked to the other side of the Oval Office.

"Um…making decisions?"

Bing scoffed as he slid into a chair opposite the desk. "You were out to lunch!"

"Please! Do you know how many meetings I go to every day?" Darcy said with an irritation he didn't quite feel. "Forgive me if I lose focus in one of them!"

Bing pointed an accusing finger. "It isn't *one*, and you know it. You're spacing out during most of them, and it's getting worse."

For God's sake! It wasn't that bad. Darcy took a deep breath. "I haven't been sleeping well. I guess I need more coffee in the morning."

Bing pinched the bridge of his nose, squeezing his eyes closed. "Another cuppa isn't going to make a difference, Darcy! You've seen the approval ratings."

Yeah, he had, but he'd been trying not to think about them. "We'll bounce back."

"Not without a major legislative success we won't."

"The renewable energy bill—"

Bing interrupted. "Is toast unless we can get more legislators on board, and we haven't."

Darcy surged to his feet. "I've been trying! I've been talking to them." If only his voice didn't shake so much…

Bing shook his head wearily. "They won't listen until these congressional hearings are over."

"There's not much I can do about that," Darcy said. "There's this thing called separation of powers that prevents me from interfering in the legislative—"

"Bullshit." The word rumbled out of Bing. Darcy's eyebrows rose; his friend rarely used foul language. "You know there's no evidence. They can't find anything that shows you had any contact with anyone at the USDA about that contract. They've hauled everyone from Mr. Bennet to the Secretary of Agriculture in front of the committee, and the story is the same."

Darcy regarded Bing sardonically. "Yes, thank you. *I* know I didn't do anything wrong. You don't need to remind me." Bing rolled his eyes, stoking Darcy's anger. "You and I both know they're just dragging the hearings out so they can do the maximum political damage. They're aware there's no evidence."

Bing folded his arms over his chest. "So what are you going to do about it?" When Darcy didn't respond, Bing flung his arms up in the air. "Five months ago, you would have been racing around this office figuring out what kind of leverage we could use on those guys and how we could get the media on board with the story of what actually happened. You'd be organizing the staff, inspiring them. Instead you're just sitting there like—like a lump of cold mashed potatoes."

Darcy blinked. "Mashed potatoes?"

"Don't laugh. It was the best analogy I could think of on the spur of the moment."

Slumping down into his desk chair, Darcy let his head sink to his chest. Maybe there were ways he could have put pressure on some legislators to finish the damn hearings. He'd been avoiding the whole subject, which inevitably brought back reminders of Elizabeth and how she was no longer on this continent. Of course, she was never far from his thoughts anyway.

"A lot of the Republicans will listen to reason, particularly since they want to work with you on the infrastructure plan. Their biggest problem is Wickham, and we can—"

"Actually, I received some news today," Darcy said, searching through the piles on his desk for a specific folder. "A few weeks ago, the SEC found some irregularities in the venture capital firm Wickham and his uncle run. They pursued an investigation." Darcy found the right folder and showed it to Bing. "They found evidence of insider trading in seventeen deals Wickham's firm made."

Bing rubbed his hands together gleefully. "Awesome! When are they going to nail the guy and send him to prison?"

"They're about to."

"Why aren't you thrilled about this?" Bing frowned at Darcy.

"I'm worried about Lydia Bennet. She's living with Wickham. When the SEC raids his New York condo, she'll get caught up in the whole thing, maybe even arrested. She probably doesn't even know what insider trading is."

Bing scratched the back of his neck. "Forgive me, but isn't this the woman who accused you—on television—of kidnapping her sister?"

Darcy stared down at the damning papers. "Yeah, but she's a kid. I don't even think she's twenty yet. Wickham used her. You know how he is."

"You're too nice."

Darcy couldn't meet Bing's eyes. "It would kill her."

"Lydia?" Bing raised an eyebrow.

"Elizabeth. She...and her family have suffered enough because of me."

Bing shook his head and then blew out a breath. "Okay, let me talk to Jane." He held out a hand to forestall Darcy's objection. "I won't say anything about the SEC, obviously. But maybe the family can get Lydia to come home without making her suspicious."

Darcy considered for a minute. "Okay. She's probably sick of Wickham by now. It might not take much of an incentive to get her to leave."

Bing grimaced in agreement.

"Good." Darcy nodded briskly. I'll have Peter set up calls with McCray and Ramirez. They must be unhappy about the hearings and searching for a way out."

Bing smiled as he stood. "That's the Darcy I'd like to see more often."

Darcy sat up straighter in his chair. "I try...but it's hard."

Bing pivoted to leave the room but turned back before he reached the door. "I think you should call her."

"Lydia?" Darcy said, deliberately misunderstanding.

Bing's eyes narrowed. "You know who I mean."

"Need I remind you that she's in Indonesia?"

"They have phone service there."

Darcy gave his friend a cold look. "Not all of my problems have a ready solution. She made her decision, and it was probably the right one for her. I'm not going to second-guess her."

Bing shook his head sharply. "I don't think Elizabeth knows what's best any more than you do." Before Darcy could reply, Bing had exited the room, closing the door smartly behind him.

***

"So then Lydia decided she did want the hat after all, and she tried to grab it. Of course, Kitty ran away," Jane said with a tolerant smile on her face. "Around and around the kitchen, living room, dining room. All the time Kitty is shrieking, 'She'll ruin it! She'll ruin it for sure, Mom! Someone stop her!'"

Jane set down her tea cup, laughing a bit self-consciously. Elizabeth managed some convincing chuckles and then took a sip of tea to cover her absent enthusiasm.

Of course, she was pleased that Lydia had returned home. For five months, the youngest Bennet had refused all pleas from the family. Convinced that George Wickham was in love with her, she had dropped out of school and lived in his New York condo, no doubt expecting to become a kept woman.

However, it became apparent that most, if not all, of George's wealth was illusory. Under the pretext of inviting Lydia to their father's birthday party, Jane, Kitty, and their mother had gotten on the phone to declare their inability to live a Lydia-free life any longer. Lydia had agreed to return "for their sake," but once she'd slunk back to their parents' house, she'd proclaimed herself to be very ill-used and deceived by her one-time boyfriend. Hearing the saga long distance through emails from Jane, Elizabeth had breathed a huge sigh of relief. Their mother had supplied all the pampering Lydia believed to be her right, which soon renewed her previous state of extreme shallowness.

The timing had proved fortuitous; two days later it was revealed that George and his uncle were under investigation by the SEC for insider trading and other shady business practices. Thankfully Lydia had departed before the SEC raided George's condo and carried away boxes of papers.

The congressional investigation into the USDA contract, which had already been faltering due to lack of evidence, had been dealt an additional blow by the arrest of a principal committee member. Although the hearings had not been formally disbanded, On-a-Stick's lawyer seemed confident that it was only a matter of time before the contract was restored.

Elizabeth had welcomed the news, not only because she wouldn't be forced to testify but also because Will's approval numbers were finally rising.

However, not all voters' opinions of him had improved; many still believed he had coerced Elizabeth despite her repeated denials. He still walked on thin ice politically, and it was by no means certain he would win the passage of his renewable energy bill. She hated that she was still being used as a weapon against him; however, there was no way she could help except to stay far away from him.

Nobody except her family and Charlotte had known she would arrive home for a month-long vacation, and Elizabeth planned to keep a low profile. The media had mostly left her alone in Indonesia, and she was happy to avoid their scrutiny.

Elizabeth had seen Lydia only once for an awkward dinner at their parents' house. Although she loved her sister, she still found it difficult to forgive her. It had been easier to avoid Lydia by staying at Jane's apartment during her visit.

Lifting her eyes from her tea cup, she met Jane's knowing look. "Lydia does regret her actions, you know," Jane said.

Elizabeth snorted. "She regrets that George Wickham didn't turn out to be the Prince Charming she expected, not the damage she did to my life or Will's."

Jane leaned forward, regarding Elizabeth earnestly from across the coffee table. "I do think that deep down she's sorry."

Elizabeth sighed. "Maybe. But she never apologized to me or said anything to indicate regret."

"Yeah, she's infuriating," Jane conceded.

Elizabeth took another sip of her tea, wishing it was late enough that she could retire for the night, but they hadn't even had dinner yet.

"Are you happy in Indonesia?" Jane asked suddenly.

Elizabeth rolled her eyes. Jane had asked this question in one way or another every day over the past week. "The work I'm doing is very valuable," Elizabeth answered carefully.

Jane sighed. "You always say that."

Elizabeth shrugged. "It's true."

"You don't look happy." This was the most direct observation Jane had made so far.

Elizabeth ran a hand through her hair. "What do you want me to say? It's only been about six months, Jane. I miss him, but I'm fine." Her words weren't even convincing to her own ears. "I don't know if I'll sign up for another overseas assignment when my two years are finished. It's—maybe I'm getting too old for constant travel."

Jane gave her a level look. "There's this guy at work who's cute and single—"

Elizabeth held up a hand. "Gah! No. I am so not ready for that."

"Didn't think so." Jane's smile was smug.

Elizabeth gave her sister a poisonous glare. They both knew she was hanging on by a thread, but it was what she needed to do. Why did Jane need to rub it in? Before Elizabeth could say something cutting, Jane's phone chirped. She pulled it out to scrutinize a text. "Oh, Bing's in the area and wants to stop by." Instantly Jane began tapping back a message.

"Great," Elizabeth said with absolutely no inflection. The one good result of her disastrous near love affair with the president had been that Jane and Bing had come into contact again, talked about their misunderstanding, and decided to try dating once more. Elizabeth was not surprised that they had already reached the drop-by-your-apartment stage. If any couple was meant to be, it was Jane and Bing. And Elizabeth was happy for her sister.

She was.

But she was just as happy to avoid Bing. Besides Jane, they only had one thing in common, and Elizabeth didn't want to even think about him. "Maybe I should go to a coffee shop or something." Elizabeth stood, collecting her tea cup.

"There's no need for that!" Jane admonished.

"You should have some privacy."

Jane rolled her eyes. "It's not like we'll fall into bed the moment he arrives. You've been AWOL every time he's come over, and I know he wants to see you before you escape back to Indonesia."

"Sure." Elizabeth mustered a bright smile to hide her gritted teeth. Maybe she could keep it short by suddenly remembering she needed to watch her favorite reality show about rich bachelors living on a deserted island and forced to compete for a recording contract. She picked up Jane's cup and fled to the kitchen where she didn't need to guard her expression.

Elizabeth put the floral cups in the sink under the window with the yellow floral curtains while standing on the blue floral rug. Jane had good taste; everything went together beautifully, but the apartment was almost aggressively cheerful. Some days Elizabeth couldn't get outside fast enough.

Her gaze was caught by Jane's small countertop television. Even in Indonesia Elizabeth couldn't leave her television off all the time, but she'd been fairly successful at avoiding images of Will there. How did he manage to be on every screen of every television in Jane's apartment all the time?

Now she couldn't tear her eyes from the sight of him shaking hands with the president of South Korea. They waved as pictures were taken, and then Will escorted the woman and her husband into the White House. Did he have a little gray at the temples? Had he lost some weight? Elizabeth scrutinized the image. His eyes were ringed with dark circles. Damn his staff! Weren't they feeding him and making sure he slept? Wasn't anyone paying attention?

It's not your business, Elizabeth.

Jabbing savagely at the remote, she turned off the television and directed her gaze out the window toward the apartment building across the street. How long would it be until she stopped flinching at the sight of him? It had been almost six months. Maybe she should return to Indonesia early. There she was usually too busy to notice the hollowness in her chest cavity—except in the evening and at night and in the morning. And sometimes the afternoon.

And Jane thinks I might be ready to meet another guy. I have nothing left inside me to give someone new. Her knees were suddenly weak; Elizabeth braced herself on the sink, staring out the window to stave off tears. Her mind repeated the mantra from the past six months: *It will get better.* Elizabeth still believed it, but she was beginning to despair about when "better" would arrive.

Out in the living room, the front door opened and closed. Bing. Elizabeth straightened her shoulders and finger-combed her hair, hoping her face wasn't too haggard. She ground her teeth, suddenly angry with herself for letting Jane guilt her into staying.

I should have begged off with an emergency meeting at work or claimed a sudden need to go to Mom and Dad's to feed Mary's parakeet while she's out of town. I could stop on the way there to buy Mary a parakeet. Maybe I can chat with Bing for a minute or two and then fake an attack of gout or sudden-onset deafness.

Peals of laughter and the sounds of kissing emanated from the living room. Maybe an intense round of tonsil hockey would allow Elizabeth to slip out of the apartment unnoticed.

"Lizzy!" Jane called. "Bing's here!"

Or maybe not. Elizabeth took a deep breath. *I can do this. Sit and chat for five minutes and then notice a sudden urgent craving for tapioca pudding from 7-Eleven.*

Somehow she slapped on a smile as she trudged into the living room. Bing's blond surfer looks and easy smile hadn't changed. She offered her hand, but he entrapped her in a hug instead.

"Elizabeth. It's so good to see you."

She merely nodded. *Yes, and if I had my way it would be a long time before I saw you again.* After an awkward pause, they all sat, Bing and Jane side by side on the sofa with their hands comfortably intertwined while Elizabeth took the stiff-backed wooden rocking chair. And then...

Crickets.

Surely there was some innocuous topic of conversation she could initiate, but Elizabeth's mind was blank except for the incessant drumbeat of Will, Will, Will. "Great weather we've been having," she finally blurted out.

Bing glanced at the overcast skies outside the window. "Er, it does make a change from all that sunshine."

Well, that killed two seconds.

Elizabeth wracked her brain. Surely there was another topic that might not lead back to Will. *Say something! Anything!* She opened her mouth, unsure what would emerge. "How do you feel about tapioca pudding and parakeets?"

Jane's eyes widened comically.

"How is your job going?" Bing asked at the same time.

Elizabeth latched onto the subject, pretending she hadn't spoken. "Good. It's good," she said quickly. "I'm doing good work. Making a difference."

"That's good."

Elizabeth nodded. "Yes, it is. It's good." Okay, this was possibly the stupidest conversation in the history of humankind.

Silence stretched between them again. Ugh, so awkward. It was like there was a huge hole in the middle of the living room floor, and yet they were all determined not to talk about it.

There had to be something to discuss besides pudding and parakeets. Elizabeth had stored away some interesting anecdotes about Indonesia, but she couldn't recall any at this moment. "Did you know that Jane got a promotion at work?" Elizabeth said rather desperately.

"I did." Bing squeezed Jane's hand affectionately. "I'm so proud of you." Jane gave him a fond smile that somehow hollowed out Elizabeth's chest even more.

"Well, somebody will need to take charge of the USDA contract once we get it," Jane said modestly.

"I'm sure it'll be soon." Bing's tone suggested he had more to say on the topic. Dangerous territory.

"I hear you two have a hot date this weekend," Elizabeth inserted quickly. Jane had already told her all about it, but she didn't mind hearing about it again.

"Yeah," Bing drawled, relaxing as he put his arm around Jane's shoulders. "I secured a reservation at Le Reynard for Saturday. They say Chef Pierre Bessette is a genius..." He quoted a review about the restaurant, but Elizabeth was only half listening. Her mind was occupied with concocting escape plans.

Bing's soliloquy petered out. Elizabeth wracked her brain for another safe topic. Taking a deep breath, Bing leaned forward, and Elizabeth had the bizarre sensation she was about to be subjected to a sales pitch. "Could you meet with Darcy while you're here?"

I guess we're going to talk about the hole after all.

The mention of his name was akin to a mild electric charge through her body. She bolted upright, noticing at the back of her mind that all her extremities were tingling. "That wouldn't be a good idea."

Bing jumped up from the sofa and started pacing around Jane's sparsely furnished living room. "He doesn't have enough votes for the renewable energy bill."

Her stomach lurched; that was not good news, but how did apply to her? "Non-sequitur much?"

He waved irritably at her as he stalked past the windows. "We've been working on this for almost a year. We're so close, but it's in danger of going down in flames. He could get a couple more votes on board if he just tried harder—if he spent more time working with the staff, inspiring them. But he's...not bringing his A game."

Elizabeth's whole body was hot. "That's not my fault," she bit out.

"No. Of course not." Bing shook his head vigorously. "I..." He rubbed his forehead. "I just thought you might help him get back on track."

The anger abruptly drained out of her body. *Oh.* "I-I can't. Nothing has changed...."

Bing ran both hands through his hair, making it stand on end. "I know, I know. If you started dating him, the press would be all over you again. It's inevitable, but—"

What?

"Wait!" Elizabeth held up a hand. "Do you think I broke it off because of the *press*?" Her voice soared into the upper registers.

"Lizzy, " Jane said in a patient tone usually reserved for someone about to have a breakdown, "you never actually explained why you did it. You just came to my apartment and cried on my shoulder."

Bing blinked at her. "Why else would you have—?"

Didn't anyone understand? Elizabeth was suddenly on her feet. "Being associated with me and the rumors of coercion were hurting his presidency. You know this!" She waved her arm at Bing. "You showed me the secret poll."

Bing put both hands on the mantelpiece as if to steady himself. "Maybe I shouldn't have...." His gaze turned pleading. "But that scandal is over. Congress will drop the investigation soon, and the SEC has indicted Wickham."

Elizabeth rubbed her forehead with the heel of her hand. *He just doesn't understand.* "Bing, I'm still a member of the Bennet family, and Lydia started this whole thing. He could never forgive her."

Bing opened his mouth, closed it, and rubbed his jaw thoughtfully, then opened it again. "Never forgive her?" Bing echoed. "I shouldn't be telling you this, but Will knew Wickham and his uncle were about to be indicted, and he asked if Jane could lure Lydia home before she became caught up in it."

Jane's head jerked back. "That's why you suggested—!"

Bing nodded as he continued, "If the press discovered he'd done that with advance knowledge...it wouldn't look good. But he thought she deserved a chance to escape Wickham's scandal."

Elizabeth fell into the nearest available seat. He had forgiven Lydia. "I...can't believe he did that for her..."

Bing gave her a level look. "He didn't do it for *her*."

It took Elizabeth a moment to grasp his meaning, and then she flushed.

"Can't you at least talk with him?" Bing asked softly. "He's not sleeping well. He doesn't concentrate at all."

Elizabeth closed her eyes, unable to forget the image of Will on television. "Can't you get him to eat more?" The words escaped her mouth before she could stop them.

"I've tried." Bing's hands clenched into fists. "If you talk to him, it might help with that...and other things..."

"You know it's not that easy. I bet you've done polling on whether voters still think he's coerced me." Bing winced. "You have, haven't you?" When Bing said nothing, Elizabeth plowed ahead. "And it probably shows that the majority of voters still think he might have coerced me—even though Congress didn't find any evidence."

Bing sighed. "Yeah. Fifty-two percent. But it's going down."

"And if the press thinks I'm in his life again, that percentage will shoot right back up."

Bing didn't deny it.

"There's must be some way to convince them that you truly love him!" Jane, ever the optimist, exclaimed.

Bing shook his head. "I don't see how. She can be a guest on every talk show in the country, but her own sister claimed the president was forcing her. As long as your family has that contract, people will be suspicious."

"I'm not asking my family to give up that contract. It saved the business," Elizabeth said fiercely.

Bing held up placating hands. "Of course not."

"There must be something you can do!" Jane wailed.

How many times have I said that to myself? "I don't know what, short of visiting every house in America to explain how I really feel."

"Just talk to him." Bing reached out a beseeching hand to Elizabeth.

Damn. It was as if he was offering her the forbidden fruit. She wanted it so badly but knew she couldn't have it.

"Please," Bing said.

Elizabeth was standing again, her eyes searching the room for her purse. There it was by the door. "I can't. I just...can't," she murmured, stumbling toward the door. Grabbing her purse, she yanked the door open with one hand. She paused on the threshold, not looking back at Bing or Jane. "I'm sorry...I'm so sorry."

Elizabeth closed the door quickly so she wouldn't hear their response.

***

For a few seconds after she woke, Elizabeth didn't know where she was. Then it came back to her. Charlotte's sofa. After wandering around D.C. in a daze for several hours, Elizabeth had called Charlotte with a pathetically transparent lie about having fought with Jane. Charlotte hadn't questioned it, merely offering to leave a key at the building's front desk for her.

Fortunately for Elizabeth, Charlotte had spent the night at Bill's. Elizabeth wasn't in the mood to hear moans from Charlotte's bedroom and cries of "That's it, Big Boy! Staple me so hard!"

She rubbed the back of her neck, rotating her head slowly. Elizabeth hadn't had a drop of alcohol, but she still felt hungover. *How was that fair?*

Leveraging her body into an upright position, she stared out the window as pieces of her conversation with Bing replayed themselves in her mind. His words had pinged through her head like errant pinballs all night, preventing her from falling asleep until the wee hours of the morning.

I'm miserable without him. She had finally admitted the truth to herself at around three a.m. One of the few things that made her self-imposed exile bearable was knowing that it was the best thing for Will. But Bing had suggested that Will was miserable without her. Elizabeth swallowed hard as her eyes burned with unshed tears. *You cried over Will last night; how about we try something productive for a change?*

At around four a.m., a nascent plan had begun to coalesce in the back of her mind. But seriously contemplating it provoked sweaty palms and a racing heart. What if she was wrong? What if Bing was wrong? What if Will hated her too much to forgive her?

No. She needed more information before she could decide. Elizabeth stared at her cell phone; the number she'd texted Bing for late last night glowed on the screen, demanding her attention. She wrapped one arm around her knees and tapped the number with the other hand. Closing her eyes, she focused on what she was planning to say.

"Hello?" said a female voice.

"Hi, Georgiana." Elizabeth swallowed past the thickness in her throat. "This is Elizabeth Bennet."

There was a pause. "What do you want?" The tone was cool but not hostile.

Her pulse pounded in her ears like a smith working a forge. "I need to ask you a question…about Will…"

Chapter Nineteen

As he waited at the bottom of the stairs, Fitz bounced on the balls of his feet with impatience. "We don't want to be late for Hilliard," he admonished Darcy when he reached the first step. Darcy scowled at him. He was the president. Everyone else could damn well wait on his schedule.

When Darcy reached the bottom, Fitz tried to set a brisk pace for their walk to the limo. In retaliation, Darcy slowed down, making Fitz grimace in frustration, which gave Darcy a little jolt of satisfaction. *It shouldn't. Instead I should be grateful Fitz has been willing to suffer me these last months.* Darcy knew he'd been a bastard, but at this hour of the morning he couldn't bring himself to care.

Impatience got the best of Fitz. "Darce, we need to—"

"I'm going to be late sometimes," Darcy snapped. "Stuff happens."

Fitz arched a brow. "Wow, someone woke up on the wrong side of the bed."

"It's seven a.m. for fuck's sake!" Darcy growled. "Why the hell do I even need to be out of bed at this ungodly hour?"

"You agreed to the interview."

It was true. Discussing global warming and the need for renewable energy with a ZNN reporter in front of the famous Washington D.C. cherry blossoms had seemed like a no-brainer at the time. But... "That was before I knew it would be at the ass crack of dawn," Darcy grumbled.

"It's the only time the Secret Service could manage the traffic," Fitz reminded him as they walked outside. O'Leary, the head of the morning's Secret Service detail, was standing by the open door to the presidential limo. They both slid in.

"Hilliard and Bing both think the interview can build support for the bill." Fitz's soothing tone irritated Darcy even more.

"Yeah, I know." Darcy waved his hand impatiently. "But I could just as easily do that in the Oval Office, and then we wouldn't need to cordon off half the Tidal Basin—"

"Actually, sir," corrected O'Leary, "it's *all* of the Tidal Basin."

"Is one interview worth causing traffic snarls all over the District?" Darcy asked Fitz as the limo lurched into motion. Darcy fussed with his tie, which had ended up being too long.

Fitz was unapologetic. "Hilliard likes the optics. Talking about spring and global warming in front of a tree burgeoning with cherry blossoms…it's a striking visual. And the bill needs help." As he spoke, Fitz batted away Darcy's hand and deftly undid the knot before retying the tie. Hilliard had insisted on a tie with cherry blossoms on it. Darcy had fussed, although he was forced to concede that it coordinated well with his blue shirt.

"I'm talking about how global warming has hurt the cherry blossoms. Shouldn't we do the interview in front of a dying cherry tree?" Darcy asked in an acid tone.

Fitz's brows drew together. "Jeez. I know you aren't exactly a morning person, but what the hell is your problem?"

Darcy pressed his lips together, averting his gaze to the car window and the sights of D.C. passing by. No way would he reveal the truth about his long, sleepless night. After resisting the urge for months, he had finally surrendered to his desire to Google the latest news about Elizabeth. Not surprisingly, he regretted it.

The first hit had been from a celebrity gossip site: a picture of Elizabeth meeting in some out-of-the-way D.C. coffee shop with an attractive blond guy who'd been identified as Zach Coughlin, an up-and-coming young producer at—coincidentally enough—ZNN. The accompanying caption had speculated that Elizabeth Bennet had finally recovered from her frightful experience with the president's manipulative ways and was now brave enough to start dating once more.

Darcy hadn't even known she was in D.C. But Zach Coughlin knew. Damn him.

The next site was even more explicit in describing how fortunate Elizabeth was to escape Darcy's clutches. Accustomed as he was to aspersions on his character, the implication that he had driven Elizabeth into some other guy's arms had set Darcy seething all night. *I knew this would happen. She's a great catch. It was a stupid hope that she would wait until the end of my term—or two terms. Still, six months didn't seem nearly long enough for her to get over a relationship… Well, it wasn't really a relationship, was it? More like an aborted relationship wanna-be.*

"Darcy?" Fitz watched him closely, his forehead creased with worry. *Shit, how bad do I look?*

"I'm fine." Darcy yanked at the tie. Fitz had tied the knot too tight, and the damn thing was choking him. "Let's just get this over with."

Fitz settled back in his seat, fiddling nervously with his cufflink, but at least he fell silent.

Before long, the limo pulled to a stop in the parking lot of the Jefferson Memorial. The lot was mostly empty except for police vehicles, a ZNN news van, and a few random cars that probably belonged to Hilliard's staff.

As he waited for the Secret Service agent to open the door, Darcy took a moment to recall his talking points about global warming. If he nailed it in one take, he could return to the White House that much sooner. "I hope this doesn't take too long," he grumbled to Fitz.

"I think you'll find it worth your while," Fitz said with a smile. *What the hell did that mean?* Before Darcy could ask, the door opened and he stepped out into the parking lot. Secret Service agents surrounded him as he strolled toward the Memorial.

By now Darcy was accustomed to security swarming around him. D.C. police officers had confined onlookers behind barricades on either side of the Memorial, and the crowds cheered when they saw him. The reaction usually lightened his heart, but today it settled over him like a heavy weight. Everyone expected so much from him. Inevitably he would let some of them down. And some days he just wished they'd leave him alone so he could nap.

Mustering a smile, he waved to the onlookers while the agents hustled him around the Jefferson Memorial and toward the Tidal Basin. The Basin was actually a kind of cove formed by a branch of the Potomac River, but it resembled nothing so much as a manmade lake. Every spring, for a brief period, the cherry trees around the Tidal Basin burst forth in a profusion of blossoms. It was a beautiful sight, which brought massive tourist dollars—and traffic—to D.C. every year.

As Darcy's group marched around the Memorial to the plaza on the other side, the Tidal Basin, in all its glory, burst into view. Even Darcy's spirits lifted at the sight. Nobody could have remained unaffected. The sun was barely up, bathing the whole scene in a warm golden light. The water was placid, with hardly a ripple marring its surface. Every tree around the water's edge was in bloom, a truly breathtaking sight.

Cherry blossoms were a common theme for Washington D.C. souvenirs, but those images always showed the blossoms as pink. They were in fact almost white, with just the palest hint of pink. It was a delicate, almost ethereal, color. Hilliard was right that it would make for good optics.

The press secretary hurried up to Darcy's side. "Good morning, Mr. President. Deena Driscoll will be interviewing you." *Good.* Darcy nodded. A seasoned reporter on science topics, Deena wasn't likely to spring any unexpected questions on him. He'd grown quite weary of replying "no comment" when asked about Elizabeth.

Hilliard continued, "We picked a spot where you'll be framed by the blossoms with the Tidal Basin in the background. Deena will ask the questions we agreed on. It should take about five minutes…" He trailed off, squinting at the Memorial.

"Unless we need another take," Darcy said.

Hilliard licked his lips nervously. "Of course, of course." The nerves didn't make any sense; they were old hands at interviews like this. Well, whatever. The whole thing would soon be over. He sighed. "Fine. Let's do it." He didn't miss the worried glance Hilliard exchanged with Fitz, but he was too weary to care about the reason.

Deena Driscoll, a petite African American woman with a bright smile, stood in front of a tree boasting a profusion of cherry blossoms. Her light pink business suit would blend well with Darcy's tie. Hilliard would be pleased.

Aside from the excited chatter of the crowds, the area was unusually quiet. Normally, traffic zipped along the Independence Avenue bridge, which bisected the far end of the Basin, but today the bridge was deserted. The relative peace was a side effect of the Secret Service's commitment to presidential safety, and Darcy appreciated it.

Here, too, onlookers crowded up against the security barricades on both sides of the plaza. Early morning visitors to the blossoms were certainly getting more than they had expected. Darcy waved to the people on both sides, receiving enthusiastic roars and waves in response.

Darcy took his place next to Deena, who shook his hand as she thanked him for coming. A production assistant hurried up and attached a small mike to Darcy's lapel. The morning was warming up, and Darcy was sweating inside his suit. *It'll soon be over. I can't wait to get back to the Beast and take off my coat.* It was difficult to smile when his only impulses were to fidget and scowl.

The producer, a young blond guy who looked vaguely familiar, counted down, and the camera's green light blinked on, indicating that it was recording. Somehow the police officers managed to quiet the onlookers. Deena positioned her handheld microphone just below her chin. "Mr. President, thank you for joining us on this beautiful spring day." Her smile was wide and genuine, a nice change from many reporters' faux newscaster grins. *It figures she'd be a morning person.*

"It's my pleasure, Deena," he replied.

Deena's eyes darted toward the Memorial. "However, before we start talking about global warming, we have someone here who wanted to address a different topic."

What? Darcy frowned at Deena and then shot a glare at Hilliard. This wasn't part of the script; Hilliard should stop the filming immediately. Thank God it wasn't being broadcast live. Darcy opened his mouth to object, but Hilliard made a rolling motion with his finger, encouraging him to continue. *What the hell?* Darcy's eyes followed Deena's gaze.

When he saw who was exiting the Memorial, all thoughts of objecting evaporated.

Elizabeth, wearing a pale pink sun dress, strode toward him. Her hair cascaded in a glorious tumble of dark waves around her shoulders and blew a little in the breeze. Her mouth curved in a fragile, tentative smile, and her eyes were darkly intent—fixed on Darcy's face. Stiffness in her gait betrayed her nervousness.

Darcy's eyes eagerly devoured the glorious sight. Starved of her presence for too long, he felt she might disappear if he glanced away. His fingers twitched with the need to touch her and… *Oh God, in a moment she'd be close enough to hear her voice.* No doubt he was grinning like a fool, and he didn't care. He had no idea why she was there; he could only soak up her presence.

Other people emerged from the Memorial, far behind Elizabeth— Bing, Jane…Georgiana? What were they doing here? And why the hell were they smiling so knowingly?

"Will." The husky way Elizabeth said his voice made Darcy's knees weak. Two last steps brought her to stand by his side; only then did Darcy realize that Deena was observing them from the side of the blond producer. Now Will recognized him as the guy having coffee with Elizabeth in the pictures on the Internet. However, she wasn't paying him the least bit of attention, and he appeared to be intent solely on filming them.

I'm definitely getting punked in some way. But he didn't care. With Elizabeth there, everything was right with the world. He said the first thing that came into his mind. "You're not in Indonesia." *Duh.*

"No." She watched him through the screen of her lashes. "I'm…not planning to go back."

Reeeallly? Excitement bubbled up inside him like carbonation. Still, this was too good, too fortuitous. It was beginning to play out like some great dream that fulfilled all his wishes. Was she really there? When he took her hand in his, their fingers curled together, deliciously warm. Yeah, she was real.

For a long moment each basked in the glow of the other's presence. Darcy could have stared into her vibrant, mossy green eyes for the rest of the day and never grown bored. But eventually Elizabeth's smile developed an anxious edge, and her brows tangled together. "Uh…Will…?"

Darcy's nerves spiked, and his breath hitched in his chest when he spoke. "Eliz-Elizabeth, what are you doing here? Why are you—? What's going on?"

Elizabeth reached out to grasp his other hand in hers so they faced each other like a couple at an altar. Her hands trembled nervously in his. When he gave her a reassuring squeeze, she returned a faint smile.

It dawned on him—finally—why he had been brought to the Tidal Basin. "There isn't any interview, is there?" he asked.

"No." Her cheeks reddened as she stared down at her sandaled feet. "I needed a way to talk to you."

"You could have called me." All around them the crowd laughed. Darcy couldn't imagine what they needed to discuss in such a public forum, but Elizabeth, Bing, and Fitz wouldn't have arranged all this without a damn good reason. "Okay." He laughed nervously. "Talk."

She took a deep breath. "Will, when I first met you, I didn't think I would like you." Another ripple of laughter from the onlookers. "In fact, we irritated each other, but eventually I realized our mutual irritation concealed a very powerful attraction. The truth is that I've never met someone who I have found so easy to talk to. So at home with. So instantly a part of me. When w-we br-broke up"—her voice cracked—"I realized that you had become a vital part of my world, even after such a short time. Without you, a big chunk of my soul was suddenly missing."

Darcy couldn't breathe; he knew that sensation exactly.

The onlookers were absolutely still, but Darcy heard several sighs. Elizabeth continued, blinking back tears. "If there's one thing I've learned over the past six months, it's that without you in my life I'm not actually living....I'm just existing, going through the motions. And I don't want that anymore. I want to be *with* you."

Her voice was thick with emotion, and she swallowed, never taking her eyes from his. "I know you think it's impossible to date while in office, so I'm not going suggest that."

Darcy's heart gave a funny twist. *She doesn't want to date? But, but...* He opened his mouth to object.

"Instead I would like to suggest..." Her eyes sought and held his as if she could see all the way into his soul. "I would like to *ask*...if you, William Darcy, will marry me?"

Several onlookers gasped, and it sounded like a few were crying. Behind Elizabeth, Georgiana, Bing, Jane, and Fitz were smiling so widely that their faces might crack. Georgiana mouthed "say yes" to her brother.

Darcy blinked rapidly, reminding himself this was not a dream, even though it seemed to fulfill every fantasy he hadn't allowed himself to indulge over the past six months.

It took a full second for her words to sink in and then another second for Darcy to reassure himself that he had heard them correctly. For another second, he could only stare at her, slack-jawed.

She resumed talking, perhaps because his silence worried her. "As you said, presidents don't usually date in office, but of course, most of them were married when they were elected. So I thought maybe marriage would..." Her words petered out, and she bit her lip as if she'd said too much.

He was stunned into speechlessness. *I should say something. I should respond.*

Her expression morphed from hopeful to worried. "But if you don't want—"

Those words released his tongue. "Yes!" he said quickly. "Oh God, yes! A thousand times yes! You're not getting away from me now." He rested both his hands on her perfectly curved shoulders. "When do you want to do it? Let's do it now. You look lovely. I like this dress! It's a great dress to get married in."

She laughed as he drew her in for a kiss. *She's mine now, and nobody can take her from me.* The applause around them was deafening.

Darcy's body was so light he could have floated away—taking Elizabeth with him into the clouds.

Elizabeth hugged him tightly and murmured in his ear, "I love you, and you're mine now. Mine."

He smiled at how similar their thoughts were.

In an instant, he understood Elizabeth's strategy, why she had made her proposal public and in front of television news cameras. With such evidence of her initiative and heartfelt sincerity—and so many witnesses—nobody could credibly claim that Darcy had coerced her.

He rested his forehead against hers. "My darling. My beautiful, devious darling."

"You don't mind being ambushed?"

He laughed. "No. Although I am regretting the audience right now."

"Oh?" Her eyes widened with anxiety.

"It makes it impossible for me to do what I really want to do," he whispered suggestively in her ear.

She shivered. "Maybe doing it in public *was* a bad idea."

"What the hell. You only get engaged once." He grabbed her, swung her into a dip, and kissed her like the world was ending.

Epilogue

"You were right," Will murmured in Elizabeth's ear.

"I usually am." She grinned at him. "About what specifically?"

"There's nothing like a wedding to win the hearts of the American people."

"I believe I said, 'There's nothing like a *love story* to win the hearts of the American people.'"

"I think the wedding may be the icing on the cake," he said. "So to speak."

She rolled her eyes; it was the third bad pun he had made that day.

As Elizabeth had hoped, their love story had captured the imaginations of the American public. Whispers that Will had coerced Elizabeth had all but disappeared when she proposed to him. Only a few fringe websites continued to flog that old narrative while the rest of the world got caught up in "Willizabeth Fever." Their engagement and the tale of their romance were the top stories on every newspaper and cable news station for weeks. On-air pundits wondered if there was anyone in the U.S. who hadn't seen the video of Elizabeth proposing.

And now here they were, greeting guests in what had to be the world's longest receiving line. Elizabeth turned to greet the next: who was revealed to be Charlotte, with Bill Collins trailing behind her. Elizabeth gave her friend a hug.

"Congratulations!" Charlotte said. "I didn't think you'd be able to pull off a Rose Garden wedding in two months, but everything is lovely."

"It helps to have the White House staff behind you," Elizabeth said. The staff could not have been more enthusiastic in embracing the idea of a Rose Garden wedding. They had transformed it into a beautiful day.

"And the American people," Charlotte added.

"Yes." Tears welled in Elizabeth's eyes when she remembered the support they'd received from Americans of all walks of life.

As soon as news of their engagement had been announced, everyone—including the media—had demanded to know when the wedding would take place. The answer had been as soon as possible. Elizabeth hadn't felt comfortable moving into the president's home with no official title, but Will had lived without her quite long enough, thank you very much.

The result was an engagement of little less than two months, which, along with Will's renewed focus and enthusiasm, had greatly boosted the president's popularity. Legislators who had opposed him suddenly ran the risk of appearing churlish. His renewable energy bill passed easily into law, and his refugee program was on its way to being implemented. The latter was particularly satisfying to Elizabeth, who planned to make immigrant and refugee children the focus of much of her charitable work as first lady.

"The staff certainly did you proud," Charlotte observed, gazing down the aisle toward the flower-covered canopy where Will and Elizabeth had exchanged vows a few minutes earlier.

They had been blessed with one of D.C.'s rare warm, but not overly humid, June days. The Rose Garden had never looked more beautiful. The aisle was lined with elegant arrangements of white and purple roses, complementing the purple in the bridesmaids' dresses.

"And Lydia even behaved herself," Charlotte continued.

"I think she was a bit afraid not to," Elizabeth said. The Bennet sisters, along with Georgiana, had served as bridesmaids—with Jane as the maid of honor. Elizabeth expected that Jane and Bing would be walking down the aisle themselves sometime next year, but undoubtedly they would plan a much lower key ceremony.

Charlotte gave Elizabeth another hug and continued down the receiving line to congratulate Will. As Bill Collins shook Elizabeth's hand and murmured congratulations, his eyes focused everywhere but on her. No doubt he was concerned about Mrs. de Bourgh's opinion; Darcy's aunt still did not approve of the match, although she had grudgingly attended the wedding.

"Remember us when you're buying staplers for the White House. We could put the presidential seal on them!" Bill said—as if he would be doing them a favor.

Elizabeth suppressed a smirk. "Do you have a government contract?" From the way Bill's eyes widened in horror, she guessed the answer was "no." But before he could reply, Will reached out his hand, and Bill moved along.

The receiving line had snaked down one aisle and wrapped around another, but fortunately it was near the end; Elizabeth was very grateful they had managed to keep the guest list to 150 people.

Elizabeth turned to the next guest, Charlotte's mother, who was listening to a Fanny Bennet monologue with great forbearance. "What a stroke of luck that Lizzy didn't find Bill Collins at all attractive," Elizabeth's mother was saying. "Or this"—she gestured expansively to encompass the entire venue—"might never have happened!"

Betty Lucas pursed her lips. "Of course. Everything worked out for the best," she agreed stiffly.

Fanny leaned closer to her friend. "I got to sleep in the Lincoln Bedroom!" she whispered loud enough for everyone to hear.

Betty gave a tight smile. "How wonderful."

Her mother had been sufficiently in awe of her future son-in-law that she had been amenable to nearly everything Elizabeth and the White House staff had suggested for the wedding. But her uncharacteristic amiability was bound to run its course, and it appeared that she was returning to form.

Fanny caught her daughter's eye. "Lizzy, did you hear? They're saying there are ten thousand people outside the White House gates!"

Elizabeth nodded. When she had dreamed of her wedding as a girl, she had never imagined it would result in souvenir booklets, postcards, or coffee table books. She had to admit that the stuffed William and Elizabeth dolls were kind of cute, but she couldn't imagine there would be a big market for the presidential wedding commemorative crock pots.

As soon as they finished with the receiving line, the entire wedding party would visit the Truman Balcony to wave to the onlookers. This was the part of the event Lydia was anticipating most eagerly; hopefully the press photographers wouldn't catch her sticking out her tongue or dabbing or something equally embarrassing. Fortunately, most of America had embraced the Bennets and their eccentricities. Hilliard's office had smartly portrayed them as "everyday Americans" despite their wealth, and associating with them had helped make Will seem more down to earth.

After the trip to the Truman Balcony, everyone could let their hair down—figuratively speaking—at a reception in the East Room.

But Elizabeth was most eagerly anticipating the honeymoon, where they would finally have a modicum of privacy. It turned out that Will's family owned a Caribbean island, so they would enjoy a week of just Elizabeth and Will—plus a dozen staff members and fifty or so Secret Service agents. But Will had promised they would be discreet.

Elizabeth gratefully shook the hands of the last couple in the receiving line, who shuffled along to congratulate Will. Surveying the crowd, Elizabeth noticed Kitty flirting with Fitz and wondered if she should warn her sister that she was barking up the wrong tree.

Caroline was chatting up Bill Collins with great animation while Charlotte watched with a cynical eye. Apparently Bing's sister had decided that being stapler queen of the U.S. would be an adequate consolation prize for having lost the opportunity to become first lady. But Bill only had eyes for Charlotte.

Despite her evident disappointment, Caroline had treated Elizabeth with cool courtesy and a minimum of disdain. Will had laughed cynically at this observation and noted that Caroline wouldn't do anything to jeopardize her access to people with wealth and power.

Mary and John Bennet were hovering near the table of On-a-Stick appetizers being distributed to the guests. Of course there were staff members to hand out the treats, but her family members were eagerly touting the virtues of the foodstuffs to anyone who would stand still long enough to listen.

Elizabeth couldn't hide a smile at the sight of the speaker of the house gamely munching on ravioli on-a-stick while a supreme court justice took delicate bites from a doughnut on-a-stick. Will had been very tolerant in allowing her family to cater the appetizers and very firm in declining her father's offer to supply dinner as well. The publicity surrounding the wedding had taken her father and various other Bennet family members on a whirlwind of morning talk shows, and On-a-Stick Inc. sales were skyrocketing.

She turned toward her new husband—a word that would take some getting used to—only to find Fitz standing in his place.

"What happened to Will?" Panic struck her. "Not an emergency?"

Fitz grinned. "No. Will just needed a little time to get away. But he said you could join him if you would like 'A place to clean up'—if that means anything to you." He gave her an apologetic shrug.

It took Elizabeth a moment to get the reference, then rolled her eyes. *The president of the United States really should indulge in better quality puns.* "Do I have time to slip away?"

Fitz shrugged. "I think I can cover for both of you for about fifteen minutes," he added. "But then they'll expect you at the Truman Balcony."

Elizabeth gave him an impish grin. "Thank you!" She handed him her bouquet. "I'll be right back."

If her new Secret Service escort thought it odd that the first lady was scurrying across the White House lawn in her wedding gown and white designer pumps, they didn't remark upon it. Fortunately, Elizabeth had become more familiar with the building's layout and was able to find the East Room without needing to ask for directions. The head of her detail checked out the secret corridor before allowing her to slip through the hidden door, but the agents agreed not to follow her.

The heels of her pumps thumped noisily on the wooden floor as she hurried down the corridor. The door swung open as she neared the broom closet—revealing Will leaning against the doorframe and shamelessly ogling her as she approached. "So this is where you swept me off my feet." He grinned.

Elizabeth shook her head. "Why didn't you tell me about your thing for bad puns?"

"I couldn't warn you while you still had a chance to get away." He waggled his eyebrows. "Now you're trapped."

She laughed while Will reached out and put his hands on her hips, pulling her toward his body. "I don't mind being trapped by you," she said.

"Have I told you how much I like this dress?" His fingers caressed the bare skin of her upper back.

Elizabeth edged closer to him, grateful that her sheath dress didn't restrict her maneuverability. "You might have mentioned it," she murmured.

"It displays every one of your curves to advantage," he whispered in her ear as his other hand trailed lightly over her hip. "And…." He swung her into the closet. Her back thumped against some shelves while a broom and a mop crashed to the floor. "You fit in here perfectly. A big, poofy skirt would not serve the purpose nearly as well."

"I must admit that I did not choose this dress with broom closets in mind."

"You should have known we would end up here."

"I should have," she said with a rueful laugh.

There was a long silence as he kissed her thoroughly, producing a surge of desire Elizabeth could feel all the way down to her toes. "What a shame we can't start the honeymoon right now," she mumbled.

"Mm-hmm." He was kissing the sensitive skin under her ear and making her shiver. "We'll have to return here when we have more time and less…restrictive clothing."

"Regular broom closet inspections are important." Elizabeth nodded solemnly. "No detail is too small for the president."

"Or the first lady," he replied.

Her eyes widened. "Oh! I guess I am first lady now. That's going to take some getting used to. I never expected to acquire a staff when I married."

He gave her a lopsided grin. "You're going to be a great first lady."

"I just hope I can do justice to your presidency."

"I'm sure you will." Careful of her tiara and veil, one of his hands skimmed down her cheek. "I am a lucky, lucky man. I still find it hard to believe *you* proposed to *me*."

She shrugged helplessly. "You weren't going to do it."

"I thought you were in Jakarta!" Will exclaimed. Elizabeth gave him an apologetic shrug. "I did fantasize about proposing, though."

"You did?" Elizabeth hadn't heard that before. "What would you have said?"

Now both his hands were roving around her back while his eyes remained fixed on hers. "I would have told you I wasn't surviving very well without you, which was true. And that you were the only person I could imagine spending the rest of my life with, also true. And if I proposed now, would you please wait six years until I was out of office?"

Wow. "I would have said yes."

His smile lit up his whole face. "Really? Yes to a six-year wait?"

Elizabeth blinked back tears that threatened. "I would have waited forever for you, but I'm very happy I didn't need to."

Will leaned in for a kiss. "Me, too, Mrs. Darcy," he murmured against her lips. "I'm ready for the rest of our lives to begin."

The End

Thank you for purchasing this book. I know you have many entertainment options, and I appreciate that you spent your time with my story. Your support makes it possible for authors like me to continue writing.

Please consider leaving a review where you purchased the book. Reviews are a book's lifeblood.

Learn more about me and my upcoming releases:

Sign up for my newsletter *Dispatches from Pemberley*

Website: www.victoriakincaid.com

Twitter: VictoriaKincaid@kincaidvic

Blog: https://kincaidvictoria.wordpress.com/

Facebook: https://www.facebook.com/kincaidvictoria

About Victoria Kincaid

The author of numerous best-selling *Pride and Prejudice* variations, historical romance writer Victoria Kincaid has a Ph.D. in English literature and runs a small business, er, household with two children, a hyperactive dog, an overly affectionate cat, and a husband who is not threatened by Mr. Darcy. They live near Washington DC, where the inhabitants occasionally stop talking about politics long enough to complain about the traffic.

On weekdays she is a freelance writer/editor who now specializes in IT marketing (it's more interesting than it sounds). In the past, some of her more…unusual writing subjects have included space toilets, taxi services, laser gynecology, bidets, orthopedic shoes, generating energy from onions, Ferrari rental car services, and vampire face lifts (she swears she is not making any of this up). A lifelong Austen fan, Victoria has read more Jane Austen variations and sequels than she can count – and confesses to an extreme partiality for the Colin Firth version of *Pride and Prejudice.*

Also by Victoria Kincaid:

Darcy vs. Bennet

Elizabeth Bennet is drawn to a handsome, mysterious man she meets at a masquerade ball. However, she gives up all hope for a future with him when she learns he is the son of George Darcy, the man who ruined her father's life. Despite her father's demand that she avoid the younger Darcy, when he appears in Hertfordshire Elizabeth cannot stop thinking about him, or seeking him out, or welcoming his kisses….

Fitzwilliam Darcy has struggled to carve out a life independent from his father's vindictive temperament and domineering ways, although the elder Darcy still controls the purse strings. After meeting Elizabeth Bennet, Darcy cannot imagine marrying anyone else, even though his father despises her family. More than anything he wants to make her his wife, but doing so would mean sacrificing everything else….

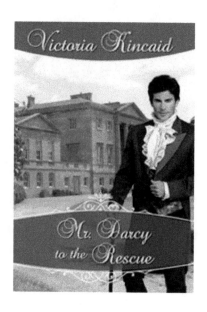

Mr. Darcy to the Rescue

When the irritating Mr. Collins proposes marriage, Elizabeth Bennet is prepared to refuse him, but then she learns that her father is ill. If Mr. Bennet dies, Collins will inherit Longbourn and her family will have nowhere to go. Elizabeth accepts the proposal, telling herself she can be content as long as her family is secure. If only she weren't dreading the approaching wedding day...

Ever since leaving Hertfordshire, Mr. Darcy has been trying to forget his inconvenient attraction to Elizabeth. News of her betrothal forces him to realize how devastating it would be to lose her. He arrives at Longbourn intending to prevent the marriage, but discovers Elizabeth's real opinion about his character. Then Darcy recognizes his true dilemma...

How can he rescue her when she doesn't want him to?

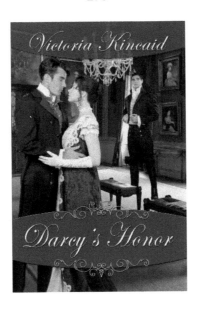

Darcy's Honor

Elizabeth Bennet is relieved when the difficult Mr. Darcy leaves the area after the Netherfield Ball. But she soon runs afoul of Lord Henry, a Viscount who thinks to force her into marrying him by slandering her name and ruining her reputation. An outcast in Meryton, and even within her own family, Elizabeth has nobody to turn to and nowhere to go.

Darcy successfully resisted Elizabeth's charms during his visit to Hertfordshire, but when he learns of her imminent ruin, he decides he must propose to save her from disaster. However, Elizabeth is reluctant to tarnish Darcy's name by association…and the viscount still wants her…

Can Darcy save his honor while also marrying the woman he loves?

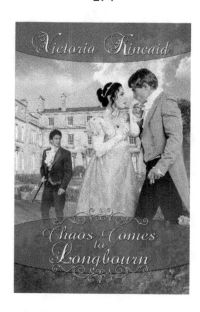

Chaos Comes to Longbourn

While attempting to suppress his desire to dance with Elizabeth Bennet, Mr. Darcy flees the Netherfield ballroom only to stumble upon a half-dressed Lydia Bennet in the library. When they are discovered in this compromising position by a shrieking Mrs. Bennet, it triggers a humorously improbable series of events. After the dust settles, eight of Jane Austen's characters are engaged to the wrong person.

Although Darcy yearns for Elizabeth, and she has developed feelings for the master of Pemberley, they are bound by promises to others. How can Darcy and Elizabeth unravel this tangle of hilariously misbegotten betrothals and reach their happily ever after?

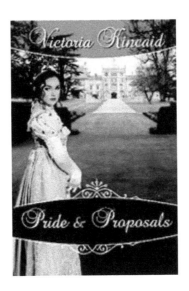

Pride and Proposals

What if Mr. Darcy's proposal was too late?

Darcy has been bewitched by Elizabeth Bennet since he met her in Hertfordshire. He can no longer fight this overwhelming attraction and must admit he is hopelessly in love. During Elizabeth's visit to Kent she has been forced to endure the company of the difficult and disapproving Mr. Darcy, but she has enjoyed making the acquaintance of his affable cousin, Colonel Fitzwilliam.

Finally resolved, Darcy arrives at Hunsford Parsonage prepared to propose—only to discover that Elizabeth has just accepted a proposal from the Colonel, Darcy's dearest friend in the world. As he watches the couple prepare for a lifetime together, Darcy vows never to speak of what is in his heart. Elizabeth has reason to dislike Darcy, but finds that he haunts her thoughts and stirs her emotions in strange ways.

Can Darcy and Elizabeth find their happily ever after?

The Secrets of Darcy and Elizabeth

A despondent Darcy travels to Paris in the hopes of forgetting the disastrous proposal at Hunsford. Paris is teeming with English visitors during a brief moment of peace in the Napoleonic Wars, but Darcy's spirits don't lift until he attends a ball and unexpectedly encounters…Elizabeth Bennet! Darcy seizes the opportunity to correct misunderstandings and initiate a courtship.

Their moment of peace is interrupted by the news that England has again declared war on France, and hundreds of English travelers must flee Paris immediately. Circumstances force Darcy and Elizabeth to escape on their own, despite the risk to her reputation. Even as they face dangers from street gangs and French soldiers, romantic feelings blossom during their flight to the coast. But then Elizabeth falls ill, and the French are arresting all the English men they can find….

When Elizabeth and Darcy finally return to England, their relationship has changed, and they face new crises. However, they have secrets they must conceal—even from their own families.

When Mary Met the Colonel

Without the beauty and wit of the older Bennet sisters or the liveliness of the younger, Mary is the Bennet sister most often overlooked. She has resigned herself to a life of loneliness, alleviated only by music and the occasional book of military history.

Colonel Fitzwilliam finds himself envying his friends who are marrying wonderful women while he only attracts empty-headed flirts. He longs for a caring, well-informed woman who will see the man beneath the uniform.

A chance meeting in Longbourn's garden during Darcy and Elizabeth's wedding breakfast kindles an attraction between Mary and the Colonel. However, the Colonel cannot act on these feelings since he must wed an heiress. He returns to war, although Mary finds she cannot easily forget him.

Is happily ever after possible when Mary meets the Colonel?

A Very Darcy Christmas

A Pride and Prejudice sequel. Elizabeth and Darcy are preparing for their first Christmas at Pemberley when they are suddenly deluged by a flood of uninvited guests. Mrs. Bennet is seeking refuge from the French invasion she believes to be imminent. Lady Catherine brings two suitors for Georgiana's hand, who cause a bit of mayhem themselves. Lydia's presence causes bickering—and a couple of small fires—while Wickham has more nefarious plans in mind....The abundance of guests soon puts a strain on her marriage as Elizabeth tries to manage the comedy and chaos while ensuring a happy Christmas for all.

Meanwhile, Georgiana is finding her suitors—and the prospect of coming out—to be very unappealing. Colonel Fitzwilliam seems to be the only person who understands her fondness for riding astride and shooting pistols. Georgiana realizes she's beginning to have more than cousinly feelings for him, but does he return them? And what kind of secrets is he hiding?

Love, romance, and humor abound as everyone gathers to celebrate a Very Darcy Christmas.

Printed in the USA
CPSIA information can be obtained
at www.ICGtesting.com
LVHW022304261123
764989LV00034B/732